Christmas
with my
COWBOY

BOOK YOUR PLACE ON OUR WEBSITE
AND MAKE THE
READING CONNECTION!

We've created a customized website just for our very special readers, where you can get the inside scoop on everything that's going on with Zebra, Pinnacle and Kensington books.

When you come online, you'll have the exciting opportunity to:

- View covers of upcoming books
- Read sample chapters
- Learn about our future publishing schedule (listed by publication month and author)
- Find out when your favorite authors will be visiting a city near you
- Search for and order backlist books from our online catalog
- Check out author bios and background information
- Send e-mail to your favorite authors
- Meet the Kensington staff online
- Join us in weekly chats with authors, readers and other guests
- Get writing guidelines
- AND MUCH MORE!

**Visit our website at
http://www.kensingtonbooks.com**

Christmas
with my
COWBOY

Diana Palmer
Lindsay McKenna
Margaret Way

ZEBRA BOOKS
KENSINGTON PUBLISHING CORP.
http://www.kensingtonbooks.com

ZEBRA BOOKS are published by

Kensington Publishing Corp.
119 West 40th Street
New York, NY 10018

All Kensington titles, imprints, and distributed lines are available
at special quantity discounts for bulk purchases for sales promotion,
premiums, fund-raising, educational, or institutional use.

Special book excerpts or customized printings can also be created
to fit specific needs. For details, write or phone the office of the
Kensington Sales Manager: Attn.: Sales Department. Kensington
Publishing Corp., 119 West 40th Street, New York, NY 10018.
Phone: 1-800-221-2647.

Zebra and the Z logo Reg. U.S. Pat. & TM Off.

First Printing: October 2017
ISBN-13: 978-1-4201-4469-7
ISBN-10: 1-4201-4469-3

eISBN-13: 978-1-4201-4470-3
eISBN-10: 1-4201-4470-7

10 9 8 7 6 5 4 3 2 1

Printed in the United States of America

Contents

The Snow Man

DIANA PALMER

Dear Reader:

This Christmas story is one I've had in the back of my mind for a long time but never got around to writing. It was fun to work with, and I hope you enjoy it. The greatest blessing it brings me is being able to work with my editor, Tara Gavin, again, and to be included in an anthology with my good friends Margaret Way and Lindsay McKenna!

Thanks so much to Kensington Books for the opportunity to be included in this group of stories, and especially thank you for the beautiful bouquet of snow-white roses that you sent me for my birthday! You are a lovely company and I am so fortunate to get to do stories for you! Thank you from the bottom of my heart.

And much love to all my readers from your biggest fan,

Diana Palmer

*To my friends Coco and June
and the Purple Lady (also named June!),
and all my other friends who never miss a signing.
This one is for you, with love.*

Chapter One

Meadow Dawson just stared at the slim, older cowboy who was standing on her front porch with his hat held against his chest. His name was Ted. He was her father's ranch foreman. And he was speaking Greek, she decided, or perhaps some form of archaic language that she couldn't understand.

"The culls," he persisted. "Mr. Jake wanted us to go ahead and ship them out to that rancher we bought the replacement heifers from."

She blinked. She knew three stances that she could use to shoot a .40 caliber Glock from. She was experienced in interrogation techniques. She'd once participated in a drug raid with other agents from the St. Louis, Missouri, office where she'd been stationed during her brief tenure with the FBI as a special agent.

Sadly, none of those experiences had taught her what a cull was, or what to do with it. She pushed back her long, golden blond hair, and her pale green eyes narrowed on his elderly face.

She blinked. "Are culls some form of wildlife?" she asked blankly.

The cowboy doubled up laughing.

She grimaced. Her father and mother had divorced when she was six. She'd gone to live with her mother in Greenwood, Mississippi, while her father stayed here on this enormous Colorado ranch, just outside Glenwood Springs. Later, she'd spent some holidays with her dad, but only after she was in her senior year of high school and she could out-argue her bitter mother, who hated her ex-husband. What she remembered about cattle was that they were loud and dusty. She really hadn't paid much attention to the cattle on the ranch or her father's infrequent references to ranching problems. She hadn't been there often enough to learn the ropes.

"I worked for the FBI," she said with faint belligerence. "I don't know anything about cattle."

He straightened up. "Sorry, ma'am," he said, still fighting laughter. "Culls are cows that didn't drop calves this spring. Nonproductive cattle are removed from the herd, or culled. We sell them either as beef or surrogate mothers for purebred cattle."

She nodded and tried to look intelligent. "I see." She hesitated. "So we're punishing poor female cattle for not being able to have calves repeatedly over a period of years."

The cowboy's face hardened. "Ma'am, can I give you some friendly advice about ranch management?"

She shrugged. "Okay."

"I think you'd be doing yourself a favor if you sold this ranch," he said bluntly. "It's hard to make a living at ranching, even if you've done it for years. It would be a sin and a shame to let all your father's hard work go to pot. Begging your pardon, ma'am," he added respectfully. "Dal Blake was friends with your father, and he owns the biggest ranch around Raven Springs. Might be worthwhile to talk to him."

Meadow managed a smile through homicidal rage. "Dariell Blake and I don't speak," she informed him.

"Ma'am?" The cowboy sounded surprised.

"He told my father that I'd turned into a manly woman who probably didn't even have . . ." She bit down hard on the word she couldn't bring herself to voice. "Anyway," she added tersely, "he can keep his outdated opinions to himself."

The cowboy grimaced. "Sorry."

"Not your fault," she said, and managed a smile. "Thanks for the advice, though. I think I'll go online and watch a few YouTube videos on cattle management. I might call one of those men, or women, for advice."

The cowboy opened his mouth to speak, thought about how scarce jobs were, and closed it again. "Whatever you say, ma'am." He put his hat back on. "I'll just get back to work. It's, uh, okay to ship out the culls?"

"Of course it's all right," she said, frowning. "Why wouldn't it be?"

"You said it oppressed the cows . . ."

She rolled her eyes. "I was kidding!"

"Oh." Ted brightened a little. He tilted his hat respectfully and went away.

Meadow went back into the house and felt empty. She and her father had been close. He loved his ranch and his daughter. Getting to know her as an adult had been great fun for both of them. Her mother had kept the tension going as long as she lived. She never would believe that Meadow could love her and her ex-husband equally. But Meadow did. They were both wonderful people. They just couldn't live together without arguing.

She ran her fingers over the back of the cane-bottomed rocking chair where her father always sat, near the big stone fireplace. It was November, and Colorado was cold. Heavy snow was already falling. Meadow remembered Colorado winters from her childhood, before her parents divorced. It was going to be difficult to manage payroll, much less all the little added extras she'd need, like food and electricity . . .

She shook herself mentally. She'd manage, somehow. And she'd do it without Dariell Blake's help. She could only imagine the smug, self-righteous expression that would come into those chiseled features if she asked him to teach her cattle ranching. She'd rather starve. Well, not really.

She considered her options, and there weren't many. Her father owned this ranch outright. He owed for farm equipment, like combines to harvest grain crops and tractors to help with planting. He owed for feed and branding supplies and things like that. But the land was hers now, free and clear. There was a lot of land. It was worth millions.

She could have sold it and started over. But he'd made her promise not to. He'd known her very well by then. She never made a promise she didn't keep. Her own sense of ethics locked her into a position she hated. She didn't know anything about ranching!

Her father mentioned Dariell, whom everyone locally called Dal, all the time. Fine young man, he commented. Full of pepper, good disposition, loves animals.

The loving animals part was becoming a problem. She had a beautiful white Siberian husky, a rescue, with just a hint of red-tipped fur in her ears and tail. She was named Snow, and Meadow had fought the authorities to keep her in her small apartment. She was immaculate, and Meadow brushed her and bathed her faithfully. Finally the apartment manager had given in, reluctantly, after Meadow offered a sizeable deposit for the apartment, which was close to her work. She made friends with a lab tech in the next-door apartment, who kept Snow when Meadow had to travel for work. It was a nice arrangement, except that the lab tech really liked Meadow, who didn't return the admiration. While kind and sweet, the tech did absolutely nothing for Meadow physically or emotionally.

She wondered sometimes if she was really cold. Men were nice. She dated. She'd even indulged in light petting with one of them. But she didn't feel the sense of need that made women marry and settle and have kids with a man. Most of the ones she'd dated were career oriented and didn't want marriage in the first place. Meadow's mother had been devout. Meadow grew up with deep religious beliefs that were in constant conflict with society's norms.

She kept to herself mostly. She'd loved her job when she started as an investigator for the Bureau. But there had been a minor slipup.

Meadow was clumsy. There was no other way to put it. She had two left feet, and she was always falling down or doing things the wrong way. It was a curse. Her mother had named her Meadow because she was reading a novel at the time and the heroine had that name. The heroine had been gentle and sweet and a credit to the community where she lived, in 1900s Fort Worth, Texas. Meadow, sadly, was nothing like her namesake.

There had been a stakeout. Meadow had been assigned, with another special agent, to keep tabs on a criminal who'd shot a police officer. The officer lived, but the man responsible was facing felony charges, and he ran.

A CI, or Confidential Informant, had told them where the man was likely to be on a Friday night. It was a local club, frequented by people who were out of the mainstream of society.

Meadow had been assigned to watch the back door while the other special agent went through the front of the club and tried to spot him.

Sure enough, the man was there. The other agent was

recognized by a patron, who warned the perpetrator. The criminal took off out the back door.

While Meadow was trying to get her gun out of the holster, the fugitive ran into her and they both tumbled onto the ground.

"Clumsy cow!" he exclaimed. He turned her over and pushed her face hard into the asphalt of the parking lot, and then jumped up and ran.

Bruised and bleeding, Meadow managed to get to her feet and pull her service revolver. "FBI! Stop or I'll shoot!"

"You couldn't hit a barn from the inside!" came the sarcastic reply from the running man.

"I'll show . . . you!" As she spoke, she stepped back onto a big rock, her feet went out from under her, and the gun discharged right into the windshield of the SUV she and the special agent arrived in.

The criminal was long gone by the time Meadow was recovering from the fall.

"Did you get him?" the other agent panted as he joined her. He frowned. "What the hell happened to you?"

"He fell over me and pushed my face into the asphalt," she muttered, feeling the blood on her nose. "I ordered him to halt and tried to fire when I tripped over a rock . . ."

The other agent's face told a story that he was too kind to voice.

She swallowed, hard. "Sorry about the windshield," she added.

He glanced at the Bureau SUV and shook his head. "Maybe we could tell them it was a vulture. You know, they sometimes fly into car windshields."

"No," she replied grimly. "It's always better to tell them the truth. Even when it's painful."

"Guess you're right." He grimaced. "Sorry."

"Hey. We all have talents. I think mine is to trip over my own feet at any given dangerous moment."

"The SAC is going to be upset," he remarked.

"I don't doubt it," she replied.

In fact, the Special Agent in Charge was eloquent about her failure to secure the fugitive. He also wondered aloud, rhetorically, how any firearms instructor ever got drunk enough to pass her in the academy. She kept quiet, figuring that anything she said would only make matters worse.

He didn't take her badge. He did, however, assign her as an aide to another agent who was redoing files in the basement of the building. It was clerical work, for which she wasn't even trained. And from that point, her career as an FBI agent started going drastically downhill.

She'd always had problems with balance. She thought that her training would help her compensate for it, but she'd been wrong. She seemed to be a complete failure as an FBI agent. Her superior obviously thought so.

He did give her a second chance, months later. He sent her to interrogate a man who'd confessed to kidnapping an underage girl for immoral purposes. Meadow's questions, which she'd formulated beforehand, irritated him to the point of physical violence. He'd attacked Meadow, who was totally unprepared for what amounted to a beating. She'd fought, and screamed, to no avail. It had taken a jailer to extricate the man's hands from her throat. Of course, that added another charge to the bevy he was already facing: assault on a federal officer.

But Meadow reacted very badly to the incident. It had never occurred to her that a perpetrator might attack her physically. She'd learned to shoot a gun, she'd learned self-defense, hand-to-hand, all the ways in the world to protect herself. But when she'd come up against an unarmed but violent criminal, she'd almost been killed. Her training wasn't enough. She'd felt such fear that she couldn't function. That had been the beginning of the end. Both she and the Bureau had decided that she was in the wrong profession. They'd been very nice about it, but she'd lost her job.

And Dal Blake thought she was a manly woman, a real hell-raiser. It was funny. She was the exact opposite. Half the time she couldn't even remember to do up the buttons on her coat right.

She sighed as she thought about Dal. She'd had a crush on him in high school. He was almost ten years older than she was and considered her a child. Her one attempt to catch his eye had ended in disaster . . .

She'd come to visit her father during Christmas holidays—much against her mother's wishes. It was her senior year of high school. She'd graduate in the spring. She knew that she was too young to appeal to a man Dal's age, but she was infatuated with him, fascinated by him.

He came by to see her father often because they were both active members in the local cattlemen's association. So one night when she knew he was coming over, Meadow dressed to the hilt in her Sunday best. It was a low-cut red sheath dress, very Christmassy and festive. It had long sleeves and side slits. It was much too old for Meadow, but her father loved her, so he let her pick it out and he paid for it.

Meadow walked into the room while Dal and her father were talking and sat down in a chair nearby, with a book in her hands. She tried to look sexy and appealing. She had on too much makeup, but she hadn't noticed that. The magazines all said that makeup emphasized your best features. Meadow didn't have many best features. Her straight nose and bow mouth were sort of appealing, and she had pretty light green eyes. She used masses of eyeliner and mascara and way too much rouge. Her best feature was her long, thick, beautiful blond hair. She wore it down that night.

Her father gave her a pleading look, which she ignored. She smiled at Dal with what she hoped was sophistication.

He gave her a dark-eyed glare.

The expression on his face washed away all her self-confidence. She flushed and pretended to read her book, but she was shaky inside. He didn't look interested. In fact, he looked very repulsed.

When her father went out of the room to get some paperwork he wanted to show to Dal, Meadow forced herself to look at him and smile.

"It's almost Christmas," she began, trying to find a subject for conversation.

He didn't reply. He did get to his feet and come toward her. That flustered her even more. She fumbled with the book and dropped it on the floor.

Dal pulled her up out of the chair and took her by the shoulders firmly. "I'm ten years older than you," he said bluntly. "You're a high school kid. I don't rob cradles and I don't appreciate attempts to seduce me in your father's living room. Got that?"

Her breath caught. "I never . . . !" she stammered.

His chiseled mouth curled expressively as he looked down into her shocked face. "You're painted up like a carnival fortune-teller. Too much makeup entirely. Does your mother know you wear clothes like that and come on to men?" he added icily. "I thought she was religious."

"She . . . is," Meadow stammered, and felt her age. Too young. She was too young. Her eyes fell away from his. "So am I. I'm sorry."

"You should be," he returned. His strong fingers contracted on her shoulders. "When do you leave for home?"

"Next Friday," she managed to say. She was dying inside. She'd never been so embarrassed in her life.

"Good. You get on the plane and don't come back. Your father has enough problems without trying to keep you out of trouble. And next time I come over here, I don't want to find you setting up shop in the living room, like a spider hunting flies."

"You're a very big fly," she blurted out, and flushed some more.

His lip curled. "You're out of your league, kid." He let go of her shoulders and moved her away from him, as if she had something contagious. His eyes went to the low-cut neckline. "If you went out on the street like that, in Raven Springs, you'd get offers."

She frowned. "Offers?"

"Prostitutes mostly do get offers," he said with distaste.

Tears threatened, but she pulled herself up to her maximum height, far short of his, and glared up at him. "I am not a prostitute!"

"Sorry. Prostitute in training?" he added thoughtfully.

She wanted to hit him. She'd never wanted anything so much. In fact, she raised her hand to slap that arrogant look off his face.

He caught her arm and pushed her hand away.

Even then, at that young age, her balance hadn't been what it should be. Her father had a big, elegant stove in the living room to heat the house. It used coal instead of wood, and it was very efficient behind its tight glass casing. There was a coal bin right next to it.

Meadow lost her balance and went down right into the coal bin. Coal spilled out onto the wood floor and all over her. Now there were black splotches all over her pretty red dress, not to mention her face and hair and hands.

She sat up in the middle of the mess, and angry tears ran down her soot-covered cheeks as she glared at Dal.

He was laughing so hard that he was almost doubled over.

"That's right, laugh," she muttered. "Santa's going to stop by here on his way to your house to get enough coal to fill up your stocking, Darriell Blake!"

He laughed even harder.

Her father came back into the room with a file folder in one hand, stopped, did a double take, and stared at his daughter, sitting on the floor in a pile of coal.

"What the hell happened to you?" he burst out.

"He happened to me!" she cried, pointing at Dal Blake. "He said I looked like a streetwalker!"

"You're the one in the tight red dress, honey." Dal chuckled. "I just made an observation."

"Your mother would have a fit if she saw you in that dress," her father said heavily. "I should never have let you talk me into buying it."

"Well, it doesn't matter anymore, it's ruined!" She got to her feet, swiping at tears in her eyes. "I'm going to bed!"

"Might as well," Dal remarked, shoving his hands into his jeans pockets and looking at her with an arrogant smile. "Go flirt with men your own age, kid."

She looked to her father for aid, but he just stared at her and sighed.

She scrambled to her feet, displacing more coal. "I'll get this swept up before I go to bed," she said.

"I'll do that. Get yourself cleaned up, Meda," her father said gently, using his pet name for her. "Go on."

She left the room muttering. She didn't even look at Dal Blake.

* * *

That had been several years ago, before she worked in law enforcement in Missouri and finally hooked up with the FBI. Now she was without a job, running a ranch about which she knew absolutely nothing, and whole families who depended on the ranch for a living were depending on her. The responsibility was tremendous.

She honestly didn't know what she was going to do. She did watch a couple of YouTube videos, but they were less than helpful. Most of them were self-portraits of small ranchers and their methods of dealing with livestock. It was interesting, but they assumed that their audience knew something about ranching. Meadow didn't.

She started to call the local cattlemen's association for help, until someone told her who the president of the chapter was. Dal Blake. Why hadn't she guessed?

While she was drowning in self-doubt, there was a knock on the front door. She opened it to find a handsome man, dark-eyed, with thick blond hair, standing on her porch. He was wearing a sheriff's uniform, complete with badge.

"Miss Dawson?" he said politely.

She smiled. "Yes?"

"I'm Sheriff Jeff Ralston."

"Nice to meet you," she said. She shook hands with him. She liked his handshake. It was firm without being aggressive.

"Nice to meet you, too," he replied. He shifted his weight.

She realized that it was snowing again and he must be freezing. "Won't you come in?" she said as an afterthought, moving back.

"Thanks," he replied. He smiled. "Getting colder out here."

She laughed. "I don't mind snow."

"You will when you're losing cattle to it," he said with

a sigh as he followed her into the small kitchen, where she motioned him into a chair.

"I don't know much about cattle," she confessed. "Coffee?"

"I'd love a cup," he said heavily. "I had to get out of bed before daylight and check out a robbery at a local home. Someone came in through the window and took off with a valuable antique lamp."

She frowned. "Just the lamp?"

He nodded. "Odd robbery, that. Usually the perps carry off anything they can get their hands on."

"I know." She smiled sheepishly. "I was with the FBI for two years."

"I heard about that. In fact," he added while she started coffee brewing, "that's why I'm here."

"You need help with the robbery investigation?" she asked, pulling two mugs out of the cabinet.

"I need help, period," he replied. "My investigator just quit to go live in California with his new wife. She's from there. Left me shorthanded. We're on a tight budget, like most small law enforcement agencies. I only have the one investigator. Had, that is." He eyed her. "I thought you might be interested in the job," he added with a warm smile.

She almost dropped the mugs. "Me?"

"Yes. Your father said you had experience in law enforcement before you went with the Bureau and that you were noted for your investigative abilities."

"Noted wasn't quite the word they used," she said, remembering the rage her boss had unleashed when she blew the interrogation of a witness. That also brought back memories of the brutality the man had used against her in the physical attack. To be fair to her boss, he didn't know the prisoner had attacked her until after he'd read her the riot act. He'd apologized handsomely, but the damage was already done.

"Well, the FBI has its own way of doing things. So do I." He accepted the hot mug of coffee with a smile. "Thanks. I live on black coffee."

"So do I." She laughed, sitting down at the table with him to put cream and sugar in her own. She noticed that he took his straight up. He had nice hands. Very masculine and strong-looking. No wedding band. No telltale ring where one had been, either. She guessed that he'd never been married, but it was too personal a question to ask a relative stranger.

"I need an investigator and you're out of work. What do you say?"

She thought about the possibilities. She smiled. Here it was, like fate, a chance to prove to the world that she could be a good investigator. It was like the answer to a prayer.

She grinned. "I'll take it, and thank you."

He let out the breath he'd been holding. "No. Thank *you*. I can't handle the load alone. When can you start?"

"It's Friday. How about first thing Monday morning?" she asked.

"That would be fine. I'll put you on the day shift to begin. You'll need to report to my office by seven a.m. Too early?"

"Oh, no. I'm usually in bed by eight and up by five in the morning."

His eyebrows raised.

"It's my dog," she sighed. "She sleeps on the bed with me, and she wakes up at five. She wants to eat and play. So I can't go back to sleep or she'll eat the carpet."

He laughed. "What breed is she?"

"She's a white Siberian husky with red highlights. Beautiful."

"Where is she?"

She caught her breath as she realized that she'd let Snow out to go to the bathroom an hour earlier, and she hadn't scratched at the door. "Oh, dear," she muttered as she realized where the dog was likely to be.

Along with that thought came a very angry knock at the back door, near where she was sitting with the sheriff.

Apprehensively, she got up and opened the door. And there he was. Dal Blake, with Snow on a makeshift lead. He wasn't smiling.

"Your dog invited herself to breakfast. Again. She came right into my damned house through the dog door!"

She knew that Dal didn't have a dog anymore. His old Labrador had died a few weeks ago, her foreman had told her, and the man had mourned the old dog. He'd had it for almost fourteen years, he'd added.

"I'm sorry," Meadow said with a grimace. "Snow. Bad girl!" she muttered.

The husky with her laughing blue eyes came bounding over to her mistress and started licking her.

"Stop that." Meadow laughed, fending her off. "How about a treat, Snow?"

She went to get one from the cupboard.

"Hey, Jeff," Dal greeted the other man, shaking hands as Jeff got to his feet.

"How's it going?" Jeff asked Dal.

"Slow," came the reply. "We're renovating the calving sheds. It's slow work in this weather."

"Tell me about it," Jeff said. "We had two fences go down. Cows broke through and started down the highway."

"Maybe there was a dress sale," Dal said, tongue-in-cheek as he watched a flustered Meadow give a chewy treat to her dog.

"I'd love to see a cow wearing a dress," she muttered.

"Would you?" Dal replied. "One of your men thinks

that's your ultimate aim, to put cows in school and teach them to read."

"Which man?" she asked, her eyes flashing fire at him.

"Oh, no, I'm not telling," Dal returned. "You get on some boots and jeans and go find out for yourself. If you can ride a horse, that is."

That brought back another sad memory. She'd gone riding on one of her father's feistier horses, confident that she could control it. She was in her second year of college, bristling with confidence as she breezed through her core curriculum.

She thought she could handle the horse. But it sensed her fear of heights and speed and took her on a racing tour up the side of a small mountain and down again so quickly that Meadow lost her balance and ended up face first in a snowbank.

To add to her humiliation—because the stupid horse went running back to the barn, probably laughing all the way—Dal Blake was helping move cattle on his own ranch, and he saw the whole thing.

He came trotting up just as she was wiping the last of the snow from her face and parka. "You know, Spirit isn't a great choice of horses for an inexperienced rider."

"My father told me that," she muttered.

"Pity you didn't listen. And lucky that you ended up in a snowbank instead of down a ravine," he said solemnly. "If you can't control a horse, don't ride him."

"Thanks for the helpful advice," she returned icily.

"City tenderfoot," he mused. "I'm amazed that you haven't killed yourself already. I hear your father had to put a rail on the back steps after you fell down them."

She flushed. "I tripped over his cat."

"You could benefit from some martial arts training."

"I've already had that," she said. "I work for my local police department."

"As what?" he asked politely.

"As a patrol officer!" she shot back.

"Well," he remarked, turning his horse, "if you drive a car like you ride a horse, you're going to end badly one day."

"I can drive!" she shot after him. "I drive all the time!"

"God help other motorists."

"You . . . you . . . you . . . !" She gathered steam with each repetition of the word until she was almost screaming, and still she couldn't think of an insult bad enough to throw at him. It wouldn't have done any good. He kept riding. He didn't even look back.

She snapped back to the present. "Yes, I can ride a horse!" she shot at Dal Blake. "Just because I fell off once . . ."

"You fell off several times. This is mountainous country. If you go riding, carry a cell phone and make sure it's charged," he said seriously.

"I'd salaam, but I haven't had my second cup of coffee yet," she drawled, alluding to an old custom of subjects salaaming royalty.

"You heard me."

"You don't give orders to me in my own house," she returned hotly.

Jeff cleared his throat.

They both looked at him.

"I have to get back to work," he said as he pushed his chair back in. "Thanks for the coffee, Meadow. I'll expect you early Monday morning."

"Expect her?" Dal asked.

"She's coming to work for me as my new investigator," Jeff said with a bland smile.

Dal's dark eyes narrowed. He saw through the man, whom he'd known since grammar school. Jeff was a good sheriff, but he wanted to add to his ranch. He owned property that adjoined Meadow's. So did Dal. That acreage had abundant water, and right now water was the most important asset any rancher had. Meadow was obviously out of her depth trying to run a ranch. Her best bet was to sell it, so Jeff was getting in on the ground floor by offering her a job that would keep her close to him.

He saw all that, but he just smiled. "Good luck," he told Jeff, with a dry glance at a fuming Meadow. "You'll need it."

"She'll do fine," Jeff said confidently.

Dal just smiled.

Meadow remembered that smile from years past. She'd had so many accidents when she was visiting her father. Dal was always somewhere nearby when they happened.

He didn't like Meadow. He'd made his distaste for her apparent on every possible occasion. There had been a Christmas party thrown by the local cattlemen's association when Meadow first started college. She'd come to spend Christmas with her father, and when he asked her to go to the party with him, she agreed.

She knew Dal would be there. So she wore an outrageous dress, even more revealing than the one he'd been so disparaging about when she was a senior in high school.

Sadly, the dress caught the wrong pair of eyes. A local cattleman who'd had five drinks too many had propositioned Meadow by the punch bowl. His reaction to her dress had flustered her and she tripped over her high-heeled shoes and knocked the punch bowl over.

The linen tablecloth was soaked. So was poor Meadow, in her outrageous dress. Dal Blake had laughed until his face turned red. So had most other people. Meadow had asked her father to drive her home. It was the last Christmas party she ever attended in Raven Springs.

But just before the punch incident, there had been another. Dal had been caught with her under the mistletoe . . .

She shook herself mentally and glared at Dal.

Chapter Two

Dal didn't leave when Jeff did. He remained standing on the front porch, both hands in the pockets of his jeans.

"Where's my cat?" he asked when Meadow was about to choke, holding back harsh words.

She paused and looked up at him. "Your cat?"

"My cat. Jarvis." His upper lip curled. "Maine coon cat. Male. Red. Remember him? You should. He spends more time down here than he does at home!"

Jarvis. She grimaced. His cat came to visit frequently. He was in love with Meadow. He'd find a way to sneak in the house and perch on the back of her chair. He'd rub her head with his face and purr and try to sit in her lap. He weighed almost twenty pounds, and he was beautiful. His big bushy tail—reminiscent of a raccoon's—was his finest feature. It was the trait that had prompted the breed's name.

"I haven't seen him today," she confessed.

"A likely story."

"I can prove it!"

She went back into the house, leaving him to follow. He unsettled her with that soft, easy step of his. She knew that he hunted elk and deer in the fall. He knew how to walk quietly. It was disconcerting when he did it in her house.

"Jarvis!" she called, confident that she could prove he wasn't inside.

A loud meow came from the bathroom.

Dal's eyes widened. "You locked my cat in a bathroom?" he exclaimed.

"I don't know how he got in there," she wailed. "I didn't even see him come in the house. I just had the door open for a minute or two while I took the trash out back," she added. "I certainly didn't see him in the bathroom!"

"He loves water," he said. "He sits in the sink when I'm not using it, and he loves the bathtub."

"Odd, isn't it? For a cat, I mean."

"Maine coon cats aren't like other cats. They're more like dogs," he said when she opened the bathroom door and Jarvis came trotting out, as if he owned the place. "You can teach them to play fetch and obey commands."

"Sure," she murmured. "I can just see you herding cats."

He gave her a brief appraisal, taking in the loose jeans and beige turtleneck sweater she was wearing. "You don't wear dressy things anymore."

"Waste of time," she said, averting her eyes. "I don't have time to train a man to live with me."

He made an insulting sound in the back of his throat. "Don't hold your breath waiting for any man to move in here," he returned. "Miss America you're not!"

"You are the most insulting man I've ever known," she burst out. "What is your problem?"

"You," he said. "You're my problem. Do you have any idea how much your father sacrificed to keep this place going? He devoted his life to it. And here you sit watching YouTube videos to learn ranching!"

"Who told you that?" she demanded.

"Is it true?"

She bit her lower lip.

He didn't move closer, but his stare penetrated. "Is it true?" he repeated coldly.

She threw up her hands. "They help! My father never taught me ranch management! And my degree is in languages, predominantly Spanish. That was my major."

His eyebrows arched, asking a silent question.

"I wanted to help go after drug lords in south Texas," she muttered.

"And look how that worked out for you," he mused.

She stamped her foot. "Will you take your redheaded cat and go home?"

He picked up Jarvis, who purred and cuddled in his arms. "Will you tell your white rat over there to stay out of my house?" he countered, indicating Snow, who was sitting just inside the dog door, laughing with her blue eyes and lolling tongue.

She wondered what she was going to do to keep her pet at home. Then she remembered what this tall, offensive cattleman had just said. "Snow is not a rat! She's a treasure!"

"I don't want her in my house," he said coldly.

"Then take out the dog door!"

He looked briefly vulnerable. "Not yet," he said. "I'm not ready."

She felt guilty. She knew what he was saying. He mourned his Lab. He didn't want to change anything. He probably still had her toys in a box somewhere, and her bed. It was the only sensitive thing about this hard man, his love for animals. It was absolute. She'd heard about him sitting up at night with heifers who were calving for the first time, rousting out the entire bunkhouse to help find a missing calf. He loved his livestock. He'd loved his old dog, too.

Meadow understood. She'd had a cat at her father's house who'd been in the family for twenty-three years when he died. He'd come into the house, a stray kitten, when

Meadow was born. Mittens had been such a part of her life that when he died, when they were both twenty-three, she grieved for months.

She'd felt stupid about her grief until she read on a pet website that people's companion pets were just like furry children. People raised them, trained them, provided for them, loved them, as if they were human. And when they died, people mourned them, sometimes excessively. It was natural. Pet owners knew this, even if those who'd never had pets didn't.

"I wouldn't let Daddy throw away Mittens's bowls or bed, and I kept her bowl exactly where it was when she was alive," she confessed softly. "I mourned her for months."

His face was shadowed. "I've still got Bess's bowl in the kitchen. I had her for fourteen years. I've mourned her more than some relatives who died."

She nodded. "I read this article in a magazine, about grief. People who don't have pets don't understand how traumatic it is to lose one. The article said that grieving for an animal isn't an aberration. It's a natural reaction when you've cared for the animal every day since you got it. They're like furry kids," she added slowly. "It takes a lot of time to get over it." She glanced at Snow, lying down in the hall, her blue eyes staring at Dal lovingly. "I got Snow from a shelter in St. Louis. She lived with me in my apartment until I came back here. I was . . ." She hesitated. "I was grieving myself to death over my mother and Mittens. I thought getting another animal might help me." She smiled. "It did. Snow took the rough edges off the grief."

"That's why I have Jasper," the tall man replied quietly. "He does help ease the pain of losing Bess."

"I'm sorry Snow keeps bothering you," she said. "I'll try to make sure she doesn't wander when I let her out."

He was still holding Jarvis, absently smoothing his big hand over the animal's head. "Jarvis moves like greased lightning," he confessed. "I usually confine him to his room and the fenced patio in the daytime so he can't run out. But he's so fast that my part-time housekeeper can't keep up with him. He's sneaky as well."

She laughed. "Next time, I'll check all the rooms when I leave doors open."

He shrugged. "I guess I could put a piece of wood over the dog door and nail it shut." He glanced at Snow. "She was a rescue?"

Meadow nodded. Her face tightened. "The shelter said that her owner had her chained in his yard and often neglected to feed her or give her water. When she howled, trying to get loose, he hit her. When she went to the shelter, she was eaten up with fleas and mange and she wouldn't eat the first couple of days. The vet honestly thought she was going to die. I happened to go in the day she was scheduled to be . . ." she swallowed, hard, "put down. It wasn't a no-kill shelter. Snow saw me come into her cage and she looked as if she'd won the lottery. She was all over me. I took her straight to the vet and let her stay there until they got her well. I visited her every day. When I brought her home, she turned into the finest dog I've ever had. She loves to ride in the car." She watched Dal's face go hard at the revelation about Snow's abuse. "To this day, a raised hand makes her run away. She's terrified of sticks. I have to use a Frisbee if I play with her outside."

"Was he arrested?" he asked.

She shook her head. "The laws haven't quite caught up with animal abuse where I lived when I got her. It was a small town outside St. Louis and the man was a local politician. But they did get Snow away from him and put her up for adoption."

"Pity he didn't live in Raven Springs," Dal said through his teeth.

She smiled. "I was thinking the same thing."

He grimaced. "Well, I'll get home. You're really taking that job with Jeff?"

"Yes."

He arched an eyebrow and smiled. The smile told her the truce was over. "I can see him now, handing you a single bullet for your gun and holding his breath if you have to fire it."

"I can hit what I aim at!" she shot back.

He shook his head and turned away.

"I can!"

He looked over his shoulder. "Your dad and I did finally get the bullet out of the tractor housing," he said casually.

She flushed red. She felt her hands clenching at her sides. "I was only sixteen and I'd never fired a gun!"

"I was winning skeet shoot competitions when I was ten."

"Mr. Perfect," she muttered.

"Miss Imperfect," he drawled back.

"That's *Ms.* to you!"

"Oh, sure. You're a manly woman, all right, just like your dad always said."

She was shocked. "What?"

He turned. His distaste was evident. "He said that you loved competing with the men at work, always trying to stay one step ahead of the people in your unit. He said you'd never think of getting married because you wouldn't want to give up control of your life to another person."

She felt her heart sink. Her father had said that about her, to her worst enemy? Why?

He noted her lack of response. "Not my problem, any way you look at it," he added with a faint laugh. "I like my women feminine and sweet. I'm dating a florist. She grows orchids in a back room. She loves to work in the garden." His face hardened. "If I were of a mind to marry, she'd be the woman I'd choose. But women are treacherous. I learned that the hard way. They'll play up to you, flatter you, do anything to make you think they care. Then when they've got you where they want you, they'll take up with another man and laugh themselves to death about how stupid you were."

She began to understand him, a little. He'd been burned, and he was shy of fire. She searched his hard face. "I had to go and interview a prisoner in a criminal investigation. I said something that hit him the wrong way and he attacked me, right there in the interrogation room." She swallowed, hard, fighting the fear all over again. "I never thought any man would attack me physically, not like that. He broke a bone in my face and I think he would have killed me if I hadn't been able to scream." She wrapped her arms around herself. "It sort of . . . ruined me about . . . men."

He caught his breath. "Did you talk to a psychologist?"

She nodded. She smiled sadly. "She was very nice. But do you know what it costs to go into therapy and stay in it for years? I didn't have the money. So I went as long as the Bureau was willing to pay her." She drew in a long breath. "Honestly, it didn't help all that much. I'm still afraid that it might happen again. He was very quiet. He even smiled at me. I thought he was a gentle sort of person . . ." She stopped. The memory stung.

He scowled. That didn't sound like any manly woman he'd ever heard of. He'd dated a policewoman once and watched her subdue an escaping suspect. She was small, but the prisoner didn't have a chance. She wrestled him down and cuffed him. She even smiled while she was doing it.

Meadow wasn't like the policewoman. She had a sensitivity he hadn't expected. Her father had exaggerated some of her characteristics. He wondered now if he hadn't done it to throw Dal off the track. It even made sense. Dal was forceful and aggressive, even with men. But he was also persistent with the women he pursued, and he generally scored when he wanted to. If he'd known what Meadow was really like under the mask she showed the world, he might have found her even more attractive than his florist.

Was Meadow's father afraid that he might want Meadow, who was already fascinated by him, and leave her devastated after a brief affair that she might not be able to avoid? He wasn't sure he could answer that question, even in his own mind. She was very attractive. He didn't want to be drawn to her, but he was. She was religious. She'd expect the works, marriage, a ring. He couldn't do that. The florist knew he was obsessed with freedom. It was a casual thing. Meadow would be . . . different.

Meadow noticed the way he was looking at her, and it made her nervous. She crossed her arms over her breasts and shifted a little. "I'll try harder to keep Snow at home," she said to provoke him out of his glowering expression.

He shrugged. "Nail Jell-O to a tree while you're at it," he murmured as he turned away with his cat.

"The same thing applies to your cat," she said.

He just kept walking.

She closed the door and leaned back against it with a sigh. It was hard going when she was near him. The past kept prodding her.

He'd probably long forgotten, but when Meadow had turned eighteen, there was a Christmas party in Catelow that she and her dad attended. The one that ended in the humiliating punch incident. She'd just started college that semester, and she was gung ho on her new experiences.

She'd bored a cattleman so badly with her revelations about History 101 that he'd smiled, excused himself, and actually left the building.

Dal had been dancing with a pretty blond woman, but she went to the restroom and he went to the punch bowl at the same time that Meadow did.

Meadow had adored him from the first time she'd ever

seen him, wearing stained work chaps and a sweat-darkened chambray shirt with disreputable boots and a battered black Stetson. He was tall and handsome. Women were always flocked around him at any social gathering. He never seemed to tire of the attention, although he played the field. There was no serious companion at the time.

She'd looked at him and remembered the coal bin incident and her ruined red dress and his nasty comments about her looking like a streetwalker. Arrogant pig!

The band was playing a lazy tune. People were dancing. Meadow was wearing a frilly cocktail dress with black high heels. Her blond hair was soft and thick around her shoulders. She'd used just enough mascara to outline her big, soft green eyes. She wasn't pretty, but she could be attractive when she worked at it.

Dal gave her a long look but averted his eyes to the punch bowl as if one brief glance was enough to tell him she wasn't worth pursuing.

She was putting finger sandwiches on a paper plate. Her fingers were unsteady. She'd prayed that he wouldn't notice.

In fact, he didn't. He was intent on the blond.

They didn't speak. A couple beside them was pointing to mistletoe overhead and laughing.

"Come on, people, it's Christmas! Peace on earth! Love your fellow man. Or woman!" a young man chided.

Meadow averted her eyes from the kissing couple beside her and was about to walk away when Dal suddenly shot out a big hand, caught her waist, and pulled her to him.

"What the hell," he said as his head bent. "Might as well not waste the mistletoe."

He caught her mouth under his and kissed her with instant, hot passion, twisting her soft lips under his until they parted and her head fell back against his broad shoulder with the force of the kiss.

She was too shocked to really enjoy it. Besides that, she'd never really been kissed in an adult way, and she didn't know how to respond. It didn't help that there were wolf whistles nearby while Dal made a meal of her mouth. If she'd dreamed about kissing him, and she had, it hadn't been in a public place with onlookers making a joke of it.

He pulled back, frowning as he saw the shock and uncertainty on her soft oval face. Her cheeks were flushed and she looked as unsettled as she felt.

"Nice work there, Dal." A fellow cattleman laughed.

"Hollywood stuff, for sure," a companion offered.

The blond, noticing the attention they were getting, came back and latched onto Dal's muscular arm. "Hey, stop sampling the local refreshments and show me what you've got, cowboy," she purred.

He laughed out loud, took a long sip of punch, and turned to the woman. He wrapped her up in his arms and kissed her so hungrily that Meadow turned away, sick to her stomach. The mistletoe was getting a workout.

She could still taste him on her mouth. It made her ache in odd places, the sensations she'd felt when he kissed her. She'd dreamed of it, hoped for it, since she was sixteen. Now she knew. But the way it had happened crushed her. He made it obvious that it meant nothing to him. He pulled his companion close to his side and didn't look at Meadow for the rest of the night.

She danced with a few other men, but her heart wasn't in it. That led to the drunk cattleman and the spilled punch and her utter humiliation when Dal Blake stood there laughing his head off as she tried to cope with another embarrassment. Her father had noticed her depression long before the drunk cattleman's attentions. She'd asked him to take her home.

"Let me tell you something about Dal," he said when they were inside the house and she was toweling off her beautiful, ruined dress. "He's a rounder. He doesn't believe in picket fences and kids, and he likely never will. His mother ran away with his father's best friend when he was twelve. His first real girlfriend threw him over for a real estate agent and laughed at him for thinking he was more important to her than any other man. He'll never settle down."

"I know that," she said, disconcerted. Her father hadn't spoken to her like this before.

"You've got a crush on him," her father continued gently, nodding at her shocked expression. "Nothing wrong with that. You have to cut your teeth on somebody. Just don't get too close to him. He'd break your heart and walk away. He doesn't really like women, Meda. He thrives on broken hearts."

"I noticed that," she said. She forced a smile. "Don't worry, Dad, I know he's not my type. Besides, his date was beautiful."

"You're beautiful inside, honey, where it really counts," he said solemnly. "I'd do anything to keep you away from Dal Blake. You deserve someone better."

"Aw, that's sweet," she murmured and laughed as she hugged him. "Thanks, Dad."

He hugged her back and let her go. "Now, change your clothes and come have coffee in the kitchen like we used to when your mother was alive," he added, alluding to the sudden, sad passing of her mother the year she started college, "and tell me about that history class you like so much!"

* * *

That had been years ago, but Meadow never got over the hurt. She knew that Dal Blake would never give her the time of day romantically, but it was painful to see how opposed her father was to anything developing between them.

She knew he was right. As the years passed, Dal's reputation with women became even more notorious. To say that he played the field was an understatement. He was handsome and rich, and he could get almost any woman he wanted. He dated movie stars, politicians, physicians, even a psychologist. But he never bought any of them a ring, and they didn't last long. He pushed them out of his life if they tried to get serious.

Meadow wasn't disposable. She wanted a man who could settle down and raise kids with her. Of course, that presupposed that a man would actually want to have kids with her one day. So far, her few dates had been mostly disastrous.

She'd gone out with a fellow FBI agent who spent the entire date talking about his favorite makes and models of cars and described painstakingly how he'd rebuilt the engine in a classic sports car.

Then there was the businessman who dealt in securities. He was good for two hours on the benefits of diversity in a portfolio. As if Meadow, even on her good salary, was ever going to be able to build the sort of portfolio he was talking about.

The last man she'd dated had been an electrician. She'd met him when the refrigerator and the stove both stopped working at the same time in her apartment. A faulty electrical line was the culprit. He'd fixed it and they'd talked, and he'd asked her out. His wife had phoned her the following night to ask if Meadow would like to come over and meet her and his children. Horrified, she'd almost been in tears. She honestly had no idea that he was married. The woman had relented. She was sorry. Her husband made a habit of this. She was pregnant with their third child and he was roaming. Again. Meadow apologized. She blocked the man's calls and never saw him after that.

She pretty much gave up on dating after that. It had been over a year since anyone had asked her out. She wasn't a social animal anyway, much preferring a good book to a booze-soaked party. She had no close friends. Her college roommate had married and moved to England. Her high school friends were all married and scattered to the four winds. Her mother had died soon after she moved into the dorm at college her first semester there. Her father had died weeks ago. So now it was just Meadow and her dog.

She remembered that warm, hungry kiss that Dal had given her under the mistletoe so long ago. She'd given him her heart and he never knew. It wouldn't have mattered. Her father had made sure that he wouldn't want her. He knew Meadow had no resistance to Dal, considering her feelings for him. He was protecting her, making Dal see her as a somber federal agent who didn't really like men and wanted only to compete with them and best them in her chosen profession.

It was sweet of her father to care so much. Probably he'd saved her, in case Dal had developed any feelings for her. Not that it was likely, considering how angry he got when he had to bring Snow back home or come to collect Jarvis. The only emotion she seemed to provoke in him was extreme irritation.

It would have been nice if her feelings for him had vanished. He gave her no encouragement at all. Her only memories of him were hedged in by humiliation and ridicule. But love was as hardy as a weed and just as hard to eradicate. Her heart fed on just the sight of him, as it had for so many long years.

She'd have a better chance of lassoing the moon and bringing it home. She knew that. It didn't help.

She wore a neat dark green pantsuit to work the following Monday, with soft-soled shoes. She wore her old service pistol as well, the .40 caliber Glock, in a holster at her waist.

The Juniper County Sheriff's Department had an office in the hundred-year-old county courthouse in downtown Raven Springs. In addition, there was the detention center a mile out of town, where prisoners were housed and which was under the care of Captain Rick Sanders.

Jeff was happy to see her. He introduced her to the clerk at the desk, to his two patrol officers and his chief deputy, or undersheriff, Gil Barnes, who barely had time to say hello because he was rushing out to answer a call from the local 911 center.

"It's a small operation," Jeff explained sheepishly. "We have our office here at the courthouse, where it's been for almost a hundred years. The detention center is newer, but we're mostly here in town. Not much has changed since my granddad was sheriff."

She remembered talk about his grandfather, who had been one heck of a lawman. She just nodded.

He glanced at the weapon on her belt. "A Glock?"

"I like them," she said. "They're not heavy, they're easy to use, and if you drop them in mud, they still fire."

He laughed. "Good point." He indicated the huge .45 1911 model Colt in the holster on his own wide hand-tooled leather belt. "I like something with stopping power."

"Have you ever had to shoot anyone?" she asked solemnly.

He nodded. His face hardened. "A guy who'd just killed his five-year-old son. He was high on meth and he came at me with a combat knife." He averted his eyes just briefly.

"I had a 9 millimeter pistol, like yours," he added. "I emptied it into him and he caught me by the throat. If my under-sheriff, Gil Barnes, hadn't been sent to assist by the 911 operator, I'd be dead. You might have noticed from the glimpse you got of Gil that he packs a .45, like mine. He took the man down. It was a hard lesson. Sometimes you need a weapon that will knock a man down in a deadly circumstance. That was why .45 caliber handguns were invented in the first place, for their stopping power."

Her lips parted on a rushed breath. She recalled the man who'd attacked her in the interrogation cell, where she hadn't had her firearm. She wondered if she'd have the nerve to actually kill a man who threatened her life. Her batting average in gun battles was dismal.

"You were lucky," she pointed out.

He nodded. "Damned lucky. So you think it through and decide if you want to keep that," he indicated her pistol, "or exchange it for one like mine."

She smiled sadly. "Jeff, my hands aren't made for big weapons." She displayed them. "I even had trouble with the .38 I trained with at the academy. My firing instructor said I needed to keep doing hand exercises to build up my strength. But it never really worked. I just have small hands."

He sighed. "I'll make sure you always have backup," he promised. "But that one shooting was the only one I've been involved in for the seven years I've been sheriff," he said encouragingly. "So maybe you'll get lucky."

She grinned. "Maybe I will. Okay. I'm here. I've been photographed, fingerprinted, grilled and chilled, and li-censed to carry a concealed weapon if I so desire. So what do I do first, boss?"

He chuckled. "I like that. Boss." He turned back to his desk and pulled out a file folder. "This is a photo I took off the Internet. It shows a lamp like the one that was stolen just recently. I know, it's a light case, but I'm starting you off with easy stuff. Okay?"

She didn't take offense. It was early times. "That's fine. What do you want me to do?"

"Go into Raven Springs and talk to Mike Markson at the Yesterday Place. It's our only antique shop. See what he can tell you about the lamp. If we know what it's worth and who might want it, we might get a break on a suspect."

"I'll go right now."

"He's on the main drag," he told her. "You can drive one of our cars, if you like."

"I'd rather drive my own SUV," she said. "Since I'm a plainclothes investigator." She frowned. "Did you want me to wear a uniform?"

"Not necessary," he said easily. "Wear what you like. Well, short of low-cut red dresses," he added, forcing down a helpless grin.

She glared at him. "He told you!"

He burst out laughing. "Sorry. Really. I just couldn't resist it. Dal said the whole coal bin fell on you."

She ground her teeth together. "Dal Blake is an animal," she said shortly.

He raised both eyebrows. "Well, when it comes to women, he probably is," he agreed. He chuckled. "We've been friends since high school. I'd give a lot to have his charm."

"There are other words for that," she muttered.

"Now, now," he said gently. "He'd just break your heart if you got involved with him. He's not a forever after sort of guy."

"I knew that the first time I met him," she confessed. She managed a smile. "Don't worry, I'm not breaking my heart over him. I had a huge crush on him when I started college." She forced a laugh. "It didn't survive the last Christmas dance."

He pursed his lips and whistled, laughing. "That was memorable, too. I wasn't there, but I heard about it. Old man Grayson's wife gave him hell all the way home about coming on to you, not to mention having him embarrass you by tipping the punch bowl over on your dress."

She shrugged. "It wasn't much of a dress," she confessed.

"Dal said that." He averted his eyes. He was laying it on thick, but he didn't want her looking in Dal's direction. He wanted that ranch, and she was going to eventually have to sell it. Both men needed the water rights. Jeff wanted them very badly.

She wasn't bad looking, and he didn't have a steady girl. So if courting her got him the land, why not?

"Dal can shut up," she said under her breath. "His opinion is no concern of mine."

He smiled. "Exactly. Now get out there and find that lamp."

"Yes, sir." She grinned as she went out the door.

Chapter Three

The Yesterday Place was a small shop right on main street in Raven Springs. It had a stenciled name on glass that looked a little ragged around the edges. But inside, it was warm and friendly.

The owner, Mike Markson, was bald on top and had big, kind brown eyes. He was short and a little rotund. Meadow liked him at once. He was friendly and welcoming, not the sort of man who had a hidden agenda. At least, her FBI training had taught her body language and how to notice criminal traits. This man seemed as straight as an arrow.

"I'm Meadow Dawson." She introduced herself, shaking hands with a warm smile. "I'm Sheriff Ralston's new investigator."

"Glad to meet you. I'm Mike. I've been here for so long that I feel I own half of Main Street." He laughed.

"Our family goes back three generations in Raven Springs. I lost my father just recently," she added.

"I knew your father," he replied. "Good man. I was sorry to hear that he died. Was it quick?"

She nodded. It was hard to talk about it. The wound was fresh. "Heart attack."

He grimaced. "My wife went like that," he said. "My

son never got over losing her. He and I get along, but he's more aggressive with people than I am." He shrugged. "Maybe that's good. I tend to be a little too generous in my offers." He laughed. "Gary can bargain them down to a fraction of what something's really worth."

Meadow would have called that a larcenous personality, but she wasn't about to say it to the man's father.

"I'd like you to look at something, if you don't mind," she said politely.

"Glad to. Glad to."

She pulled the Internet photo out of the file under her arm and put it on the counter.

"This lamp?" He pulled up his glasses with a grin when he bent over the photo. "Reading glasses, my left elbow." He chuckled. "Have to take them off to see anything up close." He frowned. "This is a magnificent lamp. John Harlow had one just like it. I tried so hard to get him to sell it to me, but he wouldn't budge. My son, Gary, the antique expert, had a fit over it. He offered John a small fortune for it. John said it was a family heirloom, and he couldn't part with it. It belonged to the family of President Andrew Jackson at one time. It had a history." He shook his head. He frowned and looked up at Meadow. "Why am I looking at this lamp?"

"It was stolen, just recently, from Mr. Harlow's home."

"You don't say!" Mike was shocked. "But we don't have people stealing antiques around here," he added quickly. "In fact, we hardly ever have thieves at all, unless someone's desperate for drug money. There was a case last month, a man who stole a whole steel gun case out of a local man's house and blew it open with C4." He frowned. "Neighbor heard the explosion and called police. They walked up just as the perpetrator was taking the guns out of the case."

"Tough luck for him," she agreed.

He shook his head. "Damaged one of the skeet guns. A Krieghoff, worth about fifty thousand dollars."

Her lower jaw fell open. "That much for a gun?"

"Not just any gun," he said. "A competition shotgun. They're expensive. The guy who owned it is a Class A shooter. He goes to the World Skeet Shooting Competition in San Antonio, Texas, every year and wins prizes."

"Wow." She shook her head. "I had trouble affording my Glock," she confessed.

He smiled. "I have a twelve gauge shotgun of my own," he said, nodding toward the underside of the counter she was leaning against. "Can't take chances. I have some very valuable things in here. I've never been robbed, but there's always a first time."

The bell on the front door clanged, and a tall, thin young man with brown hair and a scowl walked in.

"There's my son! Gary, this is Meadow Dawson," he said. "She's with the sheriff's department; their new investigator. Miss Dawson, my son, Gary."

"Nice to meet you," he said, but he looked apprehensive as he stared at her. He didn't offer to shake hands.

"She's here about that lamp that was stolen from John Harlow's place," the older man explained.

"I see." Gary's eyes narrowed. "Got any leads?"

"Not yet. I was just checking with your father about its worth. I'd also like to know if you have any contacts who could tell me about potential buyers for an item like this," she added to Mike.

He pursed his lips. "Not really. I deal with local people. But Gary here has some links on the Internet to specialty purchasers, don't you, son?"

Gary gave his father a cold glare. "Not many. I deal with the big auction houses back east for rare items. Very rare items," he emphasized. He glanced at the lamp in the photo. "That's a low-ticket item."

"It is?" Mike asked, surprised. "I thought there was a big demand for period antiques right now, especially ones with a history like John's."

"There was. It's gone now. It was a fad. Buying habits change quickly in antiques," the boy added offhandedly. "I'm going to get breakfast. Can I bring you something?" he asked his father.

"A bear claw and black coffee, please," Mike told him. "Take the cash out of the drawer for it," he added with a chuckle, because his son was already dipping into the register.

"Be back in a minute or two," Gary promised, waving several twenty dollar bills.

Meadow's eyebrows arched. She wondered what sort of bear claw cost almost a hundred dollars.

Mike noticed where her attention was and drew a conclusion. He laughed. "Yes, he took several twenties out of the register, you noticed? He needs to gas up that big Ford Expedition he's driving," Mike told her. He shook his head. "Gas is through the roof. Costs almost seventy dollars to fill it up with premium."

Meadow, who drove an economy SUV and put regular gas in it, was surprised. But she just laughed. "Why does he run such an expensive vehicle?"

"He does most of the hauling for me," he explained. "I bought him the SUV for that purpose. We had a pickup truck, but when it's raining, or snowing, even a tarp doesn't keep out some of the wetness. Antiques are delicate."

"I see." She smiled and went back to the photo, dragging as much information out of him as she could for her report.

When he finished, she shook hands again. "Thanks very much for your help. It goes without saying, if anyone tries to sell a lamp like this to you . . ."

"I'll phone you at once," he agreed.

She reached in her purse and hesitated. "I don't have business cards yet, but you can reach me at the sheriff's office in the courthouse."

"I have that number," he told her. "And I'll call you."

"Thanks very much. Nice to meet you."

"Nice to meet you, as well."

When she went back to her car, there was still no sign of the son who'd gone to get breakfast for his father.

She gave the information to Jeff. "He knows a lot about antiques," she said.

He nodded. "He's our local expert. He does appraisals as well."

"I met his son."

He made a face. "Gary. He's nothing like his dad. He never could hold down a job, and he tried to be a lot of things, including a truck driver." He shook his head. "If his dad hadn't helped him out, he'd probably be living in a shelter somewhere. He doesn't like work, but he loves money. Bad combination."

"I've seen it lead to trouble," she commented.

"He was in juvy a couple of times for petty theft," Jeff commented, referring to juvenile hall, where people under age were placed when charged with crimes.

"What did you think of him?" Jeff asked unexpectedly.

She grimaced. "He didn't make a great impression on me."

"His dad's been in the antique business most of his life. He does know the business, and he makes a good living."

"Good luck to him. I don't think he'll find many things that valuable around here," she sighed.

"You might be surprised," he commented. "Dal Blake has a small table that was used to sign the surrender at Appomattox," he said. "It's worth a fortune. Dal's careful to keep his doors locked. He inherited it from his grandmother."

"Wow," she commented. "That's really an heirloom."

"Yes, it is," Jeff agreed. He laughed. "But we really don't have many thefts in this community. We've been lucky."

"I'll say," she replied, recalling the many cases she'd seen back in Missouri when she worked for the Bureau.

"Feel like interrogating some suspects for me?" Jeff asked. "I've got a gas drive-away and two possible suspects. We have a photo from the surveillance camera that could be of either two men."

"I'll go grill them," she said with a grin. "I'll be back soon," she promised, and went to work.

The drive-away at the gas pump was a sad case, a crime that grew more prevalent with gas prices rising and people out of work.

"I have to get to my job," the belligerent young man groaned when Meadow showed up at his door with a copy of the surveillance camera photo. "Ma'am, the baby got sick and we had to pay the doctor up front. No gas, no job . . ."

"I understand how hard things can get," she said gently. "But stealing is still against the law, regardless of the reason."

He drew in a breath. "I guess I'm arrested," he said with resignation.

"The owner is willing to drop the charge if you'll pay for the gas."

He brightened, just a little. He dug into his pockets and pulled out several one dollar bills and a few coins. "I just pumped eight dollars' worth," he explained. He was counting money. "That's all of it." He flushed as he handed it over. "I'm real sorry. I promise I won't do it again."

"Listen," she said softly, "there are all sorts of places you can get help. Your local church probably has emergency funds for things like this. There's the Sharing Place, which has canned goods and clothes. They have emergency funds, too. You should talk to them."

His eyebrows were arching. "They help folks like us?" he asked. "I thought that was just for people who were homeless."

She shook her head. "It's for anybody who needs it. The local family and children services agency can help, too. There are all sorts of programs. There's even a truck that comes once a week downtown to distribute groceries to people who can't afford them."

He looked as if he'd won the lottery. "We got a new baby and we been going without some things to buy that new soy milk he has to have—he's allergic to cow's milk."

She smiled. "Ask your boss for an hour off and go talk to some of these people."

"Ma'am, I'll do that very thing. Thanks for not arresting me. And thank Mr. Billings at the gas station. Tell him I'm real sorry. If he ever needs anything, I'll come do it for free, to help make up for stealing from him."

"I'll tell him."

She went back to the office, sad at the state of the world.

"What's got you so disheartened?" Jeff asked.

She smiled. "I guess it shows, huh? I was just thinking how hard life is for some people. The young man coughed up the price of the gas. They have a new baby and he has to have soy milk . . ."

His eyebrows were arching like crazy.

She blinked. "Was it something I said?"

"The young man's name is John Selton. He isn't married. He hasn't got a child. In fact, he hasn't got a job," he added, holding up a sheet of paper. "He just got out of state prison for passing bad checks."

She sat down on the edge of the desk. "Well!"

"Hey, at least you got Mr. Billings's gas money back," he said, trying to cheer her.

She smiled vacantly. "Do you think that some people should never be given jobs in law enforcement?" she asked.

He chuckled. "Sometimes we have to learn that not everybody is honest."

"I've been in law enforcement for several years," she pointed out. "I was a policewoman in Missouri and I was with the FBI for two years. If I haven't learned to size up people by now, there isn't a lot of hope that I'll develop the skill."

He almost bit his tongue trying not to say what he was thinking. He agreed with her. She was the least likely law enforcement officer he'd ever met, but he was basically a kind man. So he just smiled.

He did give her a job looking up cold cases while he sent his chief deputy working wrecks with the highway patrol and his volunteer deputies checking out reports of vandalism and petty theft.

Meadow came across an interesting cold case, that of a stolen antique pipe organ that had once belonged to a famous politician. It was said to be his grandmother's. It had vanished four years earlier about the time a fire had burned down the local tourist attraction where the politician had lived.

"Are you sure it didn't burn down in the fire?" Jeff asked Meadow when she described the case to him.

"There was enough left to be sure that an organ wasn't with the destroyed furnishings," she replied. "I talked to the fire chief. He remembered the case. He said that it was very probably an arson case, but since it was set with pine kindling and newspaper, there wasn't enough evidence to trace a suspect."

"Four years ago." Jeff frowned. "I remember the case. We investigated. In fact, we had Mike Markson take a look at a similar organ we found in an antique catalog. The thing was worth over fifty thousand dollars. But the stolen one never turned up. Honestly, I'm not sure we'd have recognized it, if it had. An organ's an organ. We did have Mike and Gary look out for anybody local selling one."

"They never had an inquiry?"

He shook his head. "Mike deals mostly in period furniture and lamps, he's not musical. And Gary certainly isn't. When he saw the photo we used for comparison, he thought it was a player piano." He chuckled.

"We can't all be musical, I guess," she agreed.

He checked his watch. "Go home," he said. "It's quitting time. I like what you're doing with those cold case files, by the way," he added. "None of us ever thought about putting them on the computer."

She smiled. "It's easier to check and cross-reference them if you have them on disc," she said. "Sorry, but your filing system is . . . how can I put this . . . antiquated?"

"Obsolete," he corrected with a grin. "Don't worry about hurting my feelings." He gave her a long look. "How about supper?"

Her eyebrows arched.

"Just supper," he added lazily. "I have no plans to propose over dessert."

She burst out laughing. "Oh. Well, okay. That would be nice. I haven't even thought about what I was going to cook."

"You can cook?"

She gave him a speaking look. "I can make homemade bread and French pastries," she said haughtily. "My grandmother taught me, years ago."

"I can put those cans of biscuits in a pan and bake them," he said. "Otherwise, it's TV dinners."

"No wonder you're so slender," she chided.

He chuckled. "Well, that's mostly because I'm always running. If it isn't the job, it's working cattle."

"I forgot. You have a ranch."

He nodded. "It joins on the north side of your father's property," he said. He looked out the window. "And it looks as if our first snow is only a day or two away. We'll be out beating the bushes for stray cattle."

She frowned. Should she be worried about that? "Oh, dear," she said. "I guess I should be thinking about that, too."

"You have capable cowboys who'll do that for you," he assured her. "Nothing to worry about."

She grimaced. "I don't know what I'm doing," she confessed. "I've never had to run a ranch. Dad knew all that stuff, but I wasn't interested in learning, so I never listened to him talk about management." She sighed. "I hope the whole outfit doesn't go on the rocks because of me."

He bit his tongue to keep from making her an offer for the place right then. He had to bide his time. *Slow, Jeff,* he told himself, *you have to go slow.*

"We'll have supper at the Chinese place, if that's okay."

"I love sesame chicken," she confessed.

He laughed. "I like chow mein. But, hey, it's still Chinese."

"Got a point. What time?"

"I'll pick you up about six."

"Suits me. See you then."

She went through her closet looking for a nice dress. She had plenty of pantsuits, but an evening out seemed to call for something a little less structured and worklike. She had one nice black cocktail dress. She paired it with elegant pumps and her one good coat, a black wool one with a small mink collar. She started to put her hair up, but when she brushed it out, she loved the way it looked down around her shoulders. It softened the lines of her face, made her look more feminine, younger. In the end, she left it long.

As she finished her makeup, there was a belligerent knock at the front door. She sighed heavily. She almost certainly knew who it was, since Jeff wasn't due for another thirty minutes.

With resignation she opened it, and there, in the snow, stood Dal Blake with Snow. The dog rushed in past him, leaving Meadow to deal with him.

But the belligerence seemed to drop away as he stared at her with narrowed dark eyes. "Going somewhere?" he asked.

"Yes," she replied curtly. "Jeff asked me to dinner."

He pursed his lips as he stared at her. She was sexy as hell in that dress, and she looked pretty with her face made up. He remembered the taste of her mouth under the mistletoe at a long-ago Christmas party and hated the sudden hunger it kindled in him. He'd spent years not seeing her. She wasn't his sort of woman. No sense starting something he couldn't finish.

But his body reacted sharply to the sight of her in that tempting little dress. Jeff would certainly sit up and take notice. Why was that so irritating? He scowled.

"It's not a scandalous dress!" she blurted out, uncomfortable at the way he was watching her.

"I never said it was." He hesitated. "You look . . . nice."

Her heart jumped. She ignored it. "Thanks. I'm sorry, was Snow at your house again?"

He just nodded. He stuck his big hands in the pockets of his heavy shepherd's coat. Under the wide brim of his hat, where snowflakes were gathering, he looked very much a Western man.

She shifted. She didn't really know what to say. She'd expected a broadside about her pet, but he wasn't belligerent. Not yet, at least.

His head lifted. "Just a tip," he said after a minute. "Jeff loves heavy perfume, and he's a card-carrying liberal. If you want to make an impression, that will help."

She brightened. At least he wasn't insulting her. "Okay." She paused. "Thanks."

He shrugged. "Jeff's my friend. He's a good guy."

She smiled. "Yes, he is. He's a great boss."

"Well, your dog's home. I have work to do. See you."

"I'll try harder to keep her at home. Sorry."

He didn't even answer her. He kept walking to the horse tied to a nearby tree, the one he'd obviously arrived on. He mounted and rode away, still without looking back at her. She closed the door and went to put on more perfume.

Jeff just stared at her when she opened the door, heavy coat on but unbuttoned and her purse in hand. He smiled slowly. "Nice," he said, putting so much feeling into the one word that she flushed a little. She wasn't used to admiring males.

He looked pretty good, too, in dark slacks with a white cotton shirt, red tie, and wool jacket.

"Thanks," she said.

"Shay shay," he said.

She raised both eyebrows.

"It means thank you," he said. "One of the waitresses at the Chinese restaurant goes to college up in Denver. She's teaching me."

She laughed. "That sounds like fun."

"She'll teach you, too. It never hurts to know a little about other languages and cultures. It rounds us out."

"I totally agree."

"Well, if you're ready . . . ?"

"I am." She closed the door behind her, locked it, and put the key in her purse. She noticed when they got in Jeff's sedate sedan that he looked uncomfortable and he was coughing.

"Mind a little air-conditioning, just to stir the air?" he asked, and he sounded hoarse.

Odd, air-conditioning in freezing temps, but she just smiled and nodded. "That's fine."

He turned it on and took a deep breath. He did stop coughing afterward.

The waitress was very nice. She laughed when Jeff explained that he was teaching Meadow what the waitress taught him.

"I'll make sure I add words every time you come here," she told him with twinkling black eyes. "What would you like?"

They gave their order and settled down with cups of hot jasmine tea. Meadow was enjoying herself until the front door bell tinkled and Dal Blake walked in with a striking brunette.

Jeff glowered toward them. "Dana," he muttered.

"Excuse me?"

"Dana Conyers. She owns the local florist shop in Raven Springs," he said, his eyes never leaving the brunette. "She's a sweet woman. Sings in the choir at the Methodist church, teaches Sunday School, volunteers at the Sharing Place on Saturdays. Shame that she's going around with a man who goes through women like handkerchiefs."

That sounded bitter. She watched him watching the florist. He was a little too interested for a casual observer. It got more interesting when Dana Conyers saw him with Meadow and abruptly shifted her eyes back to Dal.

"The world's full of women," Jeff said under his breath. "Why does he have to go around with her?"

"She likes him," Meadow said. "You can tell."

He made a face. "He plays up to her. Brings her flowers. Takes her places. She's never had a real beau. But he won't marry her. He's not the sort."

"Maybe she doesn't want to get married," she ventured.

"She loves kids." He toyed with the spoon in his tea cup. "She volunteers at the Christmas party, giving out gifts to the children."

"I see." She didn't, but it was something to say.

Dal had Dana by the elbow and was guiding her as they followed the waitress past the booth where Meadow and Jeff were sitting.

Dal raised both eyebrows. "I thought you didn't date coworkers," he told Jeff.

Jeff glowered at him. "It's just supper."

Dal shrugged. His dark eyes slid over Meadow in her pretty but conservative dress, down the length of her long hair.

She just smiled. She didn't say a word.

"Do you give her more than one bullet for her gun?" Dal asked Jeff conversationally.

"Not nice." Jeff wagged a finger at him.

"I'm Dana Conyers," the brunette said to Meadow. "I think I've seen you around town."

"I'm Jake Dawson's daughter," Meadow said.

"Oh, yes, we did the flowers for the funeral," the other woman said. "I'm very sorry. He seemed like a nice person."

"He was," Meadow said, and fought tears.

"Sorry again," Dana grimaced. "It must be hard."

"Did you ever run down that lamp of Harlow's that was stolen?" Dal asked Jeff.

"Not yet. Meadow's on the case."

Dal gave her a speaking look. "Well, that certainly raises the level of confidence, doesn't it?"

Meadow glared at him. "I've been in law enforcement for years," she began.

"Did I mention that your father and I found the bullet that lodged in the tractor housing . . . ?" Dal interrupted.

Meadow's lips made a thin line. "You've told me a number of times."

"The waitress is motioning to you," Jeff said quickly, nodding toward her.

Dal smiled sarcastically. "Then I guess we should go. Good seeing you, Jeff."

"Sure."

"Nice meeting you, Miss Dawson," Dana added.

Meadow just nodded. She wasn't sure she could get words out, she was so angry. Leave it to that, that, cattleman to make her feel small! He worked overtime at it, too.

"Don't let him rattle you," Jeff said, noting her irritation. "He just does it to get a rise."

"He is the most irritating, unpleasant person I've ever known," she said through her teeth.

"And he works at it, too," Jeff returned with a grin.

She laughed. "So he does."

The waitress came back by and freshened their tea. Talk turned to work while they waited for their orders.

It was a pleasant meal. Meadow enjoyed Jeff's company. He was interesting to talk to. He'd been in law enforcement much longer than she had, from the age of seventeen, in fact, and he had a wealth of stories that he shared about life in Raven Springs, past and present.

"What's the most unusual case you've covered?" she asked.

He laughed. "The Peeping Tom."

Her eyebrows arched in a question.

"We had this guy peering in windows, always very early in the morning, when women were getting ready to go to work. It was always the same houses, too. He was barefoot, we could tell by the prints he left. He never tried to break in or anything, but just the fact that we had such a guy in the community was disturbing."

"Did you catch him?"

"Oh, yes." He forced down laughter. "He tripped over a child's tricycle and went down in a mud puddle after a spring rain. It turned out to be that he wasn't trying to look at naked women at all. He'd lost his cat and he thought one of two families had stolen it, so he peeked in early in the morning, hoping he'd see them feed the cat."

"Now I've heard everything."

"It gets worse." He was choking back laughter. "It turns out that one of the houses actually did have his cat. The little girl—the one whose trike he fell over—had taken it home with her and hidden it in her room. No litter box, you understand. Her mother did notice a smell, but she thought it was the garbage can outside the window."

"Did he get his cat back?"

"He did, with an apology from the child. However," he added, sipping tea with a laugh, "he did get probation for the peeping charge."

"He must have loved the cat."

"Very much."

"What about the little girl?"

"Her mother bought her a cat of her own, *and* a litter box," he added with a chuckle.

Meadow smiled. "I used to have cats when I was a child. I wasn't really a dog person, but I love my Snow. She's a lot of company, and she does at least howl when somebody comes up outside."

He frowned. "Howls?"

"She's a Siberian husky. They don't bark. They howl."

"Well!"

She laughed at his surprise. She remembered then what Dal had told her about Jeff's politics, so she launched into a dig at the current administration in Washington DC and the loss of the liberal agenda. It wasn't really her own position, but she wanted to impress her boss. She didn't notice at first that he clammed up and said little. It was puzzling— he almost seemed to feel offended.

Chapter Four

They finished the nice meal and Jeff escorted her out to the car and helped her inside. It was snowing heavily. He had no trouble driving in it, but Meadow noticed that he was almost silent the whole way back to her house.

"Did I say something wrong?" she asked when he pulled up at her door.

"What? Oh. No. No! Of course not," he replied.

Too many denials meant he was thinking just the opposite. She did remember that much from her years in law enforcement.

She remembered what Dal had told her. She thought about the coughing and the air-conditioning. Jeff was coughing again, in fact.

"You don't really like heavy perfume, do you?" she asked.

He made a face and pulled out an inhaler. He took a breath of it and stuck it back in his pocket. "Well, honestly, no," he confessed sheepishly. "I have allergies."

Meadow caught her breath. "I'm sorry! I'm so sorry!"

"Not your fault. You didn't know."

"And you aren't a liberal, either, are you?"

He grimaced. "Well, no. I'm a conservative."

"Oh! That man! That hateful man! And I thought he was being nice, and helping me, and all the time . . ."

Jeff's eyebrows arched. "What man?"

"Dal Blake," she almost spat the name out. Her face was flushed with bad temper. "He brought Snow back home just before you came. She practically lives at his house. I told him we were going out. He said you loved heavy perfume and you were a card-carrying liberal."

Jeff saw the light. He started laughing. "Helpful, wasn't he?"

"That man!" she repeated furiously.

"Well, forewarned is forearmed," he quoted. "Don't pay him any attention."

"Why would he do that?"

"I suppose it's best to be honest, even when it feels wrong," he said under his breath. "You see, Meadow, your land borders on his on the east and mine on the west," he said. "This ranch," he looked around, "has the best water in the county, and plenty of it. He's hoping you won't get involved with me because he wants the land. He tried to buy the ranch from your father, but he wouldn't sell. He said it was a family legacy and he was leaving it to you."

"I begin to see the light." She was looking at him askance now.

"It was just dinner," he lied, laughing. "I have no ulterior motives. But apparently, my friend Dal does."

"I was just thinking that," she said through her teeth.

"You remember that," he said, wagging a finger at her. "Water is the most important resource we have in this part of Colorado."

"At least I know where his mind is. I won't listen to any more of his helpful advice about you," she promised, laughing softly. "And I'm truly sorry about the perfume. And the long speech about liberals." She paused. "Actually, I voted for the conservative candidate myself. Most of us in law enforcement aren't with the liberal agenda. We're mostly patriotic and on the side of constitutional law."

"Me too."

He got out and opened her door, taking her arm as he helped her over a mound of snow and up onto her porch.

"I had fun," he said.

"So did I. The food was great."

"We'll do this again. Okay?"

She smiled. "Okay."

He bent and brushed his mouth gently over hers. "Sleep well."

He was gone before she could decide whether or not she liked kissing him. There hadn't been a spark, he didn't make her heart race. But it was early days. Now that she understood why Dal Blake had tried to sabotage the relationship before it began, she'd be on her guard. She and her boss could really get to know each other. She was looking forward to it.

She undressed and pulled on the long yellow granny gown she liked to sleep in, brushing out her hair after she removed her makeup. Jeff was so nice. She really liked him.

Her cell phone rang with the *Sherlock* theme. She loved the series on PBS. She pressed the answer button. "Hello?"

"How'd the date go?" Dal drawled.

"Very badly, thanks to you!" she shot back. "How could you?"

"Jeff's a good sport, even if you aren't," he mused.

"He has allergies! How could you tell me that he liked heavy perfume?"

"He's got allergy medicine," he said easily.

"It was mean!"

"So I'm mean," he replied. "At least you know now how badly he wants that ranch, don't you? He didn't say a thing about the heavy perfume and the liberal pep talk, did he?"

His tone was hard, firm. She hated him because he was right. Jeff hadn't been honest until she forced him to be. She knew that Dal, in his place, would have complained immediately about the perfume, and he'd have gone after her hammer and tongs about her improvised liberal opinions. Whatever else he was, he was honest.

"I don't care . . ." She paused. There was a loud meow from behind her.

She turned, phone in hand, as Jarvis walked into the bedroom as if he owned it and started purring and rubbing up against her legs through the gown. "Your cat's here!" she muttered.

"Nail the dog door shut," he suggested sarcastically.

"I can't! Snow wouldn't be able to get out when she needed to use the bathroom!"

"Speaking of Snow, guess where she is?"

She drew in a breath. "Well, that's just great! I'll put on a coat and bring your cat to you!"

"No need. I'll drive Snow down and meet you at the front door."

She bit her tongue trying not to make a snide remark. She didn't want to have to go out in the knee-deep snow in her gown and a coat. "All right. Thanks," she added grudgingly.

"No sweat."

He hung up.

She led Jarvis to the front door and hunted up a coat. She wasn't giving Dal the opportunity to make any nasty remarks about her being dressed for bed and trying to lure him in like a spider with a web.

She thought of herself as a giant spider in a yellow nightgown and started laughing uproariously.

* * *

He was there in less than five minutes, driving a ranch truck. He opened the door and let Snow out and walked her to the front door where Meadow was waiting.

He stared at her in the enveloping Berber coat. It was black, and it highlighted the long, honey blond hair curling around her shoulders. She looked worn and sleepy. Her green eyes were lackluster.

"You've just been out on a hot date. Shouldn't you look bright-eyed and joyful?" he chided.

She glared at him. "It was a nice Chinese dinner."

He shrugged. "I flew the florist down to San Antonio last week for fajitas and salsa."

"Lucky her."

He pursed his lips. "That wouldn't be jealousy . . . ?"

"As if I could be jealous of a man who once referred to me as a spider!" she burst out.

He raised a dark, thick eyebrow. "I believe the term I used was 'prostitute in training.' And you deserved it. Seventeen and trying to seduce a man my age," he scoffed. "Your father was livid."

She flushed and averted her eyes. "Teenagers get crushes on all sorts of unsuitable people," she muttered.

"So they do."

It was freezing cold. She let the door open so that Snow could run in. Jarvis came when she called him. He ran past her and jumped into Dal's arms.

"Thanks for bringing Snow back home," she said.

He was still watching her, in that odd intent way. "You should see a doctor."

"What?!"

"I mean it," he repeated, his dark eyes going narrow. "Jeff said you fell today at work."

"I tripped over a trash can," she began.

"You had two falls at Christmas, two years running," he recalled. "You told Jeff you had a fall when pursuing a criminal in St. Louis, and you hit your father's tractor with a shot when you fell here. Hasn't it occurred to you that a balance issue like that has a cause?"

No, it hadn't. She'd never really thought about how many falls she'd had. "I don't have a medical condition," she said belligerently. "I'm just clumsy."

"I don't think so," he replied. "Humor me. Old Dr. Colson is still practicing, and we're not that far from Denver. You'll have insurance that will pay for tests, won't you?"

She had private insurance that she assumed when she left the Bureau. "Yes," she said grudgingly.

"Tests never killed anyone," he added.

"I'll think about it."

He cocked his head and looked at her intently. "It might be nothing at all. But it's something you need checked. What if you were chasing a perpetrator on a high place and you fell?"

She'd thought about that once or twice herself. But she denied the balance issues because of what they might reveal if she had tests. She knew that tumors of the brain could cause them. She had headaches . . .

She lifted her chin. "Was that all?"

His eyes were on her soft mouth. "No good-night kiss?" he mused.

"I am not kissing you!"

His eyebrows arched. "Heaven forbid!" he exclaimed. "I was referring to the fact that Jeff obviously didn't kiss you. Your mouth isn't swollen." He smiled tauntingly. "The perfume put him off?"

"You . . . you . . . !" She was searching for just the right word when he put Jarvis gently down on the porch and reached for her.

Before she could get a word out, his head bent and he was kissing her. Really kissing her. So hard and hungrily that she couldn't fight him. She wanted to. She should . . .

Her mouth opened softly and he groaned and kissed her more insistently. She felt the shock of it all the way up and down her body, and she moaned, too.

His hands went under the open coat, to her waist, and then around her, bringing her against the length of his long, hard body. He enfolded her against him, devouring her soft, warm mouth in the cold while snowflakes drifted around and over them.

After a minute, he pulled back with some reluctance, one big hand going to her flushed cheek, his fingers tracing down to her swollen mouth as he studied the confusion and pleasure she couldn't hide from him.

"Now you look kissed, Meadow," he said huskily, and he didn't smile.

She still couldn't find words.

He pursed his lips. Like hers, they were faintly swollen. "At least now, when Jeff kisses you properly, you'll have somebody to compare him with, won't you?" he drawled as he moved back.

She got her voice back. "And you'll have somebody to compare your florist with!"

He laughed softly. "She doesn't have any competition," he said outrageously. "She knows how to kiss." He lifted an eyebrow. "You need practice."

She glared at him, her expression furious. "Not with you!"

"Oh, of course not. I don't need practice," he drawled, chuckling.

She wasn't touching that line with a pole. She jerked her coat closer around her, turned, walked past Jarvis, called Snow inside, and closed the door firmly, before he could follow her in. A minute later, she heard the truck start and drive away.

She looked at herself in the hall mirror and caught her breath. She was almost pretty. Her green eyes were glistening with excitement, her expression was one of absolute joy. That man! That horrible man!

He'd said that this was how she was supposed to look after her date with Jeff. He was right, although she'd never admit it to him.

It was maddening, that he'd sabotaged her date and then come down here to mock her. But why had he kissed her? It made no sense. He'd said often enough that he was in a relationship with his local florist, and he'd never made a secret of the fact that Meadow didn't appeal to him. So why had he kissed her, and so hungrily that her mouth was still swollen?

She thought that she'd never understand him. He'd said that she needed practice. Of course she wasn't experienced. She'd never been intimate with a man. He'd certainly ascertained that quickly enough, and then taunted her with it. He flaunted his own experience. Certainly, he knew what to do with a woman's mouth. He was an expert. She flushed, remembering how hungry he'd made her, with a kiss that never even got really out of hand.

She'd wanted it to get out of hand. That was humiliating, to want a man that badly and have him know it and ridicule her for it.

Had he been pointing out Jeff's obvious lack of experience with women? Well, it wasn't a drawback to Meadow. She didn't want a man who'd been used like a towel on a dirty dog.

That set her off and she started laughing. Dal was a bath towel. She shook her head, patted Snow on the head, and led her toward the bedroom. As an afterthought, she closed the bedroom door, discouraging the dog from going out.

"You'll have to wake me up if you need to go potty," she told the laughing husky. "I'm not letting you land me with Dal Blake twice in one night."

She crawled into bed, set her clock, and turned out the

lights. But she didn't sleep until it was almost dawn. And when she finally did, Dal figured prominently in her confused dreams.

She wondered why Dal had been insistent about her going to a doctor about her clumsiness. It wasn't as if she meant anything to him. He'd made her painfully aware of that over the years. She had considered a physical reason for her falls, but she had no real symptoms, and it looked like a waste of time to her. She was due for a physical the following month, anyway. It wouldn't hurt to mention it to the doctor, she supposed. But it wasn't going to be a priority.

The snow started coming down in buckets full the following Saturday. Meadow was off work, which was a good thing, because her cowboys were going nuts trying to feed and find cattle in the whiteout.

Meadow, concerned, actually dressed in jeans and boots and a shepherd's coat, went to get a horse.

"Ma'am," the horse wrangler stammered, "you aren't really going to go out and hunt cattle . . . ?"

"It's my ranch," she said haughtily. "Of course I'm going to!"

She had him saddle the horse and then she stood next to it, grinding her teeth, while she wondered how she was going to get into the saddle. It had been years since she'd ridden.

"Uh, ma'am, there's a mounting block," the younger of two cowboys pointed to it, just at the edge of the barn.

"Thanks," she said tautly.

She led the horse over to the block, stepped up on it, and sprang into the saddle. "Well," she said to herself. "That wasn't too bad . . ."

Just as she said it, her hands jerked on the bridle and the horse reared up and ran away with her.

She heard a shout behind her and then the sound of horse's hooves thundering in the snow. At least they were going to try to save her. She caught the horse's mane and tightened her legs around his sides, holding on for dear life. Her father had said something about runaway horses, but all she could remember was to hang on and don't get thrown.

She tried to guide the horse with her legs, but he was unsettled and unresponsive. She hoped he wasn't going to run her under a low limb and get her killed. She kept her head down and prayed for him to stop.

Horses' hooves sounded closer. A minute later, the horse was being forcibly slowed, and a firm deep voice called to him, calming him as he came to a stop, finally, and stood panting for breath.

"Are you all right?" Dal Blake asked, riding his horse up to hers, but in the opposite direction. "Meadow?"

Funny, he actually sounded concerned. She was trying to get her own breath. "Yes. Thanks," she panted.

"What happened?"

She grimaced as she forced her eyes up to his. "I jerked the reins when I mounted him."

"Her," he corrected with forced patience. "She's a mare."

She glared at him.

He reached down and got the reins, handing them back to her. "Follow me back to the ranch. I'm not leaving you here. And she'll need to be put up."

She wanted to argue, but she felt sorry for the horse. "All right."

His eyebrows arched. "My God, are you actually agreeing with me?"

"It won't set a precedent," she muttered.

"No doubt there. Come on. Catch up."

She followed him back to the ranch, where two cowboys stood waiting for her. She coaxed the poor horse to the mounting block, where she painstakingly dismounted. Her legs felt sore and bruised just from the short ride. She began to see that she wasn't going to be able to just go out and get in the saddle and ride all day without some preliminary rides to adjust to the horse.

She grimaced as she got to the ground, leaving one of the cowboys to lead the animal back into the barn and take care of it.

Dal glanced at the older cowboy who'd helped her get the horse saddled. "Ted, you'd better get the men out to check on the cattle. You can't afford to start losing calves."

"I was going to bring the pregnant mamas closer to the barn," Ted told him. "We're short a couple of hands today. That damned flu laid them up."

"I'll send a couple of my men over to help." He noted Meadow's open mouth. "It's what we do out here in the wild," he said before she could speak. "We help each other. Neighbors do that."

She closed her mouth and bit back a short reply. "Okay. Thanks," she added as an afterthought.

He tipped his hat. "You're welcome." He stared at her. "Jeff said he's taking you to dinner again tonight."

She flushed. "Yes. To the new steak place."

"They have good food. I take the florist there sometimes."

She ignored him. She was jealous of the florist. It would never do to let him know it. "Thanks again."

She started limping back toward the ranch house.

"You have to start out riding every day to build up those

muscles in your legs," he called after her. "Sitting in the living room knitting doesn't teach squat."

"Thank you for that brilliant observation, Mr. Blake."

There was a soft chuckle before she shut the door behind her.

She soaked in a hot tub of water, groaning at the protesting muscles. She hadn't ridden in a long time. She knew the cowboys were probably out there with the so-superior Dal Blake laughing their heads off at their tenderfoot boss. Clearly, a few more YouTube videos were going to be necessary for her to learn anything about the ranch. Maybe one or two on horse riding and how to handle a runaway. But not tonight. She had a date!

Jeff gave her a grin when he saw the way she was walking. She wore a simple gray pantsuit tonight, with a pink camisole underneath, and wool-lined leather boots with her Berber coat. One thing she had learned was how to dress for the cold.

Jeff was wearing a heavy coat, too, over jeans and a long-sleeved shirt. They'd agreed that it was going to be an informal evening. Meadow was grateful. Her legs were still killing her.

"I hear you had an adventure today," he remarked when they were walking through the line past all the delicious food that servers were putting on plates for them.

She grimaced. "I guess Dal told you."

"He said a horse ran away with you," he replied. He wasn't going to add that his best friend sounded worried about her, or that his concern had shown. "You need riding lessons. It's been a long time since you've been on horseback, hasn't it?"

"Yes, it has," she said reluctantly. "All I could do was hang on. I jerked the bridle. Apparently the horse is high strung. I should have picked a gentler one."

"Need to let your men do that for you," he said.

"I know. I was in a hurry. I just picked a horse and told them to saddle it. Ted tried to argue with me, but . . ." She grimaced. "I was bullheaded. I'm like my dad, I guess."

He laughed. "Nothing wrong with being stubborn sometimes. It's what leads to solving cold cases."

"I suppose so."

"Legs sore?"

She laughed. "Does it show?"

"Well, you're pretty much walking like a senior citizen," he added when they'd gone through the line and were sitting in a booth.

"I'd forgotten how sore it could make you," she confessed. "I always liked to ride, but I've never been good at it. I'm afraid of horses," she added, lowering her voice. "This isn't the first time I've had one run away with me. The last time ended badly. It stopped suddenly and I went over its head into a shallow stream. Hit my head." She frowned. "I was sixteen. I'd forgotten."

"Your dad took you to a doctor, didn't he?"

"I was riding with my mother, in Mississippi. Our cousin has a big farm there, and he keeps quarter horses that he'd let us ride on his place." She hesitated. "Mom took me to the doctor, but he didn't do tests. He checked me out and said I had a mild concussion. I wasn't ever in real danger."

"I see."

"But it sort of put me off horseback riding, if you get my drift." She laughed.

"I can see why!"

"This is really good," she exclaimed, having tasted the rare steak she'd ordered.

"They use a lot of spices," he said. "It brings out the flavor." He closed his eyes as he chewed and moaned softly. "Gosh, this is great!"

She laughed. "Now I understand why the place is so crowded. It's just . . ." She stopped, looking past him, and ground her teeth.

He gave her a curious look before his head turned. He saw the reason for her consternation. There was Dal Blake with the florist, attentive and smiling as they headed for a booth right beside Jeff and Meadow's.

"Well, what a coincidence," Dal exclaimed, putting down his plate to shake hands with Jeff. "What are you two doing here?"

"Eating," Meadow said without cracking a smile.

Dal chuckled. "Somebody's in a sour mood. Maybe that dessert will sweeten you up."

She just glared at him before she turned her attention to the florist. She forced a smile. "Nice to see you again, Miss Conyers."

Dana smiled back. "Good to see you, too, Miss Dawson. This is our favorite hangout on the weekends," she added with an adoring glance at Dal, who frowned and looked briefly irritated.

"It's one of several we go to," he amended. He studied Meadow in her pantsuit. "No dress?" he commented.

She pushed back her long blond hair. "It's casual Saturday," she said.

Dal looked pointedly at Dana in her brief red and white dress with ruffles at the neckline and long sleeves. She had pretty legs that were on display, discreetly enhanced by tight-fitting black hose.

"I like women in dresses," he said, and smiled as Dana flushed with pleasure at the remark.

"You just like looking at Dana's fabulous legs," Jeff chided, and then seemed to bite his tongue at the remark.

Dana's eyes brightened and she laughed. "Thanks, Jeff. That was sweet."

"She does have fabulous legs," Dal agreed, studying them with male appreciation.

Meadow did her best to ignore him, busily munching mashed potatoes with gravy.

"Obviously, Miss Dawson doesn't like having hers on display," Dal said with dripping sarcasm.

"Mine don't go all the way up, so I have to conceal them in pants," Meadow said without looking at him.

There was muffled laughter from Jeff.

Dana laughed.

"These potatoes are awesome," Meadow told Jeff. "I don't usually like garlic, but they do add a lot to the taste."

"Hard on amorous men, however," Dal said deliberately. "Right, Jeff?" he chided.

Jeff looked embarrassed. He cleared his throat. "I like garlic."

Meadow hated having her boss embarrassed. She glared up at Dal. "I like garlic, too. I'm somewhat less impressed by overbearing male pigs."

Dal's eyes twinkled. "Seen any around?"

"I'm staring right at one," she shot back.

"Uh, Dal, shouldn't we get to our food? The movie starts in an hour . . ."

"Absolutely," he told Dana, smiling as he eased her into the booth and slid in across from her.

Meadow looked at Jeff and rolled her eyes comically. He chuckled, relieved at the interruption.

All through the lovely meal, it was impossible not to overhear Dal's deep, drawling voice complimenting Dana on her appearance and referring to other dates, and places they'd been, and people they'd met.

By the time Meadow finished the last of her dessert and

her now-cold coffee, she was more than ready to get out of the restaurant by the quickest possible method.

"Are you ready to go?" she asked Jeff hopefully.

He was staring sadly toward the back of Dana's head. He caught himself and smiled. "Of course."

Jeff left a tip under his tray and nodded toward the couple behind them. He didn't say good-bye. Neither did Meadow.

Jeff caught Meadow's hand in his as they walked out of the restaurant. He seemed to do that deliberately, so that Dana would see. Meadow was getting a definite suspicion that Jeff had a case on the pretty florist.

Good luck to him, she thought, because Dal Blake was formidable competition, and he obviously liked the woman. God knew why.

"It was a lovely meal," she said when they were back in the car.

"There are a couple of good movies on at the cinema. Want to see one?" Jeff asked.

Meadow remembered that Dana had mentioned they were going there after they ate. "No, I don't think so, thanks," she said abruptly.

He chuckled. "Me neither. Dal might think we are following them around. He's possessive of Dana," he added with a bite in his tone.

"He's got no staying power," she said when they were standing on her porch. "He plays the field. If she's not careful, he'll break her heart. Dad said once that he was a real rounder."

He glanced at her, surprised by the venom in her tone. "You don't like him at all, do you?"

"No," she said shortly. "He's like a tray of hors d'oeuvres that's been passed around too much at a party. Not my sort of man. Not at all."

He sighed. "I'm sort of the opposite. I don't get out much."

She laughed. "Neither do I."

"So we might stick together, just for survival, like Chris Pratt said in that movie, *Jurassic World*," he teased.

"Not a bad idea," she agreed. "You know, you're a nice boss. And I like going places with you."

"I like going places with you, too, Meadow." He drew her to him, bent, and kissed her very gently.

She smiled. He smiled. He kissed her again, a little harder. But there was no spark. Not for either of them. And it was painfully obvious.

"Well, I'll get to sleep. See you at church tomorrow," she added, because they both attended services at the local Methodist church.

"Count on it. See you there."

"Thanks. I had fun."

"Me too!"

She waved him off and went back inside.

Chapter Five

Jeff's undersheriff, Gil Barnes, was working on a cold case that had ties to the theft of the Victorian lamp that Meadow was investigating.

He was a little taller than Jeff, built like a rodeo cowboy, with blond-streaked brown hair and black liquid eyes and a somber expression.

"This pipe organ that was stolen suddenly showed up in an antique catalog online at an auction house in New York City," Gil told her. "I think it's tied to the lamp theft."

"It's possible," she had to agree. "But it's been, what, four years since the theft?" she added.

He nodded. "Probably the thief fenced it," he said sadly. "But it might be possible to trace it. I'm going to see if the sheriff will let me fly back east and interrogate some people."

"It would be nice if you could find a link to the lamp. Do you think it might turn up at the same auction house?" she added.

"It would be a long shot," he said. "But we might get lucky."

"I still have some contacts in the Bureau, if you need them," she added. She smiled sheepishly. "Well, I have at least one who might contact me if he didn't recognize my name. I sort of messed up."

He frowned. "How?"

She drew in a breath. "Tripped over my own feet and discharged a weapon into the windshield of a bucar while chasing a suspect." The reference she used was what agents called an FBI vehicle—a bucar.

He gave her a sympathetic smile. "First case I ever worked, we'd had an ice storm and I was chasing a suspect down a long hill. Long story short, I went sideways in a skid, forgot to correct, and ended up in the river."

"Oh, gosh!" she said. "Did you get frostbite?"

He laughed. "You're the first person who was more concerned with my welfare than the car's."

She shrugged. "You can replace cars. People, not so much."

"I knew I liked you," he said softly.

She flushed. "Thanks. You're nice, too."

"And now that we've worked that out, how about getting down to business?" Jeff asked, lounging against the door facing.

"Can I have a plane ticket to New York?" Gil asked abruptly.

Jeff's eyebrows arched. "I'm not that mad."

Gil chuckled. "It's about that pipe organ cold case I'm working."

Jeff grimaced. "While I applaud your enthusiasm, I can just see myself standing in front of the county commission trying to explain why I funded a trip to New York over a pipe organ theft."

Gil drew in a breath. "It was worth a try. Okay, I'll see what I can do with the computer and Skype."

"Now that's a good idea," Jeff said.

"The plane ticket would have been a better one," the undersheriff retorted before he retreated to his desk.

"I'm still looking for the Victorian lamp," Meadow told the sheriff. "I just have a hunch that it's connected to the pipe organ cold case. Both valuable antiques, both stolen locally."

"There's a definite pattern," Jeff admitted. "But they're minor cases," he pointed out. "We have five assaults, four burglaries of jewels and cash, three attempted robberies, two forged checks . . ."

"And a partridge in a pear tree," Meadow blurted out, flushed, and then laughed as Jeff started chuckling. "In my defense, it's almost Christmas," she pointed out.

"So it is. There's a Christmas party at the civic center next Saturday. Will you go with me?"

She hesitated. "Is it formal?"

He shrugged. "I'm not sure."

"If it is, I can't go," she said sadly. "I only own one dress. I'd be embarrassed to wear it twice in a row."

His eyebrows reached for his hairline. "Why?"

"I wear . . . I wore . . . pantsuits to work." She glowered at him. "Well, it's not dignified to chase fugitives wearing short skirts and tights and high heels. It's not very efficient, either."

He cocked his head and studied her. She was wearing yet another pantsuit, this one in dark blue with a simple white blouse. She looked oddly elegant in it, but less feminine than Dana Conyers, whom he'd taken to the dance last year—before they argued. Dana wore sexy things. He loved the way she looked in them. He frowned as he thought about the way they'd argued. Dana would be at the party, he was certain of it, and with Dal.

"Do I look that bad?" Meadow asked.

"What?"

"You're glaring at me."

"I was thinking about Dana," he blurted out. "We went to the dance together last year. We had sort of an argument, and she hasn't spoken to me since."

"An argument?" she prodded.

He moved restively. "I thought her clothes were too seductive and I said so. She said how she dressed was none of my business and asked what century I lived in."

Meadow moved closer. "I used to wear sexy things, too," she said. "Well, not really sexy, but more revealing than what I wear now. I had to interview a prisoner in a jail outside St. Louis. The prisoner seemed very nice and quiet, so I had them uncuff him while we talked. I even had them bring him coffee." Her expression hardened. "It was a sexual assault case. I asked him a question that set him off. He said that I dressed like a woman who really wanted it bad, and he came at me. When I fought, he beat me up." She swallowed hard. The memory was painful. "I never wore revealing things again." She looked up at him, reading the sympathy in his hard face. "I guess Dana has been very lucky. Or maybe I'm just in the wrong sort of profession." She smiled. "Maybe I should hit Dana up for a job selling flowers." She laughed. "If I'm not armed, I'm not really a danger to the public."

"You're not a danger to anything," he said softly. "You had a bad experience, several of them, and you've lost your self-confidence. I'm going to help you get it back. I promise."

Her expression was revealing. "What if I'm not cut out for law enforcement after all? You know, when I was with the police department, all I did was paperwork. They let me train under a patrol officer, but I heard later that he said I'd be a disaster if they turned me loose in a car." She shrugged. "He was right. I wrecked a patrol car. After that, I did mostly investigative work and searched down leads. The Bureau took me on faith, but I think they were sorry about it afterward. The agent who recruited me was a friend of my father's. He helped me get into the academy."

"None of us start out well in law enforcement," he said, but he was thinking she might be right about her choice of professions. He wasn't going to put her in the line of fire, that was for sure.

"Do you want me to keep on the lamp case, or . . . ?"

"I'd like you to run down these forged checks, if you don't mind. You can speak to the security chief at the bank. His name is Tom Jones. He'll help."

She gave him a wide-eyed look. "He didn't retire from a singing career . . . ?"

"Get out of here," Jeff shot at her.

"It's not unusual to be loved by anyone . . ." She warbled on the way out.

"If you sing that song to him, wear track shoes!" he called after her. "You can take it from me that he has absolutely no sense of humor!"

She just laughed.

She realized that he wasn't giving her cases that would put her in the path of violent men. She was grateful in one way and sad in another. He didn't trust her not to mess up. He was probably right. It hurt, just the same.

But it was her job to follow orders. So she did.

Tom Jones looked nothing like the famous singing star. He was big and stocky and had thick black hair and hands the size of plates. He didn't smile. His dark eyes narrowed on her face, as if he was assessing her.

"The sheriff sent me over to ask you about some forged checks," she began.

"Come into my office and we'll talk."

He led the way into a glass-fronted office, offered her a padded leather chair, and sank into the leather of his own desk chair. "One of those suspects has done time already," he told her. "And both of them do private duty as caretakers for the elderly in our community. They stole checks from their employers and learned to forge the names. We were fortunate that both their clients noticed the erroneous charge on their bank statements and called us. We discovered the thefts pretty quickly."

"Nice work."

He smiled, if that faint drawing up of one side of his mouth could be called a smile. He laced his fingers on his chest. "The other suspect is a friend of the one we fingered," he added. "He only got a couple of thousand. His friend, the one with the rap sheet, stole thirty thousand from his client. We can put together all the information you need to prosecute them, and I'll testify in court if you need me to."

"Thanks," she said sincerely. "I'll get back to you on that. Right now, I have to do some interrogations."

"The first suspect, Russell Harris, served time for assault," he returned. "If you interview him, don't go alone. The victim was a woman."

She felt her heart jump, but she smiled. "Thanks for the advice."

"We heard about what happened to you in the Bureau," he said, surprising her. "We'll look out for you here. If you can't get a deputy to go with you, I'll go. I'm licensed to conceal carry and I'm not afraid of men who hit women."

The smile grew bigger. He was nice. "Thanks."

"It's a small community, Raven Springs," he commented. "We don't have many newcomers, so when we do, we start asking questions. In a nice way," he added. "We don't really pry, but we like to know who our neighbors are. I'm sorry for what happened to you," he added. "They should have sent a male agent with you on that interrogation. When I was with the Bureau, I made sure that female agents had backup."

"You were with the Bureau?" she exclaimed.

He nodded. "For five years. They were good years. But

I wanted roots. I have a wife and two young sons," he added, chuckling as he turned a photo to face her.

It was a good-looking group. She noticed that his wife was blond and young and pretty. "Your sons look like you," she said.

"They do," he said with a sigh. "I wanted a pretty little blond girl like my sweetheart there." He indicated the photo. "But God really doesn't take orders." He laughed.

"There's always hope," she pointed out.

"Always." He got up. "Whatever you need, just ask." He frowned. "Why did you leave the Bureau after just a year?"

"They had me filing and typing up reports," she said sadly. "It wasn't what I thought I'd be doing. At least here, the sheriff lets me do investigations and talk to people who don't wear guns."

"I'm sure he's grateful for the help," he added. "The job doesn't pay much, but it comes with a certain amount of prestige, just the same. Welcome home, Miss Dawson. You're going to like living here. Your dad was a fine man."

"He was. Thanks."

"If you need help during the winter, you can always ask Dal Blake," he added. "His place is right next door to yours, and he's a good man. He'll do what he can for you."

"I'm sure he would," she said without feeling. "Thanks again, Mr. Jones."

"No, thank you."

She turned, curious. "What for?"

"Well, for one thing, for not asking if I retired from a singing career." He burst out laughing at her expression. "I can just imagine what Jeff told you about me. Tell him that the next chess game is mine by forfeit."

"I'll tell him." She grinned. "Nice to meet you."

"Nice to meet you, too."

* * *

Jeff was grinning when she got back to the office with the printed documents she'd obtained with a court order, just so everything was legal.

"Did you ask him if he sang?"

"He said you forfeited the next chess match." She laughed.

He sighed. "Well, I guess I should. But he's a good sport. Good security man, too. He was Army intelligence overseas, and he's been both a policeman and an FBI agent."

"He told me. I'll bet he was good at it."

"He was, but he had a girlfriend—now his wife—who informed him that she wasn't lining up to be a widow with him in that sort of work. He had to make a choice, and she won. I don't think he ever regretted it. If you ever see them together, they're like two halves of a whole. Still deeply in love after two kids." He shook his head. "Surprised a lot of people when he married her. There's a fourteen-year age difference. She said love doesn't have an age limit and ignored the gossip." He laughed. "I guess love does triumph."

"I guess so." She was thinking of the age difference between herself and Dal Blake and hated herself for it.

"I wish you'd reconsider the dance," Jeff said solemnly. "You could wear a pantsuit. Nobody would gossip about you."

She drew in a long breath. "Let me think about it for a day or two, okay? I'm not really a party person. And Dal Blake will probably be there," she added darkly.

"You really don't like him, do you?" he asked, and looked pleased.

"No. I really don't. He's arrogant and blunt and impolite . . ."

Jeff held up a hand. "No time for that now. We have to get back to work. I'm sending Gil with you to interview Russell Harris. He works part-time at the Bar K Burger joint. He'll be on his lunch break in ten minutes. I've already alerted his boss that you're on the way."

She smiled. "Thanks."

"Nobody's slugging you around here. Not on my watch," he added, and looked imposing.

"Thanks, Sheriff."

"Jeff."

"No. During working hours, you're the boss. So it's Sheriff. Or boss."

"I like boss better," he commented.

"Okay. Boss."

"Gil!"

"On my way," the other man replied, sliding into his thick coat as he joined them. "Snow's started again."

"We have chains on the patrol cars," Jeff pointed out.

"I think we're going to need them. Weather forecast looks messy for the next few days."

"It's Colorado," Jeff sighed. "Snow is sort of a way of life."

"So it is. You ready to go?" he asked Meadow.

"Yes, I am."

She followed him out to the patrol car, pulling up the hood of her parka as snow peppered down on them.

"That's painful snow," she commented.

"It's sleet mixed with snow. Stings like a bee, doesn't it?" he replied.

"Yes."

He pulled out into the road and drove a mile to the small hamburger joint that sat just off the highway. There were several cars in the parking lot, but Jeff found a vacant parking spot and pulled into it.

"That's quite a crowd in this weather," she commented.

"I recognize four of those cars." He chuckled. "They're EMA."

She frowned.

"Emergency Management," he said. "They're always out if people are lost, and we've had a hiker go missing in the back woods."

He opened the door for her and followed her inside. Four

grizzly-looking men were hunched over the counter drinking coffee and eating pancakes.

"How's it going, Brad?" Gil asked the man in the shepherd's coat.

A broad, unshaven face with heavy eyelids glanced at him. "Badly," he said. "We found some tracks, but the snow covered them up along with most of anything else. Jerry's gone home to get his bloodhound. He'll find the trail."

"Yes, he will. Old Redhide is famous locally," Gil told Meadow. "He can track over anything."

Brad laughed. "He sure can. Found the Candles' little girl when she wandered into the woods after a fawn she saw, last summer. Her parents bought him what looked like a lifetime supply of chewy toys and treats for Redhide."

Meadow grinned. "I've got a husky. She loves those, too."

"A husky. Is she an escape artist?" Brad asked.

She sighed. "She is. I keep her inside, but she has a doggy door for nighttime emergencies. I haven't had to go looking for her for a long time, though. Except at my neighbor's. She loves him."

"Dal Blake." Brad nodded. "He sure misses his old Lab. Hard thing, losing a pet."

"It is," Meadow agreed.

"You here to buy us all breakfast, on account of the great job we do?" Brad teased.

Gil chuckled. "Nope. It's lunchtime, you reprobate, and we're here on another matter."

Brad's face tautened. He glanced toward the last booth, where an unkempt light-haired man was lounging arrogantly, still in his apron. "He's over there. My second cousin was the woman he assaulted. I hoped he'd never get out. But he got lucky on public defenders."

"Some do," Gil said nonchalantly. "See you later."

"Keep safe."

"You do the same."

* * *

Meadow disliked Russell Harris on sight. He was the sort of man she'd seen far too often in lockup. He still had prison tattoos on both arms, and huge biceps. He was wearing a kerchief tied around his forehead.

"You wanted to talk to me?" he drawled, glaring at them. "I haven't done anything wrong. I'm not about to break the law. I don't want to go back inside."

If he was already on probation, Meadow thought, a bad check case would most likely send him straight back to prison. She hated the pleasure the thought gave her.

"We want to talk to you . . ." she began.

"I'll talk to him," Harris interrupted sarcastically. "I don't answer to women for nothing!"

"No, you just hammer them into submission, don't you, Mr. Harris?" she asked sweetly.

His body tautened.

"If you make one move toward her," Gil said softly, his arm at an odd angle, "you'll go back in stir by way of the emergency room. Care to look under the table?" he added.

Harris knew without looking that a .45 Colt was cocked and aimed at his belly. He sat back in the booth. "I didn't pass no bad checks."

Meadow pulled out two sheets of paper. She had to wait until her hands stopped shaking to put them on the table.

"The sheet on the left has your signature on a check from your employer. The sheet on the right has the forged name of the victim in a check forging case. The signatures are the same. Yours."

"I'm not going back!" Harris said, and jumped up.

Gil had him before he could run, spun him around, tossed him down like a feather, and cuffed him so quickly that Meadow was barely on her feet before the suspect was in custody.

She noticed then that the rescue party had gathered close by in case they were needed. She smiled at them. Nice to know that law enforcement had that sort of backup from other members of the community.

They smiled back and sat down.

"You can't prove I did that." Harris was raging all the way to the patrol car. "That paper don't prove nothing!"

They ignored him. They stopped by the drive-in window to get burgers and fries and tell the boss that he was going to be short one employee for a while.

Russell Harris went into a holding cell to be processed. Meadow and Gil went back to the office with food.

The sheriff joined them for lunch.

"We should arrest cooks more often," Jeff commented between bites of his burger and fries. "Especially at lunch time. I don't guess the other suspect works at a restaurant?"

Meadow chuckled. "He works at a feed store. I don't think alfalfa sprouts would taste quite the same."

Jeff grinned.

"That was really good police work," Meadow told Gil. "Gosh, the way you took that guy down was awesome! I had an instructor at the academy who could do it like that. I never could," she confessed. "I'm too clumsy."

"I've been in law enforcement since high school," Gil confessed. "And I did a tour of duty in the Army where I was an MP. I guess I'm used to violent people."

"Good thing," Meadow commented, "because I really thought he was going to come over the table at me." She moved restively. It had brought back painful memories. "Thanks for saving me," she added.

"You'd have done okay," Gil told her. "You don't learn how to do a job unless they let you do it, mistakes and all," he said seriously. "Your bosses did you no favor by sticking you behind a desk."

She smiled warmly. "Thanks. But they did have just cause," she told him. "I have two left feet. Balance issues."

"Ever seen a doctor about them?" Jeff asked.

"Not really. I had a concussion, but it was mild."

"I saw this show about head injuries in football players," Jeff replied. "It showed graphically what happens to them over time. It was sobering. Even a slight head injury can do permanent damage."

"There was that wrestler, you remember him, who killed some people, and they said he had the brain of an eighty-year-old from all the years of being in the ring," Gil commented. "Tragic case."

"That's why football players wear helmets," Jeff said.

"Yes, but the injuries happen in spite of helmets," Gil returned. "And wrestlers don't wear helmets."

"I used to love to watch the Rock on *Monday Night Raw*," Meadow confessed. "Now I watch him in movies instead."

"*Race to Witch Mountain* was one of my favorites," Gil said.

"Oh, mine's *Central Intelligence*," Jeff added. "Nobody like the Rock. He's got a heart the size of a mountain to go with all that talent."

"And he's dishy," Meadow added with a grin.

They just laughed.

Meadow couldn't find the second bad check suspect, although she did trace him to a local motel. He was registered there weekly and had gone away for the weekend. Meadow told Jeff she'd try again on Monday, and he said that was fine but Gil or one of the other deputies would go with her. Just in case. She didn't argue. It might not be politically correct, but having a tough man for backup didn't bother her pride one bit. Not after she'd almost been killed by a suspect.

She went home weary and eager for a quick meal and bed. But when she got there, in driving sleet, she couldn't find her dog.

She went all around the house, calling Snow over and over again. Her voice echoed down the hills, but the dog didn't answer.

She knew that a nearby neighbor trapped animals in the woods. It worried her that Snow might have followed a rabbit or squirrel and been caught in a trap. There were bears in the forest, wolves, God knew what else. On the way home, she'd passed a huge elk carcass just off the road. It looked though it had just been killed. It had probably been hit by one of the huge semi trucks that passed through on the highway.

That brought another possible tragedy to mind. She got into her car and drove up and down the road until she was satisfied that Snow wasn't lying, hurt, just off the highway. But that didn't solve the problem of where she was.

Then she thought of Dal Blake. If Snow had gone to his house . . .

She pulled out her cell phone and called him. The phone rang and rang. She was about to give up when he answered it, curtly, as if it had irritated him to be interrupted.

"It's Meadow Dawson," she began.

"Your dog isn't here," he said shortly.

"Oh."

There was a question in a soft, feminine voice.

Meadow recognized it, and now she knew why the interruption had bothered Dal. He and the florist . . . She cut off the thought.

"Sorry to bother you," she said, and hung up.

She put the phone in her pocket and trudged down to the barn, where one of the older cowboys was sitting.

"Have you seen Snow, Harry?" she asked hopefully.

He looked up. "No, ma'am. Well, not since this morning, anyway. She was playing in the snow. Loves the outdoors, don't she?"

"Yes, she does." She fought tears. "I can't find her. I thought she might be at Dal Blake's place, but he hasn't seen her either."

"Suppose we saddle up a couple of horses and go looking?" he asked gently.

She almost fell on him in gratitude. "Could we?"

"Gonna be hard on your legs, you not used to riding and all."

"I wouldn't care if it broke them, if I can just find my dog," she said, and had to fight tears.

He saw that anguish and understood it. "She'll be all right. Probably just wandered off after a rabbit." He got up. "I'll saddle the horses."

"Harry, thanks," she said huskily.

"Ma'am, any of us would do anything we could for you," he said gently. "We'll find your dog."

He went off to saddle the horses. Meadow stood in the snow that was up almost to the top of her boots and shivered in her thick coat. She was wearing a wool hat that should have repelled the wetness, but it seemed to soak it up. She'd even forgotten her gloves. Well, she'd manage. She had to find Snow!

Harry led out two horses, both geldings. He gave the older of the two to Meadow by the reins. "He's old and gentle. He won't throw you. His name is Mickey," he added with a grin.

"Hello, Mickey," she said, patting his mane. "Don't toss me, okay?"

The horse lifted his head and looked at her with big, brown eyes.

"He's sweet," she said.

"Yes, he is. Let's go."

She mounted up and rode behind Harry as they started down the ranch road that led past the sheds where the pregnant cows were kept in bad storms, past fenced pastures where huge round bales of hay were protected from the elements in plastic bags.

"They look like giant marshmallows," she commented.

"So they do. It keeps the hay from rotting, though," he replied. "Not a bad thing."

"Not at all." She rode up beside him. "Harry, doesn't Mr. Smith trap animals for fur?"

"Yes, he does." That thought had occurred to him, too. "Want to ride down by his place?"

"I would."

"Okay then. It's this way."

He turned off the trail and eased his mount up a small rise, looking back to make sure Meadow was following.

Her legs were already sore and her hands were freezing, but the only thought in her mind was that she had to find her dog. *Oh, Snow*, she thought miserably, *please, howl, bark, do something to let me know where you are! I can't lose you. I can't!*

Harry noted her worried expression. He had the same thought she did, that Snow might be caught in a trap. If she was, and they couldn't find her . . . Well, it was better to think positively.

"I wish we had more people looking," he commented. "All the men are out checking on cattle, except me."

"We'll do what we have to," she replied.

"You could call Dal and ask for help," he said.

She tautened all over. "I'd rather ask the devil himself for aid."

He raised his eyebrows, but he didn't comment.

Just as they started down another snow-covered hill, her cell phone went off.

Chapter Six

Meadow recognized the phone number on the call. She'd just used it. The temptation to just let it ring was great, but her fear for Snow was greater.

"Hello?" she said curtly.

"Have you found her?" he asked.

She swallowed. Her lips felt numb. "No."

"Where are you looking?"

"Harry and I are riding down to Mr. Smith's place," she said, and knew he'd understand why without being told.

"Smith's gone to Oregon for the holidays," he said. "He's not home."

She drew in an icy breath. "His traps will still be there, even if he's not," she said shortly.

There was a pause. She heard the feminine voice again. It chilled her heart, as the snow chilled the skin that was exposed to it.

"When did you see her last?" he asked.

"This morning, at breakfast. She went out just before I went to work. I never thought she'd run away . . ." She had to stop. Her voice was choking up.

"I'll send some of my men over to look around the river bottoms," he said curtly. "There have been reports of wolves there and near Smith's place, so watch your step. Are you armed?"

She bit her lip. "No."

"Is Harry?"

She looked at the man beside her, noted the rifle in its case, and said, "Yes, he is."

"Tell him to be careful. We'll start searching."

"Thanks," she bit off. She fought tears. "She's the only family . . . I have left." Her voice broke. It humiliated her to have him hear that weakness. She just hung up.

"Dal sending men over?" Harry asked.

She fought to stop her voice from cracking again. She swallowed, hard. "Yes. He's sending some men to help. He says they'll search the river bottoms."

"Lots of wolves down there," Harry said. He noted her fear. "Wolves don't usually attack without provocation, even when humans go near them," he said. "They're part of the circle of nature. We could legally kill them, but we don't. They belong here. Like the mountains."

She managed a smile for him. "You don't think they'd hurt Snow?"

"Not unless they were starving. And there's still game around."

"Okay. Thanks, Harry."

He nodded, pulled his hat lower to protect his eyes from the driving sleet, and rode on.

The longer they searched, the more Meadow's spirits drooped. There was no trace of Snow.

Her cell phone rang. "Where are you?" Dal Blake asked.

"Have you found her?" she countered with helpless concern.

"Not yet. But we're getting Jerry Haynes to bring old

Redhide over. Do you have something of Snow's that he can get her scent from?"

"Oh, thank you!" she said, almost crying with relief. "Yes, there's her blue blanket that she sleeps on. It's just inside the back door." She hesitated. "It isn't locked. I forgot. I was so scared . . ."

"It's all right." His voice was oddly gentle. "We'll give Redhide the scent and I'll keep you posted. We'll find her," he added with such confidence that a little of the fear left.

"Okay," she said. She hesitated. "Thank you again, for helping."

"She practically lives with me," he said, and he didn't sound angry. "I feel some responsibility for her. I'll be in touch. Is your phone fully charged?"

Oh, if only he hadn't asked that. She looked at it. One bar left. She ground her teeth together. "Sort of," she confessed.

"Ask Harry if his is charged."

She did. Harry chuckled and nodded.

"Yes."

"Give me his number."

Harry called it out to her and she relayed it to Dal.

"I'll call him when we know something. Got your gloves on?"

She bit her lip, hard, and didn't answer. "We'll keep going toward the traps," she said instead.

"All right."

She hung up. They rode on.

The snow and sleet increased so that it was hard to see even a few feet ahead. Meadow was worried that Harry might say give it up until the storm abated, but he didn't. He kept going without a single complaint.

Meadow thought of Snow when she'd rescued her, of how much company the dog had been, of the happy times they'd shared. Snow had been her comfort when the world fell on her. A sweet, gentle soul who loved her mistress. She couldn't lose Snow. She just couldn't!

Harry glanced at her. "We'll find her," he said. "Old Redhide can track anything. He's famous. Even the FBI used him once to track a fugitive who ran to our county to hide. Flushed him out of an old mine within minutes of getting his scent." He chuckled. "If we've got that blood-hound, your dog is as good as found."

"Thanks, Harry," she said softly. "I'm just scared, that's all. Snow had such a hard life until I got her from the shelter . . ."

"Have to have faith," he said. He smiled. "It does work wonders."

"I'm trying. Really."

They rode on. Meadow was freezing, but she tried to hide it from Harry. The men all knew she was a tenderfoot, rancher's daughter or not. Her legs were killing her, too. But if she could just find Snow, it wouldn't matter. Nothing else mattered.

"That's where he sets traps," Harry said, noting a stretch of woods. "Have to go on foot out there, Miss Dawson. And watch every step. He sets bear traps, too."

"I hate traps," she muttered.

"It's how he makes his living, trapping fur. Long years ago, it was big business out west. Trappers went far and wide getting hides for the companies back east."

"I guess so." She swallowed down her fear. "Do the traps kill things fast?"

He hesitated. But he wasn't used to lying. "Not usually."

"Damn," she said under her breath.

"When he's here, he checks them periodically all day

long," he continued. "He finishes off whatever he finds fairly quickly."

"Fur." She glanced at him. "I don't own a single piece of fur. Well, except for what's on Snow," she added with a forced smile.

"Watch where you walk." He handed her a stick. "Just in case. If the stick trips a trap, it won't bite you."

She nodded. "Thanks."

They walked through the long patch of wood, but there were, thankfully, no animals in the traps. There was also no Snow.

It had been two of the longest hours of Meadow's whole life. She knew Dal and his men were searching, that the bloodhound was on the trail, but what if Snow was . . . She swallowed down her fear. Harry was right. She had to believe her dog would be all right.

As she processed the thought, Harry's phone rang.

"Did they find her?" Meadow asked in anguish.

Harry glanced at her, grimaced, spoke into the phone. "I'll tell her. We'll be right there."

"Is she alive?" she asked quickly. Better to know at once.

"She is," he replied. "Caught herself in a barbed wire fence and couldn't fight free, with all that fur. I know where it is."

He led the way. Snow was alive. Snow would be all right. She felt tears pouring down her cold cheeks, and she didn't even try to check them. Thank God, she thought, for everyday miracles.

When they got to the fence, Dal was on one knee with a pair of wire cutters, getting the last of the wire away from Snow's thick fur while she licked his hand. It was evident that she loved the tall rancher, even though her mistress avoided him like the plague.

Meadow's legs were so numb that she almost fell getting off the horse. She stumbled to the fence.

"Oh, Snow," she whispered, choking as she went down on both knees in the snow to hug her dog. There were traces of blood on her fur. "Snow!"

The big dog's blue eyes laughed at her, as if to say, *Silly human, of course I'm all right, my other master saved me!*

"Your hands must be frozen," Dal commented as he handed the wire cutters to another cowboy. "Don't you have gloves?"

"I have two pair, actually. They're in my house." She was too busy hugging Snow and getting licked to care about the criticism.

"And your jeans are soaked," he continued. "Let's get you both home."

"Snow needs to see the vet," she said.

"My vet makes house calls. He's on his way to your house." He didn't add that the vet was on retainer, or that Dana had been irritated that Dal left her to go hunt for Meadow's dog. That had irritated him. He loved animals. Dana didn't.

A young man with red hair joined them. "Hi," he said. "I'm Jerry Haynes." He introduced himself. "And this is Redhide." There was a huge bloodhound beside him, panting even in the cold.

"Hi, big guy," she said softly and extended a hand for him to smell. "Thank you for saving my baby."

Jerry chuckled. "He's a marshmallow," he commented when the big dog climbed on her bent legs and licked her face. "He loves women."

"He's wonderful."

Jerry grinned.

"We'd better go," Dal said curtly. "I've got the truck over here. I'll carry Snow for you."

"Thanks," she said softly.

He gave orders to his men, thanked Jerry, lifted Snow, and carried her to the truck.

"I'll hold her," Meadow said quickly when she opened the passenger side of the truck and climbed in.

"She's got blood on her fur," he said.

"It's just clothes," she replied. "Please?" Her green eyes had him almost hypnotized. He slid the big dog onto her lap and closed the door with a jerk.

"Snow, my baby, my poor baby," she crooned, hugging her dog close.

"Seat belt," he said.

"I'll try." She reached for it and managed to get it around her waist under Snow.

"I'll do it."

Dal reached for the seat belt and found her hand instead. Even through his leather gloves, he could feel the chill. "Your hands are like ice," he said.

"They're okay," she said. "Just a little numb." She hugged Snow close. "I was so afraid that we'd find her in one of Mr. Smith's traps."

He had been, too, but he didn't say so. He started the truck. "You need to find a way to close that dog flap at night so she doesn't wander. Or put a high fence set in concrete around the house."

"I'll buy a helicopter for the Bat Cave while I'm about it," she muttered.

He gave her a curious glance.

"I work for the sheriff's department," she pointed out. "My budget is much more Walmart than Park Avenue."

He frowned. He hadn't considered her situation. She was probably hurting for money, or she wouldn't be working at all. Pity she knew nothing about ranching. If she had, she'd at least have enough money to fence her yard.

He turned into her long driveway. "You need to sell the ranch to someone who knows what to do with it," he said bluntly.

"Your tact always amazes me."

He glanced at her. "I don't have any tact."

"And I am not surprised," she pointed out. "But thank you for saving my dog." She averted her eyes. "She's all I have."

He felt the pain of those words like a blow. He understood them. His big Lab, Bess, had been his only family. Her loss, despite the company of Jarvis, his cat, had left him bereft. Dana hadn't understood why he kept the dog dishes in their place in the kitchen. She'd started to throw them out, and he'd jerked them out of her hands. She'd laughed. *What a silly, sentimental thing to do*, she'd commented.

That had led to some harsh words that Meadow's phone call had interrupted. He and Dana argued more and enjoyed each other's company less. Dal really wasn't much for families and Dana was. It would end soon, as all the other brief affairs had ended. He didn't trust women enough to stay with one.

He got out of the truck at Meadow's front door and carried Snow inside for her, waiting while Meadow got two thick bath towels to spread on the floor to catch the droplets of blood.

"Let me see your hands," Dal said.

She left Snow long enough to show them to him. He grimaced as he touched them. "Red and raw, but no frostbite. You were lucky. Don't go out without gloves again," he instructed.

"Don't give me orders," she returned. "I don't belong to you."

"Thank God," he said with faint sarcasm, his eyes disparaging on her face. "I like my women soft and feminine."

She smiled sweetly. "How fortunate for you that you've got Dana, who's both."

"Yes. Lucky me."

He searched her eyes longer than he meant to. She felt the jolt of pleasure all the way to her toes and averted her eyes quickly to keep him from seeing. Her heart was racing like mad. She hated the effect he had on her. He was all but engaged to the florist, after all. She shouldn't even be thinking of him like that.

He was doing some thinking of his own. He was an experienced man. He knew the signs when a woman found him attractive. Meadow always had. Even at seventeen, her heart had raced when he came close. He'd been cruel to her, to make sure she didn't get close enough.

Now she was older, and she was beginning to get to him. He'd thought her hard, cold, all business. But she was vulnerable and sensitive, and she loved that dog. It was a side of her that he hadn't seen, and it touched him deeply.

But he remembered that she went to church every Sunday and she'd never had an affair. That lost her points. He might be in the market for a few nights in her bed, but he didn't do forever after.

He shoved his hands into his jeans pockets and glared down at her from under the wide brim of his Stetson. His dark eyes were expressive.

"You still want me," he drawled, and with distaste. "No go, honey. You're still not my type."

"Want you?" She drew herself up to her full height and her green eyes snapped at him. "Why, you arrogant, smug, self-righteous cow puncher! Were you always this conceited, or did you take lessons?"

He pursed his lips. "Were you always this nasty tempered or did you take lessons?" he shot back.

"I get along great with most people!"

"They must be blind and deaf."

"Excuse me?" she asked huffily.

"Not to see the horns and pointed tail or hear the sound of brimstone churning when you show up," he said with a vacant smile.

Her cheeks flushed even more than they had from the cold. "Now, you just listen here . . . !"

The knock on the door saved him. The vet, Dan Johnson, was tall and blond and pleasant. He examined Snow, pronounced her wounds superficial, and gave Meadow instructions for her care for the next few days.

"I'll leave this with you," he said, handing her a topical solution for the wounds. "I've given her an antibiotic shot. It will take care of any infection that might set in. Keep her close for a couple of days. If you see any unusual redness, swelling, that sort of thing, get her to me."

"I will. Thank you so much. I was so scared," she said, and laughed self-consciously.

"They do get next to you, don't they?" he asked, grinning. "I like German shepherds. I have two, both female, and they sleep with me." He shrugged. "I guess they're why I never married. Not much room left over in the bed," he added, chuckling.

She shook hands with him. "Here, I've got a business card. Can you have your bookkeeper send me the bill?"

He glanced at Dal, who telegraphed a message with his eyes.

"Sure, I will," he told her, taking the card.

"Thanks again," she said.

Dal knelt down to pet Snow. "I hope you get better, you bad girl," he said. "Stay out of barbed wire, okay?"

Snow licked him.

He got to his feet and followed the vet to the door. He turned. "You going to be okay?" he asked.

"I'm just cold and sore. I'll be fine," she said. "Thanks again," she added a little stiffly. "Sorry I had to bother you."

"It wasn't a bother. I was just having a hell of an argument that you interrupted. No big deal. See you."

He went out, leaving her curious about who he'd been arguing with. Surely not Dana, who obviously adored him.

Gil had received the bill of sale from the antique dealer in Kansas City, but it didn't contain any information that was helpful. When he tried to trace the owner of the pipe organ, he hit a wall. It became obvious that the man listed as the pipe organ's most recent seller was a man who'd been in a cemetery in Billings for some twenty years.

"How cool," Gil remarked. "A dead guy can still buy and sell antiques. Who'd have known?"

"Isn't Billings an odd choice of places to look in cemeteries?" she wondered aloud. "Do we have anybody around here with relatives in Billings? Maybe somebody's cousin or aunt or uncle who died recently was buried there?"

Gil smiled. "You're a wonder. That's a great idea. I'll start checking."

She grinned. It made her feel good that she wasn't totally useless. She went back to work on the check forger. She tracked him to a restaurant in the middle of town, where he was eating steak and potatoes.

He saw her coming and just sighed. He put down his fork and knife and sipped black coffee. "You're the sheriff's new investigator, yeah?" he asked with resignation. "I guess I'm arrested. My girl wanted a diamond ring, and that old man had a million dollars in a money market account. I didn't think he'd miss a couple of thousand, you know?"

She shook her head. "I'm sorry, but theft is theft, regardless of how rich the victim is."

"Well, I'll go quietly. I don't want to end up like Russell Harris," he added with a faint grin. "Gil's pretty fierce, isn't he?"

"He is."

He cocked his head. "You were with the FBI. You must be some hotshot investigator, to track me down this quick."

She hid the pride the words invoked. "Just doing my job. If you're willing to come along without making a fuss, I won't cuff you."

He got up, smiling. "Thanks. That's damned decent of you."

She walked out with him. "Been in trouble with the law before?"

"Never. This new girl, she wants lots of pretty stuff." He sighed. "Guess I should have given her up. I just work for wages, you know. Not many diamond rings lying around my old house."

"A woman who loves you won't care if you're dead broke," she said flatly.

"I know that. I just can't resist bad girls."

"Jail may tweak that mind-set a bit," she pointed out.

"That's what they say."

She put him in the back of the patrol car and got in under the wheel. "If you haven't been arrested before, you can get first offender status. Keep your nose clean and they'll wipe your record."

"They will?" He sounded enthusiastic. "Will I go to jail?"

"Maybe not for long. It's not a murder charge," she added dryly.

He leaned back. "Thanks," he said. "I should have turned myself in. Thought about it, but my girl said that was a bad idea."

"Pardon me, but your girl is a bad idea," she returned. "If you want to stay out of trouble, you'd do better to find someone less greedy."

"You may have a point."

She took him to detention to be booked. Then she went back to Jeff's office to report what happened.

"He just came with you with no fight?" Jeff asked, stunned.

"Yes. He was very polite." She cocked her head. "Why do you look so surprised?"

"Because Tuck Freeman is one of the meanest men in town," he replied. "We've never locked him up, but we've pulled him out of a couple of nasty fights where his opponents had to go to the emergency room. He's not known for his polite manner."

"Well!" she exclaimed.

"Did he say why he went quietly?"

She laughed. "Yes, he did. He said that Gil was fierce and he didn't want to end up like Russell with extra felony charges from resisting arrest."

"He's got a point," he admitted. "Gil has a reputation of his own. Not many men tougher. He could have worked in any big-city department with his background, but he likes small towns. My good luck that he liked ours. The whole county could fit inside the city limits of Denver, almost." He laughed.

"It's a nice place. I loved it here when I was little. I hated when my parents divorced and I had to leave. If I could have stayed with Dad, I'd know what to do with the ranch."

He averted his eyes. "Ever think of selling it?"

"Every day," she confessed, and missed the sudden light in his eyes. "But then I think of my father and how hard he worked to make it prosperous, and I realize that I can't sell it. So my only options are to learn ranch management or hire a professional."

"Hiring a professional can be risky," he said to discourage her. "You don't know who you can trust until it's too late, sometimes."

"That's me. I don't really trust people anymore," she said. "Well, I'll get back to work on the next case. That assault case . . ."

"No."

She stared at him.

"That's Gil's case," he said. He smiled. "We'll keep you out of dangerous scrapes, just for a little while. Okay?"

He was a very nice man. "Okay."

"Thought any more about the dance?"

She had. And something had happened that changed her mind. Her father had invested in an oil company, and the checks from the investment company fed directly into the joint checking account she and her father had started when they saw his health begin to fail. She had a windfall of several hundred dollars. More than enough to buy one nice dress and some shoes to match.

"I'll go," she said.

He brightened. "You will? That's great!"

"What's great?" Gil asked as he walked in.

"Meadow's going to the Christmas party with me."

Gil glared at him. "No fair. I didn't even have a chance to ask her."

Meadow felt valuable. She grinned at him. "I'll still dance with you, if you come."

"I can do fancy dances," Gil said, scoffing at the sheriff. "He just stands in one place and shuffles his feet."

Meadow laughed. "I don't mind."

"You can have one dance," Jeff told his deputy. "I'm

pulling rank. Now go to work before I volunteer you to direct traffic at the high school football game."

"Sadist," Gil muttered as he passed.

They all laughed.

Meadow bought a red dress. She hadn't meant to, but she kept recalling Dal Blake's blistering comments about her efforts to seduce him when she was seventeen. Red dresses had played a big part in what there was of their relationship. The first red one had ended in a coal bin, the second in a punch bowl. Third time lucky, maybe, she wondered.

But this red dress wasn't like the one that hadn't survived the accident with the coal bin. It was made of deep red velvet with black accents. It fell to her ankles. The bodice was ruffled, with wide shoulder straps that added to its elegance and made Meadow's small breasts look larger. The color, against her fairness, was flattering. So was the fit that emphasized her small waist and nicely rounded hips. She bought a pair of strappy black leather high heels to wear with it. She planned to put a soft wave in her hair for the event and leave it long, around her shoulders, and put a black silk orchid in her hair. The effect would be exotic, to say the least. And hopefully it would erase Dal's memory of the clumsy, sad young woman she'd been at seventeen.

Also, hopefully, it would erase the memory of the second red dress that had met the punch bowl, at the Christmas party where Dal had kissed her so hungrily in front of the whole crowd. Just thinking about that kiss under the mistletoe made her tingle all over, and that would never do. She'd dance only with Jeff—and maybe Gil—and leave Dal to his florist. She knew that he'd never want to dance with her. He didn't even like her.

* * *

Snow was mending nicely. She'd healed from her mishap with the wire fence, and Meadow had been meticulous about going out with her any time she had to use the bathroom during the night and early morning. When Meadow went to work, she put a pad down for accidents and bolted the dog flap shut. It wasn't a perfect solution, but it seemed to work.

At least, Snow wasn't up visiting Dal. But Jarvis was still making his rounds, snow and all. She wondered how the big cat even got through the snow, when it was almost a foot deep. He came in the dog flap late one afternoon and rolled around her ankles, purring like mad.

"You bad boy," she chided. "You're going to get me in trouble again."

He just purred some more. He even rubbed up against Snow, and she liked him. Odd animals, she was thinking as she picked up her cell phone. So odd!

The phone rang and rang. Finally, he answered it. "Hello?" he asked gruffly.

Not a friendly greeting. He'd recognized her number. "Your cat is down here," she said shortly.

"Did you lure him in with chicken treats or kidnap him as an excuse to see me?" he drawled.

She punched the red button and tossed the phone onto the sofa. A string of curses followed. She could have screamed. She only wished she had an old-fashioned telephone, one she could slam down in his ears, the pig!

Minutes later, his truck stopped outside. She waited a few seconds after he knocked to go to the front door. She had Jarvis in her arms when she opened it.

"Here," she said, handing him the big cat.

His eyebrows arched over dancing brown eyes. "No invitation to have coffee and talk?"

"I don't drink coffee at night, and I don't want to talk to you. The road is that way." She pointed.

"You sure got up on the wrong side of the bed," he commented. "Jeff lacking as a lover, is he?"

She flushed. "My private business is none of yours."

"Should I be crass and remind you that I saved your dog? The white one there who likes to follow me home?" He indicated Snow, who was sitting patiently in front of him, obviously in love with him.

She crossed her arms over her chest. "I thanked you for that."

"So you did."

She glared at him. "All you ever do is insult me. Don't expect a warm welcome here."

"It never crossed my mind," he said, studying her angry face. "You coming with Jeff to the Christmas dance?"

"Yes."

"I'm bringing Dana. She can dance."

So could Meadow, but she wasn't taking the time to tell him so.

"Do you dance?" he asked. "I've never actually seen you do it. The punch bowl got in the way . . ."

"I'm freezing." She indicated the open door behind him.

"Want me to come in and close it?" he asked in a mock tender tone.

"How about closing it from the outside?" she retorted.

"Heartless woman. If you didn't want me here, why did you lure my cat in?"

"I don't have to lure your cat, he thinks he lives here!"

"Your dog thinks she's mine." He indicated Snow licking the hand that wasn't holding Jarvis.

"I'll speak to her firmly," she said. "Now, good night."

He chuckled softly. "You improve with age."

"Do I really? Sorry, but your opinion is way down on my list of things that matter."

"Probably so." His dark eyes slid over her face and down to her soft mouth. "They'll have mistletoe at the dance."

She flushed, remembering. "Then I'm sure you and Dana will give it a workout," she said sarcastically, almost ushering him out the door.

"I might let you kiss me," he taunted.

"Never in a million years," she retorted. "I have no idea where you've been!"

And before he could reply, she shut the door in his face, despite Snow's protests. She could hear soft laughter outside before she left the room.

Chapter Seven

The really interesting thing about working in law enforcement, Meadow thought, was the endless variety of incidents that went with each new day. You never knew what might come up. There might be a vandalism charge to investigate, a complaint about a business refusing to make good on a defective product, a shooting, a domestic disturbance, a speeder. So much variety made the job interesting. And sometimes, dangerous.

As most law enforcement people knew, domestic disturbances were the things most likely to get an officer killed. From time to time, even the person who called 911 in the first place might be armed and out for revenge if the person they reported was then arrested. Shootings were not infrequent, and fatalities often ensued.

But not in Raven Springs. Nobody could remember the last time anybody local got shot. The only close call any law enforcement person had ever had, except for Jeff's shooting incident, was when Bobby Gardner ran his patrol car off the road into a snowbank and broke the windshield. Considering the tragic shootings nationally just lately involving policemen, it was a miracle that local law enforcement had remained safe.

Meadow was still working the theft of the Victorian lamp. She'd sent the photo of it out to several auction houses, but with no responses so far.

Gil said that wasn't surprising. "The pipe organ went missing here," he reminded her. "And it's just turned up at that big auction house back east. Obviously the thief hoped that nobody local would notice. He felt safe to try and sell it." He pursed his lips. "Interesting, though, the way he covered his tracks. Using a dead man's identity on the bill of sale is cagey. If we hadn't investigated, it might have gone unnoticed. The bill of sale looked legit."

"Yes, it did," she agreed. "Two antiques, which originally belonged to famous people, both stolen locally. One turns up back east, the other is still missing."

"Well, we know that whoever took both items knew their worth." He grimaced. "Problem is, we hardly ever have any such thefts here. I mean, people break in and steal money and guns, mostly. Not a lot of folks would even know the value of antiques like those."

She nodded. "How long has Mr. Markson been here?"

"He came with the town." He laughed. "He's been here a long time, and he's as honest as the day is long. And if you're thinking Gary was responsible, the boy's barely got enough energy to put gas in his truck. He isn't the breaking and entering sort. He's too lazy."

"I guess you're right," she agreed. "He'd have been my first suspect."

He studied her with a smile. "He knows antiques, and he does have ties to auction houses back east. Maybe he'd be into something like that fancy table Dal Blake owns. It's got a history that makes it priceless. There's an item that a seller could ask his own price for and get it." He frowned. "Like the Victorian lamp and the pipe organ. It isn't their antique status that makes them valuable—it's who owned them originally. Both belonged to former presidents. But Dal's table—now that's real history."

"On the other hand," she laughed, "if it went missing, it would be almost impossible to fence it without giving its history."

"True," he agreed. "But there are private collectors, you know. The sort who buy priceless antiquities and keep them in personal vaults, behind closed doors. Millionaires who can afford any amount of money."

"Let's hope Mr. Blake never has to worry about someone stealing it, then," she said.

"I wouldn't want to try and break into Dal's house," Gil chuckled, "not with that big cat in there. He actually attacked one of Dal's own cowboys who walked inside in the dark without turning on a light. It was sort of an emergency, but Jarvis didn't care. The cowboy had scratches from stem to stern. He was yelling his head off for Dal to save him, at the last."

"Jarvis is very big," she agreed. She laughed. "I guess he's ferocious enough to qualify as a watchcat, but he likes me."

"We heard about that. Spends his life at your place, like your dog hangs out at Dal's. Strange animals."

"I was just thinking the same thing."

A phone rang in the outer office and the clerk, old Mrs. Pitts, stuck her head around the door a minute later. "Somebody ran through a red light and broadsided old man Barkley's Lincoln. Who wants to save the driver from him?"

It was a well known fact locally that Barkley had bought the Lincoln new and polished it by hand. It was his baby. The other driver would be running for his life.

"I'll go," Gil said. "I may have to run down the other driver." He chuckled.

"Good luck," Meadow called after him.

"That's one nice young man," Mrs. Pitts remarked as

Meadow followed her into the outer office. "You going to the Christmas dance with him?"

"No," Meadow said. "With Jeff."

She laughed. "The sheriff doesn't get out much. He was going with Dana Conyers until she set her cap at Dal Blake." She grimaced. "Jeff's got a nice ranch, but he can't match bankbooks with Dal. Nasty piece of work, that woman. She puts on a good act—goes to church, teaches Sunday School, does volunteer work. She sells flowers, but she doesn't like them, you know?" she added suddenly.

Meadow frowned.

"You don't understand, do you?" Mrs. Pitts asked kindly. "You see, people who grow flowers fall into sort of a category. They're nurturing people, the sort who would stop to save a drowning person or help a little animal out of the road. Dana inherited the shop from her aunt. She overprices everything and cheats on vases and substitutes less expensive flowers when people call in something exotic. Got called down for it by the pastor of our Methodist church after the patron who bought the flowers told him that Dana hadn't delivered what he ordered."

"She doesn't strike me as a typical florist," Meadow had to admit. "But she's very pretty."

"Pretty on the outside, I guess," the older woman agreed. "I'd rather have pretty on the inside. A kind heart is more important than the packaging it comes in, you know."

She smiled. "I guess."

"You've known Dal Blake a long time."

"Since I was about thirteen," she agreed. "He and my dad shared bulls. He came over to the house sometimes when I was visiting."

"Your dad liked him," she said. "But he didn't want him around you when you were in high school. Even in college.

He said you could do a lot better than a man who collected hearts."

"You knew Dad?"

She nodded, smiling. "We went through school together. He was a fine man. Your mother wasn't from here. We hoped she'd settle and stay with him, but we were too rural to suit her. Sorry. I didn't mean to offend."

"You didn't," Meadow replied. "I loved my mother, but she really was something of a snob."

"Your dad wasn't. He never judged people by what they had. Hurt us all to lose him," she added. "We were glad when you moved back here. The ranch has been part of our community since his own dad founded it, way back when."

"I wish I knew how to run it properly," Meadow confessed. "I wasn't around enough to learn the ropes. Now it's too late. I have to depend on the men to know what to do. But that won't save it. We need an experienced manager. Those are thin on the ground."

"You should marry Jeff and let him manage it for you," Mrs. Pitts said wickedly.

She laughed. "He's a very nice man, but . . ." She shrugged.

"I know what you mean. He's still stuck on Dana, regardless." She shook her head. "Never ceases to amaze me how much some men love being badly treated by a woman. She snapped at him, stood him up, called him names, and he kept going back." She sat down at her desk. "That won't work with Dal Blake. He'll set her down and walk out the door. Never has been a woman he couldn't walk away from. Not even when he was younger."

The thought made Meadow sad, but she concealed it. She went to her own desk. "Well, I've got work to do. Best I get to it before I'm out the door looking for a new job." She laughed.

"Jeff won't fire you. He's too grateful for the help." She

shook her head. "It's been hard on him since our investigator left."

"I'm not making much headway on the antique lamp."

"You will," Mrs. Pitts told her. "You've got a good head on those shoulders. All you need is a little self-esteem."

Meadow's eyebrows arched in a question.

"Don't you let Dal Blake run you down," came the unexpected comment. "He'll walk all over you if you let him."

"He'd better be wearing thick boots, then," she returned.

Mrs. Pitts just laughed.

Meadow went to the town's one convenience store to investigate the theft of a jacket and a pair of boots that belonged to the owner. Nobody locked doors around here. Somebody had just walked in the back door while the proprietor was waiting on a customer and took off with the items.

The odd thing was that the thief had put on the boots. The owner recognized the tread pattern as they walked out back where fresh snow was falling.

"Now doesn't that beat all?" the man said, exasperated. "He steals my best snow boots and just walks off in them! Doesn't he know about tracks?"

"I think he may be a couple of beers short of a six-pack." Meadow chuckled. "I'll see if I can run him down."

"You be careful. Easy to get lost in them woods when snow's coming down like this."

"I will. Thanks."

She started out the back and followed the tracks. It was like bread crumbs, she laughed to herself. What a strange thief.

The trail led down the hill, across a frozen stream, and up to the back of the local barbecue joint. In fact, it led right to the back door.

She knocked, and a surprised young man opened it and gaped at her.

She looked down. He was wearing boots. Snow boots. With snow still clinging to them.

"Well, damn!" the boy burst out.

"Would you like to explain?" Meadow invited.

He let out an angry sigh. "Billy Joe stole my girl," he blurted out. "I was mad as hell. I saw her drive off from the convenience store and I threw a limb, I was so mad . . . I rolled down the hill and into the creek. Soaked my sneakers and my coat. So I went in the back door and took Billy Joe's," he added belligerently.

She noted the pile of soaked sneakers and jacket on the floor beside him.

"Go ahead, cuff me, lock me up," he muttered. "I got nothing to live for anyway, since Billy Joe stole my girl!"

Meadow grimaced. "I'm really sorry," she said, "but regardless of the reason you took them, the fact is that you did take them. I have to arrest you."

"I understand. It's okay." He drew in a breath. "What a lousy day!"

Meadow called one of the deputies to pick him up and take him to the detention center while she carried the boots and jacket down to the convenience store and had the owner identify them.

He did, but he said he wouldn't press charges. "I didn't mean to take his girl, but she liked me better and she wouldn't go away," he said simply. He laughed. "I guess some girls are hard to hold on to. Anyway, he shouldn't have to lose his job and his freedom because he pitched a temper tantrum."

She smiled. "You're a good sport."

He laughed. "She's a sweet girl."

* * *

Jeff chuckled when she told him about her morning's work. "You can't say this job is ever dull," he pointed out.

"No. You certainly can't."

She and Jeff stopped by the local restaurant to have lunch. It was buffet style. The food was good and inexpensive. A lot of people had lunch there every day.

As she and Jeff took their trays to a booth, Meadow noticed Dal Blake and Dana Conyers sharing a table nearby. She averted her eyes from them and smiled at Jeff as they unloaded their trays.

"I like the way they do fish," Jeff commented. "The cook came here from LA. He said the traffic was driving him nuts."

She laughed. "The slower pace is pretty nice," she said. "St. Louis has its share of traffic as well."

"Dana's from LA," Jeff commented, glancing irritably at the table she was sharing with Dal. "Her aunt loved it here, but Dana has champagne tastes. She'd better not be banking on Dal putting a ring on her finger. No woman's ever been able to get him to an altar."

"I'm not surprised," Meadow said nonchalantly. "He likes to play the field."

"If I had his money, I might . . . no, that's not true," he added on a sigh. "I'd like to find a nice woman and settle down. Raise a family. I'm thirty-five this year. I don't want to spend the rest of my life alone."

"There are worse things," she pointed out.

His eyes slid over her face. "Do you want to get married?"

She shrugged. "It's not high on my list of priorities," she confessed. She didn't add that nobody yet had wanted to marry her. She was everybody's kid sister at work, usually. Her dates were infrequent and usually miserable. She had no illusions about herself. But she didn't say that to Jeff.

"It's hard for people in law enforcement to settle down

with someone who doesn't share the job," he commented. "I've seen plenty of divorces since I started out. You don't want to take the job home. There are so many horrible things you have to see, things you can't tell outsiders about."

"I know what you mean," she said. "Civilians have a hard time understanding the demands of the job, much less the stress it puts on us or the sense of family it creates."

"We share things outsiders can't understand," he agreed. He made a face. "I could never talk to Dana about any of it. She said it wasn't something she wanted to hear about. She thought it was stupid to carry a gun, and she didn't like having me called out all hours on cases. She said I should hang the badge at the door and forget it until the next morning."

"That would work well when a man's beating his wife and child to death and you get called to save them."

"I know, right?" He sipped coffee. "I guess I knew it wouldn't work out. But I was crazy about her."

"You can't force yourself to love the right people." She laughed.

"Have you ever been in love?" he asked.

"No," she lied. "And I hope that I never am. My parents seemed to love each other, but they couldn't live together. I don't want to end up like they did."

"My parents were happily married for fifty years," he recalled fondly. "They died together in a wreck—went over the guardrail up in the Shoshone National Forest in Wyoming during a rain storm. Neither one of them could have lived long without the other," he added. "They were like two halves of a whole."

"Do you have siblings?" she wondered.

He shook his head. "I was an only child. I'd just started as a deputy with the sheriff's department when they died. Hard, losing both of them at once, though."

"I'm so sorry."

"Your mother died some time back, didn't she?"

She nodded. "It was just the two of us. We had disagreements, but we loved each other. It was hard. But losing Dad . . ." She stopped and sipped coffee, to keep from crying. "It gets easier, as time passes."

"It does."

Mike Markson came in the door a minute later and stopped by their table to say hello.

"How are you coming on the stolen lamp case?" he asked Meadow.

"Slowly," she said with a smile. "But it's early days yet."

"Gil tracked the pipe organ back east," Jeff told him. "It was sold through an antique dealer in Kansas City."

"Really?" Mike asked. "Who was it? I know some dealers there . . ."

"You wouldn't know this one, Mike," Jeff said as he put down his coffee cup. "He's buried up in Billings."

"Excuse me?"

"A dead guy sold the pipe organ to the dealer in Kansas City," Jeff said with twinkling eyes. "Amazing, how he managed that."

Mike whistled. "Good heavens!"

"Anyway, the lead went cold after that."

Mike shook his head. "Old man Halstead was from Billings, you know," he mentioned. "He had people up there. In fact, his aunt died just recently."

"Old man Halstead?" Meadow wondered.

"Owned the pipe organ that was stolen," Mike told her. "In fact, I had Gary drive him up there for the funeral so he could talk to the antique dealer he bought the organ from. He hoped the man might remember someone asking about it, you know, about who bought it. Someone with an unusual interest in it."

"Was there such a person?" Meadow asked.

"In fact, there was," Mike told her. "The dealer had to turn down a man who offered him a small fortune, because he'd promised it to Halstead."

"I'd love to talk to that dealer," Jeff said. "I'll send Gil up to see him, if you can provide us with a name and telephone number."

"I'll get the information when I go back to my shop and email it to you, how's that?" Mike asked, smiling.

"It would be a great help," Jeff said. "Gary not with you today?"

"He's still asleep," Mike said heavily. "He sits up all night in chat rooms, talking to people he doesn't know. If he's not playing video games online," he added. "I keep hoping he'll take a bigger interest in the business. I'm not getting any younger. But Gary's just not that into small-time antiques."

"Shame," Jeff said.

"It really is. I should have had more kids," Mike said on a sigh. "Well, I'll get lunch and then I'll send you over the information. Good to see you both."

They nodded.

"That might give us a break," Jeff commented with a grin. "I'd love to be able to return that organ to Mr. Halstead. It belonged to his great-grandmother. He loved her dearly. It's not so much the monetary value as it's the sentimental value."

"Isn't it that way with most things?" she wondered aloud. "I have my mother's sewing kit. It's old and nothing fancy, but it's priceless, because it belonged to her."

"Why aren't you two working?" Dal Blake asked sarcastically, holding Dana's hand tight as he paused by their table. "Goofing off on county time, are you?"

Meadow bristled, but Jeff just laughed. "Get out of

here. We're on our lunch hour. Even law enforcement gets to eat."

"Hi, Jeff," Dana purred. "Are you coming to the Christmas dance?"

"Yes. I'm bringing Meadow."

Dal's eyebrow lifted. "For God's sake, spare us all and don't wear a red dress, will you?"

Meadow glared at him.

"What's this about a red dress?" Dana probed.

"The first time she wore one, she ended up in the coal bin in her father's house," Dal drawled, enjoying himself. "The second time, she fell into the punch bowl and wore the contents home."

Dana was laughing uproariously. "My, you are clumsy, aren't you?" she asked Meadow.

Jeff glared at her. "Not everyone is perfect," he said shortly.

Dana flushed. "I never insinuated . . ." she began.

Jeff threw down his napkin and stood up. "Ready to go?" he asked Meadow with a warm smile.

"Yes, I am," she said, and smiled back.

Dal glared at both of them. Beside him, Dana was furious at the way Jeff snubbed her.

They walked out without another word to either of the couple still standing at their table.

"She's insufferable," Jeff said curtly, turning to Meadow at the squad car. "Don't let her get under your skin. She loves to needle people."

"I'm impervious," she lied with a laugh.

"I try to be. She loves to rub Dal Blake in my face," he added curtly. "She even told me that if I'd been a little richer, she'd never have thrown me over for him."

"What a sweetheart," she muttered.

"He wasn't much kinder, with that remark about your

dress. You ought to wear a red one just to spite him," he added.

She grinned. "In fact, I bought a new red one," she replied. "And I don't plan to end up in the punch bowl this time."

"I'll make sure you don't." He glanced toward the other side of the parking lot, where Dal was putting Dana into his big Lincoln. "We'd better get back to work."

"Ready when you are, boss," she said easily. She put on a good act, but her heart was breaking. Dal was heartless. She should be grateful that he didn't like her. A man like that would rip her pride into shreds. But part of her was still seventeen, hanging on his every word, so much in love that it hurt to even look at him. She hoped she could keep those impulses under control. The last complication she needed in her life was to give Dal Blake the idea she couldn't live without him.

The snow came suddenly, in such a blizzard that Meadow couldn't even see how to get to her SUV. She put on sunglasses, which helped a little. Finding her car was hard. Once she found it, under about five feet of snow, she realized that she'd have to dig it out to even get it started toward what used to be her driveway.

Shoveling that much snow would take hours, and she didn't even own a snow shovel. She stood beside her entombed SUV, with the hood of her parka pulled up over her blond hair, and tried to decide what to do next.

She heard jingling bells. She turned, and there was Jeff in a sleigh, with two horses pulling it.

He stopped the team just beside her SUV and grinned at her from under the brim of his hat. "Going my way?" he teased.

She laughed wholeheartedly. "Am I ever! Thanks so

much! I think I'd be here until after Christmas if I had to dig my poor SUV out of there."

He helped her into the sleigh and got the horses moving. "What about your cattle?" he asked.

"I talked to my foreman. He said the men would get to them even if they had to go out on snowshoes with shovels." She shook her head. "It's been a long time since I saw snow this deep."

"It's Colorado. We have a lot of snow."

She smiled at him. "This is a nice way to get to work."

"Well," he replied, "it will be until the snow melts."

She laughed. "What would you do then?"

"Leave the sleigh out back of the office and have Gil help me ride the horses home, bareback, I reckon."

She liked his resourcefulness. "They're a good team," she remarked. "I've heard that some horses can't be trained to pull sleds or any sort of loads."

"That's true. There are horses you ride and horses you use to pull wagons or sleds. Some people learn that the hard way." He chuckled. "Like old man Beasley, who hooked up a skittish mare to a little wagon and thought she'd calm down once she got used to it."

"What happened?" she asked.

"She heard a car backfire in the distance, reared up, turned over the wagon, Beasley and all, and fell in the creek. He traded me the mare for a nice draft horse."

"What did you do with her?"

"She made one of the nicest saddle horses I've ever had. There are methods to get a skittish horse used to noise, to desensitize them. I worked with her for a few weeks, and she got over her nervous episodes."

"That's nice," she commented.

He smiled at her. "I like animals."

"Yes. Me too."

She leaned back on the seat and watched the snowy

landscape slide by as the horses made a path through the snow. "Should we be singing something like 'Winter Wonderland'?" she asked with a laugh.

"How about 'Jingle Bells' instead?"

"You're on!"

They sang the popular song all the way into town, laughing in between the choruses.

The night of the Christmas dance, Meadow slid into her sexy red dress, carefully put her hair into an elegant high coiffure with synthetic ruby combs, and applied her makeup perfectly.

The result made her feel good inside. She wasn't beautiful, but if she worked at it, she could look fairly attractive, she decided as she studied her reflection in the mirror.

She thought about Dal Blake's poisonous comments about her last two red dresses and she flushed with anger. He was always insulting these days, no matter what she said or did, or wore. She wondered why he was so antagonistic. She hadn't done anything to deserve such treatment. God knew, she hid her feelings for him so well that nobody around her suspected that she even liked him. But he went out of his way to insult her.

She tried not to think back to the last Christmas dance she'd attended, when her father was alive. That dance, when Dal had kissed her so hungrily under the mistletoe, had colored her whole life ever since. She couldn't forget it. She'd had some crazy idea that he felt something for her as well, those few endless, poignant seconds when she felt his hard mouth on hers.

Of course, he'd been drinking. And he'd made sarcastic remarks afterward. When the drunk man had tried to come onto her and spilled the contents of the punch bowl over her, Dal had thrown back his head and roared with laughter.

He hadn't even been sympathetic as she stood there with punch dripping off her beautiful dress, humiliated beyond belief.

Her father, bless him, had taken her home. He'd had some harsh words to say about, and to, Dal Blake afterward. He told Meadow that the man was never going to be welcome in his home again, not after that.

Meadow had said that it didn't matter. She lived far away and Dal was kind to her father, even if he wasn't kind to her. Sometimes, she said philosophically, people just developed dislikes for other people. It wasn't logical, but there it was. The plain fact was that Dal Blake didn't like Meadow Dawson. Period.

Yes, he'd kissed her under the mistletoe, but he'd been drinking. Men under the influence often did strange things. A veteran law enforcement officer, Meadow knew that better than many people.

She'd had to cope with drunken husbands beating up wives, children, even pets during rampages while she was with the St. Louis police department. Sadly, her clumsiness had caused some issues there, long before she went with the FBI.

She was steady under fire. She never lost her calm, no matter how heated things got on the job. But she did have balance issues. She thought back to something Dal had said, about her many falls.

In fact, she'd wondered herself if there wasn't a physical reason for her clumsiness. She thought that, after the new year, she might have a doctor do some tests, just to be sure. She'd had a very bad fall while she was in high school, thrown from a horse, and she'd hit her head. She'd been dazed. Her mother had taken her to the doctor, but no tests had been done. The kindly old man did a cursory examination and assured her and her mother that it was just a light bump, barely a concussion. Nothing to worry about.

But Meadow had read that even slight head injuries could produce problems later in life. She wanted to know if she had an issue that should trouble her. That was what she'd do. She'd see a doctor. Just in case.

Thinking about Dal's comments brought back another memory, the incredible hunger in his mouth when he'd kissed her just outside her front door, when she'd come home from that first date with Jeff. She flushed involuntarily. He'd done that, and he hadn't been drinking.

She forced her mind away from Dal Blake. Two kisses, years apart, didn't make a relationship. Especially not with a rounder like Dal.

Chapter Eight

Jeff wore a navy blue suit to the dance, with a spotless white shirt and blue paisley tie. He looked very elegant, his blond hair shining like gold under the lights in the Raven Springs community center.

Beside him, Meadow looked unusually seductive. The dark-haired, dark-eyed man standing at the punch bowl found himself staring helplessly at her, drinking in the way she looked in that close-fitted red dress. He'd taunted her about the dresses because he couldn't forget the way she tasted. That last Christmas dance she'd attended, when he'd kissed her, had colored his life since. Even Dana, with all her wiles, couldn't erase the memory. Or the pleasure. The kiss they'd shared after her date with Jeff worked on his mind even more because it was fresher in his mind. He'd wanted her for a long time. Lately, it was getting worse.

And there she was, with Jeff, clinging to his arm, looking as if she belonged to him. He hated even the idea that she was sleeping with him. He wondered if she was. She looked . . . loved.

"Why are you glaring at Jeff's new deputy?" Dana chided.

"She looks ridiculous in that dress," he lied. "Like a prostitute looking for a street corner."

Dana's eyebrows arched. That was acrimonious, even for Dal. But she shrugged it off. Everybody knew that he couldn't stand Meadow. His cat kept going to her house, as her dog kept going to his. Someone should do something about those animals.

"She needs to keep that dog on a chain," Dana muttered.

"What dog?" he asked, his eyes still glued to Meadow.

"Her dog! That husky."

"Oh. Snow lives inside."

"Well, she gets out, doesn't she?" Dana asked haughtily. "And every time, she runs straight to you."

"She likes me."

Dana pressed close to his side. "I like you, too."

He shrugged. "I did suggest that she nail the dog door shut at night."

"Did she do it?"

"I guess," Dal replied. "Snow hasn't come calling anymore."

She noticed that he'd already filled a second glass with whiskey and soda. "You don't usually drink so much," she pointed out.

"Don't nag," he said shortly.

She drew in a breath. "Jeff looks very nice," she said aloud, sketching him with her eyes.

"So do you."

She laughed, surprised by the comment. She looked up at him. She knew the little black cocktail dress outlined her full figure in the nicest way. But it was good to hear the compliment, just the same. Dal wasn't known for flattery. Not that he hadn't flattered her more than usual since Meadow had returned to Raven Springs.

"Thanks," she said.

"I'm starved," he commented. "Let's see what we can find on the buffet table."

"Great idea!"

* * *

Gil showed up minutes later, in a dark gray suit with a flashy red tie. He grinned at Meadow as he joined her and his boss in the crowd.

"There are a lot of people here," the deputy commented, his black eyes flashing with humor. "I almost didn't find a parking space."

"They'd like to enlarge the parking lot, but the land they'd need belongs to Ned Turner, and he'd never sell an inch," Jeff said with a sigh. "He doesn't even like the idea of the community center itself. He says the noise every weekend drives him nuts." He threw up his hands. "If he hates it so much, why doesn't he just move farther into the national forest?"

"I expect he'd need a lot of legal paperwork done to get permission," Meadow added. "But the Forest Service does sometimes trade parcels of land. If there's some they like, they'll trade land for it. Somebody with land they want might sell it to them in return for ownership of the tract next to the community center."

"That's resourceful thinking," Jeff said, smiling as he locked Meadow's cool fingers into his.

She smiled back. "Thanks."

"Hello, Jeff," Dana Conyers said with an amused smile as she joined them with a whiskey highball in one hand. She was wearing a black lacy cocktail dress, her dark hair loose around her shoulders. She looked very pretty, something Jeff picked up on at once.

"Hi, Dana," he replied. "You look pretty."

"Thanks. You don't look bad yourself." She looked around. "I can't find Dal anywhere. He's always wandering off to talk cattle with other ranchers." She grimaced. She looked up at

Jeff with sultry eyes, ignoring Meadow entirely. "Care to dance?" she asked.

Jeff let go of Meadow's hand with an apologetic glance, set his glass on the table, and led Dana onto the dance floor. Meadow, who had no real romantic feelings for Jeff, nevertheless felt bad for him as she watched him shuffle around the dance floor with Dana in his arms. She knew how he felt about the other woman. Poor man. She was just toying with him, probably to make Dal jealous. She hoped Jeff knew. Men were so blind about women and their motives . . .

"Well, well, you found another red dress," Dal Blake drawled from behind her.

She steeled herself not to show any emotion. She turned and looked up at him. "I had a few spare minutes, so I took down the curtains and made them into a party dress," she said sarcastically.

His dark eyes slid over her like caressing hands, making her pulse run wild and her breathing erratic. Those were signs he was too experienced to miss. She was still stuck on him. He hated it. He hated her. She was a woman who had white picket fence written all over her, and he never wanted to settle down.

"Cute," he remarked. He took a long sip of his drink. "I hope you've got your men looking out for pregnant heifers. You can't afford to lose livestock."

"They know what to do," she replied. "I just let them do it." She glanced toward the dance floor. Jeff had Dana close in his arms, and she seemed to be eating it up.

"Faithless," Dal muttered, following her gaze. "Women never devote themselves to one man anymore. They play the field."

She shrugged. "It's a new world."

He looked down at her with dark, irritated eyes. "Yes. A

new world." His eyes ran over her again. "Are you making a statement, with that dress?"

She flushed. She'd worn it deliberately, to taunt him. He probably knew it already. She hated how transparent she was to him.

"It's the only really good party dress I own," she lied.

"That's right. Mustn't wear anything feminine." The smile he gave her was sharper than a razor.

She flushed. "It's hard to run down criminals in a dress and high heels," she said shortly.

He took another sip of his drink. His dark eyes slid down to her mouth and lingered there so long that it was like an imprint. She moved restlessly.

He took a step closer, so that there were only a few inches of space between them. She steeled herself not to feel anything.

"I don't like your hair like that," he commented softly. "I like it long, and soft, curving around your shoulders."

Her heart jumped. "That's why Dana wears hers long, I imagine. For you," she added pointedly.

His head bent. She could smell his minty breath, feel the heat of his hard body so close to her own. She wanted to run, but that would give away far too much.

"Long hair is sexy," he commented. His eyes were still on her mouth. He stared at it until her lips parted under the force of her quickened breath.

"Is . . . it?" she stammered.

He moved another step closer. Now he was right up against her. She could feel his warm strength, wrapping around her. "Your heart is running like an over-wound watch," he whispered. "You still want me."

She felt her cheeks burn. "I do not," she said, enunciating every word.

"Liar," he whispered.

She tried to move back, but one steely hand caught her small waist and brought her right against him. It didn't take an experienced woman to know that he was aroused. She'd never felt a man like that, not so close. It made her uncomfortable.

"You need to . . . let me go," she managed.

"Why?" The hand at her waist moved softly against her rib cage, edging closer to the underside of one small, pert breast.

"People . . . can see us," she began.

He took her glass and put it on the table, along with his. He caught her arm and moved her through the crowd, right out the side door and under the awning. It was freezing cold and she had no coat.

He pulled her roughly into his arms, inside his unbuttoned suit jacket, against the warmth of his body. "You go to my head," he ground out as his head bent. "I hate what you do to me!"

Before he finished the sentence, his hard, warm mouth was grinding into hers, demanding and insistent. There was such raw passion in the kiss that she had no defense against it. She moaned harshly against his devouring mouth.

He heard the pitiful little sound and reacted immediately. One big hand slid down her back to her hips. He pushed them hard into the thrust of his body and held them there, despite her weak protests.

"Stand still," he bit off against her mouth. "Don't make it worse."

She didn't understand what he was saying. She didn't care. He was kissing her as if the world was ending and it was the very last chance he'd ever have to get her so close. She gave in to his ardor without even a struggle, loving the feel of his aroused body and knowing that she was responsible for it. Her short nails bit into the white shirt under his suit jacket as she pressed closer, her arms going under his, her starving body shivering . . .

He groaned in anguish. He wanted to push her up against the nearby wall, pull up her dress, and make love to her so hungrily that she'd never be able to look at another man as long as she lived. He wanted her. God, he wanted her!

He'd had just enough to drink that he was near the edge of his control. He found the zipper that held the dress in place and started to move it down.

That was when Meadow came to her senses. As much as she loved what he was doing to her, she couldn't let this go on. There were people just inside the door, for God's sake!

"Dal, we can't," she moaned against his mouth.

He drew in what he hoped was a sobering breath, but he was looking at her soft, warm, sweet mouth. He bent again, forsaking the zipper, but his big hands came around and blatantly moved over her breasts, feeling the hard tips, loving her headlong response to him.

"You're sweet to kiss," he whispered, nipping her lower lip. "Come home with me," he added roughly.

She was trying to keep her senses intact. It wasn't easy. Her head was spinning, as if she'd had too much to drink. In fact, she'd only had a sip of something alcoholic. He was like whiskey. He was sweet to kiss, too, but before she could say it, his mouth was against hers again. She felt his hands moving on her, seducing her. He was experienced, and it showed. No rushing his fences here. He teased and tempted until she was aching for anything he wanted to do to her.

"Come home with me," he repeated against her mouth.

If she did, her life was over. She did at least know that. "You brought . . . Dana," she protested weakly.

"Dana." He lifted his head. It was spinning. She was

heady. He hated her. Why was he trying to seduce her right outside a building full of people?

He drew back. His hand went to his head and he scowled down at her.

"I know," she said, holding up a hand of her own. "You had too much to drink and you mistook me for your date."

"Not much hope of that. Unlike you, she dresses like a lady," he said, angry at his own weakness. "You look like a call girl!"

She hit him. It was an impulse that she almost regretted. She turned and went back inside, heading straight to the restroom to repair the damage he'd done to her makeup and put cold water on her lips to reduce the swelling. Now if only Dana didn't show up in there!

She didn't. Meadow fixed her makeup, restored her hair with the small brush she kept in her evening bag, and put cold water on her lips with a wet paper towel. After a minute or two, she felt normal enough to return to the dance floor.

She went out the door with her head high. She hoped Dal had to explain that red handprint on his hard cheek to his date. It would make her feel better about her response to him. It was an elegant dress she was wearing, even if it was red! And she didn't look like a hooker!

Jeff was standing by the punch bowl, looking morose.

"What's wrong?" Meadow asked gently.

He glanced down at her and forced a smile. "Nothing. Nothing at all. Care to dance?"

She was thinking of ways to refuse him when Gil joined them.

"Who can do a wild cha-cha?" he asked his coworkers. "Please say no," he added to Jeff, who was still looking glum. "I'd hate dancing with your left feet, boss."

That brought a laugh from Jeff. "No, I can't do a cha-cha."

Gil raised his eyebrows at Meadow.

"You bet I can," she said, and slung her little purse back over her shoulder. "You're on!"

Gil led her onto the dance floor, where the Latin beat was pulsating like a heartbeat.

Meadow could dance. Her mother had sent her for lessons, to make sure she had the social graces. It had devastated her that Meadow wanted to be a policewoman instead of a debutante. Her mother had even picked out a nice rich man for her. Meadow had dodged the introduction and gone back to work.

"You're good!" Gil exclaimed with a laugh.

She grinned. "So are you."

They moved around the dance floor, oblivious to the angry, dark-eyed man who glared at them from the side-lines.

"Well, she can dance," Dana murmured reluctantly.

"She looks like a call girl in that damned dress," he said shortly. "She should have worn something sedate."

"Why?" Dana asked curiously.

He glanced down at her. He was aware that he wasn't acting rationally. He was still vibrating from the long, sweet session with Meadow outside the building, in the freezing cold. Neither of them had even noticed it, they were so wrapped up in each other. Not in her finest hour could Dana have ever competed with Meadow, not that way. He was fond of the woman at his side, he enjoyed her company. He even enjoyed kissing her, although he'd gone no further than kisses—bad business to make a local business-woman into his mistress and flaunt it. But kissing Meadow Dawson was like walking into fire. In his experience, and there was plenty of it, he'd never come across a woman who went to his head the way she did.

But she still had white picket fence written all over her, and he wasn't a settling man.

"What happened to your cheek?" Dana asked, frowning as she noticed it.

"The call girl and I had what you might think was a confrontation," he murmured, and sipped some more of his drink. "She took offense at what I said."

"If you called her that, no wonder," Dana said, driven to defend a fellow member of her sex against such an unwarranted attack. "Dal, that's an expensive dress. There's nothing about it that would provoke any man to say such a thing. I know you dislike her, but that's just going too far."

"You're supposed to be on my side," he flashed at her.

"Well, I am. Of course, I am," she replied. "But she has a reputation that most women would envy. Even me," she had to confess. She knew people talked about her, speculated about her, since she'd been dating Dal, who everyone locally knew was a rounder.

"What sort of reputation?" he drawled.

"A spotless one," she told him. "I have a girlfriend who dated Meadow's boss in St. Louis. He said that Meadow rarely dated anyone, and she never slept around."

"Maybe she was pining for me." He laughed coldly.

"For you?"

"She's got a case on me, didn't you notice?" he asked, his eyes going angrily to the woman in the red dress, moving so elegantly on the dance floor. "She's been stuck on me since she was seventeen."

Dana didn't know what to say. She just stared at him.

"Oh, for God's sake, she's just a kid," he said when he saw the expression. "I don't seduce children!"

"She's twenty-five," she said, confused.

"She's still seventeen," he said, half under his breath, watching Meadow dance like a fairy to the Latin beat, graceful and skillful. "She fell into the coal bin, in a red dress. I laughed." He recalled Meadow's expression back then, the wounding he could see in her eyes. He'd done it deliberately, trying to ward her off. Even at seventeen, he wanted her. He'd always wanted her, always denied it, fought it. He wasn't giving in. He didn't do forever.

"If you say so," Dana replied. She smiled to herself. At least Dal wasn't stuck on the younger woman. That meant she still had a chance. "Want to dance?" she asked.

"No. I can't do Latin dances," he said resentfully as he watched Gil spin Meadow around on the dance floor.

"Gil can," Dana sighed. "He always was light on his feet."

He looked down at her, astonished. "Dancing isn't a skill!"

"Well, actually, it is," she replied. "Most men can't dance. Heavens, didn't you see Jeff on the dance floor? He can barely shuffle his feet."

Dal could dance. He didn't do it much. No Latin dances at all. But he could do a masterful waltz. Not that he had much of a chance to show off that skill tonight. This wasn't a waltzing crowd. Most of the music they played was western or country. The Latin music was just for Gil. He'd seen the man approach the bandleader earlier so he could dance with Meadow.

Dal didn't like her dancing with the younger man. He had another sip of his drink. His head was starting to feel like an overfull balloon.

"We're going to have to go soon," he told Dana. "I'm sorry. I've had too much to drink," he confessed.

"I'll drive," she informed him.

He shrugged.

Meadow and Gil came off the dance floor, panting and laughing. Her face was flushed. She looked . . . beautiful. Dal could hardly take his eyes off her. The red dress was elegant, at that. He was sorry for the remarks he'd made.

Meadow saw him watching her. The look she gave him was sizzling, and not in a sexy way. She looked as if she'd like to see him frying on a grill. There was hurt in it, too. He'd made her feel cheap, when that was the last thing she was.

He would have apologized, but very quickly she said something to Jeff. He gave a wistful glance at Dana, nodded, and dug for his car keys. They retrieved Meadow's coat and walked out the door. Dal felt as if he'd been thrown head-first into a snowbank. He felt guilty.

He turned to Dana. "How about driving me home?" he asked in a hollow voice.

She saw his expression and felt her hopes dwindling. The light went out of him when Meadow left the building. It was a revelation. Dal was crazy about the other woman, and he didn't even seem to know it.

"I'll just get my coat," Dana said with a quiet smile. Oh, well, she was thinking. Jeff had been very attentive and morose that she was with another man. They'd been quite an item around town until they'd argued. She couldn't even remember what they'd argued about. Jeff wasn't as rich as Dal, but he had that huge ranch and he was a respected member of the community. She could do worse.

Sooner or later, Dal was going to give in to his feelings for Meadow, or Meadow would leave and go back to St. Louis. Either way, Dana would survive. She had prospects. That was all she needed.

Meadow smiled as Jeff kissed her lightly on the cheek.

"Thanks," she said, trying to hide the pain Dal had given her. "It was a nice dance."

"No, it wasn't," Jeff said on a sigh.

"You're still hung up on Dana," she guessed aloud.

He shrugged. "I'm a one-woman man, but I lost the woman to someone richer," he said bitterly.

"She was glaring at us on the dance floor," she commented helpfully.

He perked up. "She was?"

She smiled. "Yes, she was."

He chuckled. "Maybe there's hope."

"Maybe there is. Thanks for taking me."

"Thanks for going with me. See you first thing Monday morning."

"You bet. Good night."

"Good night," he called as he went back to his car, started it, and roared off with a wave of his hand.

Meadow went into her house. It was quiet and dark. That was how her heart felt. Dal had said terrible things to her, hurtful things. He'd meant them. He thought she looked like a hooker. She laughed coldly to herself. She'd seen hookers on the street. She should get him in the car and drive him to Denver, let him see for himself how little she resembled the real thing in her elegant dress. But it wouldn't make any difference. He hated her. He'd made it apparent tonight.

She wondered why he'd kissed her so hungrily. Dana was his girl, everybody knew it. Had he mistaken her for Dana? He'd been drinking a lot. That was unusual. Everybody knew he rarely drank hard liquor at all. Someone in his family had been an alcoholic, his grandfather, she recalled. It must have been hard for his father. He'd been an only child. Dal would have grown up with bad memories of men who went over the edge on booze.

But he'd been drinking tonight. Why? She gave up wondering and went to bed.

Her dreams were wild and erotic. Dal figured heavily in them. Just before she woke up, he'd been kissing her again, devouring her as he had outside the building the night before. It was so sweet. He'd whispered something. She was trying so hard to hear it when Snow started howling in her ear.

She came awake at once. The white muzzle was sneaking under the covers, cold and insistent on her cheek.

She laughed and hugged Snow close. "Got to go, huh? Okay. Just a minute, sweetie. I have to go with you so you don't sneak off."

After the things Dal had said, she wasn't about to let Snow wander up to his ranch. Not again. Never again.

She threw on her snow boots and a coat, got the lead, and went outside with her dog.

She'd thought that it would be a long time before she saw Dal again, but he was sitting on the edge of Jeff's desk when she walked into his office in the courthouse.

He gave her a disapproving glance, his eyes going to the pistol on her belt, next to her badge. "You walk around with that gun all the time?" he asked.

"It goes with the job," she returned calmly, refusing to be baited. "Hi, boss," she added, with a smile for Jeff.

"Hi, kid," he said with a grin. "I've got a job for you."

"You have?" she asked warily.

"I have to be away from my house tonight," Dal said curtly. "I need someone to stay there and keep an eye on my antique writing desk. I had an attempted break-in the night I took Dana to the dance. I'm sure he'll try again, and tonight's his best chance. Everybody knows I'm going to Denver to buy a new lot of purebreds. I won't get home until near midnight."

"That would be private security," she said coolly.

"Yes, it would," he replied, "and it's a paying job. You don't work nights. There isn't anybody else," he added, with just enough acid to let her know that this wasn't his own idea.

"I sort of volunteered you," Jeff said apologetically. "If you don't want to do it, nobody's going to insist."

Dal cocked his head. "You can bring Snow with you," he said sarcastically, "since she thinks she lives at my ranch, anyway."

She bowed up like a spitting cat. "Look here . . ." she began.

"Here." Dal put a key in her hand. "One of my men's watching the house right now, but he has to leave at five. That's when you'll need to relieve him. The other men will all be out with the pregnant heifers. Another snow storm's headed our way."

She wanted to protest, but she couldn't find a way out that didn't involve slapping that smirk off Dal's sensuous mouth.

"All right," she said shortly.

"I'll leave the check on the telephone table," Dal added. "Thanks, Jeff."

He walked out without another glance at Meadow.

Nice, she thought, thanking her boss and without a single word of approval for her. That was Dal.

"Sorry about that," Jeff said when his friend was gone. "I tried to ward him off, but he's in our jurisdiction. And he's my friend . . ."

"Not to worry, I don't mind," she added. She frowned. "That was the table that one of the major surrenders was signed on when the Civil War ended, wasn't it?" she asked.

"Yes, it was. It's worth a fortune. It was handed down in Dal's family. His grandfather sold it on one of his drunken binges," he added. "Took Dal's father a year to make enough to buy it back. Sad story. It's sort of a family heirloom."

"Like the pipe organ and the Victorian lamp that belonged to former presidents." She was thinking aloud.

"I had the same thought," Jeff replied. "Our thief is very

selective about what he takes. If it's the same man—I'm assuming it's a man, because we've never had a female thief do break-ins locally—then it was probably him who tried to get into Dal's house while we were all at the dance. Good thing his foreman was in the house getting a bill of lading at the time and heard the noise in the back of the house. Chased the thief, but lost him in the woods."

"Nobody called us," she complained.

"Dal would have, but he was," he hesitated, "incapacitated at the time."

"He was with his girlfriend," she said, trying to hide her irritation.

"He was stinking drunk," Jeff corrected. "Dana had to drive him home and get him to bed. She said he slept the whole way home. One of his cowboys helped her when they got to the ranch." He shook his head. "Never saw Dal drunk in my life. He hates liquor. His grandfather beat him when he was little, when his daddy went away on cattle sales. He never got over it. Said he'd die before he'd turn into a lush."

She gritted her teeth. "Poor man," she said reluctantly.

"We get a lot of deputies who come from homes like that," he mentioned. "They go into law enforcement trying to save other kids from what they went through. Sometimes we get lucky. Sometimes we don't."

"That's true," she confessed. "We've all been there, where you try to arrest a drunken husband for beating his wife, and the wife either refuses to testify or attacks you when you try to arrest him." She laughed. "One threw a whole gallon of milk on one of our officers in St. Louis. Soaked him to the skin. We called him 'the milkman.'" She laughed at the memory. "He was a good sport."

"Don't get me started," he said. "I've got some stories of my own."

She grinned. "Okay. I'll get to work."

"Plenty of opportunities for that. There are several new files on your desk," he added apologetically.

"No sweat. It's what I get paid for."

He glanced at her. "It stung you, what Dal said about your gun."

She shifted restlessly. "He hates me. He said I looked like a call girl in my red dress."

"I'm sure he didn't mean it." He defended his friend. "You looked very elegant, I thought."

"Thanks, boss."

"Dal says things he doesn't mean. He's always sorry, and he tries to make amends. I don't know why he's so hard on you," he added, frowning. "It's not like him. He loves women. He goes out of his way to make sure the ranch wives who work for him have anything they need and a lot of things they just want."

"It's a long story," she replied, recalling the first incident, her red dress that met a terrible fate in the coal. "I know he doesn't like me. It doesn't matter. In this business, you get used to being disliked." She chuckled. "I'll just go do my job."

"Good idea. I'll go earn my paycheck, too."

"The county commission will love you for it."

"On my deathbed, maybe." He laughed.

She sat down at her desk and went to work. At least it kept her mind off Dal for most of the day.

Chapter Nine

Meadow went home and changed clothes. She wore jeans and boots and a long-sleeved blue checked shirt with a fringed vest under her shepherd's coat. She looked very Western, especially when she brought out her treasured feather-brimmed cowgirl hat to go with it. She looked in the mirror and heard Dal's harsh voice ridiculing her when he saw how she was dressed.

She went back to her wardrobe and took out a navy blue pantsuit and a modest white camisole. She thought about leaving her gun at home. Like most people in law enforcement, she knew hand-to-hand combat and how to take down an opponent, even if she'd been sadly unprepared for the one assault when she'd needed to use it. She'd been trained by a veteran of wars in the Middle East, a combat veteran who was a master trainer for their department in St. Louis. He'd been a dish, but he had a lovely wife and two sweet little boys. He didn't wander, either, not even when beautiful women flirted with him. He was quite a guy. Loved his wife.

She could just see Dal being faithful if he ever married. It was hilarious. He'd be sneaking out the back door to some other woman's house while his wife was busy in the kitchen. He'd never be able to limit himself to just one woman.

There had been plenty of women in his life. If she hadn't heard that from other people in Raven Springs, she'd have known by the masterful way he kissed her at the dance. In just a few heated minutes, she was almost far gone enough to go home with him. He'd kissed her as if he was dying, as if she was the last woman he'd ever hold in his arms. It was an odd thing. He was dating Dana, who was rumored to be experienced herself. Why was he kissing Meadow that hungrily, if he was getting what he needed from Dana? It was a question she really didn't want to answer. Dal hated her. That wasn't going to change. If it wasn't Dana, it would be some other woman. It would always be some other woman, never Meadow. Once she got that through her thick skull, maybe she could force him out of it. Memories of his ardor haunted her.

She left her blond hair long around her shoulders, hating herself for that one concession. He loved long hair. Angrily, she found a pretty elastic hair tie and looped it around her hair, making it into a ponytail.

She looked at her waist, which was bare. The gun was part of her working gear. Most burglars weren't armed; most wouldn't harm anyone in the commission of a theft. But there was always the exception. This thief had struck twice already and apparently had no compunction about breaking in. She could be in danger if he did carry. Her mind went back to the prison interrogation room and the beating she'd taken from the inmate she'd been interviewing. She swallowed hard. Dal didn't like the gun, but he didn't have her past. And he had no right to make her feel guilty about the tools of her trade.

She got her duty belt with her badge on it and whipped it around her waist. She took her Glock out of the locked drawer in the living room, loaded the clip and chambered a

round, put on the safety, and stuck it in her belt. She was
going armed, even if Dal made harsh comments and
laughed at her. Not that he'd be there, she assured herself.
He'd be gone. That was why she had the key to his house,
after all. Sad, how that depressed her.

She threw on her thick Berber coat and drew an equally
thick wool cap over her head. The snow was coming down
in buckets.

Dal's house was quiet. Snow settled in front of the dying
fire in the fireplace with Jarvis, the huge red Maine coon
cat, who'd laced himself around Meadow's pants legs and
purred up a storm.

"Sweet boy," she said softly, petting him.

She patted Snow on the head and put a few more pieces
of wood on the fire. It seemed to be the only source of heat
in the very cold room. It was comfy, though, with over-
stuffed chairs and a long sofa in the same earth tones. There
was a Navajo blanket over the chair. Meadow had seen one
just like it at an exhibit she'd gone to with her father in
Denver. Dal had been there. Meadow had enthused over the
beautiful jagged pattern and the bright colors. Dal had
made fun of her enthusiasm and embarrassed her into silence. Then, apparently, he'd purchased that very blanket
and brought it home with him. She was surprised.

She touched it, curious. She'd never been in his home
before, not even with her father, who visited him frequently. She tried to stay as far away from him as she could.
He always had something cutting to say to her.

Why had he bought the blanket she'd wanted? To keep
her from getting it? That was a laugh. The beautiful thing
had cost almost a thousand dollars. It was functional, but
still a work of art. Meadow, much less her father, could
never have afforded something so very extravagant. Not

that it wasn't worth every penny. It was meant for a house like this, for furnishings like this. Everything around her was elegant, not like the secondhand or on-sale things that graced Meadow's apartment and her father's house.

She sat down on the couch and turned the television to a game show she liked. She settled back with a bottle of Perrier water she'd found in the kitchen and made herself comfortable.

She'd gone through the movies, couldn't find one she liked, found nothing to tempt her on the local stations. So she settled down with the Weather Channel and watched the progress of the storm that was plowing into Raven Springs. It had already overcome the ranches. She'd phoned her foreman to ask about the progress of their pregnant heifers and been assured that the nighthawks were on the job.

She'd lowered the lights in the living room and muted the sound on the channel. She was very tired. It had been a long day. She'd had to track down a witness in a domestic violence case, always a tricky thing to do. The witness, an older woman, finally admitted to what she'd seen but refused to appear at trial or even be deposed. Meadow gently reminded her that the victim, a pregnant young woman, had been admitted to the hospital with injuries that cost her the child she was carrying. The witness reluctantly agreed to appear as a witness for the prosecution.

Ann Farrell, the assistant district attorney assigned to the case, had gone with Meadow to talk to the witness. Afterward, they'd had lunch and traded horror stories. Civilians had no idea what people in law enforcement had to cope with. District attorneys were also involved in the daily operations of law enforcement when they had to prosecute a case. The assistant DA was confident that she could win the case. The victim was mad enough to testify and had, in fact, already filed for divorce. Since the case was unlikely to be tried until the next circuit court session, the divorce would be through and the husband under a court order not to approach his wife or have any contact with her. A wife could testify against her husband, especially in a criminal case where the wife was the victim.

Meadow wondered privately what sort of lowlife would raise his hand to a pregnant woman in the first place. Probably, she mused, the same sort of lowlife who would chain a dog to a tree and forget to feed and water it, like poor Snow.

She reached over and ruffled the fur between Snow's ears, laughing as the pretty husky raised her head and closed her eyes. Snow was such a treasure. She loved the thick white fur with its pale red tips. She'd never had a pet as intelligent as her dog.

After a few minutes, she stretched out on Dal's cushy couch with a pillow under her head and dozed while the television droned on.

She was barely aware of a faint noise in the back of the house, but Snow heard it and got up quickly. She lifted her head, sniffing the air. She looked at Meadow with her pale blue eyes and howled faintly.

Meadow sat up. Her hand went automatically to her pistol as she got to her feet and moved on the carpet, silently, to the hallway. She heard the noise again. So did Snow, who jumped forward and ran toward the source of it.

That sound was coming from Dal's office. He'd told her about the antique writing desk that was kept there, the one she was guarding. It seemed that his concern wasn't misplaced. The thief had come back!

Her heart racing, pistol steady in both hands, Meadow moved cautiously behind Snow. She wanted to call the dog back, but her voice would alert whoever was moving around in the room down the hall. She hoped that Snow wouldn't do too much damage to him before she got there. The dog was aggressive when she needed to be, despite her usually sweet temperament.

She heard a thud. Seconds later, there was a loud yelp. "Snow!" Meadow called, and started running down the hall. To hell with stealth. Something had happened to her pet!

She got to the study where the writing table was kept. Her keen eyes noted the empty space where it had been and the open window behind it. Jarvis was meowing loudly. He was standing on the big desk, and there was a smear of blood on some bond paper that was stacked beside him, near the printer.

"Are you okay, baby?" she asked Jarvis quickly. He seemed fine, although there was blood on one of his paws.

She ran to the low window and looked out. Snow was lying on the ground, still, motionless. Her heart stopped in her chest. In the distance, there was a tall figure in a gray coat carrying a big cloth bag, like the sort artists carried their canvases in. He didn't look back. He was running.

So Meadow had a choice. Chase the thief, which was her job, or save her pet's life. It was no choice at all.

She holstered the gun and climbed quickly out the low window. As she knelt in the snow to put a hand on Snow's chest, she noticed a long piece of firewood just beside the animal, obviously the thing the thief had used on her poor pet. There was dirt on Snow's head, visible against the blinding white snow in the outside security light, probably from the wood. Snow's chest was rising and falling. She was alive! Now Meadow had to get help to keep her that way.

It was a long way to the driveway where her SUV was parked. She struggled to drag Snow around the side of the house. The dog was very heavy. She was still breathing, but also still unconscious. Terrified, Meadow found strength she didn't even know she had as she wrangled the big dog up into the vehicle and closed the door.

She had her cell phone out even as she revved the SUV and roared off down the snow-covered road, sliding a little in her haste. She'd left the window open, the door unlocked. Dal was going to be furious . . .

Snow could die! She had no time to go back and secure the house. She had the vet's number on speed dial, thank God.

There was a lot of information on after-hours care, with a phone number. She stopped in the road, turned on the overhead light, and grappled for a pen in the console. She wrote the number on her hand, having no scrap of paper except in her purse, on the floor. No time to hunt for some.

She called the number and shot the big vehicle forward, her heart shaking her with its terrified beat. It rang once, twice, three times.

"Come on, come on," she cried aloud, glancing at the dog's still form. "Please!"

Apparently angels did exist, because a soft, feminine voice came on the line. "Dr. Clay. How can I help you?"

"I'm a deputy sheriff. I was standing guard over a priceless antique when a thief managed to get into the house and take it. My Siberian husky tried to stop him and he hit her over the head with something. A piece of firewood, I think, I remember seeing one . . . she's unconscious. Still breathing. Please . . ." Tears blurred the road in her eyes.

"Bring her right on to the office. I'm less than five minutes away. I'll meet you there."

"Thank you. Thank you so much!" Meadow sobbed. She hung up. She was about eight minutes away.

Damn the snow, she thought recklessly, and stood on the accelerator. Thank God they had the snowplows out in force. At least the roads were mostly clear—the main roads, that is. She had to get from the ranch road to the main road, and it wasn't easy. The snow was deep. But she got through it, sliding onto the main highway but recovering quickly.

She glanced at Snow and reached over to smooth the soft fur. She hadn't noticed any blood around the dog's mouth, which hopefully meant that there was no fatal damage. "Hang on, baby, please hang on! I can't lose you," she whispered. Her voice broke. She couldn't bear the thought of losing her dog, her companion, her friend.

She gunned the engine, prepared to out-argue any fellow law enforcement officer who caught her speeding. Luckily the road seemed to be empty.

She spun the SUV off the road into the parking lot of the veterinary office, where another SUV was parked just at the door.

The vet came running to help Meadow get the big dog out of the vehicle and inside, onto the examination table.

"Head trauma," Dr. Clay murmured as her hands went over the still form of the dog. She opened Snow's mouth and nodded. "Good, good." She took the stethoscope from around her neck, looped the earpieces into her ears, and listened. She nodded again. Her hands probed the skull and she nodded again.

"Concussion," she said, "as you've probably guessed. We'll need to run tests, but the most immediate thing is to get her oxygenated, start electrolytes, and elevate her head. I don't feel any depressions in her skull that would indicate a skull fracture, and her heart rate is good. There may be some pulmonary issues, but we'll worry about those after she's stabilized. She'll need to be watched continuously until she comes to." She noted Meadow's terror. "I'll have Dr. Bonner relieve me, but I'll stay with her for the next few hours."

She didn't add *if she comes to*. Meadow knew from her experience in law enforcement that if a patient with a head injury didn't regain consciousness in seventy-two hours, the patient was likely not to survive.

Meadow took a deep breath. "It was my fault," she said. "Snow ran ahead after the perp. I wasn't quick enough to stop her."

"Don't blame yourself," Dr. Clay said gently. "We're human. We do the best we can. It's not your fault. Okay?"

She nodded, lips pressed together to stop them from trembling.

"I'm going to have to have help with her once I get the preliminary things started," the doctor said, and searched for the materials she needed. She had her cell on speakerphone. Meadow heard it ring, and a soft voice answered. "Tanny, I need you to come in. I have a patient, a female husky with severe head trauma."

"I'll be right there," the vet tech promised and hung up.

"She's very good," Dr. Clay told Meadow as she started Snow on oxygen with a mask. She reached for clippers and removed the fur around the dog's lower leg, just above the foot, to start a drip.

"She has to live," Meadow ground out. "She just has to."

"There are positives," the doctor said. She was elevating Snow's head with a board. "Have to turn her every half hour," she murmured to herself as she worked. "No bone fracture, her vitals are good, if a little off center. How old is she?"

"Two years," Meadow choked.

The vet nodded. "Young. And she's in great shape physically. There may be some neurological problems if . . . when," she added after a glance at Meadow's drawn face, "she recovers. Seizures, most likely. We'll have to put her on anticonvulsant medication. Look at that," she added softly, noting Snow's sudden sharp movement. The blue eyes opened and looked around. They closed and she breathed regularly. "Another good sign."

Meadow let out the breath she'd been holding. She reached out to pet Snow's soft fur. "When I get through my current nervous breakdown, I'm going to move heaven and earth to find the man who did this to her," she said through her teeth.

"If you get him, I'll be more than happy to testify," the vet said grimly. "I hate animal abusers."

"Me too."

"Dr. Bonner and I will take turns watching her, around the clock if we have to. But we'll need someone to special her once that's out of the way. It may be expensive."

"I don't care what it costs," Meadow said, choking up. "It's so hard!"

Dr. Clay patted her on the shoulder. "I know. I've been in this situation myself," she added. Her pale eyes were sympathetic. "You go home. There's nothing you can do here. Give me your cell number. I'll call you if there's any change."

Meadow gave it to her, tears running down her cheek. "She's the only family I have left," she said huskily.

"I know how that feels, too." Dr. Clay took the pad and pen she'd loaned Meadow and put the number into her own cell phone.

"Will she come out of it, do you think?" Meadow asked after a minute. "Honestly?"

"I don't know," came the quiet reply. "In cases like this, we have to wait and see. I'll run those tests. They'll help us decide on what treatments to pursue. You have to authorize them."

"I'll sign anything."

The doctor smiled sadly. "Try not to worry. I'll do whatever I can. I promise."

"I know that." She smoothed her hand over Snow's fur and ground her teeth together. "Don't leave me, baby," she whispered. "Please, fight. You have to fight."

The dog seemed to stir a little again at the words. Meadow kissed the fur behind an ear. "I'll be waiting at home, okay?"

She moved away, shaken, terrified. Her wide eyes met those of the doctor. There was really nothing else to say. It was a matter of waiting now. She signed the electronic permission form, fighting more tears.

She passed the veterinary technician on her way out the door. She was a young woman, short and dark-headed, with a sweet face and a compassionate smile.

"I'm Tanny," she told Meadow. "Don't worry, we'll take good care of your dog," she assured Meadow. "One of us will make sure you know the minute she comes around," she added with an optimism that Meadow prayed was justified.

"Thanks so much," Meadow said huskily.

"It will be all right," the vet tech said quietly. "You have to have faith. It really does move mountains."

Meadow just nodded.

She went home, dragging, worn to the bone, sick with worry. It was far worse than when Snow had wandered into the barbed wire fence and everyone had been out searching for her. She could die. If only she could do something!

Her heart jumped when she saw that Dal Blake's big truck was sitting in her driveway when she got there.

She got out of the SUV. He was furious. She winced as he moved closer, face like a thundercloud.

"You let the thief take my table right out the damned window, and you didn't even chase him! I followed his footprints to the woods, only his, yours went to the damned driveway! You left the doors unlocked, the window open . . . what the hell kind of security are you?"

She started to speak, but she couldn't get a word in edgewise.

"Next time I want someone to guard my house, I'll have Jeff send a real law enforcement officer, not some damned flighty woman who welcomes thieves into houses and walks off without even leaving a note behind!"

"Let me explain," she began.

He cut her off. "You're useless," he said icily, "as a deputy, even as a woman. You don't even know how to kiss, for God's sake! Always watching me, trying to seduce me . . . as if I'd ever want some backward virgin who doesn't know what to do with a man!"

The sting of those words went right through her. On top of the worry for Snow, it was just too much. "You go to hell, Dal Blake!" she said harshly, tears running down her face.

"That table had been in my family for three generations," he said through his teeth. "It was all I had left of my grandmother. And you let someone just walk off with it!"

She took a shaky breath. "I'm sorry."

"You're sorry! You don't know what sorry is, but you'll find out. When Jeff knows what you did, he'll fire you! No wonder you left the FBI. You can't find your left foot with a fork!"

She turned and went to the front door. Her hands were shaking as she unlocked it.

"That's it, run away!"

She did. She closed the door and locked it behind her. Then she went into her bedroom and collapsed into tears on the bed. It had been a horrible night. In many ways, it was one of the worst nights of her life.

She didn't put on a gown. She lay down on the coverlet

in her sock feet, still in her pantsuit, in case she had to rush back to the animal hospital. She thought of Snow, poor Snow, who'd been hurt trying to save stupid Dal Blake's equally stupid antique table.

He was the most horrible person in the world, and she was sure that she never wanted to see him again.

Snow. She recalled so many happy times with the rescued dog, playing in the snow, chasing along paths in the woods, sitting by the fireplace at night, with just the light of the burning logs. Snow was more than a dog, she was a companion, someone to talk to, someone to keep her company. Snow was . . . like her child.

The tears came back, flowing like hot rivers down her cheeks, into the corner of her mouth. *Please*, she prayed silently, *please don't let her die because of me. I should have chased her, I should have stopped her.* It was just one more foul-up in a life full of foul-ups. And now her stupidity was going to cost her Snow.

Belatedly, she recalled the job she was doing when the tragic events unfolded. She called Jeff at home on her cell phone.

"Snow was injured?" Jeff exclaimed. "I'm so sorry!"

"They don't know if she's going to live," she said, managing not to burst into tears. She wanted so badly to have someone to just hold her and let her cry. Fat chance of that. "I saw the thief. He had a big canvas bag, like artists carry their paintings in, over his shoulder. He was tall. I couldn't see much, but he had on a gray overcoat." She hesitated. "Oh, and Jarvis had blood on one paw. There was a smear of it on some paperwork on the desk in the study. It might belong to the perp. Jarvis was fine, but if he scratched the man, it might explain the blood."

"That's terrific detective work," he said gently. "At least it's something to start with," Jeff said. "I'll get Gil out of bed and send him over to Dal's place right now."

"Dal said I was useless," she began, and her voice wobbled.

"Yes, he phoned me," he said, and didn't add what the man had said. "Never mind. I have no plans to fire you, okay? I don't blame you for putting your dog's life over trying to catch the perp, which it's unlikely you could have done anyway if he had that much of a head start."

"I want him. Bad," she added coldly.

"So do I," Jeff replied. "Don't worry. Dr. Clay came to us from a prestigious animal clinic in New York City. She's one of the best I've ever seen. She treats my dog, Clarence."

"She's very nice. Oh, darn," she ground out. "It's been a horrible night. But I'm sorry I let the man get away."

"We'll get him," Jeff said. "I'll phone Gil right now. You take care. If you need me, call, okay?"

"Okay. Thanks."

Gil arrived at Dal's front door more than a little out of humor. He'd had the story from Jeff. This rancher had laid into poor Meadow without even giving her a chance to explain what happened. Typical Dal Blake—yell first.

"I'm here to get evidence," he told an irritated Dal.

Dal didn't even reply. He led the deputy to his study. Gil went to the desk and took out a kit to get a sample of blood from the paper.

"I need to see your cat. I hope you haven't washed his paw," he added. "There may be some dried blood on his claws. I'll need a sample of it."

"What blood?" Dal asked, frowning. He looked over Gil's shoulder.

"There's a good chance that your cat scratched the perp,"

Gil murmured. "If this is his blood, it's evidence that will stand up in court. We can get a DNA profile from the state crime lab."

"I didn't know Jarvis had scratched him," Dal murmured.

Gil didn't even answer him. He worked the crime scene, taking photos and measurements, careful to dust for fingerprints. But that was futile. Obviously, the perp had been wearing gloves.

He went around the house to the open window and knelt, looking at the tracks that started near where Snow had lain. He saw the imprint of her body. Nearby was a piece of firewood. He shined a light on it.

"That's firewood. What's it doing out here?" Dal wondered and started to pick it up.

"Leave it, please. That's evidence."

"It's a piece of firewood."

"It's probably what the perp used on Meadow's dog," Gil murmured as he put the firewood into a large evidence bag.

Dal stopped dead. "Her dog? Snow?"

Gil nodded, preoccupied with the tracks. "She's at the vet's office. They don't know if the dog will live," he added, glaring up at his companion.

Dal felt two inches high. Now the imprint on the ground and the drag marks made sense. Meadow had had to drag Snow around the house to her vehicle. Snow might die, and he'd gone flaming mad to Meadow's house and called her names . . .

"Dear God," he said on a heavy breath. "I didn't know. She tried to tell me and I wouldn't listen," he ground out.

Gil ignored him. He followed the tracks into the woods, photographing as he went. "The thief is a big man," he murmured. "Tracks are deep. They end there, at the side of the highway." He knelt again and photographed the tire tracks. "Probably won't do any good, but they might be able to match the tread pattern. I'll get pics of it, anyway."

He got to his feet. "He was carrying a big canvas bag, wearing a long gray coat," Gil added.

"He must have removed the legs, to make the desk more portable," Dal commented. "They screw on."

"I'll make a note of that."

"God, poor Meadow!" he ground out. "They don't know if Snow's going to make it?"

"No." Gil faced him, still irritated. "Head injuries are tricky. I was in Iraq. One of the men in my squad was hit by falling masonry. He went down like a sack of sand and died three hours later without regaining consciousness."

"I've seen fatal head injuries, too," Dal replied. "I was in Afghanistan."

Comrades in arms, Gil thought, but he didn't reply. He was angry at the man who'd made Meadow even more upset. He recalled how miserable she'd been at the Christmas dance. Dal had been responsible for that, as well, although Gil didn't know what was said between them.

"I need to see your cat," Gil said.

"I'll find him for you. I didn't notice his paws."

Gil said nothing. He followed the other man into the house. Jarvis was sitting in the kitchen sink, as usual.

"Careful," Dal said when Gil moistened a small square of gauze and lifted the paw with blood on it, gently squeezing the pad to make the claws appear. "He bites. Meadow can pick him up, but nobody else can. Not even me."

"She has a way with animals," Gil agreed. The cat was cooperative. It didn't offer to bite or scratch while he got the blood sample.

He put away the evidence and turned. "I'll get back to the office with these and send them to the crime lab first thing in the morning."

"Thanks for coming over."

"Jeff told me to," he replied, indicating that wild horses wouldn't have dragged him there otherwise. His black eyes narrowed. "Meadow has real self-esteem issues," he said quietly. "Good job, making her feel even worse while her dog fights for its life."

He turned and went out the door before Dal could manage a comeback. His conscience stung him as the deputy's car drove away.

He phoned the clinic and asked for Dr. Clay. "How's Snow?" he asked without preamble, when he'd given his name.

"I'm part owner, you might say," he added when she hesitated. "She stays at my house as much as at Meadow's. I'm concerned."

"She's still alive," was all the vet would concede. "We're treating her now."

"Whatever it costs," he said gruffly. "I'll take care of it. I know Miss Dawson's financial situation. It's going to be tough on her if she tries to afford the care. If you'll grab a pen, I'll give you my credit card information."

There was a visible lessening of tension. "Okay," she replied. "That's kind of you."

"I've been blatantly unkind," he said bluntly. "Maybe this will help make amends. Ready?"

"Yes."

He gave her the information and asked her to call him if Snow worsened. "Meadow doesn't have family anymore," he added. "I'll take care of her if she loses the dog."

"Don't give up on her yet," Dr. Clay said softly. "She's a fighter."

"Like her owner," Dal said. "Thanks."

He hung up and glanced at the clock. It was almost nine. He imagined Meadow hadn't even had time to grab a bite to eat. Nothing had been touched in the kitchen. He knew from her father that she loved cheese and mushroom pizzas. He dialed the number of the local pizza parlor delivery and gave them an order for Meadow, charged to the account he kept there.

Someone knocking at the door was the last thing Meadow expected at that hour. Had Snow died and the vet came to tell her in person? It was an illogical thought, but she was traumatized enough that it made sense.

She ran to open the door and found a teenager with acne and a big grin standing on her porch. "Pizza delivery," he said, handing her a box.

"But I didn't order . . ." she began, all at sea.

"It's a gift from a person who wants to remain anonymous," he said. "Already paid for. Enjoy!"

He ran back toward his car with the pizza parlor's lighted bar on top.

"Thanks!" she called after him belatedly.

"You're welcome!"

He moved out of the driveway, swerving to avoid a deputy sheriff's car that swung into it as he was leaving.

Gil pulled up at her door and got out.

"Pizza?" he mused, grinning.

"Somebody sent it," she said, eyeing him suspiciously.

"Not I," he told her with a chuckle. "But it smells awesome!"

"Come in and share it with me," she said. "I'll make coffee, too."

"I don't know . . ." He hesitated. "Eating on the job, and all that."

His cell phone rang. He answered it. "Standing on Meadow's porch. She just got a gift of pizza . . . sure, here."

He handed her the phone, and she laughed. "Jeff, thanks so much for the pizza! How did you know I like cheese and mushroom?" she enthused.

He hesitated. "Well, it was a lucky guess. Glad you like that kind," he added, happily taking credit for the gift. "You doing okay? How's Snow?"

"We don't know yet," she said sadly. "It was a vicious blow. I want to hang him up by his thumbs when we catch him," she added darkly.

"I'll start stockpiling rope," he assured her. "If you need me, you call, whatever time it is, okay?"

"Okay. Thanks. Can Gil have pizza with me?"

"Yes, he can. He has to get a statement from you anyway. Tell him I said so."

She smiled. "I will. Take care." She hung up and gave the phone back. "He says I have to give you a statement, so you can eat pizza while I'm doing it."

He rubbed his hands together. "Awesome!"

She laughed and led the way to the kitchen. She put the pizza on the table, got down paper plates, and made coffee.

"This was so sweet of Jeff," she commented when they'd gone through two slices apiece and were on their second cups of coffee.

"It was, wasn't it?" he chuckled. "They make good pizza."

"I wish I could . . ."

The *Sherlock* television series theme blasted out in the kitchen from her phone. She looked at it with apprehension and grabbed it, fumbling for the answer button. "Meadow," she said at once.

"Hi," Dr. Clay said. "Just wanted to let you know that Snow's conscious," she said, laughing. "We're going to keep her for a couple of days, but the prognosis just went from iffy to good."

"Oh, thank God!" Meadow let out the breath she'd been

holding. Tears streamed down her face. "Thank God! Thank you, too! I'll never be able to thank you enough!"

"You're very welcome."

"I'll come right over and write out a check . . ."

"Oh, Mr. Blake took care of that earlier this evening," Dr. Clay said. "He was very concerned for Snow. He says he's almost part owner. He must think a lot of her."

Meadow was almost speechless. "She worries him to death," she began.

Dr. Clay laughed. "He didn't sound irritated, believe me. He was concerned, too."

"It was . . . kind of him," she said.

"Yes."

"Can I come see Snow?"

"Whenever you want to."

"I'll finish up here and be right over!"

She told Gil the good news, beaming. Then she frowned. "Did you tell Dal about Snow?"

"Yes," he said. "I wasn't very happy about the way he treated you. I'm afraid I was less than courteous. I guess Jeff will fire me."

"Never in a million years. Suppose I write out the statement and bring it to work in the morning?" she asked. "I really want to go see Snow."

Just before he answered, his radio blared. He pressed the answer switch on the mobile microphone at his shoulder. "Go."

The 911 operator's voice came over the line. "Wreck with injuries, state highway near the Kangaroo at Raven Springs northbound."

"On my way," he replied. He turned to Meadow. "That blows my offer of a ride to the vet," he said. "Have to go."

"I'll bring the statement in tomorrow. Did you get a blood sample from Jarvis?"

"Yes, I did, and he didn't bite me."

"Wow."

He chuckled. "Animals like me. Happy about Snow. Night."

"Good night," she called after him.

She dealt with the remaining slices of pizza, more than enough for supper the next night. Snow was going to live! She was almost floating as she went to find her purse and coat.

Chapter Ten

Meadow had just locked the door when headlights blinded her, coming toward the house.

A big, black pickup truck pulled up beside her and Dal Blake got out. He looked worn as he joined her on the porch.

"I'm on my way to see Snow," she began a little coldly. He'd paid the vet bill, but she couldn't forget the way he'd treated her.

"I'll drive you. I want to see her, too," he said in a subdued tone. He moved closer, towering over her in his shepherd's coat and wide-brimmed Stetson, both dotted with falling snow.

He took her gently by the shoulders. "I'm sorry," he said softly. "Damned sorry."

She bit her lower lip. It had been such an ordeal. She fought tears. It was deadly to show weakness to the enemy.

While she was thinking it, he pulled her into his arms and folded her close, his lips in the hair at her temple.

She hadn't had comfort in years. Nobody held her when she cried, nobody except the father who had died so recently. The comfort was too much for her. It broke her proud spirit. She started sobbing.

Dal wrapped her up tight, whispering at her ear. "It's all

right. Everything is going to be all right. Snow's going to live, okay?"

"It was my fault," she choked. "I didn't stop her. I was afraid to say anything, afraid he'd hear me. She went out the window after him. He hit her . . ."

His mouth cut off the angry words. He kissed her gently, softly. "We'll get him," he said. "If it takes years, we'll make him pay for what he did. I promise!"

"She's my baby," she moaned.

He drew in a long breath. "She's my baby, too," he said tenderly. "Nuisance and all." He smoothed down her long hair, tangled by the wind where it flowed out under her cap. His hands gathered it up, savoring its clean softness. "I'm so sorry," he whispered. "If I'd just let you talk . . ."

She pulled back and looked up at him in the porch light's glare, her face drawn with worry, her eyes soaked in tears.

He wiped the tears away with his thumbs, his big hands warm and comforting where they cupped her oval face. "Stop bawling," he said quietly. "She's going to be fine."

"Dr. Clay said she might have seizures!"

"If she does, we'll handle it," he interrupted. "They have medicines to deal with them. She'll live. That's all that matters."

She drew in a shaky breath. "Okay." She swallowed. "Dr. Clay said you paid the bill."

"Yes. I thought it was the least I could do, under the circumstances. The desk was valuable," he added, "but you can't equate an antique with a pet's life. I'd have done exactly what you did, if it had been Jarvis, or Bess," he added.

She searched his eyes for longer than she meant to, flushed, and dropped them. He'd had too much to say already about her fawning over him. She pulled away from him.

"You're remembering all of it, I guess," he said sadly. "All the vicious things I've said to you, down the years." He laughed, but it had a hollow sound. "I don't suppose you've realized why."

She cocked her head, looking up at him like a curious little bird.

"Never mind." He smoothed his thumb over her soft mouth. "Let's go see Snow."

He helped her into the truck and drove her to the vet's office, helping her down from the high truck with his big hands circling her waist.

He kissed her gently and smiled. "You've been eating pizza. I tasted mushrooms and cheese."

She laughed. "Yes. Jeff sent it. I hadn't eaten anything all day. It was so kind of him!"

He didn't reply. He was going to have something to say to his friend about letting her make that assumption, though.

She glanced at him.

"Jeff's a prince," he said belatedly. He pressed the button so the vet could buzz them in. Even here, in the boondocks, security was a big deal at a vet's office. They kept a store of medicines, including narcotics. There had already been one robbery here. The owners were understandably cautious.

Dr. Clay greeted them and led them back to Snow's cage, where she was still on oxygen and a drip.

She looked at them drowsily.

Dr. Clay laughed. "We've had to sedate her. She wanted to get up and instruct us in the proper management of her case," she added, tongue-in-cheek. "Odd thing about huskies, that so-superior attitude of theirs."

"I know." Meadow laughed, settling on the floor beside Snow, to rub her fur. "She's always like that."

Snow nuzzled her hand. She looked up at Dal and panted,

her blue eyes laughing at him. He knelt beside Meadow and smoothed over Snow's head.

"Poor baby," he murmured gently.

The vet, watching the two of them, was seeing more than they realized. She just smiled.

"Will she recover?" Meadow asked after a minute.

"Yes. As I told you, there may be some neurological issues to deal with. We'll keep her under observation for a few days. I'll have Tanny special her tonight so she's not alone. If anything goes wrong, I live less than five minutes away and I'm a light sleeper," she added when she saw the new lines of stress on Meadow's face.

The lines relaxed. "Okay. Thank you. Thank you so much."

"Oh, she did all the work," the doctor said with a smile. "She's got grit. That will mean a lot while she's getting back on her feet."

"Can I come and see her tomorrow?"

"Every day, whenever you like," the vet replied.

"All right. That makes it a little easier."

"You find whoever did this to her," the vet said suddenly. "He needs to be locked up!"

"I'll find him," Meadow said, and it was a promise.

Dal drove her back home. He was reluctant to leave. "I don't like having you here on your own," he said curtly. "You can come stay at the ranch. I've got five spare bedrooms."

She swallowed and flushed, sure he was going to go right up the ceiling and the truce would be over when she refused.

"I see," he said softly, smiling at her embarrassment. "That squeaky-clean reputation wouldn't allow it."

"We all have our handicaps," she began.

"It's not a handicap," he replied, his voice deep in the stillness of snow and darkness. He searched her eyes in the porch light. "My grandmother would have reacted exactly the same. She was a tiny little woman, sweet and kind and gentle." His face hardened. "My grandfather got drunk and knocked her around. Dad was afraid of him. I never was. As soon as I was big enough to hit back, I tackled him in the living room one day and told him to leave my grandmother alone. After that, he still drank, but he never touched my grandmother."

She touched the soft white fur that peeked out of the lapel of his sheepskin jacket. "Nobody in my family drank," she said. "But I started dealing with drunks when I was seventeen and volunteered at the St. Louis police department." She laughed. "Mama had a fit. She tried to talk the captain out of hiring me, but there was a shortage of peace officers. He reassured her that they'd watch out for me. And they did. They were a great bunch of people."

"Why law enforcement?" he wanted to know.

"I'm not sure. I think I was looking for a way out of marrying this man Mama had picked out for me," she confessed. "He was a lot older than I was, very rich, and she said he'd take care of me." She pursed her lips. "Two years after that, he was arrested for dealing drugs. I was in on the bust. Mama was appalled," she added on a chuckle.

"So much for her judgment," he agreed.

"She wanted me to marry and have a family." She shrugged. "I knew that wasn't going to happen," she added sadly.

He frowned. "Why not?"

She lowered her eyes to the top button of his jacket. Snow was falling beyond the porch. "I'm clumsy and old-fashioned. Not pretty, like a lot of women. I don't move with the times."

"But you're lovely," he said softly, scowling. "Didn't you know? It's what's inside you that matters. You're tender and loving and you never quit on the people you care about. Those are virtues."

"Being tender and loving with perps is not an option," she said, trying to lighten the conversation.

"I've made you feel small for years," he said sadly. "I didn't even know why. Picking on you became a defense mechanism."

She looked up, surprised. "Defense against what?" she asked blankly.

He cupped her soft face in his big, cool hands. "Against this, honey," he whispered as he bent to her mouth.

The endearment stunned her. The kiss was . . . amazing. It was soft and gentle, respectful. It was the way you'd kiss someone you cared deeply for. All her adult life, Meadow had been rushed or grabbed or overpowered by dates. Here was a man she'd known forever, a man she'd loved with all her heart. And he didn't rush or grab. He kissed her as if he . . . loved her!

He drew back after a minute, perplexed. "When we have more time, and it's not so late," he mused, "I really need to do something about that ego. Not to mention your skill set."

"What skill set?" she asked.

"Exactly."

Her eyebrows arched. "Who's on first, what's on second . . ."

"I don't give a damn, he's our shortstop!" he finished for her, chuckling. His hands fell away. "Call me when you want to go see Snow tomorrow. I'll go with you."

"Is Jarvis okay?" she asked suddenly. "He had blood on one paw."

"Yes, Gil thinks he scratched the perp. He got blood samples." He glowered. "He's got a case on you."

"Wh . . . what?" she stammered.

"Blind little woman," he mused, searching her shocked eyes. "Can't see what's right in front of her."

"Gil's my colleague," she said. "He isn't a potential suitor."

"Are you sure about that?"

"Yes, I'm sure," she said.

He pursed his lips. "Okay, then. I was wondering how much trouble I'd get in if I had to call him out," he remarked. "Dueling with deputies is bad business."

Her lips fell apart. "Duels?"

He touched her mouth with his. "You'll work it out. One more thing," he added, and he was solemn. "I never slept with Dana. In case the subject ever comes up. And I broke it off with her earlier today, in person."

She was stunned. She didn't understand what was going on.

"You might tell Jeff, if you think about it," he added darkly. "And tell him he owes me."

"For what?"

"He'll know."

"I don't understand." Her voice faltered.

He drew her up close. "You'll work it out," he chuckled as he bent his head. He kissed her hungrily. "Don't stay up too late," he whispered into her lips. "And keep the doors locked. A man who'll hit a dog will hit a woman," he added icily.

"Dal . . ."

"Oh, I like the way that sounds," he whispered, and kissed her harder.

She gave up trying to puzzle out his odd behavior and instead kissed him back with enthusiasm if not with skill.

He let her go slowly. He smiled, his dark eyes warm and full of secrets. "Try to get some sleep. Snow's going to be fine."

She drew in a long breath. She smiled back. "Okay."

He turned and started to the truck.

"Be careful," she called after him. "The roads are slick."

"I didn't notice," he drawled with amused sarcasm, and kept walking.

She watched him swing the truck around, dazed with unexpected pleasure. He stopped in the middle of the road and powered down the driver's side window. "Will you get inside?" he called.

"Bossy," she muttered.

"Count on it. I'm a lobo wolf. You'll never tame me. But you're welcome to try," he added in almost a purr.

She laughed and went back into the house. He didn't leave until she closed the door.

She went into work the next morning with a mission. She was going to find that thief.

She downloaded some software Jeff kept that substituted for a sketch artist. She hadn't seen the man's face, but she did a fairly accurate tracing of his long form, just slightly bent, and his dark, unruly hair. As she started adding things to the portrait, she remembered the bag he'd been carrying. In her whole life, she'd only seen one of those big canvas bags once. She couldn't remember where, though.

"What are you doing?" Jeff asked when he came back in from answering a call.

"Hi," she greeted him with a smile. "I'm trying to make an accurate sketch of the man I saw at Dal's house."

He looked over her shoulder. "Not bad, Deputy," he said.

"Thanks." She glanced at him. "Dal said to tell you that you owe him. He wouldn't say why."

His high cheekbones flushed a little. "I sort of took credit for something I didn't do," he confessed. "That pizza. I didn't really send it to you. Dal did."

Her heart jumped. "He did?"

He recognized that look on her face. He just chuckled. "No more daggers at ten paces?" he teased.

"I don't really know. He's changed, all of a sudden." She searched his eyes. "He broke it off with Dana yesterday."

"He did?" He had the same expression that she knew was on her face when he'd told her the truth about her pizza.

She laughed. "So maybe I'm not the only one who's getting a surprise."

"Why would you say that?"

She was looking past him. "You might turn around," she said in a loud whisper.

He did, to see Dana in a pretty blue coat standing just inside the front door.

"Hi," she called to Jeff. "It's almost lunchtime. I was wondering if you were free."

"I'm not, but I'm reasonable," he quipped.

"Oh, you," she teased.

"Let me get my coat and I'll be right with you," he said.

"I'll wait in the car," Dana said. She gave Meadow an odd look, but she softened it with a smile and a nod that said *no hard feelings*.

All sorts of strange things were happening, Meadow thought to herself. Nice, but strange.

She finished what she could recall of the man's appearance. Gil came back in a few minutes later.

"Snow's getting deep," he told her, laughing as he brushed the snow off the plastic cover of his Smokey the Bear hat.

"I noticed. Give this a look and tell me if you've ever seen anyone locally who looked like my sketch, would you?"

"Sure." He looked over her shoulder at the screen. "That overcoat looks sort of familiar, but I can't think why. The bag over his shoulder is unusual."

"I knew an artist once, in St. Louis, who carried her canvases in one. That's the last time I saw one. I'm not sure they even sell them anymore. It looked old. I remember thinking it had a stain about halfway down . . ."

"You didn't see his face?"

She shook her head. "He kept his back to me. He was running. He was fast," she added.

"Running in snow is not easy. I know," Gil remarked.

"He had long legs." She sat back in her chair. "We don't have that many people in Raven Springs, but it's still a large number. There are probably at least one or two artists who live here and have bags made of heavy canvas." She hesitated. "Is there an art supply store?"

"Not here," he said. "You'd have to go to Denver for one of those."

"Another dead end," she muttered.

"How's your dog?" he asked.

"Better, thanks," she replied. "Dal and I went to see her yesterday."

His eyebrows arched.

"He was really sorry about what he said to me," she told him. "He paid the vet's bill."

"Nice of him," he agreed. "I was pretty hot when I had to go out there. He should never have yelled at you without knowing what actually happened."

"That's exactly what he said," she replied. She drew in a breath. "I guess we're all guilty of jumping to conclusions from time to time." Her face tautened. "I want to get my hands on the man who hit Snow."

"I don't blame you. I would, too. We might make copies of that sketch," he added, "and hand them out to businesses. Someone might recognize the man."

"Good thinking!"

"Oh, I'm a genius," he returned. "It doesn't show because I'm so modest about my talents."

"Is that so?" She laughed.

He shrugged. "I guess I'd better go watch for wrecks. Good Lord, half the people in this town should never have been issued licenses. I told that to a man just this morning. He tried to run a red light, swung the car around, and fishtailed right into a parked car with a woman sitting in the passenger seat. No major injuries, but I charged him with reckless driving just the same."

"Good for you. Maybe he'll learn from his mistake."

"Miracles happen. Can I bring you back lunch?"

She dug in her purse. "A green salad with Thousand Island dressing from anyplace you go, and thanks." She handed him a ten dollar bill.

"You're on." He left her sitting at the computer.

They passed out copies of her sketch, but nobody seemed to recognize anything about the man in it.

On a whim, Meadow stopped by the Yesterday Place on her way home to give Mike Markson a copy to display.

He stared at the sketch, frowning. "Who do you think this is, again?" he asked.

"The man who stole an antique writing desk from Dal Blake," she explained. "And took a log to my dog. She's at the vet's with a head injury," she added coldly. "I really want this guy. I want him badly. A man who'll brutalize an animal will do the same thing to a person."

Mike seemed to go pale as he studied the sketch. "Well, yes, men . . . men like that would probably hit people, indeed." He lifted his eyes to hers. "Your dog, will it be all right?"

"No thanks to the thief," she replied. "Snow was unconscious when I found her. It was a very long night until she came out of it. We weren't sure that she would."

"Poor animal. I used to have a dog," he said sadly. "A female Lab. I . . . lost her two years ago," he added reluctantly.

"I'm sorry. I love animals."

"So do I," he replied. "It was such a shock. She'd been running around, laughing, the way they do, you know, always happy. I came home and Gary said she'd run into the road, right into a car. She died instantly. It was a head injury . . ."

"I guess I really got lucky with Snow," she said. "But I'm sorry for your loss. They're like people to us."

"They truly are." He stared again at the handout. "I'll post it and see if anyone recognizes who the person is," he told her. "If so, I'll call you."

"Thanks," she said, and smiled at him.

"Any luck on the organ and the lamp?"

She shook her head. "More dead ends, I'm afraid. Nothing new. But we're stubborn and persistent. One day, we'll track them down."

"I do hope so," he said.

"Thanks for your help."

"Any time."

She started out the door and almost collided with a tall, thin man with unruly hair. It was Gary, Mike's son. He had a cut on his cheek. She wondered idly if he'd done that shaving. Men were careless with the razor sometimes. Her father had been.

He looked at her uneasily. "Deputy," he said, with a nod.

"Mr. Markson." She nodded back. She thought he looked strange, but she didn't dwell on it. She was eager to get home and see Snow. Dal was going with her. She smiled to herself as she started up her SUV and drove away. So many changes in her life. She couldn't remember a time when she'd felt happier.

"Jeff confessed about the pizza," she told Dal when they were on the way to see Snow. "He said he was sorry."

He chuckled. "He's a good guy," he replied.

"So are you. It was a lovely pizza." She glanced at him. "How did you know I liked mushrooms and cheese?"

"You've forgotten, haven't you?" he teased. "I had supper with you and your father year before last. You ordered two pizzas. Yours only had mushroom and cheese, and your father said it was because you weren't carnivorous like he and I were."

The memory came back. Dal had been sarcastic about her disdain for sausage. He'd been that way about a lot of things she liked.

"I was a fourteen karat heel, wasn't I, honey?" he asked softly, glancing her way. "It took me years to understand why I was so rough on you."

"Why were you?" she asked.

"Oh, that's not a question you should ask when I'm driving."

Her eyebrows arched.

"How's your manhunt coming?"

She was diverted. "I made up a sketch of what I remembered the perp looked like," she said, "on our computer at work. I made copies and took it by several businesses for them to post. We might get lucky."

"Did you bring one with you?"

"It's at the house," she replied. "I had several copies left over."

"I'd like to take a look at one when we get back. I've lived here all my life," he reminded her. "I might recognize him, if he's local."

"I should have thought about that."

"You've had a lot on your mind."

"True."

He pulled up at the veterinary hospital and opened the door for her.

Snow was much better. She howled when she saw them, her blue eyes laughing.

They laughed, too.

"She's responding very well to treatment," Dr. Clay said, satisfied with the dog's progress. "I think she'll be fine."

"The seizures?"

She sighed. "Well, yes, that's going to be an ongoing problem, I'm afraid," she added. "She had one earlier. But we gave her phenobarbital and she responded nicely. There's a little hesitation with her gait as well, but I think that will go away in time. The seizures are something you'll have to deal with."

"I've seen epileptic seizures," Meadow replied. "My mother had them. I got very good at giving her injections."

"What sort of seizures?" Dr. Clay asked.

"Grand mal," Meadow replied.

The vet winced. "Those can be scary."

"They always were," Meadow agreed. "But we coped. I'll cope with Snow. I'm just so grateful that she lived. Thanks for all you did."

"Just my job, but you're welcome," Dr. Clay replied with a warm smile. "I'll leave you to visit with her while I wait for an emergency that's coming in. Cat got attacked by a stray dog," she sighed. "The owner was almost hysterical."

"I can identify with that," Meadow replied.

Dr. Clay went back out front. Dal and Meadow settled down next to Snow's cage and talked to her and petted her.

"You'll be coming home, soon, in case you wondered if I was going to desert you," Meadow told her pet.

Snow seemed to laugh. Her blue eyes were bright and attentive.

"I miss you at night," Meadow confessed. "The house gets so lonely."

Snow nuzzled her hand.

"Did you talk to your dog?" Meadow asked Dal.

"All the time, just the way you talk to Snow," he replied. "She was a lot of company. So is Jarvis, but he's more arrogant and self-sufficient than a dog. He cuddles, but only on his terms."

She smiled. "We never had cats. Mama didn't like them. I love Jarvis," she added. "He's so sweet."

He held out a hand with several scratches visible. "I was late getting his supper down in the kitchen," he mused. "He took issue with me."

She laughed. "He's never scratched me."

"He loves you," he replied.

"Snow loves you," she said simply, watching the dog nuzzle Dal's big hand.

"They get along amazingly well, considering that they're supposed to be natural enemies," he commented.

"Animals are individuals, just like people," she said. "Some get along, some don't."

He was studying her, his dark eyes warm and soft. "And some call truces after years of open warfare," he teased.

She looked up at him and smiled. "Yes. Some do."

Chapter Eleven

Dal drove Meadow back to her house and went inside with her to look at the handout she'd made of the thief.

She gave one to Dal. He studied it with a frown.

"Recognize anything about him?" she asked.

"I'm not sure," he said. "I think I've seen that coat somewhere."

"Was there ever an art supply store in town?" she asked suddenly.

"Sure, years ago," he told her. "Markson bought it out and turned it into an antique store."

"He might have seen a canvas bag like that one in the sketch," she said excitedly. "I'll drive back over there tomorrow and ask him. Thanks!"

"Oh, I'd do anything to help," he said. "I'd like to have that desk back before it ends up in an auction back east. It has a history. But it's mostly the sentiment that matters to me. My grandmother loved it."

She smiled at him. "She must have been a sweet woman."

"She was. Like you." He grimaced. "I'll never forgive myself for what I said to you about that desk. It wasn't worth Snow's life."

"You didn't know she was hurt," she said.

"I didn't listen," he replied. "I tend to fly off the handle at the best of times. I'm truly sorry about what happened."

"It's okay," she said. "I just hope we can find it. We've got flyers out everywhere, even on the Internet."

"Even if it goes the way of the Victorian lamp and the pipe organ that were stolen, I'm just glad Snow's going to be all right."

She smiled. "Me too."

"I wonder," he started, "if we might . . ."

Before he could finish the sentence, a noise outside caught their attention.

A truck roared up into Meadow's driveway and slid to a halt. Dal and Meadow went out to meet the driver.

"We can't find Todd," one of Dal's cowboys called. "He went down to the Davis cabin to check on the old man. He left there in his truck, but we found it beside the road a mile from the ranch. There were no tracks off the road, anywhere!"

"I'll be right there," Dal said. He turned to Meadow. "He has a wife and a five-year-old son. I have to go."

"If I could help, I would."

"Nothing you could do, sweetheart," he said softly, and bent to kiss her warmly. "Go back inside."

"Call me when they find him. Please?"

He nodded. He strode to his truck and took off, following the other cowboy out into the road.

Todd was one of Dal's favorite hands. He was thrifty, meticulous, and one of the best horse wranglers Dal had ever worked with. He was never late for work, never absent a day. To have him missing was disturbing, especially since there were no tracks.

Dal pulled in behind Larry, his top hand, and cut off

the engine. He grimaced at the complication that had just presented itself. Charity Landers and her little boy, Pete, were sitting on Dal's porch. Todd's family.

They came running when they saw Dal.

"We have to find him," Charity said in a rush. "The snow's so deep . . ." Her voice broke.

"Where's my daddy?" Pete asked Dal, and pale blue eyes looked up at him with absolute trust. "You'll find him, won't you, Mr. Blake?"

The child fascinated him. He'd seen the little boy around, gone to the christening. But this was something new. The child loved his father, and it showed. Dal had never thought about a child of his own before.

"We'll find him, Pete," he promised, and hoped he could keep the promise.

Just as he finished speaking, a car came up the road and stopped at the house. Todd climbed out, thanked the driver, and walked to the porch, where he was smothered with kisses by his wife and son.

"We thought you were dead or something!" Charity wailed.

"Daddy, we was scared!" Pete cried into his dad's throat as he was held close. "I love you so much, Daddy!"

"I love you, too, son." He kissed Charity. "Now, now, I'm fine. The damned truck quit. I had to hitch a ride into town to get a wrecker, then the trucks were both out, so I had to hitch a ride back home . . ." He paused. "Sorry, Dal, I left the truck parked on the highway, but they said they'd send the first wrecker they had free—lots of people stuck in the snow, he said. I'll have to go back and wait for it."

"Larry can go," he said, and nodded to the other man, who threw up a hand and ran for his truck. "You take your family and go home." He chuckled. "You've had enough adventures for one day."

"Gosh, thanks, boss," Todd said, grinning from ear to ear.

"You're welcome."

Pete wriggled to get down. He walked over to Dal and held out his little arms.

Dal picked him up, amazed at the perfection of that small face up close.

"Thanks, Mr. Blake," he said, and hugged the big man.

Dal hugged him back. It was the most amazing feeling, that tiny body so trusting in his arms. The child was a reminder of what he'd been running away from most of his adult life. He found that he liked the idea of a son.

He laughed and put the boy back into his father's arms. "Nice kid," he told Todd.

"We think so. Night, boss."

"Thanks, Mr. Blake," Charity added.

"You're welcome." He waved them off.

The child was on his mind when he drove back down to Meadow's house.

She came out onto the porch. "Did you find him? Is he all right?"

"He's fine," he said, following her into the house. "The truck quit and he had to hitch a ride into town to get a wrecker. Forgot his cell phone." He laughed. "I've done that a time or two myself."

"And here I thought you were perfect," she teased.

He lifted both eyebrows. "Well, in some ways I am," he murmured with a long look at her figure that spoke volumes.

She flushed.

"Coffee?" he asked hopefully, smiling. "It's cold out there."

"I can make a pot," she said. "No cake, but I have cheese and crackers."

"Even better," he replied.

* * *

They sat eating cheese and crackers in a companionable silence.

"Got your pregnant heifers up?" he asked.

She nodded. "Dad's foreman is really good at his job. All I needed to do was stand aside and let him do it." She shook her head. "I almost made a mess of things. I would have asked you for help, but . . ."

"But I was being tiresome," he answered for her. He smiled. "I'm reforming as we speak," he promised. He nibbled a cracker. "Todd's little boy came running when his dad showed up. He was bawling." He shifted in the chair. "I never thought about kids," he added. "In fact, I've spent most of my adult life running away from ties."

She didn't speak. She just waited.

He noticed that, and smiled. "I enjoyed playing the field. But after a while, they all look alike, sound alike." He shrugged. "Even Dana. She was sweet and I was fond of her, but I never pictured her wearing an apron, surrounded by little kids."

"I don't think she likes kids, from what Jeff's said about her," she replied.

"He's the same way. They're the sort who'd travel, if they had money. They think alike."

She nodded.

He studied her. "You were seventeen when you fell into the coal bin," he recalled. "Didn't you ever wonder why I reacted so badly to the way you were dressed that night?"

She blinked. "Well, once in a while," she confessed.

He stared at her evenly. "You were lovely, even at that age. I wanted you. But I knew your father would kill me if I tried anything. You were years too young anyway." He sighed. "I backed away and kept backing away, especially after he told me how competitive you were around men." He laughed hollowly at her expression. "It was a lie, and I didn't realize it. He was trying to protect you from me."

"I guess so," she said. "You had quite a reputation."

"I still do," he said, and he was somber. "It will take some time to redeem it in the eyes of local people. But I'm not running anymore, Meadow," he added quietly. "I've done a lot of thinking about what I want to do with the rest of my life. I want a family."

Her eyebrows were arching. She felt her forehead. "I don't think I have a fever. How can I be hallucinating?"

"Stop that," he said. "I'm serious."

"Me too. What have you done with Dal Blake?"

He chuckled. "I guess I don't sound like myself." He cocked his head. "Suppose you and I start going out together? We can even go to church next Sunday."

She caught her breath. "The minister will pass out in the pulpit."

"Probably, but if he does, more people will show up the next Sunday out of curiosity." He chuckled.

"Are you really serious?"

He pushed away from the table, got up, picked her up in his arms, and dropped into a cushy armchair in the living room.

"Let me show you how serious I am," he murmured as he bent to her mouth.

With a little advance warning, she might have saved herself. But he was so familiar to her, so dear to her, that she didn't have a single defense. He drew her up, wrapping her against him, while he made a meal of her soft, parted lips.

She linked her arms around him and gave in to the sweetest temptation she'd ever known. She didn't protest, even when she felt his lean hands go under her blouse, against soft, warm flesh.

"No maidenly protests?" he murmured against her mouth.

"Depends," she managed to say.

"Depends on what?"

"On whether you want children right now."

He lifted his head. "What?"

"Well, I don't know beans about precautions, despite all those lectures I survived in high school and college," she said.

He chuckled. "Point taken." He bent again. "So we'll just maul each other a little bit and I'll go home and have a cold shower."

She pressed close, loving the warm strength of him against her, the slow tracing of his fingers against her breasts inside their lacy coverings. He was potent. She hadn't realized just how experienced he was until she was almost ready to plead with him to undress her.

Unexpectedly, she had an ally. A big, bushy red tail interposed itself between Dal's mouth and her nose.

He tried to get past it, but it kept slapping Meadow's nose.

She drew back a breath. "Dal? There's a furry cushion on my lap."

"I noticed." He kissed her again.

"Dal, it's not moving."

He chuckled. "I noticed." He sat back and drew in a breath. "Jarvis, you pest, how did you get in?"

"Dog door," she said, brushing her mouth over his nose.

"It was a rhetorical question," he murmured.

"That was a rhetorical answer."

"Jarvis!" he groaned as the big red cat banged him in the chin with his head, purring all the while.

She petted the big cat. "He's just jealous."

"Of whom? You or me?"

"That's a very good rhetorical question . . ."

She sat up, her eyes wide and blank.

"What is it?" he asked.

"Jarvis. Blood on his claw. Scratch on Mike Markson's

son's cheek. Antique store. Former art supply store. Canvas bag . . ."

"My God!" Dal exclaimed as she shot off his lap. "It was right under our noses the whole time!"

She was already diving for her phone and dialing. Jeff answered on the first ring.

"Slow down, slow down." Jeff laughed. "Start over."

She did, listing the facts that had suddenly jelled in her mind. "It's got to be him!"

"I never even connected the bag," he replied. "Okay, I agree that we've got probable cause, but we can't do a thing without a search warrant. And I don't want to go waltzing into Markson's store unless I'm sure what we're looking for."

"I'll write up everything I know," she said. "Meanwhile, is there any way we can get back the DNA results on that blood Gil sent off?"

"I'll make a few phone calls. I do know someone at the state crime lab."

"All right!"

"Meanwhile, I'll get Gil back in here and have him put together all the facts he's gleaned about the antiques that were stolen earlier."

"Gary hasn't had time to travel anywhere. Odds are that the desk is still in his possession," she said. "Probably right there in the store."

"I wouldn't doubt it. But we won't say anything. I don't want to spook him."

"His poor father," Meadow said sadly.

"He'll get over it. We can't let the boy get away with this."

"I know. It's just sad," Meadow said.

Dal pulled her close against his side. She said she'd meet Jeff at the office first thing in the morning and hung up.

"I solved a crime," she said, all eyes.

He chuckled. "Indeed you did." He bent and kissed her nose. "I'm proud of you. It's just . . ." He sighed.

"Just what?"

He cocked his head. "Despite that cool sheriff in the movie *Fargo* who was solving crimes with a belly the size of a basketball, I really wish you could consider a less dangerous line of work. While you're pregnant, at least."

Her eyebrows arched. "I'm not pregnant."

He pursed his lips and his dark eyes twinkled. "Yet."

Her lips parted. She didn't know quite what to say.

"I'll go through my grandmother's rings tonight when I get home," he said softly. "She had four different engagement rings because she couldn't decide on just one. She had all the money in the family. So what do you like best, emeralds, rubies, sapphires or diamonds?"

"Rubies," she said at once.

"I'll bring the ring down to your office in the morning and we'll have a late breakfast, after you're through solving crime. Okay?"

Her heart soared. "Okay!"

He lifted her up against him and kissed her hungrily. "I'm not leaving because I want to," he whispered. "But it is a small community, and I don't want people casting doubts on that spotless reputation your father was so proud of."

"Thanks," she whispered back.

He grinned as he let her go. "See you in the morning."

"Good night."

"When can we bring Snow home?" he asked.

"Tomorrow." She glanced toward the door, where Jarvis was sitting. "Is he staying?"

"I don't know. Are you staying?" he asked the cat.

Jarvis looked up at him, meowed, and went trotting back to Meadow. She just laughed.

* * *

The next morning, armed with a search warrant, Meadow, Gil, Jeff, and an assistant district attorney presented themselves at Mike Markson's store as soon as he unlocked it.

He ground his teeth when they handed him the warrant.

"I'm sorry, Mike," Jeff said quietly. "Is Gary here?"

He drew in a long breath. "He was up late last night making phone calls out of state," the old man said sadly. "He's sound asleep." He grimaced. "He did it, didn't he? I suspected, but I didn't really want to know." He swallowed. "The writing desk is in his room. I was going to call you. I couldn't let him get away with stealing something so precious."

"Did you know about the other thefts?"

Mike shook his head. "He's my son. I love him, even if he's done bad things. But I won't harbor a thief in the business I've spent my life building up."

Jeff put a hand on the old man's shoulder. "Has he ever been in trouble with the law?"

Mike shook his head. "Not even a parking ticket."

Jeff smiled. "Get him a good lawyer. He can plead first offender status. If he keeps his nose clean, his record will be wiped."

"Really?" Mike's face brightened. "Really?"

The assistant district attorney turned to him. "Yes. Really. But he'll have to be put on probation, and it won't be an easy ride."

"I'll make sure he does what he's supposed to," Mike said firmly. "I messed up once with him. Never again."

Jeff and Meadow smiled.

"Let's go talk to him," Jeff said.

Gary wasn't really surprised to see his visitors. He gave up without a struggle. He even confessed to the thefts and offered to give the names of his buyers. He was taken to detention, booked, and assigned to a cell pending arraignment.

"Didn't that work out unusually well?" Gil asked with a chuckle when they were back in the office.

"I know something else that's going to work out unusually well," Meadow mused as she watched Dal come in the door.

"Hi," Jeff said.

"Hi. I came to steal your deputy for a late breakfast."

"But we hardly know each other," Gil protested. "And you haven't even brought me flowers!"

"Shut up," Dal muttered. "I'm not taking you anywhere. Your socks don't match."

Gil looked down and grimaced. "Not my fault. I didn't have the lights on when I got dressed."

"He's taking me out to breakfast," Meadow pointed out.

"Yes, and he's proposing," Dal added, holding out an open jeweler's box. "You said rubies, I believe?"

Meadow caught her breath. She'd envisioned a small stone in a small ring. This was a wedding band studded with rubies and a solitaire that looked to be about two carats.

"Will you?" Dal asked with a warm smile.

"Will I?" she stammered.

"Well, if you want the works . . ." He led her to a chair, seated her, went down on one knee, removed his wide-brimmed hat, and said, "Miss Dawson, will you do me the honor of becoming my wife?"

She threw her arms around him. "Yes. Yes! Yes!"

"I think that means she will," Gil translated.

Jeff and Gil laughed. Meadow fought tears. She'd loved the silly man half her life, and here he was, offering her the one thing in the world she wanted most. She wondered if she could die of happiness. But she didn't want to find out!

* * *

So they were married, at Christmas. Snow came home, with some lingering neurological issues that eventually resolved themselves. She and Jarvis the cat curled up together to sleep and never had a single argument that drew blood.

Gary did get first offender status. The items he'd stolen were recovered, including Dal's writing desk, and returned to their rightful owners. Gary got his act together, went back to school, and became an asset to the community, to the delight of his father.

Dal and Meadow found they had more in common than they'd ever dreamed. Tangled together in Dal's big king-sized bed, Meadow fought to catch her breath after a first time that exceeded her wildest dreams.

"Gosh!" was all she could manage.

He chuckled. "Now you see why I had to practice so much in my younger days," he teased, looming over her. "I was getting ready for you."

"Awww," she drawled. "That's so sweet."

He moved down against her, his mouth moving lovingly against hers. "And that's what I love most about you, Mrs. Blake," he whispered.

"What?"

"That you never throw my past up to me," he said solemnly. He lifted his head. "I'll make you a solemn promise, too, Meadow," he added. "I'll never cheat on you. Not if we're married for fifty years."

She smiled and kissed him. "Okay."

"But you're going to see a doctor and find out why you keep falling," he said sternly.

She curled back into his arms and slid one long leg around his. "It's nice that you care about me," she whispered.

"It's nice that you care about me, too," he said, and kissed her again. He rolled her onto her back, slid between her legs with a husky chuckle, and proceeded to coach her in the art of mutual pleasure. It took a long time. And eventually, it produced a sweet result: their first son.

The doctors discovered a minor lesion in Meadow's brain that accounted for her clumsiness. There actually was a physical reason for it, and a treatment. Knowing that it wasn't a brain tumor or something likely to kill her made it bearable. It stemmed from the concussion she'd had in her teens, an accident that she'd never realized would have such far-reaching repercussions.

Dal worried about her job in law enforcement. He never asked her to quit, but she knew him very well. Her clumsiness could lead, so easily, to tragedy under the wrong circumstances. So she had a long talk with the sheriff and the district attorney. And soon afterward, she had a new job.

By the time their son, Teddy, was a toddler, Meadow was comfortably working as an assistant district attorney, having put away her badge and gun for a future less dangerous and more satisfying than the law enforcement career she gave up. The following year, she gave birth to a second son, whom they named Seth. Their ranches combined to form one huge conglomerate, with Dal at the helm. So she and Dal lived happily ever after on a ranch in Colorado, with their sons, and Snow and Jarvis—and a few thousand head of cattle. And celebrated many wedding anniversaries at Christmas. Meadow finally had her snow man . . .

Kassie's Cowboy

LINDSAY MCKENNA

Dear Reader,

I am such a sap for Christmas stories! They are always uplifting, you have to have a box of tissues nearby and there's always a happily ever after. That's the kind of Christmas gift that keeps on giving.

I'm thrilled to be with my sister Kensington authors to share our wonderful heart-felt stories with all of you.

"Kassie's Cowboy" features Kassie Murphy, who runs Kassie's Café in Wind River, Wyoming. She was abandoned at birth and adopted by Jade and Marshall Murphy. There has always been a hole in Kassie's heart because she's always seen herself as "thrown away."

During high school, Kassie experienced "puppy love." She fell in love with Travis Grant. He began to heal that hole in her heart because for the first time in her life she felt wanted, desired and she was able to bond with Travis because he loved her deeply. But at eighteen, he had to go into the Marine Corps (his father, Red, had been in the Marines). He was desperately torn between staying with Kassie and following in his father's footsteps. In the end, he left. And it broke Kassie's heart in a new and painful way.

This is a story of redemption. Of two people whose hearts had been broken in different ways, and each trying to find their way forward. Love, as we all know, has its own ways with us. After a four-year absence, Travis comes home, broken by his experiences in war, and he becomes a loner, unable to fit into normal society any more.

And on a wintery morning, with a blizzard approaching, Fate takes over. And neither Kassie nor Travis will be the same again.

Drop by my website! www.lindsaymckenna.com. There is a special Kassie and Travis contest going on!!! Wonderful gifts for the winner!

Merry Christmas!
Lindsay McKenna

To Tricia S.
who has always been at my side as a friend
Thank you for all that you do for me!

Chapter One

A blizzard was coming. A bad one. A blue norther and a five-dayer, as Wyoming ranchers referred to the deadly weather front.

Travis Grant fed his two horses, made sure all the windows were shut and the area as warm as it could be. His two geldings had thick winter coats and would weather this blizzard, no problem, in his two-story, one-hundred-year-old barn. They were well fed and completely protected from the harsh, brutal elements to come. He'd also placed a heavy canvas well-padded horse blanket on each of them every night. Wyoming winters got way below zero.

It was barely dawn, a lighter gray ribbon along the clogged, cloudy western horizon. Pulling his sheepskin coat collar up a little tighter around his exposed neck, Travis heard the howling of the wind slamming against the western barn wall like invisible fists pummeling the aged wooden surface. Gale-force winds would precede this blue norther, and more than likely three to six feet of snow would be dumped on the Wind River Valley as it passed through like a slow-moving freight train.

Travis lived near the center of the Wind River Valley, about six miles away from where Maud and Steve Whitcomb had their hundred-thousand-acre Wind River Ranch where he worked four months out of the year as a wrangler.

His cowboy boots echoed and thunked hollowly along the old oak planking. He slid the door shut to the horse barn and went into his furniture-making studio, which was right next to it. In there, since returning home from the Marine Corps and too many deployments to Afghanistan, he'd found a way to make money and deal with his PTSD instead of committing suicide, like so many of his vet friends already had.

Turning on the overhead lights, his gaze moved through the thousand-foot rectangular room. It held his projects, all handmade furniture for clients who had ordered specific pieces from him.

Walking across the oak floor that shined dully beneath the fluorescent lights, he trailed his fingers across a reddish-colored mahogany top of a four-drawer dresser that was closest to where he stood. It was nearly finished, the deep crimson gleam of the wood beautiful beneath his hand and the patient waxing he'd done on it all day yesterday. It was a beautiful hardwood from South and Central America.

In creating furniture he'd found solace, maybe even a tiny corner of peace, by working alone in here from dawn to dusk, his anxiety tamped down, which was a godsend. Hard physical work like wrangling or creating furniture kept his PTSD anxiety volume turned down to a dull roar. He could use his woodworking tools, his hands, his chisels and sanding paper, to create beauty even though anxiety lived inside him like an angry, stalking monster 24/7/365.

He meandered through the clean room, a bit of satisfaction flowing through him. The scent of the different types of wood, the organic beeswax polish he used, made him breathe a little deeper. It was like a tack room in a barn, in one sense; the fragrance of leather saddles, bridles, martingales, the neatsfoot oil and saddle soap applied to all of them from time to time always calmed him, too.

In one corner he had a black potbellied stove that radiated enough heat to keep the studio toasty warm. Having just made the fire for the coming day's work, Travis walked over, opened the latch, and placed a couple more pieces of wood he'd chopped a week ago into it. Shutting it, he went to a small kitchenette where he made his coffee. Recently, he'd installed a small fridge with comfort foods such as cheese, milk, fruits, and veggies he liked to nosh on. The steel double sink was a place to wash his hands and the few dishes he dirtied daily.

For the next five to seven days, as this blizzard roared through northwestern Wyoming, Route 89, a north-south two-lane highway, would be closed. Wyoming simply did not have enough snowplows to quickly clear the one-hundred-mile stretch of Wind River Valley. It would take days to open it back up after the snow rapidly accumulated, so truck and civilian traffic could flow freely back and forth once more.

The studio was warming up. He checked the progress on each of his six projects. Thanks to Steve Whitcomb, owner of the Wind River Ranch, his career as a furniture maker had suddenly and unexpectedly taken off. Steve was a world-class architect, and he'd invited *Architecture* magazine to send out a reporter to do a story on him and his master carpentry craftsmanship last year. He'd had three pieces of furniture under way at that time, trying to make a living between being a wrangler on their ranch during the summer months and creating beautiful furniture the other eight months of winter. That one article catapulted him from being a nobody to a somebody in the world of high-class handmade furniture.

He was forever indebted to Steve for his support. He and his rancher wife, Maud, had already ordered and bought two pieces from him. The money was more than good and he'd been able to buy this small farm that sat along Route 89. It only had five acres, a fifteen-hundred-square-foot single-story turn-of-the-century cabin on it, a two-story barn, corrals, and a huge garden area. For him, it meant safety, solace, and finding the peace that eluded him since getting PTSD.

Seeing the flash of headlights through his double-paned window, he scowled. Who the hell was out at this time of morning and driving in the imminent deadly weather conditions? The beams had turned in a full circle on Route 89. That meant someone had hit black ice and was spinning out of control.

Damn.

He pulled his black Stetson down a little tighter on his head, hauled on his thick elk skin gloves to protect his hands from the plummeting temperature, and quickly headed out of the barn. The wind was hard, battering against his body as he ran to the garage. He hit the door opener and waited impatiently to get to his huge Dodge Ram three-quarter-ton pickup inside. His dirt road was muddy and iced, as well. He backed the truck out, a sense of urgency filling him.

Probably some stupid tourist or a person who didn't really understand Wyoming blizzard weather, he thought as he drove slowly through the ice-covered mud ruts. They'd already gotten two feet of snow a week ago, and the plows had just finished pushing it off the sides of the highway into high white banks. There was no way he could speed down his quarter-mile driveway or he'd spin out, too. Mouth tightening, Travis saw that the car, a bright red one, had spun out and was now tipped on its side in the huge ditch next to the entrance gate of his property.

Travis parked behind the gate and climbed out, seeing steam rising from beneath the bent hood. He couldn't see who was in the vehicle because all the air bags had deployed, and there was no movement. That bothered Travis. The windshield wipers on the car were still, indicating the car's engine was off. All he could see as he slipped and slid down the short slope of mud and snow were the layers of deployed air bags. His mind automatically began to tick off potential medical issues. As a trained recon Marine, Travis was more than knowledgeable about medical emergency situations, what to do and how to handle them.

The wind, sharp and cold, tore at him, his ears unprotected, tingly and burning as they began to freeze in the dropping temperature. Was the person in this car injured?

As he reached the car door, he could only see the outline of a person beneath the limp air bags. Eyes narrowing, he knocked on the window, but there was no movement. He called out. No answer. The driver could be unconscious. *Double damn.*

Travis didn't need this complication with a blue norther blizzard bearing down on the area shortly. There was no way an ambulance would try to make it out here from the small hospital in Wind River, twenty miles away. The first responders knew better than to drive after the road had been shut down by the sheriff's department, according to his weather radio, an hour ago. This car and driver were probably the last to make it onto Route 89 before they closed the gates. No Wyoming person would ever go out in this kind of killing weather.

He yanked open the door. It grudgingly gave way.

"Hey," Travis called, pushing the air bag out of the way. "Are you all right?"

His heart crashed in his chest.

There, lying unconscious, slumped in her seat belt, was Kassie Murphy!

His mind blanked out briefly as he froze, as so many images from their past—talks, kissing her, then leaving her—slammed through him. Travis shook himself out of his state, reaching in after yanking off a glove, two fingers pressed gently against the side of her slender neck, searching for a pulse. Her black hair, thick and luxurious, had swirled around her shoulders, covering part of her face. Worse, as he felt for a pulse against her carotid artery, he saw just how pale she'd become. And then, as he swiftly perused her for other injury, he saw a thin trail of blood leaking out from beneath her hairline along her left temple.

Kass! No! No, this can't be happening!

Travis felt as if his whole, carefully structured world had just shattered. The woman he loved was unconscious. Injured.

And he'd left her after returning to civilian life a year ago, telling her they'd never make it in a relationship because of the severity of his PTSD. He'd released her, wanting her to have a chance at real love with a normal man, not someone as wounded as he was. Kass had cried the day they'd had that gut-wrenching conversation. Her tears felt like acid eating away what was left of his heart. He loved her enough to release her. There was no way he was going to accidentally injure her again by living with her. It just wouldn't work.

His heart leapt in his chest. A pulse! There! It was strong and steady. That was a good sign.

Swallowing hard, tears jamming into his eyes, Travis fought them back. He heard her moan, her parted lips closing for a moment as she began to become conscious.

"Kass? It's Travis. Stay still, you've been in a car accident. I'm going to unsnap your seat belt and get you out of here. Just hold on . . ."

In no time, because she was a lightweight compared to his six-foot, nearly two-hundred-pound frame, she was in his arms. Her head lolled against his shoulder, brow tucked beneath his jaw, completely limp in his arms.

She was fading in and out of consciousness. Travis moved swiftly through the mud and ice, climbing and awkwardly scrambling up the ditch wall. Once on top, he made it over to his Ram truck. Holding her with one arm around her torso, balancing her against his thigh and body, he got the passenger-side door open.

"Kass? Can you hear me?" he rasped, quickly sitting her up in the cab, careful not to bang her head on anything. Hands trembling, he belted her in.

No answer. She was out cold again. There was blood dribbling down her cheek now from that cut on the side of her head.

Closing the door, Travis hurried around to the driver's side, hopped in, and got the truck turned around. Looking out on the highway, he could see the asphalt here and there gleaming with huge patches of nearly invisible black ice across it. For a moment, he'd thought about trying to drive to the hospital in Wind River, but then better judgment descended over him. He'd have to take care of Kass here, at his home. He had medical knowledge, although he wasn't a surgeon. But he would know shortly just how badly Kass was injured. Then, he could make a professional determination.

Heart pounding, he drove slowly, trying not to jostle or jerk Kass around in the seat belt. She hung like a limp rag doll in the harness. He'd settled her head against the seat, used an extra blanket as a way to keep it from moving around too much, possibly injuring her spinal column as a result. No, he had to take it slow and easy getting back to his cabin, glancing at her every now and then.

Kass seemed to start coming to for a moment and then plunged back into unconsciousness. She was so damned pale! His mind spun, wondering why she was out in weather conditions like this in the first place. Kass knew better. She'd been born and lived in Wyoming all her life.

Travis swallowed hard, several times, raw, haunting emotions washing through him like an unwelcome tsunami. What were the odds, the chances, of Kass being out in this kind of storm? What had spurred her to try and beat a blue norther that was barreling down on them, to try and get home? She wasn't a flaky, brainless woman. Just the opposite. They'd not seen each other for almost a year. And yet, here she was, unexpectedly dropped back in his life again. He tried to separate his anxiety from the PTSD and the worry over her condition. Terror that she could be badly hurt rolled through him. He felt a desperation coupled with his love of her that had never died. It had never gone away. Ever.

How many times had he tried to push her from his mind? His thoughts? Travis had lost count. It had been so damned hard to do it, too. The last three months, Kass was in his mind and heart even more strongly and he didn't know why. Up would pop one of their many spirited conversations, her laughter, that dancing, happy look in her eyes when she was with him. Remembering when she kissed him, letting him know she desired him as much as he desired her, that tore him up the most. He came to the conclusion he was missing her terribly and that was why his life was shared daily with memories of what they'd had before he released her.

So many mistakes. So much water under the miserable bridge that he called his life. He'd left Kass crying at age eighteen, getting on a bus for Marine Corps boot camp in San Diego, California. Because she had loved him with a teen's love, he knew he'd broken her heart.

They'd never gone to bed during their high school years. There was just something in Travis, that old-fashioned

Western ethos that one did not go to bed with the woman he loved until they were married. That age-old belief had prevented it from occurring. It was just a part of who he had been, at least at that young age of immaturity, innocence, and ignorance. That Travis was gone forever, thanks to many deployments and too much combat. He was a changed man, and he'd never be who he was before.

And when Kass had heard he'd come home after his enlistment was up in the Marine Corps, she had driven out to see him at Maud and Steve's ranch. Travis hadn't been expecting her to show up, to welcome him home with that sunbeam smile of hers. He'd been gruff with her, stoic, and short.

Once more, he'd hurt her with his rudeness. He couldn't help himself because his PTSD was so damned virulent and it controlled him. He was trying to adjust to civilian life, grateful that Maud and Steve had given him a part-time wrangler's job so he could make enough money to survive. But there was no way he could handle a relationship with any woman, much less Kass, who he'd never stopped loving. And once again, he'd sent her away.

Coming to a halt at the front of his log cabin, he parked and shut off the truck engine. After giving Kass one more glance, reassured she was still breathing and still unconscious, he hurried to the door of his cabin and flung it open. Hurriedly, he went back to the passenger side of the truck. Opening the door, he released the seat belt around Kass and gently eased her into his arms and against him. She was boneless.

The first hard, almost icy snowflakes from the blue norther struck at his exposed face. It felt like sharp little knives hitting his flesh as he carried her from the truck. Travis knew these blizzards as well as anyone else who lived in frigid Wyoming. First, the hard, icy crystals, then later, a deluge of heavy, wet flakes that would swiftly coat the area in many feet of snow.

The fury of this storm ate at him because he might have to try, despite the danger, to drive Kass to the hospital in Wind River.

Shutting the truck door with the heel of his boot, Travis took her directly to his bedroom. Laying her gently on the bed, he formed the pillow beneath her neck to ensure her airway was kept open. As carefully as he could, he laid her out on the bed. Only then did he cross the living room and kitchen to shut the door and lock it.

Walking quietly into the bedroom, he saw her thick, black lashes flutter. His heart bounded. Travis stood next to the bed, watching a pale pink flush begin to stain her cheeks. Kass was becoming conscious once again. But how conscious? He wanted to go to the bathroom and get a wet cloth and examine her head wound. That would have to wait. It was more important someone be with her if she awoke.

Very slowly, her lashes lifted, revealing cloudy willow green eyes. She stared up at him, the silence deepening.

"Kass? It's Travis. You had a car accident." He knew to speak in short, slow sentences because that's all her rattled brain could absorb in its present state. Instantly, he saw her soft, winged eyebrows move and confusion enter her eyes as she tried to absorb what he'd just said.

Travis leaned over her, pushing her black, slightly curled hair away from her left ear, revealing the cut she'd sustained. "Kass, you've been injured in a car accident. Can you hear me?"

"Uh . . . where am I?"

Hearing the increased bewilderment in her voice, he kept his hand on her shoulder, remaining where he was so she could look him fully in the eyes. He'd seen too much traumatic brain injury in other Marines in Afghanistan and recognized her state. "You're safe. You're going to be okay. Do you recognize me, Kass?" He squeezed her shoulder just a little, trying to get her to focus on him and on his question. She tried lifting her hand, not succeeding. Her slender hand fell against the white goose down comforter beneath her.

Her brain had been scrambled but good and Travis sat down, gently capturing her hand lying across her belly. She wore a purple nylon hip-length down jacket. Beneath she wore a pink cowl-neck angora sweater. The black wool trousers only accentuated her long legs. Squeezing her fingers, he waited. Her pupils were large and black, thin green crescents surrounding them.

He fought the urge to go get his small flashlight and pass the light across her eyes, hoping that both pupils would dilate in reaction. If they did, that was a good sign that she wasn't badly injured. If one or both pupils didn't dilate? That meant a trip to the hospital regardless of the storm danger because it meant Kass had sustained a serious brain injury. He didn't want to go there, so he remained still, watching her.

But first, Travis had to try and get Kass to recognize him, to help her understand she was in his cabin, not wanting to call it her home, because it really wasn't. Travis pushed the errant thought aside.

Kass was staring up at him now and he could see her trying to remember him. Puzzlement entered her expression. Travis felt her fingers tighten slightly around his for a moment. That was a good sign. At least there was trust between them.

He removed his Stetson, setting it on the bedstand. Pushing his fingers through his dark brown hair, he tried to lighten his voice. "Kass? Do you recognize me now? Travis Grant." The struggle in her eyes tore at him, and he held his breath. She *had* to know him! Fear wound through him.

Because of his own medical training Travis knew if she didn't, it meant either temporary amnesia, or worse, a brain injury. His fingers closed tenderly around hers. "Kass, you know me. We went to high school together. We were the best of friends . . ." And he choked back the rest—*and we were in love, with so many dreams . . . but all of them are dead now because I killed them.*

Chapter Two

Kass blinked slowly, assimilating the man's low, gruff voice. She knew him, but her brain felt like it was in pieces, not whole or functioning properly. Her brows moved downward and she closed her eyes for a moment. His face flashed before hers from another time. It was Travis! Instantly, her lashes lifted.

"Uh . . . where am I?" she managed, struggling to speak. It was a fight to put only a few words together. Instantly, she saw the stress in his expression dissolve. His pale blue eyes, which had always reminded her of a raptor on a hunt, filled with what she thought was happiness.

"You're safe. You're going to be all right. Do you recognize me?"

Kass felt his large hand covering her gloved one that lay across her belly. A warmth sheeted through her because now so much was downloading about Travis and herself from the past. She heard him call her name again, but the words he spoke jumbled briefly. All she could do was weakly squeeze his hand in return.

Seeing the patience in his eyes, feeling his hand around hers was like being in one of the torrid dreams she had about Travis and herself. But this was real. Wasn't it? It felt real. There was pain throbbing off and on in her head.

"Take your time, Kass. You have a small head injury." He lifted his hand away from hers, gently moving her hair aside. "There. I think the air bag deployed and it was one of those defective ones. You have about an inch cut in your scalp and it's bleeding."

Feeling his finger trace near her injury, she became aware of it, felt the warm blood still trickling down from her temple. When he lifted his hand away, Travis enclosed her hand once more, and it meant everything to Kass. She tried to form more than one or two words. Why was it so hard to form a sentence and speak?

More than anything, Travis was here, with her. She couldn't remember how she got here. His hip was resting lightly against hers. She was in a bed, his, she guessed. The room didn't look familiar to her.

"W-where am I, Travis?" She felt relief that she could speak, even though her voice seemed like it was in a tunnel and there was an echo from it. Instantly, she saw his eyes narrow upon her, but they were filled with warmth and care. For her? He'd told her a year ago that there was nothing left between them. That he didn't love her. She should go and find a whole man who could make her happy. All of that roared back to her as she clung to his narrowing gaze upon her. He continued to hold her hand, as if he knew she needed him as an anchor right now.

"You're in my cabin, Kass. Do you remember driving your car and spinning out on that black ice on Route 89?"

Car. She was in a car? Why couldn't she remember? "N-no . . . but how . . ."

He shrugged his broad shoulders. "I don't know where you were coming from, Kass. I was out in my furniture studio when I saw headlights spinning around in a circle on the highway in front of my house. I knew someone had spun out on the black ice. When I went to help, I found you. I brought you here to my cabin."

It took a good minute for her to process his explanation.

"Listen," he told her quietly, slowly enunciating his words, "I'm going to get my medical flashlight. I need to check your eyes out. I'll be right back."

Just his hand leaving hers filled her with momentary panic. Kass watched him ease to his feet, turn, and walk out of the room. Looking around, Kass knew she was in a bedroom. Her head ached and she felt very tired. The thunk of his cowboy boots on the floor made her open her eyes. Travis was back with his flashlight. He sat down facing her.

Gently cupping her cheek, he said, "Kass? I'm going to slowly move the light across your eyes a couple of times. I need to see if your pupils dilate properly. Just stare into my eyes, okay?"

Licking her lower lip, she whispered, "O-okay." Travis gave her a kind look and she instantly relaxed. His palm was calloused, her skin prickling with unexpected pleasure over his intimacy with her. She was like a sponge, absorbing it eagerly. A memory flowed through her, of him telling her good-bye at the bus station as he left for Marine Corps boot camp. Along with that were a lot of old emotions she'd felt as he'd told her good-bye, given her one last kiss on the mouth, and then, he was gone.

Travis moved the flashlight slowly back and forth across her eyes as she stared up at him. How much she still loved him! Heartache transcended the pain in her head. Relishing his hand on her jaw, having him keep contact with her was all that she wanted. Right now, she was highly emotional. Far more than usual. He said she had a head injury. Could that be why? Kass didn't know. As he removed the flashlight and took his hand away from her jaw, she saw relief in his face.

"Good news," he told her, setting the flashlight on the

bedstand. "Your eyes are equal and reactive. You don't have a brain injury, Kass. I'm sure you're feeling pretty scattered right now, but maybe in a few hours, you'll feel more like your old self. May I tend to your injury here?" He pointed toward her left temple.

"I remember," she whispered.

"What do you remember?"

"Y-you were a medic . . ." She saw him give her a brief smile, his hand coming to rest once more on hers, giving it a squeeze.

"Yeah, that's right. I was a recon Marine and we all held an EMT certification. I'll be right back, Kass. Just rest."

She closed her eyes, feeling better, warm and safe. She'd always felt protected when she was with Travis. So many memories were returning now . . . good ones, mostly. Their time together as children growing up and seeing each other in elementary school every day. Their playfulness. Their laughter. They were always being happy in one another's company. That had never left her, she realized. Kass heard him enter and opened her eyes. She saw he carried a small first aid kit.

As always, she realized just how handsome Travis was. He wore a red and black checked flannel shirt, the long sleeves rolled up to just below his elbows. The jeans fit him wonderfully and she enjoyed the play of light across his strong, impassive face. He wore that game face when he wanted to hide his feelings. Kass didn't know where that awareness had come from, but it felt accurate to her.

"I brought a bottle of water back," he said. "Are you thirsty?"

"No . . . not right now. My head really hurts, Travis."

"I'm sure it does," he said, opening up the kit. "I'm going to clean your cut and stop the bleeding. Scalp wounds always bleed a lot, but you won't lose much blood, so don't worry." He tucked a large dressing beneath her left ear. "This won't take long," he promised.

"Can I close my eyes?"

"Sure. Are you tired? Want to sleep?"

"I just feel . . . washed out . . ."

"Understandable," he said, pulling on a pair of latex gloves. "You got jostled around when your car spun out of control. And you either hit your head on the side of the window or a piece of metal exploded from the air bag when it deployed, and cut you here." He gently used gauze to daub away the blood.

"I don't remember."

"You will, in time. For now? You're in a warm, safe place and I'm going to take care of you."

Closing her eyes, she focused on his fingers moving her hair aside to closely examine her injury. Travis was incredibly gentle, the pain seeming to reduce as he quickly cleaned up the area of the injury, placed antibiotic ointment across it and then a small dressing.

Hungrily, Kass enjoyed his touch. How badly she needed Travis! The ache in her heart had never gone away since he told her to find another man. A "whole man," whatever that meant. All of that grief and hurt gripped her heart once more. And here she was, with a man who no longer loved her. What kind of karma did she have?

Kass was unable to fight her need of Travis or his masculine nearness. He worked quickly, efficiently, and he was done much sooner than she wanted. His touch was balm to her aching heart.

"There," Travis murmured, pleased, "all done. How do you feel now?"

Opening her eyes, Kass felt her throat tighten, watching him remove the latex gloves and put everything neatly back into the first aid kit sitting on the bedstand. "Okay," she answered, her voice strained. And then he turned, easing strands of her hair away from where he'd bandaged the cut. Her scalp prickled with pleasure. How much she needed his contact right now because hot tears were pressing into the backs of her eyes.

"It's probably going to take a day or two for you to really start feeling normal, Kass. Are you warm enough here? Or would you like something to eat? Drink?"

This was the first time she was experiencing Travis Grant after returning from the Marine Corps. He'd been so abrupt and cold to her at the Wind River Ranch when she'd heard he was finally home for good. She'd driven out there with her heart pounding with joy, finally able to see him and tell him how much she still loved him. Kass knew it was a long shot to hope that their love had survived the years he had been in the Marines. Once Travis left the valley for the military, she very seldom heard from him. That told her a lot, but she didn't want to believe it. There was nothing left between them.

More anguish drifted through her as she saw him tidy up the medical kit and close it. This was the old Travis she knew in high school: caring, sensitive, and able to reach out and help others. Not the gruff, iconic wrangler at the Wind River Ranch from a year earlier, who rebuffed her and told her to walk out of his life forever. That there was nothing left between them.

Kass had been abandoned shortly after birth, the unknown mother placing her at the doorstep to the Wind River Valley Fire Department office doorstep. Luckily, it was July and warm. A firefighter coming on duty discovered her and brought her inside, immediately calling the hospital. In the meantime, their paramedics made sure she was okay, and she was. Kass had no memory of any of that time, of course. Her adoptive parents, Marshall and Jade Murphy, had smothered her with love. She grew up with a family who wanted her. But when they told her, when she was fourteen years old, that she had been adopted, that no one knew about her mother, it had devastated Kass's world.

It had been quiet, sensitive Travis Grant who had held her as she cried after that. He tried to ease some of her pain by listening to her after her sobs lessened. He had been her stanchion from the time she entered the first grade. Kass was sure she'd fallen in love with him even then, although at age six she knew she wasn't mature enough to realize much of anything. Only that she liked him.

Travis had been drawn to her just as powerfully, and they'd been the best of friends. It was in high school that their love first expressed itself. Travis didn't care if she'd been abandoned by her real mother. He pointed out that Jade and Marshall loved her with all their hearts, and she was wanted by them. Travis had always been the voice of reason when she, so overly emotional on this topic, felt adrift and alone. Travis always made her feel wanted. So did her adoptive parents, but in a different way. Kass never pooh-poohed her parents' love for her. They'd given her everything she needed, but the hole in her heart from learning that her biological mother walked away from her had never healed.

And when Travis came home from the Marine Corps and confronted her, told her that he didn't love her anymore, that hole in heart had grown even larger. She'd struggled this last year, throwing herself into more work with her restaurant than ever before, trying to forget him. But she couldn't. It was impossible.

And now? She was lying in Travis's bed. In his home. Her brain was coming back online now and she remembered the car she was driving and how in less than a split second it had spun out of control on the unseen black ice. And then she'd lost consciousness.

Frowning, she watched Travis get up.

"You okay here by yourself? I have some work to attend

to out in my woodworking studio. I can come in and check on you in about an hour."

"Go ahead," she whispered, fighting back tears. "You have your life. I don't want to interfere in it." She saw him frown, giving her a hard look, open his mouth to say something, then think better of it and close it. "I'll be okay. I can take care of myself, Travis."

Kass didn't mean to sound ungrateful. After all, Travis had rescued her from death. Every year in Wyoming, people died out in the middle of nowhere during the winter, hypothermia killing them before anyone knew they needed help and rescue. "I'm feeling pretty up and down right now," she offered.

"Yeah, a bruised brain will do that to you, Kass. I'm sure you're going to feel like you're on an emotional roller coaster for a while. I'll come in and check on you. Okay? I don't mind doing it."

She saw the softening in his expression, regret, she thought, in his blue eyes as he stood there studying her. His voice, too, wasn't gruff and hard, either. Not like that morning when he told her he didn't love her and to leave. Swallowing, she gave a slow nod, because to move her head fast made her dizzy for a moment. "That's fine. Thank you."

Kass watched him start to leave, then he hesitated and turned his head, holding her gaze.

"Listen, if you need anything? I'm just outside the front door, in the barn. My furniture studio is in there and that's where I'll be working."

"I don't feel like standing up and walking anywhere yet. I think I'll just rest here."

Nodding, he said, "Are you sure you're warm enough? I can get you a blanket if you want before I leave."

Now the younger, thoughtful Travis, the boy who was unselfish, was here, and Kass was grateful. The Marine Corps had hardened Travis in ways she'd never seen in him before. He'd changed. *A lot.* And it was a shock to Kass on every level. The boy she'd fallen in love with was gone. Was that part of Travis dead? Never to be seen again?

"No, I'm fine. I'm warm enough with my jacket on. Thank you."

"Okay," he said, frowning, watching her. "I'll be back later."

Kass watched him saunter out of the room, leaving the door partly open. The hollow sound of his boots hitting the oak floor diminished. She thought she heard the front door open and then quietly close.

He was gone. *Again.*

What was going on? Why had this happened? Closing her eyes, Kass pressed her fingertips to her brow. A lot of the pain was gone and she was sure it was because of Travis's caring touch. There was such a gentleness to him and she'd grown up with that side. And just now? She'd seen a hint of it again. Not the same as before, but he was caring and concerned. Her dark humor side told her that if he really didn't care one whit about her, he'd have left her in the car unconscious and let her freeze to death.

The Travis she knew would never do that. Not ever. Feeling tired, Kass yearned for sleep. She pulled off her gloves and let them drop beside her, placing her hands across her belly. She could hear icy snowflakes hitting one of the two windows in his bedroom. The wind, too, was howling off and on. How lucky she'd been to spin out right in front of his home. Kassie believed in guardian angels, but this incident hinged on unearthly. What were the chances she'd lose control of her car right in front of this man's door?

What kind of sick cosmic joke was being played on her and Travis? Kass couldn't reconcile the fact that he was tender and caring toward her. If there was no love between them, why had he acted that way? It didn't make sense, and a huge part of her heart wanted desperately for him to love her as he had before.

She couldn't get kicked to the curb again like that. Being abandoned once by him had done major damage to her. Kass didn't have the guts or whatever it took to rise again and fight to regain his love. There was something in his eyes that told her he still loved her even if he wouldn't admit it to her. She had a woman's knowing, and it had never led her wrong. Exhaustion swept through her, and the last thought Kass had was that maybe her guardian angel had gotten her to Travis, to his doorstep. After all, it was December and she dearly loved Christmas. Was it possible that this might be their third and last chance to allow love to enter their lives?

Chapter Three

Ah, hell, he couldn't work! Frustrated, fighting his love for Kass, Travis was emotionally self-destructing in his studio. Unable to concentrate, her face hovering before his eyes, he gave up on sanding a chair he was finishing up.

He'd seen the love she still carried like a torch for him reflected in her beautiful, large green eyes. It was there! *Damn!* And his stupid heart responded to it, begging him to wrap his arms around her, drag her against him, and hold her so tightly that it would squeeze the air from her lungs. The ache in his heart went straight to his fractured soul. The agony was excruciating to Travis because he was trying to protect Kass from him. She didn't deserve half a man.

Travis had barely been able to hold himself together while he tended to Kass's wound. To touch her, to smell that subtle orange scent among her ebony strands, damn near did him in.

He paced the studio, unable to focus. Having her literally crash into his life had exploded all his carefully closeted, suppressed love for her. Seeing her injured? The terror over her possibly being dead when he opened that car door had ripped him wide open as he looked inside, staring at her limp, unmoving body. It felt like someone had wrenched his heart out of his chest and was pounding it with a sledge-hammer. He briefly wondered if he'd pass out or die of a heart attack in that moment, it was that visceral. All he could hear was that heavy, pounding sound in his ears, his heart screaming out for Kass, despite everything going on in those fragile moments.

How the hell could he go to her in this condition? How? Pacing like an imprisoned animal, Travis felt as if he were going to die if he didn't go back to Kass and tell her the truth: that he'd *never* stopped loving her. How badly he'd hurt her. *Twice now.* He'd left her for the Marines, and then he'd denied his feelings when he came back. This was the third time. Of all the people in the world, she didn't deserve this from anyone, especially him.

He knew she'd been abandoned at birth, and as he grew and matured, he'd seen how that wound had always shad-owed her life, still staining it to this day. She'd been sum-marily jettisoned by a mother who didn't care enough to keep her newborn daughter. It didn't matter to Travis the reasons to give up a baby. One did *not* throw a child away, no matter what the reason, in his worldview.

He was fierce when it came to family. One took care of their own. Period. They didn't abandon a newborn or an older child. Not ever. How he'd hurt for Kass over the years, but the bittersweet realization was that he, too, had abandoned her.

Because of that life-altering experience she'd endured and bravely lived through, Kass was a survivor. Travis was sure he'd torn the scar off her stained past by pushing her away from him, lying to her that he didn't love her when he really did. He saw the fear deep in her eyes that he was going to hurt her once more. He was sickened by himself and that he couldn't be the boy who she had grown up with.

That part of him was dead. He'd become a very different man in order to keep himself alive during combat.

Travis felt adrift. That created uncertainty within him. But it didn't stop Travis from wanting Kass, wanting what he couldn't have. All he would do was make her life miserable if they reconnected in a relationship. Up and down. Unpredictable. Hurting her daily in large and small ways. God, he didn't want to ever do that to her again.

Pushing his fingers distractedly through his hair, he felt so damn torn up, unable to think clearly or be decisive. Kass was the innocent in this sordid mess of his life. He thought that being tough with her, lying and telling her he didn't love her anymore, would break their tie to one another forever. Kass would be free of him to find a man who would truly cherish her as she so richly deserved. Travis knew better than anyone that Kass was worthy of happiness.

A huge rock sat on his chest, making it hard for him to breathe, and he fought himself to not tell her the truth. Travis knew if he did Kass would run toward him, arms open, not away from him. She was never fazed by emotional fear. Maybe because she'd been abandoned like that, the worst possible fear coming true, that other fear seemed insignificant in comparison.

There was nothing he could do to change who he had become since joining the Marine Corps. Kass was stuck at his cabin with him for at least five days until this blue norther roared through and the snowplows could get the five or six feet of snow off the main roads. What was he going to do until then? It took such energy and focus to live with and deal with his constant anxiety. By the end of the day with the harsh emotions that prowled through him, he was exhausted physically as well as emotionally. Now? He had all his hidden, yearning love for Kass exploding through him, as well.

He sat down, placing his hands over his face, shoulders hunched, so much fear, need, and love for this woman avalanching through him that he felt utterly paralyzed for a moment. There was no way to change what had just happened. The accident wasn't Kass's fault. She shouldn't have been out in this weather, but that was beside the point. And really? He was glad that if she had to spin out, it was at his place and not somewhere on a lonely stretch of Route 89 that had nothing nearby. She might have been found frozen to death by some snowplow driver days later.

Rubbing his face savagely, Travis felt his life as he had reimagined it crumbling before his very eyes. Nothing was going to be the same after Kass came here. She was lying in his bed! How many times had he dreamed of exactly that? Her in his arms, warm, willing, and loving him as fiercely as he made love with her. They had all been wishful dreams because in the jaded eye of daylight as he sat on the edge of his bed, waking up, Travis knew it would never work. He couldn't even save himself. How the hell could he stop Kass from loving him? No matter what he did, she'd remained true to him.

Glancing at his watch, an hour had flown by. Looking out the window, he saw fat, heavy snowflakes covering the area. The wind had diminished, but there were still gusts of fist-like power from time to time.

He wanted so badly to go to Kass, to explain everything. In his heart, Travis knew she wouldn't care about his PTSD. She would take him "as is," and that scared the hell out of him. Why did he want her so desperately? As a young girl, she'd been the radiant sunlight in his life. Her smile always warmed him, made him feel wanted and loved even when they were in elementary school. They had been inseparable. He'd absorbed every wonderful minute with Kass. And she enjoyed him just as much.

Cursing softly, Travis pushed to his feet, wiping his damp palms against his jeans, heading for the door. It was time to go check on Kass. And he was so damned scared it rivaled the worst combat missions that he'd somehow survived.

Kass was sitting up on the edge of the bed, her head hanging slightly forward, getting her bearings. She'd slept deeply and had just awakened. Warm now, she'd removed her purple coat and set it on the other side of the bed. Outside the opened heavy drapes, she could see snow falling heavy and fast. It was so thick she couldn't see the Wilson Range mountains that paralleled Route 89, north to south.

A soft knock on the partly opened door caught her attention. Lifting her chin, she saw a shadow briefly and then Travis pushing the door open a little more, peering into the gloom in her direction. Their eyes met. He looked like hell. Even though she wasn't fully recovered, she could feel the tension around him. It was in his eyes, the set of his mouth, as if he were expecting to get yelled at or hit by someone. He literally filled up the doorway.

"Hey," she croaked, straightening a little, "I think I'm going to survive, Travis."

"You look better," he said, taking a step into the room. "What can I get you, Kass? How's your head?"

She managed a slight, one-cornered smile, trying to make him feel less worried about her. "I'm still dizzy, but not as bad." She lightly touched the bandage on the cut. "And no pain. That's amazing. You're truly a healer." She fell into his turbulent blue gaze.

"That's good to hear." He hitched his thumb across his shoulder. "I finally got through to your restaurant manager, Carly, and told her what happened. I also called Jade to let her know that you're okay. She asked if you could call her back when you feel better. She's relieved to know you're going to be all right."

"Oh, good, you called Mom. I know she expected me back at a certain time. I'm sure she was worried sick. Is Carly going to shut the restaurant down? We usually do when a blue norther comes through."

Nodding, Travis said, "Yes, for the next three to five days. She said for you not to worry about the place. So far, they still have electricity in the town."

Grimacing, she muttered, "That may or may not last."

"Right," he said. "But she said the backup generator is ready to roll out and use, so you won't lose all your food in the freezers and refrigerators."

"That's great. Carly is so responsible, but then, she's a combat military vet like you. She was in the Marine Corps and was assigned to small fire bases in Afghanistan the four years she was in."

"I'll have to meet her sometime," Travis said.

Giving him a wry look, she added, "You two are a lot alike, believe me."

He stuck his thumbs in his waist belt. "Oh?"

"Loners."

Grunting, Travis said, "War will do that to you. What can I get for you, Kass?"

She looked around. "I drank most of the water you gave me." She motioned toward the bedstand and the plastic bottle. "Now I have to go to the bathroom. Could you tell me where it's at?"

He eased away from the wall, taking his thumbs out of his belt, walking over to her. "I'll do better than that." He slid his hand around her upper arm. "Let's get you to stand up slow and easy. Okay? I have you, and if you get dizzy, tell me. We won't move until the dizziness passes."

Warmed by his protectiveness and caring, she pushed to her feet. Travis's hand was roughened and calloused, but then, the man was a wrangler as well as a master carpenter working with wood. Both jobs would create callouses and skin toughness. She slowly stood.

"Oh . . ."

"Dizzy?"

"Yes."

"Lean on me, Kass. Put your arm around my waist. That way, you won't pitch and fall. How are your knees feeling? Are they solid or not?"

It was such a private pleasure to wind her arm around his narrow waist. "Yes . . . they're fine. It's just my head . . . I feel like things in the room are whirling. It's crazy." His arm went across her shoulders and he drew her against his tall, solid form, standing quietly, allowing her the time she needed in order to adjust.

"That's vertigo. A lot of blood is moving around, and it might take a minute or two, but it will pass. You can close your eyes. That will help."

She did, feeling his arm become a little more firm around her shoulders, more supportive. How delicious to fully lean against his left side, her brow resting against his shoulder, just standing there with Travis. He smelled of the cold Wyoming air, of a clean evergreen fragrance she was sure came from his studio where he was working on a piece of pine, perhaps. And then there was that special scent that consisted of his own unique maleness. Dragging in a deep breath, secretly enjoying the intimacy, Kass had never felt happier.

"My dizziness passed," she told him, looking up, drowning in his pale blue eyes. Kass could swear he wanted her. She could feel it, but it didn't show in his expression. She didn't want to read anything into his embrace other than helping her up so she wouldn't fall. "Which way to the bathroom?"

"At the door, we'll turn left and mosey down the hall," he told her, allowing her to choose the pace for them.

"You have a beautiful home, Travis. I love the wooden beams, the color of the wood."

"It's made of cedar." He allowed her to make the turn, her steps none too steady yet. "How are *you* doing?"

"A little cautious," she admitted, tightening her arm around his waist for a moment as she made the turn into the hall. The wood was gleaming beneath the overhead lights strung along the passageway, and she could see the color of the floor reflecting back, reminding her of gold and crimson.

"It's okay," he murmured, gesturing to the right. "A few more steps and you'll be in a nice, big bathroom."

Halting at the open door, Kass was impressed with how clean and sparkling it was. She always supposed men were sloppy when living alone. Travis certainly wasn't. Placing her hand on the doorjamb, she reluctantly released him. "I think I can make it now. Thank you." Lamenting his arm unwinding from around her waist, she could feel him silently assessing her condition from where he stood nearby.

"When you're done, would you like to come out to the kitchen? I've got to start figuring out what to make for lunch pretty soon. I thought you might like something to drink?"

"Coffee sounds wonderful if you have some," she said, touched by his care. His eyes were alive with so many emotions that Kass couldn't translate them all. She felt as if he were torn up about something, but she didn't know what. "Let me try to make it under my own steam once I'm done in here."

He took a step away. "Of course. You just call if you need help, though?"

"I will," she promised. Reaching out, she briefly moved her fingers down the flannel fabric along his lower arm. Touching Travis was like feeding her dessert. "Are you sure I'm not being a pain in the ass by being here?"

One side of his mouth quirked and he gave her an amused look. "Hey, you're stuck here with me for the next five or so days, Kass, so get over that thought. Okay?"

She felt heat stealing from her neck, sweeping into her jaw and then settling in her cheeks. The look Travis gave her was of a man wanting his woman. It was there for a split second, and then it was gone. Kass swore she was imagining it because being here with Travis, alone, the intimacy strong and swirling between them, was a dream come true. "Okay," she managed to say, her voice thick with emotion. "I'll get out there, I promise you."

He lifted his hand, barely grazing her mussed black hair across her crown. "Kass, you are one tough lady. But you were always like that, able to bounce back from things most people never would."

Her scalp prickled pleasantly and she felt like a cat wanting to purr beneath his palm. "We all have crosses we have to carry," she said, becoming more somber.

"There's lots to talk about," he agreed, moving away. "Call me if you need help. Otherwise, I'll put on a pot of fresh coffee for us."

Her heart skipped beats as she watched him saunter down that hall, casual, relaxed, and oh, such a hunk of man. Kass felt embarrassed by her female hormones jumping up and down at that point as she quietly closed the bathroom door. Travis deserved better than her body heating up, wanting him, feeling that gripping sensation in her lower body. How long had it been since she'd made love? *Far too long.* And the aphrodisiac scent of him was driving her right over the proverbial cliff.

Should she be like this after such a serious auto accident? Was it her rattled brain? And was she still going up and down emotionally as Travis had said she would? Kass didn't know.

She went to the sink and washed her hands, the fragrance of the almond soap heavenly to her. How many men would have a fragrance in the soap they washed with? None that she knew. Except for Travis. He surprised her in the best of ways. At least these five precious days would give her a window into him. And that was an unexpected treasure to Kass. A Christmas holiday gift all its own that she would cherish for the rest of her life.

Looking around the white subway tiled bathroom, she loved the layered, colorful red, yellow, and orange tiles that were in a horizontal stripe on each wall. The place was so clean and smelled so good. She had expected very male-colored towels, something in gray or black or brown. But no, there were two fluffy orange towels with bright yellow washcloths. She loved the colors. And she'd never been in a home that Travis lived in. Now she was getting to see another aspect of him, and it was one of cleanliness, and yet he loved color. He wasn't like most men she'd known, and that was another positive box checked in her desire for him.

That discovery about color and cleanliness moved her heart. Kass loved color, too. Her restaurant had black and red leather booths, the walls white, the semitransparent white curtains frilly with red velvet hearts polka-dotting them. When she'd taken over the restaurant from her retiring mother, she'd done some remodeling. The windows were enlarged and she had more double-paned ones put in, giving the place a much brighter, lighter look than before.

The Formica counter at her café was a bright red with brushed steel around the edging. The rainbow color of stools that followed the U-shaped counter were anchored to the polished blond oak floor. She'd brightened up the counter, ordering new Formica the exact same colors as the stools.

As she continued to examine Tyler's sense of style, she appreciated the splash of the three strips of color on the tiled wall in front of her. There was so much more to Travis than she'd ever realized.

Kass glanced into the mirror, seeing the darkness beneath her eyes. Her hair was a mess. She tried to tame it, put it into place with her fingers, and didn't want to look so disheveled. She wanted to look pretty for Travis, but Kass could see she looked like she'd been in an accident. What must he think of her looking like this? Kass loved playing with her long, black hair that fell down her back. It was slightly wavy, and she often tamed it into a set of pigtails when she worked at her café. Or a ponytail.

Travis had looked at her hair, and she noticed he liked touching the strands. Each time, she saw pleasure burn in his eyes as he slid a curl between his thumb and index finger. He was a tactile person, her heart whispered to her. Taking a washcloth, Kass washed her face and neck and felt better. Felt prettier. She'd gotten rid of the thin trail of dried red blood down her temple. Even if she didn't look better, she felt better, and that lifted her spirit.

Excitement and anxiety threaded through her as she opened the door and stepped out into the hall. She could hear soft bluegrass music in the background, coming from the living room. Travis was in the kitchen, his back to her. She could smell the coffee percolating and it made her smile. Keeping one hand on the smooth cedar wall, she slowly made her way down the hall.

The cabin was toasty warm and when she glanced into the living room, she saw a big black iron potbellied stove in one corner of it. Travis had built red fire brick behind it on two walls, and the stove stood on the same brick, but they were white in color. For just a moment, she wanted to memorize every part of his home because this place spoke of the man, not the boy who she'd known all her life. It seemed so long ago to Kass.

Right now, she felt like a child in a candy store, not knowing where to look next. Each piece of furniture, each rug, each lamp, told her something intimate and surprising about Travis that she'd never known before.

In a way, Kass felt as if she were in one of her dreams with the only man she'd ever loved. And even though he'd made it clear he no longer loved her, she couldn't help feeling at home in this cabin with him. This was a gift to her. A parting gift, for sure. But at least the next five days would give her a glance into his life as an adult. All she knew was the gangly, awkward, and shy eighteen-year-old who had left her for the Marine Corps. The man who had returned was breathtaking to her. Beautiful in all ways male. Even the timbre of his voice sent waves of longing coursing through her. There was no way to stop the pleasure or sensations that Travis caused her by his mere presence.

Hesitating, Kass knew she was living on borrowed time with Travis. Once this blizzard passed and the roads were plowed, she would be gone from his life. *Forever.*

Not wanting to think about that, Kass swallowed hard, trying not to feel the sharp, cutting sense of abandonment once again. Travis had told her he was no good for her. When she'd asked why, he said he couldn't explain it, that she wouldn't understand even if he did tell her. Travis had been hard and gruff with her at that time, unlike now. Here, he was sensitive to her needs, gentle and so caring that it made her ache for what they might have had but now never would.

In the other corner of the cabin stood a six-foot-tall blue spruce. It was perfectly formed, thick branches, and beautiful but undecorated. Kass wondered why. Maybe she could find out. Maybe they could team up like they did as teenagers, work on a project, have so much fun and laughter doing it. How badly she wanted at least to share that with Travis before she had to walk out of his life for good.

Chapter Four

Travis turned, sensing Kass coming across the living room. She had tried to clean up, her black hair, once mussed, now in soft waves around her pale face and shoulders. Each step she took was slow and measured. He could see she still didn't have her balance back. Kass would reach out and trail her fingers across the back of a chair or the couch, keeping them available should she start to fall.

Why hadn't she asked him for help? That hurt, but Travis thought he knew why: He'd made it clear that she wasn't wanted in his world at all. Was it possible for a heart to hurt so much as it did right now in his chest? Sorrow ate at him. He quickly dried off his hands, dropped the towel on the counter, and walked toward the rectangular hickory dining room table and four chairs that surrounded it.

"I'll get there," Kass promised, grit in her tone, forcing a tight, wan smile.

"Let me help." He came to her side, slipping his hand beneath her right elbow. "You should have asked me for help, Kass."

She gave him a slanted look. "Hey, after being dumped

on the step of the fire department shortly after birth, I got it, Travis."

"You're very independent," he agreed gently, cutting his steps to half his stride. She leaned into his hand and he felt gratified that even now, Kass trusted him. She should. But he didn't deserve her trust because he'd broken it too many times already. "And that's not a bad way for a woman to be today," he added.

"You're right."

Reaching the table, he pulled out the chair for her. "Have a seat. I'll get the coffee in a minute. Do you like cream or sugar?"

"No, just black, thanks." She slowly sat down in the chair. "I guess I'm not as spunky feeling as I thought I should be."

He helped her slide the chair closer to the table and forced himself to remove his hand from it. "A good night's sleep will make you feel a lot better tomorrow morning," he promised, going to the kitchen.

Kass's face was pale. Her eyes were still filled with darkness. Her steps had been hesitant and unsure. How much he wanted to hold her, cradle her gently in his arms and allow her to lean on him. Travis knew he could make her feel better. But to what end? To do it after he'd informed her she wasn't needed in his life any longer would be cruel. And uncaring. No, he had to keep his hands to himself and be the model gentleman to her. That was all.

As he poured the coffee into two turquoise-colored ceramic mugs, he wanted to spoil her. Care for her. Make her smile. Needing, once again, to hear her laughter. She had a musical laugh and her eyes sparkled at such times. Travis wanted all of that to be shared with him. But he'd seen the shadows in her eyes and sensed that she was trying to be a good guest in this terribly awkward circumstance they found themselves in. Neither of them were comfortable at the moment.

Coming over to the table, he slid the mug toward her. "Are you hungry? I'm pretty good at making eggs and bacon."

She gave him a slight smile and slipped her hands around the large mug. "No . . . thank you."

Sitting down opposite her, Travis fought the need to sit closer to Kass. His heart yearned mightily for her nearness. His head warned of the dangers of such a choice. "I knew this blue norther was coming, so I went over to a rancher's place nearby and bought beef. Are you up to a New York steak tonight? I could throw some Idaho potatoes into the oven to bake. I've even got some sour cream in the fridge."

"That all sounds good, Travis, but my stomach is on the fritz."

His brows fell. "Nausea?"

"Um, yes. Sometimes. It comes and goes."

"You probably have a mild concussion, Kass. You'd like something lighter to eat, maybe?"

"Yes, I think so, but I'm not hungry right now, anyway." She picked up the mug and cautiously sipped the steaming black coffee.

Travis watched her lips and slid his gaze away from her for a moment. Kass had the most beautiful mouth he'd ever seen on a woman. Her lips were shapely, full, the corners dimpled. What would it be like to kiss her now, not as a young teen girl, but as a woman? He remembered in high school how sloppy and untrained his kisses must have been.

Setting the mug down, Kass said, "Do you have any canned soup? Maybe chicken soup?"

He brightened. "Yes, I do. Does that sound good to you now? Or for lunch?"

"It does. And some saltine crackers? Do you have those?"

Nodding, he said, "I do."

She looked at the clock. It was nearly eleven a.m. "Maybe in an hour or so? I'm not hungry right now, Travis."

"Understandable. What were you doing out on 89 with this weather coming in?"

With a grimace, she said, "I was attending a funeral for a dear friend of mine, Val Thomas. She died in Salt Lake City. I went down two days ago. I knew Val's whole family, and I wanted to spend some time with them afterward. When I heard a blue norther was coming in, I said good-bye and hoped that I could drive home before it hit."

"I'm sorry about your friend."

"Val was one of my parent's waitresses. She quit about three years ago to go back to Salt Lake and take care of her ninety-year-old mother, Tess. They were so very close. When Tess passed six months ago, I went down for her funeral. Val didn't look good. She'd just buried her mother and afterward, she'd gone to the doctor. She had a brain tumor and he told her she wouldn't live more than two months. It was an aggressive form of cancer. So she stayed with her family. She had two grown children who were married and with kids there in Salt Lake City. They cared for her while she was in hospice. She managed to live six months. Val had that kind of toughness of spirit, a real fighter. One of her daughters was pregnant at the time, and Val fought to stay alive until the baby was born in the fourth month of her illness. She got to hold her grandbaby, and pictures were taken, which will be priceless to all the family. As it was to Val."

"Tough break," Travis agreed quietly, seeing the grief in Kass's eyes even now. "I'm really sorry."

Her mouth moved into a sad line and she whispered, "Thanks."

"So having an accident on the way home was the cherry on the cake?"

"You could say that. Perfect end to a very bad time."

And now Kass was with him, unwanted, released and told never to come back into his life. The self-reproach he felt deepened and widened within him. It was an awful time for Kass. Far worse than he'd imagined. How must she really be feeling about being here with him, of all people?

Pushing the mug slowly between his hands, he said, "And then you landed here, with me." Travis forced himself to look up and hold her sad gaze. "Helluva fix, Kass. This can't be comfortable for you under the circumstances, but I'm going to make every effort to make you feel welcome here. All right?"

"It's a hell of a fix, Travis. I feel like a shuttlecock in a badminton game getting whapped back and forth. Only it's intense and emotional."

"And I know how hard that can be."

She gave him a sharpened look. "Are you saying that because of your deployments to Afghanistan or about us?"

Twinging inwardly, Travis knew she had an unerring ability to hit a target dead on. Kass had always been super intuitive, even as a child and teenager. He was not surprised by her bold, accurate question. Kass wasn't PC about much at all, but that was one of the many things he loved about her. "Yes, about Afghanistan." He didn't dare try to start adding an explanation. Travis didn't know what to expect from Kass in reaction, but he saw her eyes grow sympathetic.

"Did you hear from town gossip that when I took over the café, I started hiring women military vets as waitresses? There were so many of them who had PTSD, and I wanted to try and help them if I could." She opened her hands. "They needed support, a friendly ear, and they are the hardest workers, completely reliable, and the most trustworthy group I've ever seen. I'm so glad that I did that for them. They've made the café a star here in the valley."

"No . . . I didn't know that, Kass. I knew that Steve and Maud Whitcomb at the Wind River Ranch made it a point to hire military vets. That's why I went to them first when my enlistment was up and I was coming back to the valley. I'd been over at Charlie Becker's Hay and Feed, and he told me they were hiring military men and women coming back from the wars."

"Yes, there's a huge effort in our valley to hire men and women vets. I thought maybe you knew all about it since you've been here for a year."

Shrugging, he said, "I don't go to town unless I have to. I pretty much stay here, create furniture for orders I've received, and I live a quiet life. I'm not privy to much gossip. The way I live now is what I need."

"Carly, my manager, saw combat in Afghanistan, too. On some nights, when it was slow, we'd sit in the back booth near the kitchen and I'd just let her talk. It seemed to help her, to take a load off her shoulders she was silently carrying. I could always tell when she was wrestling with an anxiety attack or flashback. The ladies who work for me, being vets and all having PTSD in some form or another, look out for one another. They have clued me in on flash-backs, how a smell, a sound, a shadow, or a face could sud-denly throw them back into a moment where they were in a life-and-death situation or it was terribly threatening for them."

Surprised, Travis sat there digesting her softly spoken ad-mission. He saw the concern in her expression, but even more, that husky voice of hers was like balm to his smarting conscience and guilt. "I didn't know this . . . I wish I had . . ."

"My lady vets have taught me a lot over the years," she confided wryly, sipping her coffee. "They had to get me accustomed to PTSD and what it really meant, and what it was doing to each of them. They all had different symptoms from it. We'd sit down after the café closed, drink coffee, and they'd share. That's what I like about women: They talk, they open up, and they aren't afraid to be emotional. It got so that at least every couple of weeks, we'd close the café at quitting time and then we'd gather in the back booths and just talk. I listened a lot, Travis. I had no idea what was going on inside them. They all handled so many awful symptoms with such silence and grace. They seemed so outwardly confident. And they didn't mess up food orders, they were fast to serve customers, efficient, and my regulars, even the tourists, loved each of them. I just had no idea of the minute-by-minute anxiety or other feelings they carried within them. Or being in crowded circumstances, or the noise getting too loud for them to handle."

"All of that will send us into even more anxiety," he admitted darkly, frowning.

"They taught me, Travis. I used to have the music playing loudly but they finally fessed up and told me that it put them on edge. That it made them anxious. We discussed it and I decided to do two things. First, I would play classical and semi-classical instrumental music. Secondly, I would keep it only as a soft background. They were grateful. And to my surprise? My customers loved the new type of music. They told me it made them feel relaxed. It was a win-win for everyone." She sighed. "They're in so much pain all the time. I sometimes wonder if you got shot with a bullet that it would be kinder, faster, quicker to heal up from than the emotional and mental cruelty that PTSD evokes in all of them. There's no end to their suffering. It galls me, and I wish I could take the horrible feelings they carry out of them forever."

Trying not to stare at her or have his mouth drop open, Travis choked up. How badly he'd miscalculated Kass's ability to comprehend and understand what he lived with daily. It shocked him. "It's a 24/7/365 ordeal," he agreed heavily. "And it never goes away."

"Well," Kass said, "Carly told me that there would be what she called 'windows' where the anxiety seemed to lessen or sometimes just disappear within her for a little while. She called them 'rest periods.' She lived for those hours and sometimes days. They came and went. There was no rhyme or reason for it to come or go, either."

Something broke within him. Travis couldn't say what it was exactly, only that it felt like a dam holding back millions of gallons of water had suddenly burst, and just the pressure relief from it doing so was astounding to him. His whole chest and shoulders felt lighter now, and he was afraid to name the emotion that he now felt: happiness. How long had it been since he'd been happy? He couldn't name a time when he'd felt like that for the last seven years of his life. Kass had been the only one who had made him happy. He saw her staring at him, puzzlement in her expression. Casting around for something to say, he muttered, "Yeah, it comes and goes."

"Does my talking about this make you uncomfortable, Travis?"

Shaking his head, he took a hot drink of coffee. "No, it's okay." He'd always felt safe talking to Kass about anything and everything.

"Then what's that look on your face? You're really hard to read when you don't want people to know how you're really feeling."

Giving her a sour smile, he said, "I'm surprised that you know as much as you do about PTSD. I didn't realize you were hiring women vets. I've never been to your café, so I didn't know. I think Charlie Becker mentioned it once, but I was so busy because I was caught up in a flashback that it went in one ear and out the other."

"Do you get flashbacks, too, Travis?"

"Yeah, which is why I don't go into town too often. It makes me feel claustrophobic, Kass. It's nothing I can control. If I have to go to town, I do, but I'm tense and edgy for days afterward. I have to wind down those feelings that there's a Taliban sniper hiding around the corner of a building or on a roof, waiting to blow me away."

"Oh." She studied him. "Carly has a problem with tight places. She was in a special black ops unit, a top-secret one that was testing out women in combat. She volunteered for it while she was in the Marine Corps. There's one place she won't go in our café, and that's a very small, darkly lit room. She'll ask another waitress who doesn't have that kind of reaction to go in there to get the supplies we need for the cook. They work with one another's issues, and that kind of teamwork has helped all of them."

"I'm sure that helps her a lot. I wish more people were sensitive to our issues."

"Is that why I never see you in town, Travis? You can't handle a town environment?"

As always, Kass was intelligent and very quick to put puzzle pieces together to see a larger pattern. "Yeah." He moved uncomfortably. "I lost my best friend in an Afghan village while we were searching for a specific enemy. A Taliban sniper was on another rooftop and killed him. Ever since then I can't handle a town too well."

"I'm so sorry," she said, reaching out, briefly touching his hand wrapped around the mug. "That makes sense to me now." And then she rolled her eyes. "I thought the reason you never came into town was because I was working and living there. We'd have run into one another, for sure."

More grief plunged through him. "No . . . no, that was

never the reason I didn't go into town often, Kass. My wounds have *nothing* to do with you." He saw relief come to her face.

"I guess, even though we're not in a relationship with one another," she said, "I always wanted to always remain friends with you, Travis. I know I didn't say it at the time you told me that things were finished between us a year ago. I was too upset to think to say to you that if I could, I'd still remain your friend, if you wanted. But I never told you until now."

There was fear, anxiety, and need clearly written in her features. Kass would never be able to hide how she felt from him.

Feeling his throat tighten, it took everything Travis had not to tell her the truth. Instead, he rasped, "We'll always be friends, Kass. I haven't been avoiding you. Since coming home I guess I've been avoiding life in particular and people in general." He gestured around the cabin. "This place is like a shell that protects me. Well, that and my furniture studio next door. I feel safe in both places. There's no noise, just natural sounds, which I need and it calms me. I have two horses to care for, and when there isn't six feet of snow on the ground, I go riding. And I have my furniture business, which feeds me tranquility and it focuses me."

"Wood is natural. It should be soothing. Anything that is from nature is always helpful, Travis." She gazed around the small, cozy cabin. "I hadn't thought of this beautiful cabin as a clamshell, but you know, you're right. There's a warm feeling in here, not too large or small, and the fire popping and crackling in the stove always makes me happy and relaxed. It must for you, too?"

Stirring, Travis stood up, his cup empty. "Yes, it does. Do you feel like coming out to see my wood studio?" He was desperate to have her see who he was now, to under-stand where he was at. Travis didn't know why, only that he felt driven to show her where he spent most of his time every day. Something deep within him told him that she would understand.

"I'd love to do that," Kass said, pushing the chair away. "Thanks for the coffee. It tasted really good. I should find out what kind of beans you use."

"It's local. Charlie Becker sells them."

She smiled a little, her fingertips on the table as she rose. "Charlie is always selling lots of little things to folks around here. He's so necessary to all of us."

"Yeah," he said, coming around the table, sliding his hand beneath her elbow, "Charlie is a permanent fixture around here, plus, he's just an all-around good person, and so is his wife, Pixie. She makes the best baked goods in the county."

Straightening, she stood for a moment. "Oh, Pixie is famous for them! I think the whole town knows when she bakes a fresh batch of cookies or some of her wonderful brownies or cupcakes. Everyone comes over to get some of them over at the feed store." She gave him a glance. "I'm still a little dizzy, Travis."

"Do you want to delay going to the studio? Would you rather lie down for a while or something?"

"No . . . no . . . just let it pass." Kass sighed and gave him a wry look. "Tell me how long it will take my poor pea brain to heal and I won't have this whirling sensation?"

"Probably be gone by tomorrow morning after a good night's sleep, Kass."

"Good to hear." She moved with him toward the door. "I can hardly wait to see what you make, Travis. I remember in high school you took every woodworking class available. Your dad taught you carpentry from about nine years old, onward, as I recall." She smiled up at him. "That hasn't changed about you at all. Charlie was raving about the furniture you make. And of course, Maud Whitcomb thinks you walk on water. She proudly calls you a master carpenter."

Travis opened the door. Outside, the snow was falling heavily now, being whirled around by gusts of wind now and then. There was an enclosed screen porch that protected the area from the elements. He led her down to the end of it, opening a screen door that led to a sheltered passageway. There was a roof over it and the bottom half of it was made of wood slats. The top half was screened in, as well.

He guided Kass into the studio at the end of the passageway. Opening the wooden door that he'd carved with a mountain scene and a grizzly bear by a stream, he flipped on the lights. Kass had stopped and was running her fingers across his carving, making a sound of pleasure. It made him feel so damned good. He eased her inside the large, rectangular room.

"Oh," she said, standing to one side as he came in and shut the door. "You're busy, Travis!" She smiled, gesturing around the room filled with furniture at different points of construction. "And it smells so good in here!"

"It's the different scents from the wood I use," he said. "Where would you like to start?"

"Tell me what happens from the beginning. I know Maud said that you get orders from all around the world."

"Let's go to the right, then," he urged, cupping her elbow, guiding her along the wall where sawhorses sat with different kinds of wood spanning across them. "When the phone rings and I'm at the other end of my studio, it's a run to pick it up in time to answer it."

"It's a huge place, Travis, but looking at the couches, the stools and chairs you're making, you need this kind of room."

He brought her to a halt at his rolltop desk. "Here, have

a seat," he said, pulling out the oak chair on rollers. "Sit down, and if you'd like I can kind of talk about what's going on in here?"

"Sitting is good," she agreed.

Travis waited for her to get comfortable, standing to one side. "I get phone orders here." He gestured to the desk where the black landline phone was placed.

"Who knows about you?" she asked, staring up at him.

"Steve, who is a globally known and an important architect, had one of their major magazines do an article on me. Since that article came out, I have more orders than I can fill."

"He helped you build your business, getting the word out, and so you became known sooner than usual."

Nodding, Travis rested his fingers lightly on her shoulder for a moment. "Yes, he did and I'm grateful." He wanted to continue physical contact with Kass, but he forced himself to remove his hand.

The urge to touch her was a fierce need and drive within him, something that made him feel damn near euphoric when it happened. He saw the subtle change in her expression when he made contact with her shoulder. She liked it, too. But Kass had never been coy about the fact she'd loved him, even when he was gone for so many years. He'd found out from Charlie Becker that she still carried him in her heart. That was the depth of her commitment to him. And it wasn't something he wanted to root out or destroy. But how could he change their present circumstances? Her understanding of PTSD through her waitresses blew him away, and it planted a seed of hope in his heart, too. Travis was unsure if it could grow or not. He only had five days with Kass to find out more about her and whether that seed could take root or not. A slice of him was serious about trying to reestablish a serious relationship with her. It wasn't a logical need, it was his heart crying out for her.

Could it honestly happen? Travis didn't think so, and he was afraid to hope because everything else had been torn from him during his combat deployments. He thought hope had been destroyed, but now, he discovered, it had once more, taken up residence in his badly injured heart. War and combat remade everyone who went through it. How could hope really grow and survive in the brutal desert of his PTSD?

Fighting his internal thoughts, Travis gestured around the room. "I have mostly hardwoods that I work with in here. Some, as you can see, are stacked in the first third of my studio. It's where I go to choose the wood for the project."

"Do people have a favorite wood they want for their furniture?"

"Yes. My local clients, here in the valley, prefer oak. My East Coast clients like cherry and mahogany, darker, reddish-colored furniture."

"It's an eight-month winter here in Wyoming, and the skies are always dark," Kass murmured. "Blond oak is light, and Wyoming folks sure don't have a lot of sunlight in those months. It makes lots of sense people here would want lighter-colored wood."

"That's true," he said, giving her a look of praise for her insight. "I hadn't thought of it that way, but you're right. Also, the folks around here like a softer wood like white pine. Over there I'm doing a set of six chairs for someone in Jackson Hole. All are made of it."

"Interesting," Kass murmured, smiling a little. "Do you get orders from the Midwest?"

"I do. They like elm, hickory, and some oak."

"Do you get overseas orders?"

"Yes, and they prefer bamboo. It's a tough wood to work with, and I had to teach myself how to deal with it. Bamboo is one of the most resilient, longest lasting of all woods in the world. Except maybe for ironwood, from the American

Southwest, which I find nearly impossible to work with. It's just too dense and hard to carve."

She gave him a soft smile. "You know, when you talk about your woodworking, you relax. I can actually see your shoulders drop, Travis."

He felt heat flooding his face. "You never did miss much, Kass. It's true. I love working with any kind of wood. Just running my hands over a smoothed piece, sanding it, makes me relax."

"Do you play music out here on your iPod?"

He pointed to a radio sitting on top of the desk. "That's a 1930s wood radio made with a blond oak casing. I bought it at a Goodwill store in Salt Lake City right after I got home."

"I heard you playing bluegrass music in your cabin."

"Yes, my favorite. I play it out here, too."

"So not all noise bothers you?"

He gazed down at her upturned face. The overhead track lighting brought out the blue highlights within her black hair. She was so beautiful. Clamping down on his desire, he said, "That's right. I do well with one or two people around, too. If I get in a crowd, I seize up and I have to get out of there. And music, unless it's too loud, is usually soothing to me. I guess you might say I'm reordering my world around the fact I need quiet and calm."

"Carly's a lot the same way. Now people can actually hold a conversation in my café at normal voice levels." She grinned. "Everyone likes it that way, I discovered."

"Sounds like they've been good teachers. Did you mind making those compensations for them, Kass?"

"Gosh, no! When I turned down the music and bought classical music from Pandora radio from the Internet, they loved it. And my ladies were able to relax, too. Sounds just tensed them up and there was no reason for me not to change the environment for them."

How wrong he'd been about Kass and himself. For a

moment, Travis let himself long for what he really wanted: to marry Kass, have a life with her. Could it really happen? What about children? There were so many unknowns about being a parent with PTSD, and that scared him to death. The last thing he wanted to do was hurt Kass again. Feeling trapped between what his heart wanted and what his head was screaming at him, he decided to wait some more. "You've always been a relaxing person to me, Kass," he admitted, holding her gaze. "I guess I just never realized how much you knew about PTSD and how it affects all of us."

She stared up at him, the silence stretching between them. "And because of that? Does that change anything between us, Travis?"

Chapter Five

Kass awoke slowly. She was snug and warm in Travis's bed, but he wasn't there with her as much as in her dreams last night. The heavy burgundy velvet drapes were closed to keep the heat from escaping through the double-paned windows. She turned her head, seeing the clock read nine a.m. Drowsy, Kass reran all their talks from yesterday. She felt hope for the first time since Travis had come home.

Rubbing her eyes, she sat up. Travis had given her one of his white T-shirts to wear, plus a pair of his blue-striped pajama bottoms. They hung on her. It was like wearing Travis around her, and she loved that feeling. Her black hair tumbled across her shoulders as she slowly eased out of bed and slipped her feet into a pair of his big, roomy sheepskin-lined slippers.

Her mind, without coffee to stimulate it, was like a slug. She wondered if the blizzard was still blowing. Keying her hearing, it sounded like wind gusts were still pounding against the outside of the cabin's windows. She had to get up and take a shower.

Later, dressed in another of Travis's dark blue T-shirts, a pair of his thick gray wool socks, and a pair of his jeans with the leg cuffs rolled up to just below her ankles, she made her way through the silent cabin. It was still snowing. She could see the buildup of white stuff on the outside of the windowsills. Peering out the kitchen window, which faced north, she saw the entire landscape covered in white for as far as she could see. Guessing about three feet of new snow had accumulated since her car crash, she was grateful to be inside where it was warm and dry. The snap and pop of wood in the potbellied stove soothed her.

As she went to make coffee, she saw a scrawled note from Travis. It read, *I'm out in my studio. I made coffee earlier, plus an omelet. It's in the fridge and you can warm it up in the microwave oven. Make yourself at home. I'll be back in to check on you later. T.*

His thoughtfulness trickled through her as she saw a bright orange ceramic mug sitting nearby. Her stomach growled and she went to the fridge and found the omelet, a combo of sliced mushrooms, cheddar cheese, and chunks of sausage within it. Never had she been happier. She loved Travis. Her feelings for him had never gone away, and now they were throbbing within her like glowing coals that were about to burst into flames. She so badly wanted to forge that connection of being friends with him, if nothing else. Kass didn't hold out hope for him to change his mind about them, either.

She decided to stop thinking so much and just warm up her breakfast. With a couple cups of coffee fortifying her, she would be ready for whatever the day would bring.

Kass had just finished putting the dirty dishes in the dishwasher when Travis walked in from his studio.

"Hey," she called. "I'm up and alive." She instantly saw

him smile as he shrugged out of his fleece coat, hanging it up on a nearby wall hook.

"And you look better. How's the dizziness?" he asked, walking over to her, retrieving a mug from the cupboard.

"You know, I didn't even realize it was gone," she admitted, standing aside. "You were right—a good night's sleep was all I needed."

Travis poured himself some coffee. "Come and sit with me at the table."

She poured herself a third cup and followed him. Travis pulled out her chair and she thanked him, sitting down. He sat at her right elbow. Kass loved the intimacy it established. He was wearing a light blue flannel shirt, had rolled up the sleeves to just below his elbows. The pair of jeans he wore had a slight dusting, here and there, of what she thought might be wood sawdust. "What time did you get up?"

"Early. I don't sleep well at night, toss and turn. Usually, I'm up around 0500 . . . I mean five a.m."

"Military speak," she teased, sipping her coffee. The expression on his face with his unshaven, shadowed stubble made him look even sexier to her.

"Yes, I fall into it regularly," he warned with a slight hitch of one corner of his mouth. "You work with women vets, so I'll bet you're pretty used to our lingo."

Nodding, she said, "That and so much more. My ladies have more or less adopted me." She laughed a little. "They take pity on me that I'm a civilian floundering around in the sea of military language they use like shorthand among one another. Lucky for us, our cooks are both military vets, so I'm the only one left out without a translator."

"But I'm sure they translate for you?"

She loved the calm she saw in Travis's expression. He seemed much more at peace this morning, unlike yesterday. "They do. I get so I talk their language, not the civilian one."

"You're one of us," he murmured, sipping his coffee. "I was hoping your dizziness would be gone, Kass." He pointed to the blue spruce in the corner. "I thought we might trim the tree sometime this afternoon if you wanted. I'm sure you're probably bored just sitting around here with nothing to do."

"I'm not bored," she said. "I love this cabin. You're right, it's like a clamshell, it's so safe feeling."

"When I came home, my parents told me that this place had sat empty and for sale for three years. I was able to buy it pretty cheaply. I had money saved from being in the service but was worried if I could afford much of anything at all. I got lucky."

"Do Red and Melba like your place?"

"Yes, my dad helped me set up the studio when I came home." He gestured toward the living room. "My mom, bless her, did all the buying of furniture, the decorating and making it into a home for me."

"She did a nice job. Do you get to see them often?"

"About once a month I drive up to see them, and I have Sunday afternoon dinner with them and we catch up with one another."

"I know when you were a teen, your dad was teaching you how to fix cars in his garage business. Do you still do that?"

"Naw. I'm mechanical minded, but I love carpentry and making things with my hands, not fixing car engines. I don't mind it, but it's not my passion. My grandfather was a master carpenter, and I think that gene got passed on to me instead of the mechanic's one my dad has."

"I'm sure your folks are glad you're home."

Somber, he nodded. "My mother worried about me nonstop. That was the bad part. They knew I was always in combat areas of Afghanistan. No place was safe. My dad was in the Marine Corps for four years, so he knew more than he'd ever tell Mom. It would only have intensified her worry for me while I was over there."

"Melba and Red would always come to the café on Saturday and have lunch. I got a chance to talk with them and catch up on what you were doing." Because they had, at one time, expected her to become their daughter-in-law, but she didn't go there.

Travis shook his head. "Kass, I haven't treated you like you deserved. I stopped emailing you after two years into my military life."

"I know." She shrugged. "Melba told me you got transferred into black ops, that often you couldn't get to a computer or Skype. I got it. I understood it."

He gave her a sad look. "I'm no longer the boy you grew up with, Kass. Combat has changed me forever."

"And is that why you stopped communicating with me?" Years earlier, Kass had felt hurt at being left out of the loop. Melba's explanation had helped her understand why, but not completely. Once more, she felt abandoned, but her love for Travis was so strong it overwhelmed those feelings and kept them in the background of her life.

"I was a bastard to you, Kass. I got into combat and I lost so many of my friends. I was scared and yet, I always wanted to be there for my unit. My world changed and I didn't know how to tell you that. You being a civilian, never seeing what I saw or what I survived, just made me that much more aware of the mountain that had grown up and stood between us."

"You didn't think I'd understand if you shared your experiences with me?"

"No . . . I didn't." Giving her an apologetic look, he said, "Kass, I didn't go into the military thinking all this would happen to me. You and I had a pact with one another when

I left for the Marine Corps. We'd get married when I got settled into my new career."

"But that never happened."

"No," he muttered, "it didn't. I loved you, and I had dreams for us. You and I talked about them often. But getting thrown into black ops upended the world as I knew it. It was so damned different, demanding, and it was always life-and-death surrounding me. I wanted to escape it, but I couldn't."

"It had to be so hard on you, Travis. I can't imagine some of the things you saw and experienced."

"And that's what drove me away from you, Kass. I've had a lot of time to think about what happened and why. And now? Being home a year? Getting away from all that terror and threat environment? I see how much I've changed. I have so much to atone for with you that I don't even know where to start." He reached out, closing his hand over hers, squeezing it gently. "I've hurt the one person I loved the most, in ways that I can't even begin to imagine."

She felt the roughness of his hand on hers, hungrily absorbing it, listening to his explanation. "But you're trying to set things right now, Travis? You said you wanted to be friends with me?"

Nodding, he said, "Yes. If you'll have me as a friend. I turned my back on you years ago, Kass. And it wasn't your fault. It was all on me."

"You left the valley, Travis. You entered an alien world that was so different from how you grew up here with me."

He released her hand, curving it around his mug once more. Voice low and thick, he held her gaze. "You're right. I never looked at it that way. It was alien compared to my life here."

"I want to be your friend, Travis. We have too much of our lives entwined. I'm happy to be there for you."

"You've always been so forgiving, Kass. I never understood why, but you are. You're giving me a second chance with you."

"I was thrown away at birth, Travis. I know what it's like to not be wanted. Even though you disconnected from me after you went into black ops, I never gave up hope on you. Melba and Red always kept me in the loop about you. Even with them, you were out of touch for months at a time. I know they lived for an email or a Skype from you. I got that you were into a very different world than ours. Sometimes, Red would pull me aside and tell me a lot more than he'd tell Melba. He helped me comprehend that combat world you lived within, and I was so grateful to him for doing that for me."

"You never gave up on me, did you?"

"No . . . never. Not then, not now."

He sat up, moving and twisting his shoulders, as if to get rid of so many heavy, invisible burdens he still carried. "I don't deserve your forgiveness, Kass, but I'll take it."

Reaching over, she briefly touched the back of his hand. "There's nothing to forgive. That's the past, Travis. All we have is what is right in front of us. I learned a long time ago to live in the moment. That's all we'll ever have. The past is something we learn from." She smiled a little. "I also like looking at the past when something happy or good happened, too. Heartwarming memories feed me on bad days."

He sat there mulling over her words. Finally, with effort, he said, "You have a heart larger than the state of Wyoming, Kass. I don't think I could do what you're doing. Forgiving me. Wanting to start over."

"I'll take whatever you offer me, Travis. Friendship is a good place to start." She saw his eyes tear up for a moment, and then he swallowed hard, and they were gone. She felt him battling a wave of unexpected emotion that had to be flowing through him. It served to tell Kass just how fragile

Travis really was. He was dealing with deep war wounds, and that was the culprit that had made him excise her out of his life. At least, that was what she intuited. "You're a good person, Travis. You've been caught in a vise called war and you've seen too much, and it's hurt you in ways most of us will never understand or experience. I know that because of the vet ladies who work at my café. They've told me horror stories and later, alone, I've cried for them. It breaks my heart what war does to people. It doesn't matter your gender. It's a terrible wound you live with forever."

"Yes," he said heavily, giving her a glance, "it does change you. I'm glad you've had the ladies there to help you understand at a deeper level what we're all going through."

"You need to trust me, Travis. I can feel you're afraid you're going to somehow hurt me. Is that true?" Kass wasn't going to sugarcoat anything between them. She saw surprise flare in his eyes, and then he became sad looking once more.

"Yeah, that's part of it, Kass. It's not me not trusting you, though."

"Oh?"

"I'm afraid to entrust myself to you." He held up one of his hands. "I've killed a lot of men. I won't ever forget the face of any of them for the rest of my life, Kass. When I close my eyes at night, I see them parading past me, and the firefight I was in when it happened. When I can go to sleep, there's a good chance once or twice a week, I'll get a nightmare about one of those events, and I come up swinging sometimes."

"So you're sleep deprived, Travis. That was one thing my ladies have always wrestled with, too. It's hard to function eight hours a day when you're dragging. It's hard emotionally on you, too."

"Yeah, I get short-tempered. I never used to be like that, but I am now. I'm afraid I'll take my anger or irritation out on you. And you don't deserve that."

"I've had my ladies get short with me. We talk about it after the café closes. There are no secrets among us, Travis. And I'm well aware you're short on sleep. You have shadows beneath your eyes. I'm sure you didn't sleep well last night."

"No, I didn't," he admitted, scowling down at the mug between his hands.

"Look, how can I help around here, Travis? We've got four days together, maybe more, if this blizzard keeps dumping snow on us."

"I just want you to heal up, Kass. You don't need to do anything around here. You've just come out of a level three concussion. You need to rest."

She laughed a little and sat back in the chair, giving him a humored look. "Remember, I run a business. Our café is open at six a.m. and we close at nine p.m. I'm there at five a.m. every day and I leave work at ten p.m. I'm on my feet running all day long. I'm not used to sitting around. I honestly need something to do. I'm a Type A person at heart. If you have something that needs to be done, tell me. I can help."

"Do you feel up to moving around at the speed of light right now, Ms. Type A?"

She loved him for gently teasing her. Kass could see concern in his eyes for her, that she might not be fully healed yet. "Yes. Maybe not the speed of light, but I can putter. I'm not a hundred percent and I admit that. But at least let me do things around here for you. I'll feel better and it's a way of thanking you for taking me in."

"Why don't we trim the tree later this afternoon?"

"Do you have ornaments, Travis?"

He smiled a little. "Yeah, my mom made sure I'd have a

lot of the older ones. You know, the paper ones we made as kids in grade school kind of thing? She kept all of them in boxes, a scrapbook of my growing-up years."

"The past is important in that one sense," Kass said softly. "Those good memories I was talking about earlier? Maybe that's what needs to be done to help you, Travis."

"What's that?"

"Remember our past together? The great times we had as kids and teens growing up?"

He pushed the emptied mug aside. "Sometimes I do. That's not a bad idea you have, Kass. I've been so consumed with combat, with what happened. I need a distraction, maybe. Some of the good things that happened to me in my life to replace the bad ones."

"It's understandable. But maybe remembering some *good* times might help to offset the bad ones a little bit? What do you think? We can talk about our past and what we did together. I found out from my ladies that they were fixated like you were, on all the horrible things that happened to them. I started prodding them and asking about the good things, the happy moments, the laughter they'd had in their lives. It worked. It kind of helped each of them reset their own emotional barometer. It didn't cure them and it didn't stop the flashbacks or nightmares, but they learned when it happened to force the mind and memory onto something good to come up with instead. In many of them it helped shorten their downward spiral, or it lessened the emotional impact on them."

"I'm open to anything. The VA gave me antidepressants and sleep meds. Both of them made me worse. I said to hell with it. I dropped them into the wastebasket and never looked back."

"My ladies had the same reaction to them. There's a physician's assistant in town, Taylor Douglas. She's one

Lindsay McKenna

rung below a medical doctor and she's a specialist in PTSD.
Two of the four of my ladies have gone to her with almost
miraculous results. They had high cortisol, which is what
causes that horrible anxiety everyone gets. She has something called an adaptogen, which once taken for a short
period of time turns off the cortisol that's flowing 24/7 in
your bloodstream. It returns control over that hormone
back to the brain where it belongs. Both my ladies reported
that within three days, Travis, their anxiety was gone."

He stared at her. "Seriously?"

"Yes."

"Has the anxiety come back? How long ago did they
take adaptogen?"

"Let's see . . . Laura took it for only thirty days under
Tayor's guidance. And that was a year ago. She's never had
her anxiety return. Lily took it nine months ago, with the
same result. Mackenzie and Grace have appointments with
Taylor. They've seen how well Laura and Lily are, and they
want the same thing. That anxiety is, as far as I'm concerned, the number one symptom that nearly anyone with
PTSD has to wrestle with. It also stopped their hypervigi-
lance and the feeling they were being stalked by the enemy
to be killed. As Taylor explained it to me? She said the hormone cortisol is there to help us survive situations of
danger and threat. Usually, it turns off after the incident.
But when you're in war and threat is around you for six to
nine months? The cortisol is 'on' all the time because
you're in danger all the time. And then it can't shut off.
The adaptogen puts the Master Gland in your pituitary
back into control and it shuts off the cortisol until or if it
is ever needed again. You have to admit that coming back
into civilian life that we aren't under constant life-and-
death threat. So? The cortisol, according to Taylor, remains

off and no longer flowing into the bloodstream to keep us hypervigilant and anxious."

"I have that very same anxiety," he grumped. "I'd give anything to get rid of it. That's the symptom that keeps me awake at night."

She reached out. "Then when this blizzard is over, give Taylor a call and make an appointment. The adaptogen is very cheap, and Taylor will guide you through it and be checking the lab tests on you within that thirty-day period."

He nodded. "Yeah, that sounds hopeful."

"Laura and Lily both saw a lot of combat, Travis. You're a lot like them in your symptom picture from what you've shared with me."

"Are they married?"

"No. Not yet, at least. I know Laura is sweet on a wrangler, Cody, who works at Maud and Steve Whitcomb's ranch. We're all hoping something blooms between them and we can have a wedding sooner, not later." She smiled. "But Laura is afraid."

"Afraid of what?"

"Afraid she'll be a burden to Cody. She's seen a lot of the marriages of PTSD warriors self-destruct."

"Having this stuff," Travis warned, "does tear a marriage apart, Kass. I've seen it with my buddies who went home after so many deployments. It tore their marriages apart within a year."

"I know," she said. "My ladies all have stories about other women they knew who were also in combat going home and their marriages blowing up in their faces and getting destroyed. It's such a sad thing."

"But this medicine that Taylor has? Do you always have to take it?"

"No, usually not more than once for thirty days. Taylor is monitoring you at all times with lab tests. It does require a medical person to be involved. You can't do this on your own. There's some testing before you take it to see if your cortisol is outside normal bounds. If it is, then she'll probably give you the adaptogen. And once the anxiety leaves you, she'll retest you at the thirty-day time to see if the cortisol is back within normal bounds."

"Is it for Laura and Lily?"

"Laura has a little bit outside normal, but she was in a firefight where her team got overrun. She was one of the few survivors from it. Taylor told her that she'd probably never have 'normal' cortisol levels, but the adaptogen has taken away ninety-five percent of her anxiety. She can live with five percent, believe me."

"That sounds so damned hopeful to me."

"I've seen both ladies change back to who they used to be before combat and PTSD. It doesn't mean they don't still have flashbacks or nightmares, but at least they can sleep at night, they aren't irritable, angry, and hypervigilant like they were before. Now they no longer have these symptoms, and it's changed their entire world." She rubbed her hands together, giving him a sudden grin. "That's what we're all hoping, anyway!"

Giving her a sour look, he said, "I think I'd like to have Taylor's phone number."

"Best holiday gift you could give yourself," Kass told him, rising and going to the other side of the door and lifting her purse from the hook it hung on.

Waiting until she sat down and opened it up, drawing out her cell phone, Travis added, "Once more, you're saving my life, Kass."

She gave him a warm smile. "Don't look at it that way, Travis. I want the boy I grew up with to come back to me. I know he's still in there. I sense it." She quickly got her text up. "Give me your cell phone info and I'll give you Taylor's information."

Travis had his cell phone charging on the kitchen counter. He unplugged it and turned it on. "Okay, give me my new lease on life," he teased, holding her softened green eyes. "I'll do anything to make this anxiety go away permanently."

Chapter Six

The blizzard was amping up in strength and the amount of snow falling was rapidly increasing from where Travis stood by the spruce tree near the window. He'd put on Christmas music that played quietly in the background. If Kass hadn't dropped out of the blue and back into his life, he wouldn't have trimmed the tree at all. It was all he could do to cut it down and bring it in the house. He just didn't have any desire to celebrate anything, even Christmas, anymore. That was how far he'd sunk into his depression.

Kass had come back into his life, and suddenly, he felt the power of hope once more flooding his soul. As he hung a paper ornament carefully on the end of a branch, he was amazed how one person could completely turn his life upside down and inside out in the best of ways. Kass had always been like that for him: a lucky charm, a lifeline, and a life giver. It was just who she was. How could he have let her go?

"Hey," Kass said, pointing to the decoration he was hanging, "isn't that your first dog, Champ?" She had the box of Christmas decorations on the coffee table, gently pulling them out, not wanting to tear or destroy any of the more fragile ornaments.

He hesitated. "Yes, my collie," he said.

She grinned, straightened, and walked over to him. Pushing her hair away from her face, she looked up at the branch. "He was such a beautiful collie, Travis. And so loving. He was your best friend for the first twelve years of your life."

He carefully affixed the decoration dangling on a gold thread, allowing it to hang on its own. Savoring Kass's closeness, her bright, warm spirit, his hands fell to his side. Slanting a glance over at her, he said, "This must be good memory time," he teased, understanding why she'd come over to assist him. Kass was never in a person's face. Rather, for as long as Travis could recall, Kass would quietly ease into a person's space and somehow, in her own gentle, quiet way, get the person to see something they hadn't seen before. He saw her pink lips curve, her eyes shining with laughter.

"Absolutely. Remember how Champ loved to chase that old, raggedy white tennis ball you'd always throw for him?"

He nodded. "Yeah . . . good times. And then I'd toss you the ball and he'd run toward you."

"And then I'd toss the ball back to you." She smiled fondly. "He got an awful lot of exercise that way."

"Sure did."

She looked around. "Have you ever thought of maybe going down to the no kill shelter in Wind River and picking out another doggy companion for yourself? That might give you some company and lift your spirits a bit, Travis."

He desperately wanted to turn and ease his hands around her shoulders and draw Kass close to him. It was eating him alive and now, he was fighting a new battle within himself: to draw Kass as close as he could. "No . . . I honestly hadn't thought about that." He reached out, unable to stop himself, sliding his finger beneath a curl that refused to leave her temple, and guided it behind her delicate ear.

He saw her eyes grow lustrous over his unexpected touch. As if inviting him forward, to touch and explore her some more . . .

There had been a slight hitch in her breath as he'd done it, too. For a moment, Travis froze. And in the next second, he pulled his hand away, wanting her so badly, but so afraid she'd reject him on that more intimate level. Friendship didn't mean going to bed with one another, he sourly reminded himself. And as he took a step away from Kass, bitterness coated his mouth. Travis had no one but himself to blame for the awkwardness now hovering between them. This was his fault. All his fault.

Clearing her throat, Kass took a step back. "Hey, are you ready for another decoration?"

Sensing her sudden nervousness, he nodded. "Sure." He turned to go to the box.

Reaching out, her hand coming to rest on his lower arm, she whispered, "Stay here . . . let me get it for you." Flashing him a small smile, Kass added, "I'm looking for particular decorations from when we were kids."

Her hand felt warm and comforting upon his arm. A shock of pleasure moved up his limb and he felt bereft as her fingers left it. "Sure, go ahead. Find another positive memory for me," he said, trying to sound teasing.

Standing there, watching the way Kass walked, that wonderfully feminine sway of her hips, those long legs, made him burn for her. His mind kept telling him it was too soon to be intimate with her. His heart, however, had a mind of its own, and it was pushing him hard to make more intimate gestures toward Kass, that she would be open to them and desired him as much as he did her. He felt like a man stretched between two opposite ropes, being pulled apart from the inside out.

"Ah!" Kass crowed, a glow in her face. "Here's the one

I was looking for!" Triumphantly, she held it up for Travis to see. "Remember when you made this one? Your first horse? That Appaloosa pony, Spot, that your parents bought for you when you were seven years old?" She brought over the paper decoration, laying it in his opened palm.

"Remember how we sat at your mom and dad's kitchen table with crayons and paper and scissors, drawing this picture, then cutting it out? Your mom was urging you to make a decoration for the tree that you'd always like to look at."

He studied the black pony with a white rump and the huge black spots all over it. "Yeah, I do." Looking into her eyes that danced with such joy, he said, "But you were the one who told me to draw and color Spot for the tree. You knew how important that pony was to me at that time." His mouth curved faintly as he gently touched the cardboard, memories flowing back to him.

"True," she murmured. "I remember how surprised you were when your parents gave Spot to you on your birthday. You'd just had appendicitis surgery three months earlier and been laid low with it. You had to have our teacher, Mrs. Herot, get all your lessons together for you so that you could keep up with them at home. Your mom did home-schooling with you during that time."

"It was tough on me. I was used to running around and then, bam, appendicitis. And it sidelined me but good."

"That was because there was a secondary infection from the surgery," Kass said. "I remember my mom bringing me over to visit you every week."

He warmed to her low, emotional tone. "You have no idea how I looked forward to spending a few hours with you, Kass. You lifted the depression I was feeling then. I missed school, I missed all my friends. You caught me up on what they were doing. You were the only one who came to my house and visited me, though."

Shrugging, she said, "I just put myself in your shoes, Travis. How would I feel if that had happened to me? Not being able to go to school to be with my friends and have fun?"

He hung the horse on a lower branch. "I've never had anyone as loyal as you were, Kass," he murmured. "And it took me a long time to realize the gift you'd given me."

She patted his shoulder. "You were always there for me, Travis. Remember when we were ice-skating on that pond outside my home? I slipped and sprained my ankle and couldn't walk. You were twelve, and you picked me up in your arms and you carried me back to my house all the way down that snow-covered path without dropping me."

"You were a lightweight," he teased, smiling fully. "And you were wriggling around, kept telling me not to let you fall."

"Well, you were weaving around with me. What was I to think?"

Chuckling, he said, "You probably were thinking I'd drop you and break one of your legs."

Kass wrinkled her nose. "No, I wasn't. I was clinging to you, my arms around your neck so tight, you probably felt like I was choking the air out of you."

"That's okay. We both survived."

"That was a nice day," Kass sighed, going back to the box on the coffee table. "You stayed with me. My mom put a package of frozen peas over the ankle and the swelling went down a lot. You and Dad went out to the kitchen, and he made us both a cup of hot chocolate."

So many good memories. Shaking his head, Travis said quietly, "I've got to be the lamest-brained cowpoke in the county, Kass."

Looking up, she said, "Why?"

"Just talking about these times makes my anxiety reduce a lot. It's never done that before."

"Maybe because you have some human company?" she wondered, bringing over a picture of his parents that he'd made and then glued a red ribbon around for a frame. "It can get awful lonely out here, Travis. Don't you get lonely?" She searched his eyes as she handed the picture to him.

Just the soft touch of her fingertips brushing his palm sent wild tingles up into his wrist and lower arm. "Yeah," he admitted, "I get lonely, Kass."

She stood back, her hands clasped in front of her, watching him as he placed the framed picture up near the top of the tree. "I wish you hadn't put me off-limits to seeing you. I might have been able to help you."

His mouth quirked. Placing the framed picture on the tree, he shook his head. "I wasn't in the right space when I got out, Kass. I wasn't thinking straight at all. At that time, I felt like a wounded animal, and all I wanted to do was crawl in a hole and pull it in after me." He saw sadness come to her eyes. Her mouth was so delicious looking. She wore no makeup because she had none on her. Kass had always had natural beauty that he preferred.

She stood there, holding his gaze. "I'm glad you're in a different space now. Does this mean you might drop into my café from time to time?"

"I'd like that, Kass. I guess by having you here it's making me aware that I've hidden too much."

"You like my company, huh?" She grinned playfully, turning and going back to the box.

She was always elfin, challenging him, but not in a bad way. He smiled a little. "Yeah, I do like your company. I'm not happy about how it happened, but I'm glad you're here, Kass. I really am." Travis saw her lift her head, a tender expression coming to her face as she held several decorations between her hands. "I hope," he added, "that you feel the same. Or do you wish you were home?"

"No, I like right where I am. My mom knows I'm okay,

and everything will be fine at the café while I'm on vacay here. Talking to her yesterday evening made her relax." She lifted up two decorations. "Which one next?"

"How about Tommy, the cat we had?"

"Good choice." Sighing, she gave the yellow cat with the darker stripes of buff color across his back. "For being a tomcat? He just loved you." She walked over and placed it in his hand. "Tommy adored you," she said. "Whenever you came home after school, that cat was sitting on the porch, waiting for you."

"I remember." He hung the cat decoration between Spot, his horse, and the one above it, the framed picture. "I think he thought I was a cat in disguise." Turning, he saw Kass smile gently.

"I think Tommy thought you were an odd-looking two-legged son of his." She chuckled.

"He lived to be sixteen. I was in the military and Mom had to email me and tell me that he'd died."

She gazed up at the cat ornament. "I always liked Tommy."

"He loved you as well as me," Travis said, giving her a warm glance. "Any time you came over, he was in your lap or purring around your legs, telling you hello, that he liked you."

"I loved him, too. I love all things."

"You have a huge heart," Travis agreed. "Tell me something. What do you want for Christmas?" He saw her cheeks redden a bit.

"It's a silly thing," she said, waving her hand as she walked to the box.

Travis followed her. He sat down, watching her move her long fingers delicately through the box, sifting through the fragile paper decorations. Having no right, but his body responding anyway, he wondered what it would feel like to have Kass's fingers trailing all over his naked body as they made love with one another. Swallowing hard, he forced himself to stop going in that direction. "Tell me," he urged. "No present is silly."

"You'll probably laugh," she said, sitting near him, the ornaments in her hands. "My mom's grandmother, who died when I was very young, has a broken rocker. I was trying to find someone to fix it, but it's a very old rocker and the people who could fix it didn't want to try and find the right replacement parts for it. They said that it would take an antique wood specialist to carve another one for it, match the color of the wood and all that stuff."

"Then this isn't a gift for you, but for your mom?" How like Kass. She never thought of herself; she always thought of others first. Travis wondered if that was because she was an orphan. Since she had no one, anyone who would want her would become more important in her life than herself. He said nothing, but this was something he hoped to discuss with her later because he wanted to understand her drive on a deeper level.

"Yes, for my mom. She cried when it broke. She rocked me every day in it after they adopted me. And when I was older, maybe three, she would rock me in it nearly every night, reading me a story. I loved those times with her. I love that beat-up old rocker."

"Maybe I could do some work on it for her? I work almost entirely with eighteenth- and nineteenth-century designs. Everyone wants a replica from that period, it seems. Would you let me take a look at it?" He saw her face light up, hope suddenly spring to her eyes.

"Seriously? You would?"

"Sure. When 89 is cleared off after this blizzard and we get a wrecker in here to take your car out of the ditch, I can drive you home. Maybe we could stop at your folks' home and I can check it out? Do you think your mom would mind?"

"I'd love that! Oh! This is a wonderful idea, Travis, because your woodwork and the furniture in your studio is so beautiful."

He felt heat, need, and his heart opening beneath her sudden joy. "Okay," he said, "we'll do that. In the meantime, do you have a rocking chair in your home?"

"No, but I've always wanted one. However, I don't want a modern-day rocker, Travis. I want an old one like my mom has." She gave a shy shrug. "I guess . . . well, I guess it's because it reminds me of all the love, holding and kisses she would always give me when she was rocking me after feeding me a bottle, or later, she'd read from a book, finish a chapter, and then tuck me into bed. That rocker holds so many wonderful memories of nights with her. My dad would read to me at night, too. They took turns, but both came in to kiss me good night afterward."

"Those are nice memories," he agreed in a low tone, touched deeply by her reaction. She had no family hand-me-downs from earlier generations. That pained him in another way. His folks had hundred-year-old furniture pieces that he loved to this day and the provenance, or stories, that they held was meaningful to all of them. It was like having their family with them, even though they had passed on.

Kass had no such things in her life. She had to be lonely in a way he couldn't begin to fathom. The loss in her eyes was telling, even though she was trying to keep a light tone. Travis knew her too well, and dammit, he wanted to do something to ease her terrible losses.

"Would you," she ventured hesitantly, "come and have Christmas breakfast with me and my folks? It will only be us." She gave him a pleading look.

"My parents have already asked me for Christmas Eve dinner, Kass."

"But this would be Christmas morning. Mom makes her and me a wonderful breakfast and then we all open our gifts. My dad died a decade ago of a heart attack. I know Red and Melba told you about it. If you can find an arm for that rocker, wouldn't you like to be there to see my mom's face? I know she'll be so surprised and grateful. Please say yes, Travis? It would mean so much to me." She pressed her hand against her heart.

His chest exploded with such a fierce love for Kass in that moment, he couldn't speak. Travis was afraid she'd take his hesitation as a negative. He gave a nod of his head. Gulping, he rasped, "Yes, they told me of your dad's passing, and I'm sorry you lost him. And yes, I'd like to do that, Kass. I'm sure I can find the right arm to fix Jade's rocker."

"Oh, thank you!" She leaped up and bent over him, throwing her arms around his shoulders, squeezing the daylights out of him.

Travis managed a partial laugh, slid his arms around her shoulders, and gently squeezed her. "You're welcome," he said in a gravelly tone, his face pressed against the cool silk of her hair.

Chapter Seven

Travis put the finishing touches on Jade Murphy's antique rocker. The sun was shining brightly through the double-paned windows at the other end of his studio, making the hickory wood glow gold beneath his final polish of the new arm he'd installed to fix the rocker.

Kass's mother had a 1775 Windsor rocking chair, bought in Philadelphia a year before the Declaration of Independence.

He had placed a tarp beneath the rocker, kneeling beside it, sliding his fingers lightly along the curved and polished wood. Kass had thought that he could buy a new arm for Jade's rocker. What she didn't realize was that there was nothing available in the design of the rocker arm. He'd spent a day finding the right color of hickory and then creating and shaping the new one for it, and then installing it.

Pleased with the satiny finish of the wood beneath his fingers, he stood and picked up the rocker, taking it directly into full sunlight near the huge window. Outdoors, the landscape was nothing but blindingly white, glistening snow.

The deciduous trees were barren and naked, the evergreens coated heavily with white. The sky was so blue that it hurt a person's eyes to look up at it for any length of time. If they were lucky, they might even get sunshine over the Christmas holiday, which would be rare but mightily welcomed in this part of Wyoming.

Setting the rocker down in the light, he moved it slowly around at different angles, making sure the new rocker arm exactly matched the color of the rest of the wood on the antique rocker. It did. Satisfaction moved through him. This had been a labor of love. And he was glad to do it. Yes, this rocker meant the world to Kass. And he wanted to give her the world.

Setting it aside, Travis wiped it down one last time with a clean cloth that had some lemon oil on it. The citrusy scent wafted and mingled with the fragrance of the different woods that permeated this place where he loved to work. He wondered if Jade or Kass knew how much a chair like this would bring on the auction block. Antique buyers would easily spend ten thousand dollars to purchase such a rocker. *Probably more.*

This piece had been handed down through Marshall Murphy's family from 1775 onward to the present. Kass's father was given the rocker by his mother when he married Jade at age twenty-two.

Travis had seen the eagerness in Kass's eyes when she realized it was possible for him to fix the beautiful antique for her mother. The grateful smile she gave him when he said he would repair the rocker still burned like warm, glowing coals in his heart.

God knew, he wanted to *give* Kass the world. As he finished up the oiling, he straightened and threw the cloth into a basket that would eventually find its way to the washer.

Kass was always on his mind. When Route 89 was

navigable once more, five days after the blizzard started, he'd driven her to Jade's home. There, he met Kass's warm, outgoing mother. Jade showed him the broken rocker, pain in her expression over its need for repair. Carefully examining it, Travis told her he was sure he could fix it like new for her. That he'd bring it over to her on Christmas morning when he had breakfast with them. Jade was thrilled. Kass beamed and she gave him such a proud look, his heart expanded until it felt like it would burst inside his chest.

The skin on his cheek tingled in memory of the light kiss that Kass had given him after he'd loaded the rocker in the back of his van that he used to transport furniture, covered it with a tarp, and tied it down so it wouldn't fall over and incur more damage. Long ago, he'd installed special straps and connectors on the vehicle to take his furniture safely to the buyer after he'd made it.

Not expecting that kiss, Kass had pushed up on her toes, rested her hands against his shoulders, and kissed his cheek, murmuring an emotional thank-you for doing this for her mother. It had happened so quickly, Travis didn't have time to react. He'd inhaled the scent of her hair, the strands smelling faintly of oranges. His skin tightened beneath his clothing where Kass had placed her hands lightly against his shirt. To say his body erupted into a five alarm fire was an understatement. She'd kissed him shyly and he could see she wasn't sure he'd like her doing that to him.

He did like it. A little too much, maybe. Travis had enough wits about him to say, "Can I get another kiss from you on Christmas morning, too?" He'd seen Kass's eyes shine with joy, the curve of those wonderful, sweet lips of hers blossoming in answer, that he wanted to grab and kiss her breathless right there on the spot. A real kiss on her mouth, not on her cheek, either. One that would make her sag against him because her knees had buckled from the sensuality of his mouth moving, coaxing, and capturing her lips hungrily against his.

For the last few weeks since he'd taken Kass home, he'd been restless, wandering through the silent cabin, wishing she was still there to keep him company. Hungering for her thoughts, her keen intelligence, how she saw him and the world around her, he pined for her company. Twice, he'd driven his Dodge Ram truck the twenty-mile trip into Wind River to see her at her café. He'd had coffee at the counter and had ordered a piece of her homemade cherry pie. Travis hadn't really tasted the food. He'd come to connect with Kass. He'd managed to have a few off-and-on conversations with her, but she was flying around the busy place taking orders, delivering food, or working back in the kitchen. Her café was the most popular one in town and where all the locals ate, because locals knew where the good food was served. He had got to meet a number of the vet waitresses, all heroines in his estimation. He'd never seen waitresses as happy as these but he knew why. Kassie had listened to them, absorbed their wounds and done something positive and healing for them. They all loved her and that was obvious in every way.

Travis had wanted to ask her out and take her away from the hubbub of the restaurant for a while. He was too much of a coward to ask her, afraid of being rebuffed. Why had Kassie kissed his cheek? Was it just a peck that was impersonal, a sweet thank-you for him agreeing to fix her mother's rocker and that was all? He ached to ask her, but the café was so busy it was impossible to get some focused, quiet time with her.

Best of all, he'd seen her joy when he'd walked into the café those two times. It had taken everything not to open his arms to Kass and kiss her senseless right in front of eighty or so patrons. *Not yet. Probably never.* But he hoped, just the same, that the silent, intimate look of welcome she'd given him each time was the look of a woman who loved her man and was glad to see him once again. Kass had unearthed the love he'd always held for her in those five days she'd recovered at his cabin. She had triggered hope in him once again, whether he deserved it or not.

She had magically turned his dreary gray life into something magical. He got up every day and looked forward to seeing her when he left his bedroom. He imagined her out in the kitchen busily whipping up an omelet, frying bacon, or making pancakes for them. Kass was a whirlwind of activity, but she'd always been like that.

By the fifth day, the snowplows had reopened Route 89, and vehicles could once more come and go. He'd seen how sad she'd become because she had to leave him. He was sad, too, but had said nothing. That old rocking chair of Jade's was a lifeline between them right now, and he was glad to repair it for her mom, who was well respected by everyone in the valley.

As he placed the repaired rocker aside at the other end of his studio, he covered it gently with a light tarp. Tomorrow afternoon, he looked forward to Christmas Eve dinner and opening presents with his parents in Wind River. They had always opened gifts the evening before, not on Christmas morning. Walking over to a Chippendale dresser he'd made for his mother, he ran his hand lightly across the glowing waxed surface.

Travis had painstakingly done thorough research on the Chippendale style, and then it had taken him six months to find the right wood, cherry, and then to hand hone and create a copy of a dresser he found online. He'd even mimicked the dovetails that held the drawers together. His mother would love it because she'd always appreciated the grace and beauty of Chippendale furniture, but it was so expensive no one could afford it in their hardworking middle-class family.

Tomorrow he'd place it in his van, and he could hardly wait to see her face. He'd already called his dad, who was going to meet him outside, and they'd carry it into their bedroom. All the while, his mother had to sit in the living room, on the couch, her eyes closed, and wait for the gift to arrive.

Kass had seen the piece, and he'd told her the story about it. She suggested buying some red or green ribbon, making a big bow out of it, and setting it on top of the dresser for his mother. The second time he'd met her at her café, he'd done just that. He'd walked down the wooden sidewalk, rows of stores tightly packed together, and dropped into Charlie Becker's Hay and Feed store.

It was decorated with Christmas trim, a well-decorated tree in the corner, and Pixie's homemade sugar cookies on a huge red platter for all to eat at the counter. Charlie's wife's baking ability made Pixie the queen of the small town. Everyone dropped into the feed store whether they needed anything or not. Pixie was always making cookies, cinnamon rolls, blondies, brownies, and other goodies that she stashed in the back on the coffee service table or put up on the front counter where everyone could come in and get some free bakery goods.

That was one of the many reasons Travis had wanted to come home. He'd grown up here, and as a kid, he used to run over to the feed store, race inside the door, and Charlie would invite him to take one cookie. Kids had a habit of grabbing as many as their little hands could hold, and he'd trained them all to leave some for others. Travis liked the morals and values visible in the valley.

And there, in Charlie's store, he'd found a bin full of bows of different sizes and colors, so it was his lucky day. He'd bought some and then took one of those highly decorated sugar cookies from the platter next to Charlie's cash register.

And having Kass once more in his life? Well, that was an unexpected Christmas gift to his heart, whether she knew it or not. He could hardly wait to see her on Christmas morning.

December 25

Kass couldn't remain still. She checked herself once more in the mirror. It was nearly nine a.m. Travis was to arrive any minute now. Her mother was out in the kitchen putting the final touches on their holiday breakfast.

Smoothing her hands nervously down her nubby dark green velvet slacks, she nervously fiddled with the crisp white cotton blouse that had long sleeves with feminine ruffles around each cuff. Her hair was freshly washed and dried, the shining ebony strands loose and free. Grabbing the hip-long vest from the back of the chair, she pulled it on and tidied the collar, which had lace around the edges of it. Jade had knitted that bright red vest for her years earlier, a Christmas gift, and she loved it. Her mother had given her a set of round gold earrings last Christmas, which she put on. Her heart beat in anticipation of Travis coming to their home. How she'd longed for this morning to come! Would he like the gift she'd made for him? They hadn't talked about exchanging Christmas gifts, but Kass wanted to make something for Travis anyway.

The doorbell rang.

She started. *Oh!* Giving herself one last look, she saw her pink lipstick was in place. Her cheeks were naturally ruddy. Turning, she hurried down the hall.

"I'll answer it, Mom!" she called.

"Okay, honey."

Their old oak door had a large glass in a cathedral shape on the top third of it and she spotted Travis standing patiently. He wore his black Stetson hat and a warm sheepskin coat with the collar drawn up. How handsome he looked! Her heart swelled with such love for this man that she could barely contain herself. When she pulled open the door, she smiled up at him. In his left arm he had a Christmas bouquet of flowers, red and white roses.

"Hey," he said, "you look beautiful, Kass."

Heat spread from her neck to her face as she stepped aside, allowing him into the mudroom area. "Thanks."

"Here, these are for your mother," he said, transferring the large bouquet into her hands. "I didn't want to show up without something to thank Jade for all the trouble she's gone to for me," he said, removing his hat and wiping his feet on the bristly rug just inside the door.

"These are beautiful," she said, shutting the door behind him. "I know she'll love them! Come on in. You can hang your hat and stuff on those hooks." She gestured toward the wall.

"Something sure smells good."

"Mom's making her famous French toast. She puts peanut butter on them after they're done and she has Kahlua syrup to drizzle over them. They're delicious. Come on in." She touched his forearm. Travis was dressed in a pair of charcoal gray chinos and a bright red long-sleeved flannel shirt with a black leather vest over it. In her eyes, he looked more than handsome.

"Never had that combo before," he said, hanging up his coat and hat.

"You'll love it," Kass assured him. Impulsively, she approached him as he turned, placing her hand on his broad shoulder and looking up at him. This time, he seemed to be expecting that kiss she'd promised him a few weeks ago. The look in his eyes, a man focused solely on her, the heat she saw burning in them, his raw need of her, all conspired to make her heart race.

Travis cupped her shoulders, aware that the flower bouquet was between them, and he leaned down, brushing her mouth with a kiss. Glorying in his scent, surrounded by that evergreen fragrance, the icy cold temperature outside, Kass closed her eyes, relishing his mouth moving tenderly across hers with invitation. His fingers tightened a little on her shoulders as their mouths clung hungrily to one another, silently coaxing her full participation in their mutual joy.

All her senses melted as his mouth slid and cajoled and took hers with gentle command, making her heart thunder in response. As Travis deepened that wonderful soul-infusing kiss, she returned it with equal fervor, matching his need of her.

Lost in his male fragrance, his large hand monitoring how much pressure he put upon her shoulder, their ragged breaths mingling and moist, a soft sound rose in her throat, a sound of utter satisfaction and celebration. At last! They were really kissing one another! Dazed as he reluctantly left her wet lips, her lashes barely lifting, Kass burned in the narrowed look he gave her. He moved his hands across her shoulders, caressing her, letting her know he wanted to share so much more with her. And so did she. Kass stepped back, lamenting his hands releasing her. Her whole body was humming with need, the throbbing heat increasing in her lower body.

"Wow," she murmured, giving him an awed look, "that kiss is a gift of its own, Travis Grant." She saw his cheeks grow ruddy and realized that he was just as moved and shaken as she was.

"I didn't want to kiss your cheek," he admitted wryly, moving toward her, slipping his hand to the small of her back, turning and leading her out into the spacious living room area.

"I didn't either," she admitted, her voice husky, catching the surprised look in his eyes but seeing pleasure burning in them, too. As she led him toward the open concept kitchen on the other side of the living room, she added, "And I liked what we shared back there, Travis. A lot." Again, she saw him color and wondered why. Didn't he know by now how much she liked him? Loved him? That the love she held for him had never died? And then she saw that faint curve of one corner of his mouth, his hand lightly caressing her back in response to her words.

"You're a gift to me, Kass. I like what we share."

"I like being your gift, Travis. But you're mine, too. Don't you ever forget that. You may not be wearing a red ribbon on your head, but you are all of that to me."

Travis gave her a cocky smile. "Yeah?"

"Oh, yeah," Kass murmured, her lips lifting. "We'll talk more later. I want you to give my mom the flowers. She'll love that you thought of her like this."

He took the bouquet and nodded.

Only last week while sitting with Maud Whitcomb in one of the booths at her café did Kass find out that Travis was not only famous in the world of high-class furniture making but was considered one of the finest up-and-coming young furniture craftsmen in America. In one year! That amazed Kass, but she wasn't surprised. Travis had always been a person who worked hard, was responsible, paid attention to details, and finished what he started. He took great care and pride in everything he ever did.

Maud had told her that he was probably one of a handful of people in the valley who was making a very, very good living moneywise. It was well known their valley had more people below the poverty level than almost any other county in Wyoming.

Looking at the bouquet of winter flowers, the size of it, Kass believed it. She knew flowers very well, and the bouquet had huge white and red roses, deep purple linanthus with lavender-colored Viburnum berries. The silvery-green sage was tastefully scattered throughout it, emphasizing the beauty of all the various flowers together, along with small, silver flowers here and there, and made of the metal. Even the silver foil around the flowers, tied off with a bright red bow, shouted of being very expensive.

She knew of only one place, fifty miles away, up in Jackson Hole, where such a florist would have something this rare and beautiful for sale at this time of year. Travis had spared no expense on it, and a fierce love for him giving her mother such a stunning bouquet made her want to cry. Swallowing several times, she choked back the tears. He was a hero in her heart.

More than anything, Kass was glad for Travis because she knew he came from a middle-class family who worked hard every day of their lives. It was nice to see Travis break through that glass ceiling of sorts and be paid well for his master carpentry skills. But now he was sharing his hard-earned money in the form of this incredible bouquet. She saw her mother turn, her eyes going wide, as Travis stopped in front of her, offering her the bouquet.

"For you, Mrs. Murphy. Merry Christmas."

For a moment, Kass wasn't sure if her mother was going to faint or not. She stepped around Travis and came to Jade's side, her arm going around her waist to steady her—just in case.

"Oh . . ." Jade whispered, handling the bouquet as if it

were fragile glass, "these are so beautiful, Travis. And call me Jade, please."

He smiled a little, rocking back on his heels, hands jammed into his pockets. "Yes, ma'am . . . I mean, Jade."

"These are stunning," she whispered. Touching some of the fragrant blooms, she added, "Where on earth did you get something like this, Travis? I've just never seen anything like this. Not ever. Not around here, at least."

He gave a shy shrug. "Well . . . er . . . I drove up to Jackson Hole. There's a wedding florist up there. I made her a piece of furniture earlier this year and I saw how pretty her flowers were. I went to her, told her about you, and she put this together. When I told her your name was Jade, she went over to another canister and brought the silver sage back." He hesitantly pulled a hand out of his pocket, pointing at the sage in the bouquet. "I think it looks real pretty. I could never put a bouquet like that together to save my life." He grinned unevenly.

"This is just the most beautiful bunch of flowers I've *ever* been given!" Jade gushed, showing them to Kass. "Aren't they lovely?" she asked her daughter.

"Very," Kass murmured, leaning over, smelling the flowers. "Mmmm, they smell so good. Try it, Mom."

Jade nestled her face into the flowers and inhaled.

Kass gave Travis a look of thanks and smiled. Her heart took off as he smiled back. She could tell he was nervous that maybe Jade wouldn't like the flowers, but she loved them. "Mom? How about I go find the right size of vase for them? I'll put them on the table and we can admire them as we have breakfast together."

"That would be wonderful, honey, thank you." She gently set the bouquet in Kass's awaiting hands. Then she stepped forward and threw her arms around Travis's shoulders, squeezing the daylights out of him.

Kass saw the surprise and then the joy in his face as her mother hugged him hard. His arms came forward and he gently hugged her in return.

"You're welcome," he managed, his voice off key as they separated.

Jade shook her head. "And you've fixed my rocker, too? I get this wonderful bouquet *and* my rocker back all in one day?"

He gave her a bashful grin. "Yes, you do. It is Christmas, after all."

Chapter Eight

Kass stood back as Travis carried out her mother's rocker. He'd thoughtfully placed a big floppy red bow on top of it, giving it a Christmassy look. She saw her mother's face glow with delight as he brought it over and set it in the place where it had been for as long as she could remember.

Jade moved her work-worn hands reverently across the top of the rocker and then one hand on each arm. She murmured with delight, pleased, and Travis colored as he stood nearby. Plainly nervous, Kass could see the anxiety in his eyes as her mother moved her hands over her beloved rocker. She knew how badly he wanted to please her. Jade turned and again hugged the daylights out of Travis. He turned a deeper red in the cheeks, but there was a look of relief in his face, too. Kass grinned. This was good for Travis to be encircled by loving women.

She stood near the tree. "I have a small gift for you, Travis," she called as Jade finished hugging him and led him toward the tree.

"Oh?"

Smiling, Kass heard the surprise in his voice. She leaned down and retrieved the package that had a silver bow on it and placed it in his hands. "It's not on the scale of Mom's rocker looking like new, but I thought you might be able to use this." Her fingers touched his, and never had she felt so happy as she did making contact with him once more. She saw his Adam's apple bob and felt his emotions rising even though he tried to appear cool and calm as he carefully held the bulky gift between his hands.

"Sit on the couch, Travis," Jade invited. "Kass worked hard on that gift she's giving you. I'll go make us some fresh coffee and we'll chat a bit after you open it up."

Taking her suggestion, Travis looked over at Kass, "Only if you sit with me while I open it."

"Wouldn't have it any other way. Come on."

In moments, they'd sat down. Travis placed the lumpy gift on his lap. "What is it?" he coaxed her, pulling off the ribbon.

Snorting, Kass said, "Open and find out, big guy." She warmed beneath his shy grin.

"I didn't expect this, Kass. You shouldn't have. You work so hard anyway. I don't know how you could find time."

Shrugging, she said, "I'd do it on breaks at the café. No worries." A thread of anxiety moved through her. Would Travis like her gift? He tore off the paper, revealing the dark blue knit scarf. His hand stilled over it and she saw satisfaction come to his expression. He picked it up, feeling the weight and softness of the yarn.

"How did you know my old muffler was wearing out?"

"No secret to that one. In the five days I spent with you, I saw you wear it a lot. There were holes in it. It was worn out, Travis." She gestured to the gift. "I measured it one afternoon when you were out in the studio, and this one is the same width and length as your old one."

Nodding, he said, "This is the perfect gift for me, Kass. I like ones that you can use, that are practical." He set it on his lap, lifted his right hand, and pulled her gently toward him. "Thank you," he rasped, and then kissed her gently on the mouth.

Kass had closed her eyes, not expecting his kiss, but it served to once more show his thoughtfulness. A perfect rejoinder to the happiness she'd seen in his eyes. Travis understood how busy she was and that she'd taken the time from her own demanding schedule to think of him. As their mouths left one another, she whispered, "Thank you . . . that's the best gift I could have ever received from you." She didn't want him to remove his hand, but he did. Her mother was in the kitchen and he was being circumspect because he was in her house. Kass was pretty sure that her mother knew how much she loved Travis. She'd told her mother about spending those five days at the cabin with Travis. Kass didn't swerve from telling her the truth: He brought her joy, rekindling the fires of her love for him to bright, burning life.

Travis set the scarf aside and stood up. "Do me a favor?"

"Sure. What?"

"Just sit there for a moment? Close your eyes. I have a gift for you, too."

"Really?" Kass gasped, staring at him. He gave her such a confident male smile that she burst out laughing. "You sneak! You had a gift for me all along? Why didn't you tell me?"

"Because," he said, "I wanted to surprise you. Now, just sit there and I'll be back in a minute."

Kass could barely sit still. She heard her mother come into the living room. Setting the tray down, she placed steaming mugs of coffee on the coffee table in front of the couch.

"Close your eyes, Kass," she chided, smiling as she straightened.

"Oh . . . right." She quickly scrunched them closed.

When Travis returned to the room, her mother made a sound of surprise and pleasure.

"Oh, Kass!" Jade whispered. "Oh, oh this is such a beautiful gift, Travis!"

Kass *almost* opened her eyes. She knotted her hands in her lap, sitting straight up, barely able to remain still. *What* was it?

"Okay," Travis said, "Merry Christmas, Kass. You can open your eyes now."

He stood back, watching Kass's face as she saw the Windsor rocker with a huge red and green bow atop the rail. She gasped and shot to her feet, her hands flying to her opened mouth, eyes huge with shock.

For a moment, he wasn't sure what she was going to do: yell, scream, cry, or maybe do all three. Huge tears formed in her eyes as she stared at the beautiful rocker.

"Where," she managed to croak, forcing herself to move around the coffee table to where the rocker sat in the center of the room.

"It's English oak. About twenty feet of the tree was found in a bog in England. The color is black because it's been buried in that peat bog for thousands of years. I traded some South American wood a carpenter friend of mine wanted. He was the one that found this bog oak. It's very, very rare wood."

Kass reached out as if dazed, her fingertips barely gliding across the shining black wood. "H-how did you know, Travis?" And then she choked, tears running down her face. Turning, she stared at him, at a loss for words, the tension swirling powerfully between them.

"Remember our conversation about Jade's rocker at the cabin? That you had daydreams about having a Windsor rocker just like hers? And when you had a baby, you said you wanted to rock her or him in your own special rocker, just as Jade rocked you in hers." His throat tightened.

"I wanted to make part of your dream come true for you, Kass. I know you love the color black, so after you left, I made a call to my friend in England." He made a weak gesture toward the shining ebony rocker. "I wanted to give you a gift filled with hope because that's what you've done for me when you were with me those five days. You made me realize I was living half a life until you got dropped in on me."

Kass turned, opening her arms, flying into his embrace. She made a soft, sobbing sound, arms tightening around him, her head nestled beneath his chin.

Stunned by her move, Travis saw Jade's face crumple with tears of happiness, her hands clasped between her breasts. How badly he wanted to hold Kass tightly, hold her forever. Leaning down, he pressed several small kisses to her soft, silky hair. "It's all right, Kass . . . it's all right . . ." he said, his voice going low with emotion, feeling her shake, feeling her arms so tight around him, making him so damned happy he didn't know what to do. He held Kass, rocking her a little in his arms, and she finally stopped crying and eased away from him just enough to look up into his eyes. Her gaze was dark green with dappled gold in their depths that took his breath away.

"Thank you," she quavered, lifting her hand, grazing her fingertips against his cheek and jawline. "You gave me a future gift."

Travis had no idea what she meant by a "future" gift. He managed an unsure smile, sliding his hand across her shining mass of black hair. "It can be whatever you want it to be, Kass. It will last as long as you live and then some. Maybe you can pass it on to the next generation." He lifted his head, looking toward Jade's rocker near the tree. "It will easily outlast your mother's rocker. Being nearly fossilized, the wood isn't going to wear out or wear down."

"My forever rocker," Kass murmured, cupping his cheek.

She leaned up, brushing his mouth with a kiss. "This is the first morning of the rest of my life," she said in a rasp.

"Come home and stay with me," Kass entreated Travis after she said good-bye to her mother and they left for the day, taking the stairs down the sidewalk. He was holding her hand and it felt so good. Already, Travis had placed the bog oak rocker into his van and tied it down to take it to her house.

Travis nearly missed a step when she'd asked him that. Sliding his hand beneath her, he slowed, holding her up-turned gaze. "How do you mean that, Kass? Do you want me to stay and have dinner with you tonight?"

"No. I mean stay with me until tomorrow morning. Until I have to leave for work."

Travis halted and stared at her. He tightened his grip around her elbow just slightly. "You sure about this?"

"Never more sure." She saw his lips twitch, that hunger mixed with amusement come to his eyes as he considered her bold request.

"Am I going to be your Christmas gift?" he teased, giving her a playful look.

"Oh yes. And I'm going to be yours, too. It's time, Travis. How long have we waited? How many years? Aren't you tired of waiting? I am."

He resumed walking her to her pickup on the other side of where his van was parked. "I came to that conclusion a few weeks ago. I was damned lonely, Kass. I have never felt as bereft as after you left. I felt like I was living half a life again."

"Me too." She halted at her car. "Follow me home?"

Opening the door for her, he said, "I'll follow you any-where you want to go from now on."

It took all of ten minutes for Kass to drive to the south

end of Wind River and turn into her icy driveway. Her small twelve-hundred-square-foot white home with dark green shutters had its roof still spotted with lingering patches of snow. There was a two-car garage, and she hit the door opener and then drove in. It was wide enough for Travis and his van.

Her heart was pounding with anticipation. She was shaken by the gift he'd given her. She'd expected nothing and yet, he'd given her something so utterly meaningful to her that it felt like an avalanche of fierce love.

Or maybe a wall that had stood between them for all those years had finally tumbled down, leaving an opening in her heart to love Travis with all of herself in every way. That was what Kass wanted. This was a magical day and she'd surprised herself at her boldness with him, letting him know in no uncertain terms that she was ready for him to walk back into her life. Forever, if she had anything to say about it. All she needed to hear from him was that he wanted the same thing she wanted: a forever relationship between the two of them.

The sunlight was in the south, the rays bright, but the day was below freezing, so Kass didn't feel any warmth from it. She opened the door to her home and Travis carefully eased the ebony rocker inside. Leading him through the kitchen, she guided him to the open concept living room.

"I think the rocker would look nice in that corner," she said, pointing to near where the decorated Christmas tree stood. It wasn't a very tall one, just about four feet in height, but she'd lovingly decorated it last week. There was no way Kass was ever going to miss this wonderful holiday. She watched Travis nod and then gently place it nearby. "It looks perfect there," she murmured, meeting his gaze, feeling his need of her in every possible way.

Holding out her hand, she whispered, "Come with me? Come sit down? We need to lay our cards out on the table for one another, Travis." She saw him give her an intense look and then he came forward, pulling her hand into his.

"Yes, we need to talk first," he agreed.

Kass curled up in the corner of the couch, her legs tucked beneath her. Travis sat such that her knees rested upon his hard, curved thigh. He reached behind her shoulders, his arm settling around them, drawing her close to him. It felt wonderful to cuddle with him, as if she were in some kind of unfolding dream that would never end.

Sighing, she laid her head on his broad shoulder, sliding her arm around his torso. "I never stopped loving you, Travis," she began in a low voice fraught with feeling. "After you left for the Marine Corps, I ached with grief and loss. And over time, I began to realize when you left our valley, you left me for good, too."

He made an inarticulate sound, drawing her more deeply against him. "That isn't true, Kass. It isn't . . ."

"Shhh, let me finish, all right? You need to know where I was at. How I felt about you being gone." She rolled her head just enough to catch the anguish in his eyes as he stared down at her. "I finally let you go, Travis, because it was obvious to me the relationship we'd had as children, teens, was over. I grieved a lot, but the funny thing? My heart just wouldn't give you up and let you go. And although I met some nice guys, none of them stacked up to you, who you were, your kindness and unselfishness that you gave me. They just weren't you." She sat up and turned, holding his sorrowful gaze. "And then when I heard through the grapevine that you'd come home, I was overwhelmed with joy. I got up my nerve to go see you, to really find out if it was finished between us." Turning away, her voice halting, she forced out, "And when I did? You told me to leave, that there was nothing between us. I felt as if you'd plunged a sword through my heart."

Travis winced but held her gaze, his mouth tight and tense.

"And then, this crazy, unforeseen accident," she said, shaking her head. "Crazy. But good. When I realized it was you, my heart dropped to my feet. I knew you didn't want to see me ever again, Travis. But your voice filled with so much care and urgency, the way you cared for me said something completely different. I was shaken and my brain was addled, and maybe that was good because I got to see the real you and how much you honestly cared for me even though you'd never admit it."

Opening her hand, she placed it over his heart. "Those five days were a gift for me, Travis. It showed me you still loved me. I couldn't figure out why you'd pushed me away when every time our eyes met, or you spoke, I could feel your love flowing through to me. I could *feel* it. I finally decided that something was standing between us. I didn't know what, but I knew you knew. I was hoping, after I left, that you'd drop back into my life, and you did. When you showed up at the café, I nearly buckled with joy. I wanted to cry with relief because I could see that same look in your eyes when you brought me home. You didn't want to leave me. I saw it. You never said it, but I felt it. And that gave me hope that we could have some kind of breakthrough with one another to meet on common ground, and knock down that *thing* that stood invisibly between us."

She gave him a softened look, moving her hand up his chest, caressing his shoulder. "And then giving me this beautiful black rocker? If I had any doubts about how you really felt toward me, they were all laid to rest this morning. I know you made that rocker by hand. I know how you work. And I'm sure you put in many hours on each piece of it, fashioning it carefully, bringing out the beauty of that incredible buried tree. To think it had fallen and lay in that peat bog for thousands of years made me think of us, of how much it symbolized what we've been through."

She saw him blink, questions in his eyes.

"The tree stood for a long time above ground, flourishing, growing, being beautiful, and feeling the sunshine and weather upon its leaves. That symbolically reminded me of us growing up together in the sunlight of one another, feeding and loving to be together. And then that mighty English oak was felled, maybe by a bolt of lightning, much like you suddenly leaving me. I felt like lightning had struck me and I was dazed and in shock by it all. And then the tree fell, buried in darkness, cold and alone, no longer fed and nourished by the sunlight and weather it loved so much." She offered him a sweet smile and with a graceful gesture pointed to the rocker in the corner.

"The tree was resurrected, pulled out of the peat bog, rediscovered, the man caring for it, sending the slabs of wood to you to refashion and bring to life once more. And look at it now. See how the sunlight is falling around it? It's once again aboveground, nourished, being fed, loved, and cared for." She compressed her lips for a moment, searching for the right words. Lifting her chin, she met and held Travis's gaze. "We rediscovered one another when that accident happened. You pulled me out of the cold, dark ground and resurrected my love for you, Travis. You gave me the sunlight of your care, your heart, and you fed my soul. You fed me hope that our love wasn't really destroyed. It was cyclical like this English oak's life, and we paralleled it in a symbolic sense."

Lifting upward, she placed her lips against the tight, hard line of his mouth, feeling the chaos of grief, sadness, and so many other wild emotions he barely was able to control. She kissed him gently, letting him know that it was all right. Everything was all right. And feeling his mouth relax, open, and then hungrily take hers, an explosion of unfettered joy erupted through every cell of her being. He brought his arms around her, easing her across his lap, deep into his embrace, his mouth warm, coaxing and feeding her his love once again.

Kass lost track of time, her arms entwined around his neck, the front of her body pressed tightly against his, feeling the thudding beat of both their hearts banging in unison against one another. She understood Travis was a man and they never had flowery words to describe how they felt emotionally. But he was speaking another language to her, one that was so pure and physical that she could never again question his love for her. He held her reverently, adored her lips, groaned with pleasure as she eagerly responded to his feeding her heart and soul with such hungry, needy abandon because she felt the same way.

Slowly, so slowly, their mouths parted from one another. Their breathing was roughened and shallow. Kass felt her heart beating staccato in her chest. When Travis barely opened his eyes, she saw what he wanted: her. All of her. "Would you rather show me than tell me?" she asked, her voice wispy, her lips lifting as his did, too.

"I'm not good with words, Kass, you know that. Let me show you how I feel about you."

His arms loosened and she eased out of them and stood, her knees feeling shaky. Holding her hand out to him, she whispered, "Come with me."

Chapter Nine

Travis held Kass's hand as she led him down the hall to her bedroom. He'd never been in her home before, and he liked the coziness of it. In one way, he felt dazed by the sudden shift going on between them. In another way? It was something he'd wanted with her since he left for the Marine Corps.

"In here," she said, opening the door, releasing his hand and stepping inside.

Travis liked the room. It held a queen-sized bed with an antique brass headboard and footboard. There was a brightly knitted top over it, all Christmas colors of red and green, mixed with silver ribbons woven throughout it. The floor was made of blond oak and shined, covered by two small rugs on either side of the bed. The rugs depicted Christmas scenes, and he smiled down at her.

"You really celebrate Christmas, don't you?" He saw her grin.

"I love the holidays. All of them." Kass gestured to the knit cover over the bed. "I love knitting. Mom taught me when I was twelve and over the years I've knitted a top for my bed for every major holiday."

Nodding, he wanted to simply absorb this room because it seemed to be the most intimate of all of them and spoke loudly of who the inner Kass was. Knowing she had been abandoned at birth, his gaze swept to a small baby rocker in the corner of the room. Squeezed in between the arms were three dolls and several stuffed animals. Did she some-day dream of having three children? His intuition said yes. There was so much he didn't know about her, and he was starving to know everything. This room was a major key to understanding the Kass so few really were privileged to know. He squeezed her hand.

"Your room. It reflects you, doesn't it?"

She shrugged a little painfully. "I never thought of it in that way, but you're right, it does."

"Those dolls in the rocker?"

"Yes?"

"Is that how many kids you'd like to have?"

She smiled a little. "Yes, I think three is just a perfect number."

"And the rocker? Is that the dream of having one to rock them in?"

"Sure is." She beamed up at him. "But now? Now I have a real rocker. A beautiful black one, and I just love your gift so much, Travis. You have no idea how much it means to me. It's as if you picked up on my secret, innermost dream I wanted to come true."

He pushed the door closed and then rested his hands on her shoulders, looking deeply into her happy gaze. "I'm not good with words like you are, Kass, but I want to take a moment before we love one another to say a few things." He smoothed the fabric across her shoulders, watching her eyes closely because he needed this time with her. To ex-plain a few things.

"Sure," she said, resting her hands on his waist.

Drawing in a deep breath, releasing it, he said, "I'm so sorry I've caused you so much pain over the years, Kass. I don't deserve you. I really don't." He reached up and pushed a tendril of hair away from her temple. "I love you. I never stopped loving you, although you never knew that. When I went into the Corps at eighteen, I wanted to follow in my dad's footsteps. I was only going to stay in for four years and come back to the valley to marry you. But I got into black ops, and my life, what I thought was important, changed." He grimaced, looked away for a moment and then reconnected with her gaze. "I got really bad PTSD from it. It accumulated over time until I had to get out because it was destroying my ability to be good at what I was doing."

"And then you came home," Kass said, saddened by his experiences.

"Yes."

"And then a month later, I dropped in to see you, to see if there was anything left between us," she said, her voice low with pain.

"God, that's what I'm so sorry about, Kass." He smoothed her hair with his hand, cupping her cheek, his tone raspy. "I wanted so damned desperately to see you, to run into your arms and hide. I was a mess, Kass. I didn't know what I was going to do with my life, I was screwed up in my head and my emotions. I wanted to see you, I wanted to find out if there was any love still left between us."

"But I came at a bad time, didn't I?"

"Yeah, but there was never going to be a good time, either. I was still sorting myself out, finding out who I was, fighting the PTSD symptoms twenty-four hours a day, trying to make a living. It had nothing to do with you. I was so happy to see you, but I was terrified at the same time. I was waking up at night, my hands clenched in fists, swinging in the air around me. How could I put you in bed with me under those circumstances?"

Her lips thinned. "Now I understand. Why weren't you honest with me, Travis? Why didn't you tell me that you still loved me? That what we had was still alive between us?"

Drawing in a ragged, pained breath, he said, "Because I was so afraid that I wouldn't get better, Kass. Everything I'd heard from anyone who had PTSD, it doesn't get better. It's *always there*. I felt terrified over you being in bed with me, having a flashback and striking, maybe killing you. I just couldn't go there, I just couldn't . . ." And he gave her a look of apology, his hands tightening on her shoulders.

"You were protecting me from yourself," she said simply, nodding.

The word came out anguished. "Yes."

"You didn't trust me that we could work through it, figure out some way around it, and yet still be together?"

Pain zigzagged through his chest. "At the time, no. Today? Yes, I guess this year home, stabilizing my life, my income, has all helped me, maybe matured me or made me see things differently than when I first got back to the valley."

She caressed his hand that cupped her cheek. "And if I'd known all this I could have helped you, maybe, Travis. We'll never know. But we're at a different juncture with one another now."

"A better one," he agreed, leaning over, kissing the top of her hair as he released her cheek. "But you're the one who has paid the price for it, and for that, I'm forever sorry, Kass. I never meant to hurt you. I really didn't. But in the end, I hurt you the worst."

"I'm built tough that way," she teased lamely, giving him a soft smile. Sliding her hand up across his chest, she added, "I never stopped loving you Travis Grant. Not *ever*.

Men came and went in my life, and none of them stacked up to you. My heart somehow knew that waiting, being patient, it would all sort itself out. And it has."

"You've got incredible vision, then," he muttered, "because I didn't."

"Is that why after the first two years you stopped emailing me and talking to me on Skype from time to time? You were shifted into black ops?"

"Yeah. I can't say much about it because it's all top secret, Kass, but I will tell you that I was always in enemy territory. There was no way to reach you. I was being sent out three months at a time to different areas. No phone, no WiFi, no Skype, no nothing. Even my parents were trapped in the same thing you were. When I'd get back to a fire base, I'd manage to email them a short explanation, saying I was all right but that I couldn't go into what I was doing."

"I remember that," she said. "I called your parents after I hadn't heard from you, when our communications just disappeared. I was worried. They told me you'd been deployed into black ops. At first, I didn't understand, but your dad explained it to me. I tried to reconcile myself to not hearing from you, but hoping I would. Your dad would call me about every three months and let me know they'd gotten a brief two or three sentence email from you."

"It was rough on them and rough on you," he said, sorrow in his tone. "I didn't even come home for my thirty days' leave between Afghan deployments. My skills were so badly needed and there weren't a lot of us Marines who had them, so we were desperately needed over there, Kass. What I did made a difference. Marines came home to their families instead of being overrun, attacked, and killed."

"And you're so responsible that way," she choked, grazing his cheek. "You're my hero, Travis. I may never know the full story of what you did over there, but I know you're honorable. And if lives were on the line, I can completely understand that you would do whatever you could to save lives. Just knowing that makes the years I didn't hear from you less painful for me."

"And I couldn't tell you at the time, Kass. God knows, I wanted to tell both you and my parents, but I couldn't. All I could hope for was that you would find a man who would give you the love and care you deserved. I knew I wasn't that man, although I continued to carry my love for you every day."

Tears formed in her eyes. Her voice wobbled. "And yet you continually put yourself out for the other Marines. You saved so many lives. That's important. It counts, Travis, with me. I don't like that we were separated for so long, that there was no communication between us, but I can accept why you did it, now. Before? It was just a big, black hole with a huge question mark, and I couldn't understand why you'd done it."

"I know." He drew her into his arms, pressing her gently against him, resting his chin against her hair. "I have so much to make up for with you, Kass. And I'm scared to death of my PTSD symptoms returning. In the past year my flashbacks have reduced a lot. But I'm still fearful of hurting you. Aren't you?"

She pulled back just enough to meet and hold his worried gaze. "Tell me something. When I was with you those five days in your cabin, did you ever have a flashback? Did you ever wake up punching the air with your fists?"

"No . . . never. And when I got that, Kass, that was when I started realizing that somehow, the magic of you just simply being in my life had short-circuited a lot of those symptoms. I don't know why. I have no explanation for it."

"Did they come back in the last three weeks since I left your cabin?"

He gave her a wry look. "I haven't had one. And that's unusual. In the year I've been home, they gradually reduced to about two a week. But there were none when you were in my cabin, and there's been none since you left."

"Maybe I'm your good luck charm, Grant?" she teased gently.

"No question, you are and always will be," he whispered, kissing her cheek, inhaling her special womanly scent.

"I like being your rabbit's foot." She smiled up at him. "Anything else you need to share with me?"

"Not right now. How about you?"

"No. You need to know that I'm not on the pill or anything else. I'm within the 'safe' period for not getting pregnant right now. No diseases, either. How about you, Travis?"

"No diseases, either. I wish I had a condom on me, but I don't, Kass. I can go out and buy some at the drugstore—"

"No. It will be all right as is." She gave him a warm look and eased out of his embrace, sliding her hand into his. "Come on, come to bed with me. I want to love you."

Kass could see the love Travis held for her in his eyes as he slowly undressed her where she stood with him. The late-afternoon light was druzy and almost magical to her as it moved through the sheer pink curtains. There was such concentration in his face, his roughened fingers easing the straps off her opened bra. Her skin prickled with delight as his flesh met hers. She was somewhat worried he wouldn't find her body acceptable, but she knew that was an old wound of hers and she tried to ignore it, concentrating instead on the burning look in his narrowing eyes as he revealed her breasts for the first time to his gaze. She thought she'd feel worried, but instead, hearing a soft intake of his breath, the pleasure coming to his expression, she knew she was perfect for him.

Without a word, she eased the white T-shirt he wore beneath the shirt she'd already removed upward. His body was lean and hard, his flesh warm and strong beneath her hands as she pulled the T-shirt off him. "Oh, you are sooooo beautiful, Travis," she whispered, meeting his hungry gaze. She dropped the T-shirt on the bedstand.

"Beautiful is reserved for you, Kass." He lightly moved his hands from her shoulders, all the way down her arms, and then gathered her hands into his. "You're the stuff dreams are made of, sweetheart. You're mine. You always have been, and I'm yours."

Her heart melted at his ragged, emotional words. It was as if she was in one of her torrid dreams, loving Travis and him loving her. He scooped her up into his arms and laid her gently on top of the bed and then joined her.

Without a word, she helped him take off her slacks and socks, and then it was his turn. In no time, they were naked, staring at one another, and she felt heat scalding her lower body, an ache centered deep within her, wanting him. All of him. He brought her over and they lay side by side, his hand on her hip, looking deeply into her eyes. Kass shouldn't have been surprised when he asked her what she liked and didn't like. He wanted to know ahead of time so that he knew how to pleasure her. And she asked the same of him, seeing that slow smile pull up the corners of his mouth, pleased that she was considerate as well. They both had enough experience, understanding that different people didn't always want the same thing. Knowing what her partner wanted was crucial to Kass.

Her heart blew open, sweeping her into a fierce love for Travis as she asked him to lie on his back and allow her to truly love him, to acquaint herself with him in every possible way, to understand his reactions, what pleasured him the most so that she could give him what he desired. She wanted to touch him, smooth her palms across his dark-haired chest, feel his muscles contract with pleasure and watch him close his eyes, borne on the wings of mounting ecstasy beneath her exploring fingertips. Each groan that rumbled up through his chest sent sizzling and tantalizing surges of heat through her.

Oh! How often had she dreamed of doing just this? Feeling the difference in his skin texture from his broad, capable shoulders to the thinner skin along the sensitive nape of his neck. Sliding her breasts tantalizingly across that powerful chest of his, her nipples hardening, begging to be touched. He couldn't keep his hands still as she worshipped him with her tongue, her teeth, nipping him here and there, kissing him afterward, listening to the raspy, harsher sounds of enjoyment, heightening her own need of him.

Sliding her hands around his thick, hard thigh and then drawing them downward, she closed her eyes, memorizing Travis as she never had before. The only pain she felt was the number of scars on his body from being in black ops.

As she urged him to turn over onto his belly, she saw swollen, bruised spots on his back, hips, and upper legs that would never go away. Those areas she hesitated, licked with her tongue and then kissed each one of them, wanting to will away the pain he surely felt when it happened. She had never seen a man with so many scars, white and pink, indicating age, and more recent ones that he'd collected as a Marine. Her pride in him, the courage he had, rippled within Kass. This man had gone through hell and survived it somehow. Only when she would lightly trace such a place on his hard body would he instinctively flinch. Kass would then lean down, lick the sensitized area, and then press her lips softly against the brutalized flesh. And then, almost a miracle in itself, she would hear him release a held breath of harsh air and relax beneath her delicate ministrations, as if understanding she was doing it as an act of love. And that love was ultimately healing. Tenderness swept through her as she finished the head-to-toe exploring.

As she rose and came back, he turned onto his back. She settled her leg over his hips and he gripped her hips, guiding her against his erection.

It was her turn to moan as the juices of her body met and surrounded him; the pressure he applied downward on her hips as she slid against him sent her into a keening cry of gratification. He knew exactly how to intimately get a woman's body anchored and tease her until she orgasmed. And that's exactly what she did, the explosive pleasure erupting within her, making her cry out, her fingers opening and closing against his chest as he held her in place, continuing to give her the ultimate satisfaction.

Fierce love for him swept through her as she was flung out into a night of stars surrounding her. Faintness rimmed her consciousness. It had been years since she'd experienced an orgasm, and it was so violently intense that it stunned her. Never had she felt such rippling pleasure as he was giving her right now.

Eyes tightly shut, she felt herself spinning and falling. It was only seconds later when Travis guided her body against his like a warm coverlet, her cheek resting on his shoulder. She was shuddering with heat swamping through her until all she could do was gasp for breath, hold on to him, and ride that blazing wave of incredible beauty and satisfaction. She was breathing hard and shallow, her body contracting, the flood of heat tunneling through every cell. Never had she felt such power from her own body. As his arms slipped around her torso, his lips against her temple, her cheek, she turned her face just enough so that her mouth engaged with his.

If there was such a thing as being reborn, Kass was in that moment as their mouths clung hungrily to one another, his arms tightening, holding her against him until she felt herself melting into him and they became one living, breathing human being with no beginning or end. The joy bubbling through her now was infectious and she could feel how much Travis loved her—had *always* loved her, just as she had always loved him.

And then he entered her, slowly, acquainting her body with him. A new level of celebration began as they joined. Flung into a new, heady level, Kass sat up, hands against his chest, moving in rhythm with him, their breath ragged, their hearts thundering with adoration for one another, culminating in another orgasm and his climax.

Later, she snuggled against him, her brow against his sandpapery jaw, strong, caring arms around her, roughened fingertips stroking her spine, caressing her hips in the aftermath. Even now, her lower body was contracting with memory, and the wavelike effects of the heat continued to flow outward, unabated. The man clearly knew how to love a woman fully and completely.

As she barely forced open her eyelids, the light had changed in the room, early dusk filling it. A sigh of contentment filled her as he continued to stroke her back, worshipping her with small kisses along her hairline, caressing her, letting her know in the warming silence settling around them as they lay together that he loved her more than anything else in his world.

And she loved him.

That was the last barely coherent thought that Kass had because she drifted off into a galaxy of sunlight warming her, rainbows before her closed eyes and the thudding of his heart beneath her palm where it lay upon his chest. Her own heart was thudding in unison with his. They were still one with one another, and she absorbed the moment as never before. One with each other. *Finally . . . finally . . .*

Chapter Ten

"For the longest time, Kass, I thought I couldn't dream of ever having you like this: in my arms, in bed together, talking . . . loving one another . . ." Travis had fallen asleep after they'd made love the first time. Kass had nuzzled her way beside him, sleeping deeply with him. They'd awakened, almost on cue, sensing one another in the way only lovers could do, and made love once more around three a.m. They had fallen, exhausted, into one another's arms afterward, as if trying to make up for all the lost time they had been separated from one another.

The first hint of dawn surrounded them through the two windows, and that was when he'd awakened. Kass slept innocently in his arms, her black hair a shining cloak spread across his shoulder and part of his chest as she remained pressed up against the length of his body. He'd lain there for a good fifteen minutes, watching her sleep, feeling the soft rise and fall of her breasts, the limpness of her arm around his waist. And she'd just drowsily come awake on her own, as if sensing once more her mate was awake and ready to meet the new day.

"I was just thinking the same thing," she said, her voice

scratchy with sleep. Moving her fingers slowly up across his chest from his waist, she tangled them in the silky dark hair across it.

"Maybe we're both in the same dream?" He tried to make light of it. Her thick black lashes lifted up to reveal not only sleep-filled eyes but a deep lover's warmth for him alone.

"No . . . you have to believe that dreams do come true, Travis Grant. We're proof of that. Don't you think?"

A slow grin of acknowledgment tugged at the corners of his mouth. Sliding his fingers through her unruly hair, he watched the low light bring out the bluish highlights in some of the strands. "Proof is in the pudding, Ms. Murphy." Kass smiled then, a drowsy, fulfilled smile that made his heart soar with joy. More than anything, Travis wanted to please this woman who had artlessly loved for so long and without any expectation of ever coming together with him.

She rubbed her hips against his. "Sure is, cowboy, sure is."

Already, despite two times last night, he would want her again sooner, not later. He cupped her flushed cheek, drowning in the warm look in her green eyes for him alone. "I have an idea. How about we get up, take a nice hot shower together, fool around, and then I'll make us breakfast? I know you have your manager opening up the café, so you don't have to be there at the crack of dawn. You can spend some time with me."

Her lips curved. "Yes, she'll open the café. And you're right, I'm starving to death, Travis."

"Oh? For me or for food?"

She laughed and eased up into a sitting position, sliding her fingers through her hair, pushing it behind her shoulders. "Oh, you are not only food for my soul but food for my heart, and don't you ever forget that."

He liked the rich purr in her husky voice. "Do I get to wake up like this with you from now on?"

She pulled her knees up toward her body, wrapping her arms around them, giving him an amused look. "Yes, always. Tell me something. Did you have any bad dreams last night?"

"I didn't sleep enough to get any, Ms. Murphy."

Trying not to laugh out loud, Kass struggled to maintain her serious demeanor. "Did you have any nightmares?"

"Nope." He reached over, caressing her arm. "None."

"Any flashbacks?"

"Not one."

"See? I'm good for you, Travis Grant. Whether you think so or not. When I'm around? You're *fine*."

He became more somber, sliding his fingers down her leg covered by the blankets, coming to rest over her foot. "That's true. The five days you were at my cabin, just a room away from me, I stopped having them. I slept the best I've ever slept since coming home a year ago. It was only later that I realized it was because you were in the vicinity, Kass." He held her tender gaze. "It's you. All you. There's something I can't explain that goes on when you're near me. You're pure magic."

"Love is like that," she whispered. "Love heals, Travis. I know it does. Jade and Marshall Murphy took me in as a tiny baby and I'm sure I was feeling horribly abandoned, although I have no memory of it. But their love put me back together again, gave me a reason to fight to survive, to live and learn to love myself. The biggest gift they gave me was not feeling as if I'd done something wrong and deserved to be abandoned. I carried such guilt about it in my early teens."

"Yes, they loved you more than life. They were a childless couple, from what my parents said, and they desperately wanted a baby. And there you were."

"But it was more than that," Kass murmured, lying down, facing him, her hand on her head, propped up. "Growing up, they didn't tell me I was adopted. It hit me hard when they did, but I remember my mom and dad surrounding me with love after they sat me down. And it wasn't always about a hug or a kiss. They know *how* to love someone else. So many little things . . . well . . . like what you just did for me this morning is a good example of that in action."

"How so?" Travis asked, caressing her cheek, watching that lambent need for him leap to her eyes.

"You made me that Windsor rocker. How many guys would do that for a woman? It showed your love for me. It showed me you not only listened to what I told you but you did something about it. You understood just how important, how symbolic, that rocker is to me. I know not every man is a master carpenter like you are, Travis, but you understand my gist?"

He brought several strands of her hair over her shoulder, watching them catch the dawn light. "Yes, I get it. And look what you did for me. You saw that ratty, old, worn scarf I wore when I had to go outside to bring more wood in for the fire, and you knitted me a new one. Not only that, you used the same color because you knew I liked blue and you wanted to please me."

"I like doing little everyday things for you, Travis. I'm going to spoil you rotten." She sizzled beneath that hungry look he gave her. "So, do we need to talk about where we're going to live together? And telling our parents about us and our plans?"

"It's on the schedule," he said. "Where do you want to live, Kass?"

She shrugged. "I loved your cabin. I love that you have two horses we can ride on that five acres. And there's so many trails in that immediate area that we can go on when the snow finally leaves."

"I live about twenty miles south of town, though."

"I can drive it daily. That doesn't bother me."

"But if you had your choice?"

She sat up and leaned over, kissing him tenderly. Moving inches away, she whispered, "You need your cabin right now, Travis. It gives you a sense of being a womb, it gives you a sense of safety, and that's vital. You're still healing daily from combat. You're comfortable there, and that wood studio isn't something you could replicate here in my little house anyway. I just don't have the room or acreage to build something like that next to this house. You have two horses to care for, too."

"But do you like living there?"

She sat up, the blankets falling around her waist. "Of course I do. I love your horses, too. And I'd love to get us a dog and maybe some cats, too, after we move my things to your cabin. It's a beautiful little place, and it's fine for us right now."

"Until," he said, reaching out, capturing her hand, "you get pregnant and the first child is on the way. What then?"

Kass hesitated, the silence stretching between them. "Are you serious about that, Travis? About me having a baby? It will change our lives forever."

"I think if we have a year of being together, I'll know a lot more about my PTSD and how it's acting. I don't want to bring a baby into the world if I can't be a partner and be a true father."

"I think that's a smart plan. It also gives us time to reacquaint with one another and get used to living under the same roof." She grinned. "I'm going to love that!"

* * *

December 31

Kass wanted their New Year's Eve meal to be perfect. She'd taken a week off, leaving her manager in charge of the café, and worked hard to make their cabin homey as never before. Because she was an avid seamstress, she'd found some heavy winter fabric of a lighter lavender color for their bedroom windows, instead of the darker burgundy which kept the room gloomy in her opinion. She'd pulled Travis into looking at it, talking about his favorite colors, and this was one of them. Getting them made up and hung brought a new level of coziness and lightness to that room.

She created new kitchen curtains, taking the drab-looking tan-colored ones down. Now they were a festive pale yellow embroidered with spring flowers and frilly feminine ruffles. Winters were so long and hard in Wyoming that she decided to create a tablecloth of the same fabric as well, to add color and life to those long, dreary winter nights. Spring always promised rebirth, and she liked that hopefulness. Travis liked the colors, too.

Her mother had knitted them a housewarming gift of a thick, soft multicolored afghan that could lie on the back of the long couch in the living room. The colors were the same as the flowers in the kitchen curtains.

Maud and Steve Whitcomb were thrilled that Travis and Kassie were finally together. Their housewarming gift was expensive but wonderful. They had gifted them with a 9 x 12 rug that had a flower meadow running through the rich green grass, the blue sky above it. Travis loved it and so did she. His parents had given them a snowmobile so that they could ride together and get out on winter days for some fresh air and sunshine, even when it was below freezing.

Sometimes during that week off from the café, so busy with making their cabin a real home for both of them, Kass would stop, shake herself, look around, and wonder if she was in some kind of beautiful, unending dream. It just seemed so natural for them to be together like this. Travis had not had one nightmare or flashback since she'd moved in with him. They made love nearly every night and sometimes during the day. It was as if they were trying to make up for lost years and being apart.

It was touching, and Kass often felt her heart break as Travis opened up a little more about his years in the Marine Corps. He wasn't only behind enemy lines, he was out there alone, without backup, calling in air strikes on some of the most dangerous Taliban leaders in the country. If he'd ever have been caught, they'd have beheaded him. That always sent a shiver down her spine whenever she thought about what he'd told her. No wonder the man had PTSD.

For the last week, Travis had forbade her from coming into the wood studio. She loved going in there and watching him work, the long graceful strokes with a planing tool, smoothing and shaping wood that just seemed to surrender to his knowing hands and good heart. She was amazed and mesmerized how Zen-like he was when crafting furniture. It were as if he and the wood were one.

Once, she'd asked him if he'd ever had PTSD symptoms while woodworking, and he said no. Maybe that was a key. She had meditated since she was in her mid-teens, finding that it helped her stop being so antsy and restless and allowed her to settle into a calmer, more grounded state. At some point, she would approach Travis about trying meditation as a way to dial down his anxiety and other PTSD reactions. It was worth a try.

Hearing the door open, she looked up. Travis came in and shut the door. He was wearing the canvas apron he always wore when doing woodwork.

"Dinner is in two hours," she said.

"I know. Do you have a minute?"

"Sure." She saw the enigmatic expression on his face, and she wondered about it. Something was up, that was for sure.

"Can you come with me?" He held out his hand toward her.

Slipping her hand into his, she smiled. "What? Is my imprisonment over? Can I come out into your wood studio and visit you every now and then?" She saw his cheeks flush and he shrugged.

"We'll see." Opening the door for her, he led her out, shutting the door behind them.

"You're acting awful mysterious, Grant. What's up?"

"Oh . . . nothing . . . just something I want to show you, is all."

He was *such* a master of understatement, she was finding out.

"Right," she teased, walking with him to the studio door.

He turned. "Okay, you have to shut your eyes now. I'll lead you in and I'll tell you when to open them. Okay?"

"Okay, cowboy." In his heart he was a wrangler, but his wonderful creativity as a master carpenter was also a part of him. She closed her eyes, trusting him fully as he led her into the warm, woodsy-smelling studio. Hearing the door shut, she waited patiently.

"Open your eyes, Kass."

She did and gasped. There, just in front of her was a bog oak Windsor baby cradle. It was the same color of black wood that Travis had used for her rocker. "Oh, my God, Travis!"

"Do you like it? I got the drawing plans from a friend of mine in Pennsylvania."

"Like it? I love it!" She moved forward, hands outstretched, touching the rounded top of one end of it. There were two simple curved upward rockers that the body sat on. The curved wood made the cradle look elegant in its simplicity. Travis went to the other side of it and crouched down. "This cradle has wood slats around all four sides. That way, there's air movement and you or I can see our baby from any angle and see what she or he is doing." He moved his hand on the gleaming ebony surface. "Here we can put in a small, flat but comfy mattress. You can then sit in your rocker, and with your toe on one of the rockers, our baby will fall asleep in no time." He looked up, grinning. "What do you think?"

She crouched down opposite him, a hand on each end of the cradle. "I think it's perfect, Travis. So this is what you were doing out here while telling me I wasn't allowed to come in?" She saw him flush, that little-boy look cross his face.

"Yeah. I wanted it to be a New Year's gift for you, Kass. It's a new year and we're with one another. I wanted something that would symbolize the future for us."

Tears burned in her eyes as she slowly rose, releasing the cradle. Coming around one end, she threw her arms around him, pressing herself tightly against him, not caring if she got a little sawdust on her from his canvas apron. Travis wrapped his arms around her, kissing her hair, her neck and shoulder.

"I love it," she breathed brokenly, the tears winding down her cheeks. Looking up, she pulled back enough to meet his concerned blue gaze. "And I love you!" She pushed up on her toes, seeking and finding his mouth, closing her eyes and melting beneath the passion that always simmered just below the surface of Travis.

As they separated, their breathing a little shallow and fast, he said, "There's one more gift for you." He opened his arms, caught her hand, and had her sit down on a flowery sofa he'd just finished for another order. She sat there, watching him remove the heavy canvas apron and lay it aside. Walking over to a set of eighteenth-century mahogany bedstands, she saw a small gold-wrapped gift sitting on one of them. Travis scooped it up, turned, and smiled as he approached her, holding it out in her direction.

"Here, this is for you . . . for us, Kass. Open it up."

Travis sat down beside her, his arm around her shoulders as she shakily pulled the red ribbon from around the gold wrapping.

"What is this," she muttered, opening the box and finding another box within it, this time wrapped in silver foil with a blue ribbon.

"I'm going to make you work for it." He laughed a little, kissing her temple.

Kass gave him a dirty look. "Who knew you were this cagey, Grant?"

"I'm black ops, Darling. That says it all."

"Well," she said, tearing open the paper after pulling off the ribbon, "this had *better* be worth it, cowboy."

He merely smiled a catlike smile.

Kass gasped as she opened the smaller white satin box. Inside it was a set of silver wedding rings. The engagement ring had seven emeralds set in graduated sizes, the largest in the center. It was completely transparent, the facets bringing out the evergreen color of her eyes. She looked over at Travis, who had lost his smile but was studying her intently.

"Will you marry me, Kass Murphy?"

Stunned, she stared at him. Recovering, her voice low with emotions, she said, "You know I will!" His boyish grin returned and he squeezed her shoulders gently.

"I love you, Kass. I never stopped loving you. Now? This all seems like a continuing dream to me. I'm afraid I'll wake up and you won't be here at all."

She grimaced. "You don't know how many times I've thought the same thing, Travis. But it's real. We're real."

She held out the set of rings to him. "Slip the engagement ring on my finger?"

"With pleasure." He eased the emerald encrusted ring out of the box. "This is platinum, by the way. Maud has a jeweler in New York City and I went to her a week ago, asking her if a woman could have emeralds for a wedding ring instead of diamonds." He slid the ring on her finger. It went easily, as if always meant for her hand. "She laughed and said yes, took me to her jeweler's website and showed me several wedding ring sets. When I saw this one? I knew it was for you." He lifted her hand, pressing a kiss to the back of it and then releasing it. "You look beautiful wearing it, Kass."

Disbelievingly, she held it up to the row of lights above them. "They are so gorgeous, Travis. Yes, I love them!" She turned, kissing him long and hard, letting him know how happy she was.

Snuggling with him, Kass laid her head on his shoulder, content as never before. "This has been just the best Christmas of my life, Travis. And it's because of you."

"I feel the same way, Darling." He slid his fingers through her strands, revealing her temple and ear. "We've got a long way to go, but I've never been more hopeful than with you at my side."

Sighing, she whispered, "Happy New Year, Travis. Maybe by next New Year, we might be welcoming our child into our lives."

He nodded, kissing her brow. "I'd like that, Kass, and I know you would, too."

"First," she said, laughing a little, "we have to get married!"

"Let's go to bed and talk about that."

She gave him a teasing look, easing out of his arms and standing before him. "Come on, cowboy, let's get a nice, hot shower together and then race one another to the bed. Last one in is a rotten egg!"

Her Outback Husband

Margaret Way

Dear Reader,

I have always had a special love for Christmas, walking hand in hand with my father beneath a starstruck sky to Midnight Mass, wearing the prettiest dress in the world, a present from my darling Irish grandmother, Margaret Fleming. Born on her birthday, August 7, and named after her, I always called her "Mags." It was Mags who passed on to me her love of language and her gift of the gab.

These days Christmas has become a time of remembrance. Remembrance of the loved ones I've lost, the empty seats at the table. "Remembrance like a candle burns brightest at Christmas." Dickens, I think. Hearts can and do soften in an irrepressible outpouring of good will, setting the scene for reconciliation as in my Christmas novella, where hero and heroine once again get caught up in the season's celebration of love.

The very best to you and your family,
Margaret Way

Prologue

The sky was so intense a blue it was said to be the most beautiful sky on the planet. Queensland Blue, it was called. Darcey, who had travelled much of the world—a marvellous twenty-first birthday present from her father—had no quarrel with that. Queensland Blue every time. Blue skies, after all, were part of the state's character.

She stood on the open terrace of the MacArthurs' riverfront apartment, half imagining herself in heaven. This was Brisbane, the state capital of the vast state of Queensland, well over a thousand kilometres from Planet Downs, the MacArthur historic cattle station in the Channel Country in the far South-west. The Channel Country was a vast area, covering a quarter of Queensland. It had been, in days gone by, the heart of the great Sir Sydney Kidman's pastoral empire. With a prehistory of the fabled inland sea, the Channel Country, criss-crossed with innumerable water courses, was the most distinctive landscape on the continent.

This was the place where the legendary explorers perished so tragically trying to find that inland sea. It was still in the twenty-first century an extremely daunting area, with the mighty Simpson Desert right on the doorstep. It was also the home of the nation's glamorous cattle kings, like her beloved husband of eighteen blissful months, Scott MacArthur.

Her face glossed over with sunlight, she raised her arms to the sky as if she could pull down some of that glorious blue on herself. It was another perfect day in early November. What passed for winter in subtropical Brisbane had been so mild it had slipped imperceptibly into spring. The golden wattles, the nation's emblem, had finished blooming and now it was the time of the jacarandas. Within a week, the jacarandas would be joined by the crimson flaunting of the poincianas. Both great shade trees when in blossom created near-unworldly beauty throughout the city. The jacarandas, the first to unfold, dazzled the eye with blossoms. Darcey could see the purplish blue haze that hovered over the opposite bank of the river and as far as the eye could see.

Scott, an experienced pilot, had flown the Beech Baron home the day before. He could never be long away from the top job. It had only taken an extra day before Aunt Rachael rang to ask if she could come to lunch when Darcey had all but given up on inviting her.

"But of course! That will be lovely!" Darcey's answer was more courteous than strictly honest. No one could accuse her aunt Rachael of being a fun person. Fun was pretty much a curse word to her aunt, but family harmony was important. From time to time she and her aunt had lunch at one of the city's expensive restaurants. It was always her aunt's choice, for if the decision were left to Darcey, they would finish up at the nearest accredited McDonald's.

"Something light, perhaps a salad?" Darcey suggested. She ran through the contents of the fridge in her mind. Cold meats, ham and turkey, smoked salmon. Leafy greens for the salad, plump red tomatoes, cucumber, capsicum, fennel, and always Queensland's superb avocados dressed with virgin olive oil and lemon, a dollop of mild American mustard. She wasn't about to run out for truffles and other delicacies her aunt fancied. Fresh raspberries and strawberries for dessert with whipped cream would be fine, she decided.

"That will have to do, my dear!" A groan of forbearance. Her aunt's voice, though cultured, could sometimes sound like a mechanical device about to start up.

"I'll see you at one p.m. sharp!"

Darcey only just stopped herself from saying *aye aye!* She was used to her aunt's peremptory style, though she had seen any number of people reel away from it. Sophie, her mother-in-law, had very early on observed Aunt Rachael had "all the warmth of a fridge." Most people would agree. Be that as it may, her aunt always acted with rigorous integrity, and to hell with those who disliked her.

With Scott's blessing, Darcey had remained in the city to attend a piano recital by a visiting virtuoso she greatly admired. Once her aunt found out, she invited herself along. The two of them had become close in a difficult-to-describe way since Darcey's mother, Ysobel, Rachael's younger sister, had died in a tragic accident eight years before. Up until that terrible day Darcey had lived a wonderful life with a great certainty to it. Tragedy played out. She was aware of that. But far from home. She had been in grade 12, her final year before university, head girl at her prestigious all-girls school. Her ultimate goal was to become an architect like her multiple-award-winning father. Both her parents were highly artistic. Everything had been planned.

Only all her plans fell apart in a single violent incident. Nothing mattered after that. No joy. No laughter. A great silence. Anyone who understood grief understood that. Ever since her mother's death she had begun preparing herself for future disastrous events. She had naively thought there would be warnings in life. Only warnings didn't come

over a period of time—sometimes they struck from a clear
blue sky. As important to her as was her much loved and
respected father, Paul Gilmore, mothers were irreplaceable.

"Mummy!"

Was there another word in any language to match it?
Was there another word more primal?

"Mummy, I want to speak to you!"

Never again. Not even in her dream-riddled sleep when
she saw her mother walking away from her, farther and
farther, though she cried out to her to stop.

Resignation. Acceptance. That was all that was on offer.

And torment.

Aunt Rachael, the elder by nearly ten years, was childless, an unmarried woman by choice.

"Some guy had a lucky break!"

The irrepressible Sophie again.

Even so, it had to be remembered Aunt Rachael had
done her very best to take her sister's place. Even the people
who thoroughly disliked her gave her credit for that. Up
until then Aunt Rachael had not been what one could call a
loving aunt. Hitherto distant, overnight she became the
closest relative Darcey had, except for her father, who after
four years of surviving an avalanche of pain and grief had
married a longtime colleague and family friend Anne
Matheson, a lovely woman. Darcey had thoroughly ap-
proved of the marriage. Her father had suffered enough.

Life went on. There were no options but to fight or fold.
Life was chaos; governed by chance. There was good fortune
and appalling bad luck. Bad things happened to bad people.
Bad things happened to good people.

Things just *happened*.

The only solution was to keep moving or fall into limbo.

She had tried and *tried*, but she had never been able to verbalize her loss. Not until she met Scott, who understood everything.

Scott, my husband, my perfect lover, my soul mate.

Given such perfect weather, she had decided they would dine on the patio. There was a gentle breeze wafting from the east. She had opened up a blue and white striped beach umbrella, and it shaded the glass-topped circular wicker table with its four matching chairs. The handsome apartment had a bank of floor-to-ceiling glass doors to take in the view, high ceilings, large light-filled rooms, comfortable furnishings, and gleaming polished wooden floors with a scattering of Kashan rugs.

Best of all, it overlooked the sparkling sheen of the Brisbane River. Everyone loved the river. It cut a swathe through the city, meandering mile after mile into the suburbs.

The annual Riverfire festival centred round the river. Commuters travelled from one bank to the other in catamarans, the CityCats that plied up and down the river day and night. Brisbane was a city of some two million people with a diverse, highly educated, multicultural population. Third largest city in Australia, it was a great place to live, not the least of it being its wonderful climate. The country's tourist destination, it was less than an hour's drive to the fabulous beaches of the Gold Coast and a short plane trip to the World Heritage listed Daintree Rain Forest and the Great Barrier Reef.

From her high vantage point, Darcey could see the flow of people strolling along the network of riverway pavements: parents with their children, couples holding hands, committed joggers, a teenager on roller skates, earphones plugged in, showing off his arabesque. Some were storing up the beauty around them in video cameras, the sun-spangled water and the ecstatic flowering of the great shade trees.

Days like this, one wanted to shout with the joy of being alive.

The final table presentation looked good enough to please even her downright critical aunt. Radiant white linen and lace place mats and matching napkins, pretty china, sparkling glassware. She had placed vases everywhere filled with lovely sweet-smelling spring into summer flowers she had bought at the local market. Once she had thought catastrophe couldn't happen when one was surrounded by flowers. Tragically it did, but she couldn't live without flowers blooming all around her. Her mother had been the same. Her aunt favoured valuable sculptures in onyx or bronze, difficult to shift around. Everyone had their methods for getting through life.

Her aunt arrived, and they ate lunch. The salad was fresh and crisp; the ham slices, thick and succulent; the dinner rolls, freshly baked, but her aunt was toying with the meal, showing none of the delicate gourmandising motions and tiny mews of appreciation she employed when savouring treats. Maybe she should have tried Peking duck? It was clear something was on her aunt's mind, twisting and turning, desperate to get out.

"You'll have some berries and cream?" Darcey offered in her gentle, melodic voice.

"No thank you, dear." Rachael slumped back in her chair, rather rudely pushing her plate away. Thin as a rake and intensely proud of it, Rachael bore a striking resemblance—and one she played up—to the notorious Duchess of Windsor, wife of the abdicated King Edward VIII. She owned and ran a very successful art gallery which she had opened less than a year after her sister, Ysobel, had been killed. It was Rachael who had put Ysobel Gilmore's name on the map, selling her paintings like hotcakes except for the best, which Paul Gilmore had kept for himself and his daughter.

Few people liked Rachael Richardson, though oddly enough they fawned over her at showings and invited her to their dinner parties. Such was the level of social hypocrisy. Some called her a cold woman, if not full in her face, but all were ready to concede she was very good at what she did, finding promising young artists and pushing their work.

"Something is obviously troubling you." Darcey tried to catch her aunt's deep-set dark eyes. The truly remarkable thing was her aunt in no way resembled Darcey's physically beautiful, artistically gifted mother. They might have been a different species. No lighthearted chatterer, her aunt was rarely *this* quiet. Aunt Rachael was a woman who liked to talk when others were obliged to listen.

Darcey couldn't truthfully admit in her heart to *loving* her aunt. The difficulty arose because her aunt wasn't a *lovable* woman. There was a certain *voraciousness* about her which inevitably brought to mind an image of a rapacious bird. That being said, Aunt Rachael was *family*—her beloved mother's sister. Darcey felt a strong moral obligation to her aunt, and she trusted her implicitly. Her high regard was commensurate with the fact her aunt, whatever her deep personal grief over the loss of her younger sister, had always been there for her.

It was Aunt Rachael who had held the fort until her architect father was located out on a home site. He had rushed home, shocked out of his mind by the news, hardly believing what he had been told. Darcey still remembered flying into his arms. They had closed strongly around her as the two of them wept torrents. That image would remain in her head forever.

Aunt Rachael had been amazingly strong, but no one could say she was a demonstrative woman. No warm embraces. Even her rare pats were awkward. Darcey couldn't even remember Aunt Rachael kissing her own sister. Some people just couldn't abide hugging and kissing, Darcey always told herself. In the main they weren't happy people. Happy times were strictly parcelled out.

"Can we go inside, dear?"

Her aunt was already rising before she had a chance to say yea or nay.

"Of course. Coffee?"

"Perhaps a good idea."

The tone would have shot arrows of concern into anyone.

It took no time to have the freshly ground coffee in the French press. Her aunt sat silently, apparently buried in thought, until Darcey brought the coffee over and set it down on the long rectangular coffee table that separated the two ivory leather-upholstered sofas with their bright scatter of silk cushions.

"The last thing I want is to upset you." Rachael shifted a pretty ceramic pot filled with sweet peas well out of the way. For some reason she was puffing out her thin cheeks. "But it's my duty, Darcey. My *overwhelming* duty . . ." She reached for her coffee, took a scalding gulp as if she were parched. When she finished that, she took another. She surely had to have an asbestos tongue?

"*Tell* me." Darcey who would never be completely free from anxiety, felt her stomach begin to tie itself in knots.

"What *is* the best way?" Rachael debated, piercing the side of her hair with her long, red-lacquered fingernails. Diamond rings she wore on three fingers of her right hand and endlessly tinkered with gave off dazzling flashes of light.

"You must have thought that out before you rang me."

"It couldn't be worse for you." Rachael's brusque tones vibrated with anger. "I've waited for Scott to leave. I know how much you love him."

"*Love* him? I adore him." Darcey was severely taken aback. "I thought you were very fond of him too."

"I am. *I am!*" Rachael's voice rose steeply. "But there it is. You're going to be devastated by what I have to say."

"Just *say* it," Darcey urged, her whole being on guard. She was no good whatever at revelations.

Rachael stared into Darcey's face, speaking deliberately as if she were dealing with a nitwit. "Much as it grieves me to tell you, Darcey, Scott, your husband, *had . . . a . . . one-night . . . stand . . . with . . . your . . . friend . . . Becky*."

The pain she felt was so sudden and unexpected it was like being shot. She could hear her aunt's baleful tones coming at her in *s-l-o-o-w* motion. Her whole body was giving way to a slow *whoosh*. The terrace floor seemed to be giving way beneath her. She was about to plunge to her death, forty feet below, her head and her body cracking against the concrete sidewalk. Seconds passed. It might have been hours.

Scott, Becky!

Then, like a gift from God, air rushed back into her parched lungs. Blessed clarity returned, dispelling the darkness around her.

Easier to believe the pope gave up being Catholic.

Scott had a one-night stand with her friend Becky? She had never heard such rubbish in her entire life. She was going to need an explanation *right now.* She had unerring faith in her husband. How dare anyone, Aunt Rachael included, say such a thing about Scott. She hated it. *Hated it!* Her feelings went far beyond resentment. She was *outraged.* She wanted to chase her Cassandra of an aunt right out the door. Then lock it. Have a whole bunch of new locks installed.

"I have the *perfect* answer to that, Aunt Rachael," she said in an angry, deeply offended voice. "It's an abominable *lie*! Scott is a man of integrity respected by everyone who knows him. It could *never* have happened. Scott loves me. I love him. We couldn't be happier. He would *never* betray me. I could never betray him. Never!"

Memory caught at her. The two of them together, she locked in her husband's close, loving embrace.

"Nothing will ever go wrong for you again, my darling. I won't let it. For every problem there is a solution. We'll find it together."

"According to your friend, he *did*," Rachael retaliated like a woman who wanted to bring back public hangings. "Stranger things have happened. It was August. Remember, one of your panic attacks erupted. It landed you in hospital. They kept you in overnight. All three of us were at your bedside. Scott, Rebecca, and I. Scott offered to drive Rebecca home, don't you remember? I had my car."

Darcey clenched her hands in case she lost it and pitched something at her aunt's head. For years before she had met Scott she had lived her life on autopilot, working hard to block out her grief, completing her architectural degree. It was what her mother had wanted. Achievement gave some meaning to her life. She was older now. Stronger. A much loved married woman. She had toughened up. Nevertheless the cautionary voice in her head that never went away advised her to breathe in and out. It was an exercise her psychologist had suggested for whenever she thought one of her panic attacks could be imminent.

Breathe . . . in . . . out.

In . . . out . . .

That's it, Darcey.

No hurry.

It was exhausting.

She thought of Scott, her strength, her sanctuary, her raison d'être.

"How do *you* know all this, Aunt Rachael?" Her low, sweet tones had taken on a remarkable sharpness. "I can't believe Becky would be fool enough to come running to *you* to confess, considering the scorn you have for her. You treat Becky 'like shit.' Her words, not mine."

"Vulgar creature! If the cap fits, wear it," Rachael said, curling her thin lips disdainfully. "She didn't confess. I would have slapped her face hard. How did I come to know? I followed them. I was worried on your account. I'm a very perceptive woman. It was all I could do not to go inside the building and knock on the door."

"I'm surprised you didn't."

Rachael was further taken aback by the tart tone. "Scott has tremendous sexual charisma. Even I can see that. You must know Rebecca was and still is strongly attracted to him."

Darcey couldn't deny it. "What of it?" she whipped out. "Scott attracts a lot of women. It's part of his natural aura. It's quite unconscious. He's not the man to get hung up on personal vanity."

"All the more potent for it."

"He certainly wasn't attracted to Becky." A white energy was moving through Darcey. She wanted her aunt to disappear. Vaporize. It shouldn't be hard. She was as skinny as a broomstick.

Rachael shrugged. "You know what men are," she offered. "Men who radiate energy. The build-up of energy has to find release. Rebecca is a pretty girl. She would have invited Scott in for coffee. We had been hours at the hospital. You can be certain once inside, she gave Scott the come-on.

One thing leads to another, as they say. I'm sure she doesn't mean a thing to Scott, but you had something of a relapse at that time, my dear. Sadly they're always waiting around the corner. Manlike Scott simply wanted sex."

Darcey pinned her aunt's dark eyes. God knows what lay hidden behind them. She wanted her aunt out of the apartment before her sense of alienation was complete. "So my husband was desperate for sex with Becky when he could get it freely from me the next day?" She had never come into direct conflict with her aunt. Now could well be the day.

Rachael compressed her lips, clearly rattled by the dramatic shift in Darcey's manner. "I've no need to hear that, my dear," she said with more than a hint of reproof. "Please don't go biting my head off."

"Don't make the mistake of thinking I'm not up to it, Aunt, especially when you attack my husband. Sex is a dirty word with you, is it? None of us would be here without it. Even you. You didn't arrive in a Hermès handbag. You certainly know how to draw an exaggerated picture of my panic attacks. *Erupted?* Really?"

"I see nothing wrong with that word, Darcey. I'm sorry if it offends you. "

"It does. You need to promise me you won't use that word again. I go *quiet*." It was true. No moaning. No screaming. No crying out. Silence with a complete absence of calm. Just inner desolation. The last attack had come right out of the blue. Now she understood why. Her aunt, who had come into the world thinking *clinically,* had an unfortunate way with words. Words were weapons. They could blast holes in one's self-confidence and self-esteem.

"The attack did come on quite suddenly. That's all I meant." Rachael gave a tight smile that had no connection with warmth.

"My panic attacks have been few and far between, Aunt Rachael. That was the only one I've had since I married Scott."

"I know, dear girl. I was there. I'm sorry."

But she's not sorry.

"I do have a tendency to be too explicit," Rachael said with a rare show of self-criticism. "I know some people view me as a cold person. I'm not."

"Don't let's explore that. So while you're parked on the street in your latest Mercedes, thinking dark thoughts about my husband and my friend, you surmised illicit sex was going on?"

"Is that so amazing?" Rachael's eyebrows joined up with her widow's peak. Surely it had grown farther down her forehead? "Men have thoughts about sex umpteen times a day. They're such unfaithful creatures. I never, never, never trust them. Please don't be angry with me, Darcey. You mean more to me than anyone in the world. You bring out all of my protective instincts. I want you to be happy above everything else. I know the panic attacks go back to the unresolved issues you still have with your mother's death."

Darcey felt the blood drain from her face. "You're suggesting I'm neurotic?"

"Good heavens, no!" Rachael said, not half convincingly enough. "That would be crossing the line."

"Yet you constantly dance around it?" Darcey realized of a sudden that was true.

"Please calm down, dear," Rachael urged. "I have issues myself, but I'm a strong woman. I wish I could say you are too, but we both know you're not." It was a diagnosis delivered with her aunt's usual abrasive candour.

If only she were a conjuror and could wave her hands and make her aunt disappear.

Hey, hey, go away!

"No one knows you better than I do, Darcey." Rachael studied her niece's face, the lithe nymph-like body as if seeking fault. "I've tried to help, but you're always expecting hell around the corner."

True.

"But then you're young," Rachael conceded generously. "I'm actually surprised how well you've done. You're a beautiful, vulnerable young woman, just like your mother. You're the image of her."

"I see her every time I look in the mirror." Darcey's thoughts had become like caged birds, banging away against her skull. She needed *quiet.* She needed Scott. This wasn't *real* drama compared to the death of her mother. These were cruel, callous, *lies.* Was she supposed to take it without answering back? No way!

"You need to live with *trust,* my dear," Rachael insisted as though trust was a clause in a contract she was drawing up. "It takes trust every time. Not deceit. I finally got around to tackling Rebecca. After all, I wasn't one hundred per cent sure. I was only going on a hunch, but I played it to the hilt. All in a day's work for me. The stupid girl panicked. Blurted it all out. The whole mess."

Darcey thought she might just freak out. And for once be extremely *noisy* about it. "My God, Aunt Rachael, do you seriously believe I'm going to accept this? Becky was making it all up. She's not a happy person. It's fantasy. Becky has missed out on a lot. That was one of the reasons I asked her to be my bridesmaid. Her parents divorced. She doesn't get on with her father. Her mother has married a man she loathes. She's always short of money. I've helped her out on many an occasion."

"More fool you!"

The question was out before she gave it thought. "Did you *ever* in your life love a man?"

For a split second Rachael's eyes turned hard, ruthless, *black.* "I've buried the past, Darcey."

"I believe you."

Rachael speared her hand through her hair again as though immensely irritated by the shift in the conversation.

Only Darcey had caught a glimpse into her aunt's soul. "Only the past is never past, as Faulkner once said. So you *did* love someone?" Unwittingly she had struck a nerve. God knows who it could have been. She pictured an obsessively dedicated scientist who one day would discover some mind-blowing drug. He and Aunt Rachael would be able to talk about it for hours on end. Even in their twin beds.

"The question doesn't require a reply. Let's say I too know what betrayal is." She reached for her niece's hand across the table.

Darcey withdrew it.

A rare slight.

"Do you seriously think I wanted to tell you this?"

"You do like your dramas."

"What else could I do? It's terrible, but you have to know. Scott has to admit his mistake up front."

Darcey rose, unable to tolerate another word against her husband. Nothing felt right. *Nothing.* The man she loved body, heart, and soul would never betray her. Becky had been drunk. Dreamed it. "I know you mean well, Aunt Rachael, but I'd like you to leave." She had always shown her aunt great respect. But this? "I need to be alone. I'm sure you have work to catch up on. I must cancel this evening. I'll give you my ticket. You can take a friend."

"As if I would want to go now," Rachael said, jerking angrily to her feet. There was an unattractive flush on her high cheekbones. She had always prided herself on controlling her motherless niece; now her niece was as good as ordering her out. "I'm your aunt, Darcey. Your dear mother's only sibling. I've been instrumental in helping you recover from your grief. Try to remember that. I hated to have to tell you, but I have an obligation. That girl, Rebecca, is not of good character. She betrayed you. When you feel strong enough, I suggest you ask her. I can come with you for support."

"Thank you, Aunt, but I'll do the talking to Becky. Maybe you intimidated her? You do intimidation well. She wouldn't be the first person to confess to something that never happened. I assure you, I'll get to the truth."

Rachael hefted her Hermès handbag as though it were a piece of heavy luggage. "Don't let them get away with it. I know you will want to reconcile. You're so dependent on Scott, but you may find his infidelity too much to live with. No one loves you more than I do. I'm the person your mother would have appointed to be your caretaker, your protector."

"Aren't you forgetting my father?" Darcey asked in an ice-cool voice.

"I'm surely *not*! I *never* forget Paul. But where is he, Darcey? I'll tell you where. In London with Anne Matheson."

Now she knew for sure her aunt hated Anne. "It's Anne *Gilmore*, Aunt Rachael. Dad and Anne live in London for their work."

"Believe you me, Anne Matheson was always after your father."

"Nonsense!"

"What a child sees and what a grown woman sees are two entirely different things, Darcey." Aunt Rachael's grim expression implied there were some things Darcey would *never* know.

She paused at the front door. No beauty, but a striking-looking woman, impeccably groomed from head to toe, though Darcey had always found it difficult to place her aunt's style of dressing in time. 1920s? 1930s? "Every family has its secrets, Darcey," Rachael said with the air of a woman who knew every last one. "What you need to do now is focus on resolving this issue as soon as you can. Or you can simply breathe it away like you do with your exercises. As your aunt, I had a duty to put the sorry facts before you. You're the victim here, but only if you *choose* to be. Remember I'm always here for you. You are all I have left of my sister."

Were those tears that glittered in her aunt's eyes?

Gone in a blink.

Hours later, her so-called friend Becky greeted her with her game face on. That meant Becky had been psyching herself up for this encounter. In no time at all, shocked by the change in Darcey's manner, she was in floods of tears, begging forgiveness.

"It wasn't really my fault." Becky dashed a hand across her wet cheeks. "Scott dazzled me. He's such a gorgeous man. It was an aberration, impossible to resist. I'd like to kill myself."

"Put it on your to-do list," said Darcey. The bleaker the situation, the blacker the humour.

"I'm so sorry." Becky's voice had dropped into her scruffy flatties. "I'm your friend. You've given me so much emotional support."

"Don't forget the financial support. Four thousand dollars, off the top of my head."

Behind Beck's drenched blue eyes something hostile flared. "Honestly, Darcey, I'll pay you back when I can. Don't think your generosity hasn't worried me. I am just so *grateful*."

There was a dollop of poison somewhere in that.

Jealousy? Envy?

"Please stop!"

Becky started to back up against the kitchen counter, strewn with a mountain of dirty dishes. Becky was no housekeeper. The flat was a mess. "I'm as good as alone in the world. I don't have a rich father. I don't have a rich aunt. Please don't hate me."

Darcey's inner voice spoke up.

Get out.

Out. Out. Out.

She obeyed. She walked to the door, grasping the brass knob. "You're not worth hating, Becky," she said. "You're an opportunist. I see that now."

Becky dropped to her knees like a penitent. "And you're too bloody good to be true. Beautiful *and* clever. You shouldn't be both. It's not fair. I couldn't help it."

"Sounds like betrayal to me." Darcey could taste humiliation on her tongue. "I don't need negative feelings in my life, Becky. I *will* check this out with my husband."

"Oh, *do*!" Becky invited, springing nimbly to her feet. "He'll deny it, of course. They all do."

"You say that like you know all about it."

Becky looked as if she didn't need a lecture about how she spent her time. "Most women have to live with infidelity at some point in their lives, Darcey. Try to view it realistically. It was just a moment of madness. A one-off. Scott wanted it. Or rather he wanted to be *served*. You know how sexy Scott is? I'm never needier than when I'm around him. I can't describe my feelings. Maybe they're abnormal?"

"Let's stick to worthless. I never want to hear from you or see you again, Becky. I don't wish you ill, but I can't stomach your treachery."

"I'll go away?" Becky offered.

"Make it Outer Mongolia."

"Damn bitch!" Becky muttered.

"I beg your pardon?" Darcey whirled, adrenalin flushing through her blood. She wasn't about to tolerate profanity from this traitor.

Only an expression of utter *wretchedness* was moving across Becky's pretty wet face. "Not you, Darcey," she said.

"You're a true innocent, God help you. I meant your vulture of an aunt."

Then she started laughing. A crescendo of hysteria.

Darcey had to escape at all costs.

Nothing turns out as we expect. Sometimes things get better. Most often they get worse.

That night she had another troubling dream about her mother. As always she wanted to run to her, throw her arms around her, but she couldn't. In her dream state she was paralysed. She could only watch on. Only this time her mother didn't walk away from her. She faced her, mouthing words one could not hear in dreams. Only on her mother's face was an unmistakeable message.

Be warned.

Chapter One

Two years later

A splendid Christmas tree of jubilant forest green soared into the double-height entrance hall of the homestead, commanding the entire space. The branches were lavishly decked with all manner of glittering baubles, the traditional red and green, the silver and gold, interspersed with ribbons of tinsel and exquisite little Christmas ornaments that had been in the family since forever and lovingly taken out of their boxes year after year. This year there were more additions in the form of hand-painted porcelain Alessi Christmas bells and some beautiful silver Georg Jensen collectables. Decorating the tree was important and hugely enjoyable.

"Silent Night" was being wafted through the house over the state-of-the-art sound system. It was being sung by a boy soprano whose celestial voice had the power to move the two women to tears.

Samantha MacArthur, daughter of the house, was up the tall ladder. Her mother, Sophie, was on a shorter ladder on the other side of the tree busy tying little winged Cupids to the lower pendulous branches. Samantha, a beautiful young woman with the MacArthur glorious russet hair and intensely blue eyes, was working her way to the top of the tree which would be adorned with an antique white porcelain Christmas angel with 18 karat gold-tipped wings.

"I've something to tell you, Sam," Sophie whispered, from behind her hand.

Samantha had to smile. Her mother had long established herself as a *character*. "You have my full attention, Mumma," she said indulgently.

"Please come down off the ladder, darling," Sophie begged, sounding unexpectedly serious. "I don't want you to fall."

"Fall? For crying out loud, Mum. I'm not going to fall. What's the problem?"

"Please do as I ask."

Samantha obeyed. She had no idea what her mother was going on about. Her mother was full of surprises. "Okay." Swiftly she descended the ladder, the Christmas angel in hand. She took a moment to put it down on the hall console.

The words came tumbling out of Sophie's mouth. "I've invited Darcey for Christmas."

Whatever Samantha had been expecting, it was *never* that. The admission went off like a bomb, striking her dumb.

"You've *what*?" she finally asked, her voice lifting alarmingly.

"No need to shout, darling." Sophie glanced quickly over her shoulder in case someone would come running. "You'll bring down the tree."

Samantha snorted. "You're joking."

"I mean it. I've invited Darcey."

"You're only saying that," Samantha moaned. "You'd never do it. You'd *never* do it, would you, Mum?"

"I *have*. My decision. I take full responsibility."

"Sweet Jesus!"

Sophie, a lapsed Catholic, spoke up. "Dearest girl, please don't take the Lord's name. Not at Christmas."

"I'm *praying* to Him, Mum. Are you looking to me for backup?"

"Of course I am. You always back me up."

"I should have been much stricter with you." Samantha gave a frustrated shake of the head. It *was* her task, after all, to curb her mother's excesses. She and Scott had agreed on it. "You can apologize to me for not having told me sooner. Christmas is just over three weeks away. You do realize that. The invitations have gone out. Everyone will be so *shocked*, and I mean *everyone*. But no one will be as shocked and angry as Scott. He'll go ballistic."

"Scott would never go ballistic with his mother," said Sophie, believing the mother-son relationship sacred.

"There's always a first time," Samantha warned. "Oh, Mum! I never know what you're going to do from one day to the other. You invited Darcey, who betrayed not only Scott but the entire family. We all loved her. She was so beautiful and so gifted. She and Scott were set for life. He adored her. People said they had never seen two people so much in love. We all got on so wonderfully well. I don't believe this!" she wailed. "It could ruin everything, the polo match, the ball, Ashlee's chances with Scott."

"Darling girl, you well know Ashlee has *no* chance with Scott." Sophie tut-tutted at the very idea.

"But we *like* Ashlee," Samantha protested. "Or we like her enough. We've known her forever. She's utterly trust-worthy. She's not nerve-ridden like Darcey and she's always been in love with Scott."

"Scott has only ever been in love with one woman, and that's Darcey," said Sophie. "My son was shot through the heart by Cupid's arrow. There never will be anyone else for Scott but Darcey. No one will come close."

Samantha sighed volubly. She had to agree. "Be that as it may, you never saw the end coming, did you, Mother dear?"

"And haven't I done penance for that!" said Sophie.

"We *all* thought Darcey was as madly in love as Scott," Samantha lamented. "How did we get it so wrong?"

Sophie, a pretty, petite woman with golden brown hair and golden brown eyes, suddenly seized her tall daughter by the shoulders. "The aunt was the problem," she said, trying and not succeeding in shaking her daughter. "All right, I admit I woke up too late. I should have called a family conference. It was the meddlesome Aunt Rachael who dominated Darcey's young life."

"They never did find the motorist who knocked her mother off her bicycle," Samantha sidetracked, gently removing her mother's small hands. The family had been greatly saddened when they found out Darcey's mother, Ysobel Gilmore, had been out on a morning bike ride close to a quiet local park when she had been struck and killed by a motorist.

"The coward got clean away."

"No one gets clean away from causing another human being's death," said Sophie, exuding belief in Divine justice.

"Only some people lack a conscience, Mum."

"True," Sophie conceded. "Might as well say manslaughter, not accident. The tragedy had a hugely lasting effect on Darcey."

"God yes!" Samantha shuddered, suddenly feeling very sorry for her ex-sister-in-law. She couldn't *bear* the thought of losing her own dear mother. Or imagine how she would react after such a tragic event. "Even so, we all knew Scott didn't betray Darcey. You're right as usual, mum. It was the domineering aunt that caused all the mayhem. She had such a hold on Darcey."

"You can bet your life she worked long and hard on it," Sophie said. "Aunt Rachael is the key to the mystery we need to unlock. It's gone on far too long. Scott is suffering, though he never shows it. That's the *man* thing. The strong, silent behaviour that has been the norm for men for generations. Silence is the reason why men are so lonely. Silence is the reason why so many men *and* boys get sick. Women talk to their women friends, derive comfort and support. Men put on the brave manly face. But my boy can't hide his true feelings from his mother any more than you can. You really like Linc, don't you?"

Samantha's expression turned fierce. "I do not! I wish Scott had never given him the foreman's job. Anyway, we're not talking about me, Mum, we're talking about *you*. Why you invited Darcey for Christmas."

"I got permission from God," said Sophie, very simply. "I talk to Him, as you know."

"And God told you to do what?" Samantha asked sarcastically.

"Write to Darcey."

"He didn't suggest an email?"

"Goodness me, no. Way too impersonal. I wanted Darcey to know how we feel. We all miss her, don't we? Own up, Sam. You and Darcey had become very close."

"Like sisters," said a bitterly disillusioned Samantha. "But much as I loved Darcey, Mum, I love my brother more. She broke his heart. She won't have turned over a new leaf. She's still in close contact with her horrible aunt. I'm sorry, but Darcey has long since been brainwashed. I'm amazed she was allowed to go through with the wedding."

"The wedding wasn't a mistake, Sam," Sophie said. "The *divorce* was the big mistake. Both of them were so wounded they took themselves out of reach. Only I can't sit around doing nothing any longer. We can't pretend Scott will ask

Ashlee to marry him. He won't. Even if he never saw
Darcey again, it's as I said. He will never get fully over her."

"Maybe there's a limit to love," Samantha mused. "To
being *in* love. Things are wonderful for a couple of years,
then it's all over. A couple of years. That's all you're going
to get."

Very gently Sophie took her daughter's hand. "I never
fell out of love with your father from the moment I met him
to the day we lost him. He never fell out of love with me.
One day soon you'll find the right man, my darling, and fall
deeply in love."

"I hope so, Mum," Samantha said, without much con-
viction. "I don't for a moment include you and Dad. Dad
was a splendid man. We knew how happy you and he were.
It's been very hard for us: you, Scott, and me. We lost Dad.
Darcey lost her mother. We can't bring them back."

"No, but we will see them again. The bonds of love will
carry over into the next life."

Samantha laughed with tears sparkling in her eyes. "Oh,
Mum! Do you really believe that?"

"I most certainly do. I don't care what anyone says, there
is a heaven where we'll all meet up with our loved ones
again. The good ones, that is."

Samantha bent to kiss her mother's smooth cheek. "I
long for your faith, Mum."

"Give it a few more years, darling," said Sophie. "You
need to see a bit more of life. Right now, we have a job to
do. We have to bring Scott and Darcey back together again.
We were *family*. We will be family again."

Samantha stayed silent for a moment. "I don't have your
faith, Mum, though I guess it says something Darcey is willing to come?"

"True." Sophie nodded.

"When are you going to tell Scott?"

"I'll wait until he's ready," said Sophie.

Samantha raked a hand through her russet mane, visualizing what would surely be a tempestuous event. "And when's that? No one tells Scott what to do, even you, Mum."

"Being without Darcey is like torture for my son. He's under a lot of stress he won't let out. I'm his mother. It's *my* job to take care of him in a way he needs. If Darcey and Scott haven't communicated with each other, they need me. I know, because God told me."

"It's a wonder you and God didn't plan on allowing Darcey to show up unannounced," Samantha retorted smartly.

"Now, *that* would have been a problem."

"Whenever you plan to tell him, I want your promise you'll tell me first." Samantha held her mother's gaze.

"You know I can't possibly tell him without you to back me, Sam. I thought a week before?"

Samantha's face registered her grave concerns. "If you're okay with that, I guess I'll have to go along. After all, the deed is done. If either of us had any sense, we'd be running scared."

"I know he loves her," said Sophie. "Nothing has really changed. We knew Ashlee and the others would rush in to take Darcey's place. We know Ashlee and her mother have been making plans—"

"Ashlee hates Darcey, Mum," Samantha felt compelled to remind her mother.

"Well, they didn't really get on, I know."

"Wasn't there a reason for that? Ashlee has always been in love with Scott, then along came Darcey and snatched him away."

"She did no such thing. It was love at first sight."

"Only it didn't last, did it, Mum? Do you really think Ashlee will be able to control herself when Darcey shows up?"

"I'll be keeping a close watch," said Sophie.

"Only it's not settled yet, Mum. Scott will probably forbid it."

"If he's that upset, we'll cancel it," said Sophie, fingers and toes crossed.

Chapter Two

Things had moved so fast she really hadn't had enough time to consider the huge step she had taken. Now it was too late. The three-hour domestic flight from Brisbane to Longreach in Outback Queensland was coming in to land. She was to be met at the airport by someone from the station. She didn't for one moment think it would be Scott. No matter what soothing words Sophie had offered, she knew Scott would be furious his mother had invited her for Christmas.

The big question, however, was *not* why Sophie had invited her. It was why *she* had accepted Sophie's invitation. The divorce had been very public. The MacArthurs were among the nation's pioneering families.

Scott, when she had confronted him with his alleged betrayal, had reacted with a proud man's fury and utter disbelief. He had called her, among other deeply upsetting names, a "gullible little fool." According to Scott she had been hypnotized for years by her aunt. *"Aren't I supposed to come first with you, not your ego maniac aunt?"* Rebecca was "a conniving bitch with the IQ of an onion" who had never impressed him as Darcey's *friend*. Rather, Becky was a *parasite* who had fed off Darcey and her "foolishly kind heart."

The husband she had adored treating her like a hapless teenager had been the last straw for Darcey. Where was the respect? Scott's tirade had left her distraught and overwhelmed. She had retaliated from the bottom of her beaten-to-a-pulp heart. Her trust in Scott, her husband, had been profound. When subjected to his *real* opinion of her and his violent dislike of the aunt who had always been there for her threw her into a quandary that could only be solved by separation. Divorce? She had shuddered away from that at the beginning even as she was aware she had made herself dependent not only on her aunt but the husband she had adored. She had felt undervalued and unrespected. The time had surely come for her to emerge from the chrysalis of her tragic youth.

Marry in haste, repent at leisure.

The fallout from their separation had been enormous. Family and friends had taken sides as in a mammoth battle. Her father, while not exactly on Scott's side, had found Scott's alleged betrayal extremely hard to believe.

"I can see Rachael's meddlesome fingers in all this, but God knows why! She used to fancy herself in competition with your mother, believe it or not. But that could hardly apply to you."

It was impossible to believe her aunt would lie to her. Aunt Rachael had trained herself to be utterly truthful, as Darcey was herself. Aunt Rachael held to her solemn belief she had been doing the right thing warning her niece. Her opinion held a lot of sway. Rachael Richardson was known to be an upstanding woman within the wide community and a scrupulously honest businesswoman. Her devotion to her niece was well known. Besides, there was Rebecca's testimony, to which Rebecca held fast.

Rebecca had had nothing to gain but the loss of a well-connected and generous friend.

At that terrible time, both she and Scott had not been able to get their emotions under control. Both had erected huge impregnable walls around themselves, with one side refusing to acknowledge the other until the divorce had gone through. The MacArthurs were amongst the wealthiest families in the country. Darcey had been adamant she wanted no settlement. She had been advised by her lawyers to accept one. She had never in the intervening two years touched a cent of it.

Ultimately she had to confront the fact she had trusted her aunt above the husband she had professed to love. Agony though it was, her decision at the time had seemed straightforward. She couldn't live with betrayal. She wasn't the first woman, she wouldn't be the last. Could *any* man be relied upon to be utterly faithful? Aunt Rachael said not. Adultery struck at the very foundation of marriage. She had come to terms with the fact the past and her vulnerable nature had made her overly emotional. Her basic confidence had been shot to pieces by the death of her mother.

As a young girl she had experienced intense grief and uncertainty over what life might bring. Her father had organized therapy for her. The therapy had helped. She had developed to the extent she performed exceptionally well at university and made many friends. University had proved to be a "safe" environment.

Once she had graduated with a first class architectural degree, her father's old firm had approached her. Flattered, she had signed on. Her work became her life. People regarded her as a clever, capable young woman.

Everyone had their secrets.

She had returned to her old firm six months after the divorce had been finalized. This current year she had won a prestigious award for her design for a country farmhouse.

She had not exceeded her youngish clients' relatively modest budget, but she had delivered a farmhouse everyone in the farming district they lived in admired.

Since then she had gone freelance with surprising success. She was her own boss! Success had to be applauded. Her father and Anne had told her many times how proud they were of her. Indeed, they had wanted her to come to London, but as a Queenslander she didn't know how she would cope long term with the English climate and the everlasting rain. As an English dignitary once said to a visiting Arab prince, "I believe you worship the sun," to which the prince replied, "So would you if you ever saw it."

The domestic flight touched down right on time, releasing the passengers into Outback heat. The tarmac was red hot, the air thick as molasses. She was glad she had travelled in lightweight clothing, navy loose-legged pants with a double white stripe and a white cotton camisole edged in navy, with open-toed leather sandals on her feet. Her long blue-black hair she had pulled back from her face and secured in an updated knot. She was shaking with nerves inside though no one would have known it from her composed face and demeanour. One of the rewards of therapy.

The way she had acted with Scott . . . Dear God! Her cringeworthy behaviour couldn't have been farther from her norm. She had flown at him in an unprecedented rage, rejecting out of hand his instant furious redhead's response. She could still hear that hateful voice she had somehow acquired like a tinnitus in her head. Where had the hostility come from after all they had shared together? The answer? The love of her life had betrayed her. Threatened all that she had held dear. Such a loss had been unbearable for her. Didn't Scott understand that? Grief was all in the mind, her analyst had assured her, only she had not yet learned to control her mind. She could control her body. Her daily run, her hard work and devotion to her profession kept her sane.

Success or not, you're in a rut.

Then another grace note sent out of the blue. Sophie had written to her. It was one of Sophie's grand gestures. Once upon a time Darcey and her mother-in-law had been very close. Sophie had many of the same heart-warming qualities as the mother Darcey had lost. She had written her acceptance reply half sobbing all the while, signing off, *With love, Darcey.*

She wanted to go back to Planet Downs. She wanted to see the family again. They had been so kind to her. They had been shattered by her and Scott's mutual decision to divorce. Above all she wanted to see Scott again. Things had to be put right. Accounts had to be settled. Christmas surely had to be the best time for reconciliation.

Inside the large light-filled terminal it was blessedly cool. The locals back home from trips to the "Big Smoke" were being met by family members. Tourists en route to Darwin, the gateway to Australia, wandered back and forth to a lively thrum of noise and conversation.

She needed to wait for the passenger luggage to be unloaded. It shouldn't take long. She had brought two large pieces with her. The evening dress for the ball had taken up one piece alone. It wouldn't be her first ball on the station. Such wonderful times! Her memories threatened to make her cry. She had always been too emotional. After Scott, she had found she couldn't respond to other men. While she gave out no come-on signals, there were quite a few wanting to take his place. Only no one measured up to *her* Scott, the husband she had once loved with all her heart.

Even in the crowded terminal she became aware of a ripple that was stirring up the air. There was an abrupt cessation of conversation as well. What was happening? She was sufficiently curious to turn her head.

What she saw took her breath away.

A stunningly handsome man well over six feet wearing

a dark blue Lacoste polo shirt, fitted jeans, high boots on his feet had entered the terminal. He had a shock of dark auburn hair, burnished when it caught a stray ray of sunlight; hair that would catch anyone's attention.

Scott!

Her mind jammed.

She couldn't move. She couldn't speak.

Past and present blurred.

There was such a hard pressure of her every breath she might have been a woman suffering from broken ribs. Whatever she had imagined, it wasn't *this*.

Get control. Her inner voice broke in. *This isn't the time to allow your emotions to run riot.*

Scott was making towards *her*, his long strides as sleek and powerful as a big cat's. Scott was far more than just a handsome man. He radiated presence. Authority. This was a man who would come off well no matter how difficult the situation. The women in the area, true to form, were staring at him open mouthed. Some were whispering among themselves. Some were even gasping with vicarious excitement.

He isn't a visiting movie star. He's my ex-husband.

The magnitude of the man was enough to overwhelm any woman. Darcey was fearful now that she was here, she might not be able to cope. Emotional tears had sprung into her eyes. She put up a hand to snatch a teardrop away. How she had missed him! Once such an admission would have had to be dragged out of her, but in truth she had never gone beyond her heartbreaking memories. She had thought of him every single day. How many times—forty, fifty, sixty? Come night-time, she had been desperate for the weight of his body on hers, the shuddering ecstasy of their lovemaking. There had been no solace anywhere. Scott had set the benchmark against which all other men were judged. She had lived life without him, overcome by loss.

But she still had her pride. Not that it had done her any good.

He reached her in no time. Startlingly blue eyes swept over her, deliberately appraising. "Darcey, darling!"

His voice had always had a great physical attraction for her. Deep, dark, resonant, cultured. The voice of a man born to wealth and privilege. There was no love, no tenderness in his blue-fire eyes. She heard the contempt in the "darling" if no one else did. People were *smiling* as if witnessing a rapturous lovers' reunion.

"How wonderful to see you. Two years? It could be a lifetime."

For a long moment he held her sea-grey eyes. Then matching decision to action, he reached for her, folding her in tight to his tall, lean body kissing her long and hard on the mouth.

Hunger and Punishment.

Both emotions seemed to mingle in a sensual exchange that had to be born out of sheer starvation. Love might have flown, but sexual attraction never died. She did not attempt to fight his inevitable dominion. She couldn't. Their bodies fit exactly as they used to, in exactly the same places. Their bodies refused to play the game of pretence. She clung to him until he let her go, though he kept one steadying hand at her back. A habit unbroken by time.

Her mouth was throbbing. Adrenalin was blasting like a tornado through her veins. It was *too* easy to remember. The *force* of him! His arms around her! Her utter belief that with Scott she was safe.

This is what it means to belong to a man.

"You're well, surely? Tell me you're fine?" he asked, drawing back to gaze down on her, mockery in his dazzling blue eyes.

You're not the wretched heartbroken young woman you once were, Darcey.

"Peace to you too, Scott," she answered, breathless. "How glad I am to see you've conquered the ghosts of the past."

"*Ghosts?* What ghosts?" He took her nerveless arm, shepherding her towards the luggage chute as if they didn't have a moment to lose before they could be alone.

"Seriously, I applaud your positive attitude." Despite their long separation, she remained incredibly attuned to him.

"But Darcey, darling, I was always positive. You must remember that?" He kept a smile on his face for the benefit of the seriously avid onlookers. "Why have you come?"

She took a deep breath. "Sophie asked me."

"Even though you must know you've walked recklessly into my den?"

"Isn't there something medieval about that?" she asked. "You know, demons and dragons?"

"Strong emotions remain the same down the ages, Darcey. But of course, you are egging me on. That's what women do, isn't it?"

"You could have said no. I would have respected that," she said endeavouring to lessen the tremendous build-up of emotion.

"Really?" His cutting tone tossed her answer aside. "Please don't talk to me about respect."

She was silent for a moment. "Is this to be the sum of it, Scott? I rather hoped we could get through this. I don't want bad feeling between us."

His answer couldn't have been more direct. "You expect me to share that sentiment?"

"For Sophie's sake."

"You're suggesting neutral territory?"

"If it's at all possible?"

"Less of an embarrassment that way," he agreed. "I think

this is my mother's ill-conceived effort to bring us back together."

"I'm so sorry if you think that." She dared glance up at him, the strong regular features.

"Ah, the sweetness of your voice, Darcey!" he mocked. "Before we shove the matter aside, can you tell me one thing? Have you ever once thought you *should* have believed me?"

"I've come close," was all she was prepared to say.

"Manipulation by *charm*. You're so damned good at it. I'm surprised you haven't remarried." He glanced down at her lovely face with its Madonna-like serenity. Even in the searing heat she looked as cool as a lily. Her skin always did have the lustre of a pearl. He had a sharp memory of dipping his head into the skin of her face, her throat, her breasts . . . "Or can't you let go?"

"I'm fine. I have my work."

"And awards too, I hear. My congratulations. I remember the time when you wanted to make changes to the homestead."

"I don't deny it, but that was in due course. I recall you were considering it."

"I would have given you the sun, moon, and stars," he said with acid self-deprecation.

"How's Ashlee?" she asked, to change the subject.

"The same as ever." He spoke dismissively.

"Then she's still in love with you."

"Along with others." That delivered with black humour.

Only it wasn't a joke. Scott had to be one of the most eligible men in the country.

"I'm not going to marry Ashlee, Darcey, if that's what you're asking. I never *was* going to marry Ashlee."

"Does she know?"

Only then did she remember how much Ashlee Hunter

had disliked her, though *dislike* was too tame a word. She would have her work cut out for her getting a hello out of Ashlee.

"I pray she does," he said shortly.

"Hope springs eternal."

"That's the vanity of women. Why don't we forget Ashlee. She'll find the right man. I loved *you* more than I can say, Darcey. Ashlee was on the scene then, remember? We married. Marriage means getting through the highs and the lows. Or it does to me. It means commitment. Only you were just a little lost girl, not the woman I thought you were. It takes time getting over betrayal. I can't understand what possessed you to come."

"Forgiveness, Scott," she said, low-voiced.

He shrugged, unmoved. "Not yet. Not ever!" He gave her a glance that told her she was quite mad to think otherwise.

"Forgiveness on *both* sides," she suggested, her breath quaking. "You might give a thought to your own behaviour."

"*Your* accusations surpassed all understanding. Anyway, it's all history now." He gave an ironic shrug. "My mother wants you here. She's extraordinarily fond of you, God knows why. Why else do you think I've come for you? I love my mother though she *will* interfere."

"She wants what's best for you, Scott."

He gave a brief laugh. "Then one has to question her decision to invite you. I realize she wants me to find happiness again. Only, my dear Darcey, that woman certainly isn't going to be *you*."

His words would have crushed her, only her heart was already crushed. "I accept that, Scott," she said, bowing her glossy raven head. "Sophie did say you'd missed me."

"Not true," he snapped. "My mother specializes in cases of emotional drama. I'm not good at forgiveness, Darcey. Not in your case anyway. Our marriage was as substantial as a desert mirage. I expect why you've really come is to assuage your guilt."

"Like it or not, Scott. I'm *here*. I promise I won't bother you in any way."

"Thank you," he said suavely, "though I doubt you could. I've always—" He broke off as a boy old enough to know better came careening at them with a laden luggage trolley. It seemed inevitable to Darcey it would hit her. She even made a little sound of alarm, but Scott moved swiftly. He threw a strong arm around her and pulled her out of harm's way.

"You okay?" he asked with what had to be sharp, temporary concern.

"I'm fine." When she was on the fine edge of despair?

"Wait here." He strode away before she could say another word. He went after the boy, easily catching up with him. He was talking so quietly his resonant voice didn't reach her, but the boy was looking at him, his ears red, his expression over-awed and thoroughly repentant.

Darcey turned away. There were always lessons in life to be learned. Mercifully the passenger luggage had arrived. It was already rolling down the chute.

Scott, on his way back, made directly for the chute. He gave her a wry backwards glance when he pulled her two heavy pieces off the chute and set them down on the ground.

"Is this your entire wardrobe here? Just how long is it you plan to stay?" he asked sardonically, when he joined her.

Colour lit the delicate slant of her cheekbones. "It's the evening dress," she explained. "It took up most of one case."

For a split second Scott's mask slipped. There was strong emotion there. Emotion of a man who felt himself threatened by his own needs? "I daresay you'll be belle of the ball again. Just like old times. Times we both know are forever closed to us."

That painful knowledge made her wince.
Don't cry.
Dammit, I won't!

She hadn't expected Scott would have come for her in the Beech Baron for such a short flight. He had flown in one of the station's blue and silver choppers with the station's insignia, a stylized *PD*. Planet Downs was one of the very first cattle stations to be established in the mid 1880s in the Australian Outback. Indeed, the Channel Country was known to the nation as the home of the cattle kings.

Tears were trapped behind her eyes. Nothing seemed changed, she thought, her heart swelling as she looked down. How mighty was the land! So full of mystique and countless aboriginal legends.

They were across the station's south-eastern border now, in sight of the homestead, surrounded by its numerous satellite buildings. It truly was a kingdom in the middle of the wilds. A kingdom almost devoid of human habitation. The sight couldn't have appeared more dramatic to Darcey, the exile.

Planet Downs had been given its name because in the nineteenth century when it was founded, the furnace red soil was thought to be akin to the burning red soil of Planet Mars. It wasn't all that long ago NASA had revealed Planet Mars wasn't red at all, but a disappointing *brown*.

The vast landscape beneath them, however, was a fiery red in stark contrast to the thousands and thousands of golden spinifex mounds that covered the expanse like fields of wheat. Looking down, it was easy to see some of the numerous water channels that criss-crossed the region and gave it its name appeared to be running near dry. This would be of great concern, although Planet Downs

was blessed with several billabongs and creeks that held
permanent water.

The entire Outback was praying for rain. She, Darcey
Gilmore, once Darcey MacArthur, had been praying as
well. At the end of December they were into the monsoon
season of the tropical north. Fire and flood were the real
tragedies of the land. But rain! Rain turned the parched
region into a wonderland of wild flowers. Every lake, water
channel, billabong and lignum swamp on Planet Downs
overflowed, bringing in legions of nomadic birds to nest.

Once Scott had led her down a near-inaccessible wild
lignum swamp to where the pelicans had come to build
their nests. She remembered that adventure with intensity.
Scott didn't make that offer to everyone any more than to
show them the aboriginal rock paintings in the Hill Country.
These were privileges.

Chapter Three

They were greeted by a tall, trim station hand the moment they touched down. It came as a relief to Darcey that she didn't know the man. He tipped his Akubra respectfully. She smiled back.

"Put the luggage in the back of the jeep, Tom," Scott called to him. "I'll take it up to the house."

"Yep, Boss."

"Tell Linc I'll meet him at the holding yard."

"Righty-O."

Neither of them spoke a word on the trip to the house. They sat side by side like Easter Island statues. Scott circled the home driveway, pulling up at the base of the short flight of steps leading up to the homestead's broad porch. The huge building of beautiful honey-coloured sandstone, the same Helidon stone used in the construction of the Queensland University, shimmered in the strong sunlight. It was just as she remembered it, a Georgian manor house that belonged in the British countryside, never in the Australian Outback.

Memories of Home, it was called. An attempt to recreate some semblance of the homeland they had left. The original central section was flanked by two large wings. The homestead was universally regarded as a very impressive building. The wings had been added at a later date. In Darcey's view, they didn't respect the history, the spirit, or the style of the main dwelling. She knew exactly how she could change that. Once Scott had been prepared to let her. That chance was forever gone.

The luxuriant dry climate gardens she remembered looked parched. All that appeared to be thriving were the evergreen flame trees in gorgeous Christmas colour and the towering date palms that lined the long drive and gave it great drama.

"So here we are again," Scott said laconically. "Let's get straight to business." He hopped out of the jeep to unload her suitcases, carrying them up onto the porch while Darcey stood looking at him. Sophie had given her the opportunity to come, to set things right. Where was Sophie? She felt like some delicate plant hopelessly out of its habitat.

Barely a moment more and Sophie's small, slender figure came running out of the open front door, holding up her arms, just like the old days before all the grief and anger had set in.

"Darcey!"

Suddenly Darcey was crying. She didn't deserve this.

"Darcey, love!" Sophie reached her, gathering her into a hug, her body trembling with genuine delight. Her eyes too were glittering with tears.

Scott stood back viewing them both sardonically. "It's not the Prodigal's return Mother."

"Oh, I'm so happy, happy. You're going to stay for a bite to eat, darling?" she asked her son.

Scott walked swiftly and very purposefully down the steps. "I've work to do, ladies. I expect you've got plenty to talk about." His blue eyes held a brilliant satiric gleam.

"Oh, we have!" Sophie cried cheerfully. "Ask Linc back to dinner."

Scott turned on his heel. "Shouldn't you check with Sam first? Sorry. You *don't* check. How could I forget!"

"Ask him, please, dear," Sophie repeated, putting her arm around Darcey's waist and leading her into the cool of the large entrance hall where the Christmas tree in all its glory reigned.

"How beautiful it is!" Darcey exclaimed. "Quite magical." Once upon a time she had helped Sophie and Samantha decorate the Christmas tree. What joy they'd had! The carefree laughter!

Both of them were looking rather tearfully in the direction of the tree when Samantha, dressed casually in a sleeveless cotton top and short skirt that showed off her great legs, walked down the stairs. Her body language was unmistakeable.

"So you're back with us, Darcey?" she said.

"Hello, Sam," Darcey responded with her lovely gentle smile. "It was very good of Sophie to ask me." She moved towards her once bridesmaid and sister-in-law, holding out her hand. "How are you?"

"I'm well thank you, Darcey," Samantha responded. "You look as beautiful as ever. I'm sure you know inviting you wasn't exactly what Scott wanted," she added, proving her good manners by accepting Darcey's hand.

"I realise that, Sam," Darcey said, feeling cut off from the warm friendship she and Samantha had shared. "I've promised Scott I'm not going to bother him in any way."

"But you don't always keep your promises, do you, Darcey?" Samantha pointed out with just the faintest suggestion of hostility.

Sophie gave her daughter a smile that was decidedly on

the frosty side. "We've discussed all this, Samantha. There will be peace at Christmas. Darcey is our guest."

"Of course, I'm sorry," Samantha responded calmly, though there was a certain lack of Christian forgiveness in her expression.

Darcey wasn't surprised by Samantha's attitude. Samantha was a spirited young woman with the redhead's hot temper. She idolized her brother, the "finest of the finest," which meant she had an unshakable belief in his word. In Samantha's eyes, her brother could do no wrong. The wrong would always remain Darcey's.

While they stood there, a degree of tension between them, a good-natured-looking woman in her late fifties with short blunt cut orange hair, obviously dyed, an apron around her ample middle, bustled into the entrance hall, a beaming smile of her face.

"Mrs. Darcey!" she cried, clearly elated. "I heard your voice!"

Ah, the voice of angels! So much for the divorce then, Samantha thought watching on with some irony while the two came together. It was like a scene out of some tear-jerker movie. The renewal of communication. Darcey threw an arm around their housekeeper, giving Clarry an affectionate hug which was warmly returned. Clarry always had thought the world of Darcey. *A beautiful soul in a beautiful body.* Or so everyone had thought.

Even now Samantha didn't believe Darcey had been deliberately treacherous—it wasn't in her nature—more she had been a pawn in the hands of her aunt, who surprisingly had been taken in as well by a lying young tart called Becky. Probably Darcey's so-called friend had been insanely jealous of her and wanted to wreck her marriage. Why else would she have lied? She must have been extremely convincing to convince the likes of Darcey's formidable aunt.

The cause for her loss of faith in Darcey was how totally her sister-in-law had trusted her aunt's judgement. That had been so hard to understand. Gratitude, which Darcey undoubtedly felt, was *not* love. They all knew Darcey believed she owed her aunt big time, but she didn't love her aunt in the customary way. Samantha feared Scott's powerful love for Darcey could put him at risk again. Maybe their mother was right. There was no one else for Scott but Darcey.

Right or wrong.

The kind of beauty Darcey possessed had enormous *emotional* as well as sexual impact. Samantha prayed the results of their mother's well-meant experiment would not have disastrous results.

They walked up the graceful sweep of the staircase together, she and Sophie. Samantha had excused herself saying she had things to do. Darcey walked slowly, allowing her hand to trail over the gleaming mahogany handrail. She remembered how many times Scott had carried her up to bed, both of them hungry for each other.

Sophie turned towards the left wing, a short way along opening the door of the largest and easily the best of the guest rooms. Darcey knew it well.

"I hope this will do, love." Sophie sounded almost apologetic.

"It's fine. It's lovely. You're so kind to me, Sophie. I feel I don't deserve it."

"We all deserve a second chance, Darcey," Sophie pointed out. "You still love my son, don't you?" She held the starry silver-grey eyes of the young woman she still considered her daughter-in-law.

Darcey's glossy head drooped. "Scott has told me he has moved on."

"Has he? Both of you are still looking backwards," Sophie said. "There's no point in that. Both of you must look forwards. That's why I invited you here. How is your dear aunt, by the way?"

Darcey had to laugh. "She's spending Christmas in Thailand with a group of friends."

"So she's made some, has she?" Sophie asked.

"Not my concern, Sophie. I give my aunt a wide berth these days."

"I bet she can't believe it, considering the power she had?"

"I didn't have all the answers then, Sophie. Scott was right. I was too young for my age. Too easily manipulated."

"Well, you're not now," Sophie said firmly and gave Darcey a quick kiss. "Would you like me to send up tea or coffee?"

Darcey smiled. "No thanks, Sophie. Jet lag has pounced. I'll have a nap. I've been on the go since early morning."

"Of course, dear." Sophie walked to the door. "Come down whenever you're ready. I've invited our foreman Linc Enright for dinner. You'll like him."

"Enright?" Darcey frowned as she tried to slot in the name. She had a vague recollection of hearing it before. "Lincoln Enright around the same age as Scott? He's said to be George Challenor's illegitimate son?"

"Not said to be. He is, but George is a grade-A old bastard, for want of a better name. He refuses to recognize Linc. Illegitimate and all that rubbish!"

"How cruel." She remembered Challenor as a ruthless old villain, a cattleman, extremely rich.

"Indeed it is. Linc is a fine young man. These have been hard times for people on the land with the drought. Linc had been developing a small holding that went bust for all his efforts about ten months ago. Scott gave Linc a job. He's been worth every penny. Scott didn't tell Samantha until afterwards. Sam, being Sam, took it rather badly. In fact, she made a major production of it. She had met Linc several times previously without letting on. It may appear to you she doesn't like him. She does."

Darcey was silent for a moment, letting that sink in. "Well, well, well!" she said.

"Couldn't have put it better myself."

As she came down the staircase she heard the sound of voices, the women's voices overlapping the men's. She was the last to arrive for a pre-dinner drink. To her amazement she had slept for a solid three hours, but she had awakened refreshed.

Clarry had seen to it her luggage was taken upstairs, unpacked, various items folded into a tall chest of drawers, or in the case of her clothes, hung up. She had no difficulty selecting the dress she intended to wear. A short dress, silk, fluid in motion, emerald in colour. It seemed to change the colour of her eyes. It was simple yet sophisticated and it fitted her body well. Her long hair she wore in the customary updated knot. No jewellery around her throat, but she popped into her pierced ears, her mother's pavé diamond pendant earrings. Earrings she wore frequently. She had left all the jewellery Scott had given her, including her magnificent engagement ring, behind.

She hadn't bothered to open the stack of unopened Christmas cards she had received just before she left. She would open them Christmas morning. Probably the once-a-year catch-ups. She had met up with or spoken on the phone to all the people closest to her.

"Ah, here you are!" Scott was the first to speak. He sounded perfectly charming. "We feared you were going to sleep through."

"I'm sorry," she said, smiling at each face in turn. "I was a little tired, but I'm myself again."

"No apology needed," said Scott expansively. "You were hours in the air. What are you going to have?"

She didn't feel happy about nominating champagne. This wasn't a celebration. Instead she said, "A sauvignon blanc if you have it?"

"Sauvignon blanc coming up. Tasmanian. This is Linc, by the way. Linc, meet Darcey."

Of course Linc knew she had been Scott's wife. Nevertheless he came forward, a real smile on his handsome face. He lightly took Darcey's extended hand with her fine-boned fingers. "Good to meet you, Darcey. I may call you Darcey?"

"Please do. I'm happy to meet you too, Linc." Linc didn't look like a station hand. He looked like he *belonged* in this huge grand drawing room with its wall-to-wall treasures acquired down the generations. He was tall. Almost as tall as Scott, deeply tanned, good skin over good bones, wearing much the same sort of outfit as Scott. Dark dress trousers and smart informal open-necked dress shirt. Auburn-headed Scott with his blazing blue eyes wore a black shirt with pearly white buttons; Linc, sun-bleached blond wavy hair clinging to his head, hazel eyes. He mightn't have had the kind of presence that made Scott the centre of attention even in crowded rooms, but he would fan a few fires in lots of girls' hearts. Did that include Samantha who was sitting, drink in hand, the expression on her face intent, as though she had a few problems she had to sort out? Both Samantha and Sophie looked lovely in light and airy ankle-length dresses.

Darcey was amazed and relieved at how well dinner went. Scott, as heir to a cattle empire which entailed many dealings with government and fellow colleagues and cattlemen, both at home and abroad, had been raised to be a diplomat. He was the perfect host, like the Scott she had first met, but she knew better than anyone what went on behind his eyes.

Conversation ranged over a number of non-controversial subjects. Darcey didn't have to work at taking part. She had become something of a conversationalist herself. Linc opened his hazel eyes wide when Scott told him Darcey had recently won a prestigious architectural award for a country farm building.

"That's wonderful!" Linc's face was alight with genuine interest. "You must be gifted."

"Inherited genes. My father is an internationally recognized architect. He works in London these days. I always wanted to be an architect from when I was a small girl."

Architect. Not a wife.

She could see the thought in Scott's blue eyes that moved constantly over her. Her reactions were disturbing, but she was prepared for that. She had to find a way to get through to him. With the passing of time, lost bits of memory were returning, the force for good that Scott had been in her life. She had stepped closer and closer to the realization she could have made a terrible mistake. Closer to declaiming her accusations.

"Did you bring your riding gear, Darcey?" Samantha asked, sounding hopeful.

"She brought everything she owns," said Scott so laconically it raised a laugh.

"Great!" Samantha brightened up. "The cousins will be arriving tomorrow. Not a one of them knows one end of the horse from the other. Apart from Duncan, that is."

"Exaggeration, darling," said Sophie. "You remember Duncan, Darcey?"

"Of course." Duncan had been a guest at their wedding.

"Duncan is captain of the opposing polo team," Scott offered.

"You play, Linc?" Darcey turned her head to ask.

"Love it. I'm on Scott's team, needless to say."

"Why *needless*?" Samantha interjected, suddenly looking like a girl on fire.

"Because he's way better than anyone else on Duncan's team," her brother responded.

"Well, we'll see, won't we?" Samantha said, as though she wasn't expecting Linc to shine.

What was the problem? Darcey thought. She had caught Samantha staring at Linc when he wasn't looking, then hurriedly looking away. "I'm looking forward to the match," she said gently, to fill the awkward gap. "It seems so long since I attended one."

Part of the MacArthur portfolio was the ownership of one of the finest breeding establishments for polo ponies. She knew from experience polo had to be one of the most exciting and demanding sports in the world. It was hard to avoid dangerous collisions at top speed. She had worried a good deal when Scott played. Though he was one of the highest ranked players in the country, the game could be seriously dangerous even for him.

"I don't get out much," she confessed.

"That's hard to believe," said Sam in her straightforward fashion. "You must be overwhelmed by invitations to all kinds of functions."

"Not many tempt me, Sam. I work full days."

"You have to know when to stop, Darcey," Samantha said seriously. "You must take a look at the Great Hall in the morning. Nothing has changed since you had it repainted. Mum and I did the decorating, but gosh, we missed"—she caught herself up before she added *you*—"decorating isn't really our scene, is it, Mum?"

"I'm sure Darcey will have plenty of ideas," Scott broke in. "There's all day tomorrow to make any changes."

The entire station was abuzz, but Samantha found time to take Darcey out to the Great Hall where the Après Polo Ball was to be held Saturday night. Guests would stay well into Sunday, when they would begin their return home for Christmas Day, which fell on the Monday.

"Say exactly what you think," Sam invited as they walked into the vast space used for all sorts of meetings.

Darcey lifted her head. "I mean, can I?"

"Of course. You're an artist, Darcey. An architect. Do you still paint?"

"When I have time, which isn't often. I'll never be as good as my mother."

"You could be. Does dear Auntie still handle your mother's work?"

Darcey had to smile. "There aren't any more paintings left except for those belonging to my father and me. We will never part with them."

"I bet Auntie has tried to persuade you," Samantha suggested, sardonically.

Darcey didn't answer. Of course she had.

"You're not impressed?" Samantha asked, somewhat worriedly as Darcey walked farther into the hall, looking about her.

"Sam, Sam, you've done extremely well."

"Any suggestions?"

"Let me think about it." She already had a few in mind. "What's with you and Linc Enright?"

"Don't ask," Samantha said drolly.

"I *am* asking as someone who cares about you. Someone who has made a lot of mistakes."

Samantha turned to her, her blue gaze serious. "This is *vital*, Darcey. Why are you here? Do you still care about my brother? I need to know. I'm the sort of person who needs things out in the open."

"I *know* that, Sam," Darcey said, tears in her throat. "I left the love of my life. He left me. I wouldn't recommend that course of action to anyone. I work hard. I'm praised. I can't connect to any other man. What I wanted from Scott was total commitment. Total fidelity. It may have been a moment of aberration with Rebecca, but I found to my grief the kind of love I craved was unattainable."

Samantha fought down her exasperation. She could see Darcey was utterly sincere. "So you still believe Scott betrayed you? How sad that is. How *insane*."

"Well, you are and always will be on Scott's side. That's part of being a loving sister."

"Let's try again," Samantha said patiently. "We MacArthurs don't lie. Scott even as a boy was never known to be caught out in the tiniest fib. I think you should consider very seriously there may have been a conspiracy."

"You think I haven't?" Darcey's silver eyes sparkled. "Whatever faults my aunt has, she doesn't lie either."

"But that little ratbag Rebecca was surely up to it?"

"To what end?" Darcey asked, having pursued that very question endlessly. "I've never spoken to her from that terrible day to this."

Samantha shook her rich auburn head. "So where is she? You don't know?"

"I had heard she was travelling, maybe settled in Ireland. She had relatives of her mother's there."

"So where did she get the money?" Samantha asked, refusing to let go now that she had the opportunity. "Did you give her some? You used to, didn't you?"

"Sam, I gave her nothing," Darcey cried in despair. "I did tell her to disappear."

"Strange that she did. One needs money to disappear," Samantha pointed out. "Our understanding was she used to borrow from you and perhaps others to survive. She was just an ordinary working girl living from week to week."

"Day to day was more like it. Obviously she borrowed from someone to get out of the country."

"Sure it wasn't Auntie?" Samantha fixed Darcey with the piercing MacArthur regard.

"For God's sake, Sam. My aunt despised her."

Samantha gave a tight smile. "Your dear aunt despises everyone on the planet. But take note, she wouldn't be above using that Becky. One or both are lying."

"No, no!" Darcey shook her head.

"Didn't you tell me once your dad thought your aunt Rachael was secretly very jealous of your mother?"

"Well . . ." All kinds of emotions flitted across Darcey's face. "My mother was so beautiful, so gifted, so loved. She had a husband, a child."

"In short, she was everything your aunt was not. Mum and I believe your aunt might have had an enormous crush on your father. He's a very impressive man, and you said yourself that your aunt knew him first."

"Only Aunt Rachael is a man-hater, Sam," Darcey pointed out, her jaw tight.

"We *all* are, but we still love them."

Darcey walked on. "Don't go ahead with this, Sam," she begged. "You're suggesting my aunt is a monster?"

"The grim reaper." Samantha only half joked.

"She would never deliberately set out to break up my marriage. She loves me in her own way. I know she's very hurt at the way our relationship has gone."

"Shoot the messenger?" Sam asked, with perfect accuracy.

"It happens. She told me I lacked maturity."

"Is *that* what she said?" Samantha fumed.

"It's what Scott said as well," Darcey reminded her. "And that's not all."

Sam flushed. "Darcey, you broke his heart. It was like his whole world had come to an end. God, Darcey, he adored you, and you accused him of being unfaithful. It would make any innocent husband as mad as hell. I bet your aunt is pleased at the way things have turned out. She has you to herself again. She had to take a huge step back when you married Scott. She would have judged that as entirely unfitting to her exalted position in your life."

Darcey touched her temples with her fingers. "Sam, Aunt Rachael can't possibly be as black as you're trying to paint her. Dad has never once said or implied Aunt Rachael ever was in love with him."

Samantha made a face. "Maybe he thought it best to keep it to himself. I bet your aunt hates Anne?"

Darcey blushed. Only too true. "I don't know that Aunt Rachael really likes anyone. There are people like that. You've asked your questions. I repeat mine. Why are you hostile to Linc? He's a very attractive man. Is it the illegitimate thing?"

"Good grief, no," Samantha replied in an instant. "I couldn't care less about such things. The thing is, Linc hurt a friend of mine rather badly. He led her on and then dumped her. She was a real mess."

Darcey bristled. She had liked Linc instinctively. "So who's the friend? Do I know her?"

"Julie Sanderson." Samantha supplied a remembered name. "She'll be here for the polo match and the ball. She'll be staying in the house."

"Well isn't that the *strangest* thing!" Darcey exclaimed. "You believe her?"

Samantha's blue eyes glowed hotly. "How can I not? I've known Julie all my life. We were at boarding school together."

"I recall that. But what if she's trying to persuade you of something against him because she can see—as I can— Linc is deeply attracted to *you*?"

Samantha straightened her back. "Hang on!"

"Think about it," Darcey urged. "I remember Julie. She once took it upon herself to inform me Ashlee was just waiting for the moment when Scott would ask her to marry him."

"What?" Samantha couldn't hide her amazement.

Darcey gestured to the high ceiling. "I think we can make this more Christmassy, don't you? For that matter we can do some more decorating in the entrance hall and up the staircase?"

"Is that what Julie really said?" Samantha asked, still caught up in Darcey's allegation.

"With a tiny touch of menace. Julie didn't take to me any more than Ashlee did."

Samantha covered her brilliant eyes with her hands. "Oh, for God's sake!" Her tone was dismayed.

"When you think about it, Sam, it's easy to destroy lives with lies. The victim of the lies sees nothing at the time. Liars are actually believed. Why is that? I think it must go deep into the psyche of the person who is lied to. The truth is more difficult to accept. We self-destruct when we listen to liars. It could well have happened to me."

"Only one way to find out," Samantha answered, with grim determination. "The two of us could take a trip. Your aunt won't talk, but we might be able to track down Rebecca."

"I think I know the answer already, Sam," said Darcey.

* * *

The day was spent with treks to and fro to the house and conservatory to add more glamour to the decoration of the Great Hall. It took time and manpower up and down ladders. Scott saw to many of the treks, but the real power was laid on in the form of two young, very fit station jackeroos.

"It's marvellous what you can achieve," said Sophie, greatly admiring of Darcey's decorating skills. "I know this weekend is going to be a great success!"

Despite a full day on the go, she was wide awake long after midnight. Her mood was curiously glittery. On the one hand she was excited, keyed up. On the other she was assailed by a sense of hopelessness. The damage she had done, not only to the husband she had professed to adore but to his family and extended family and friends, was too extensive. She had been deported. Deposed. Lovely, warm-hearted Sophie had clearly forgiven her. Even Samantha's hostility was lessening. But Scott was *toying* with her. He knew her by heart.

Tomorrow she would come in contact with another woman who loved him. Ashlee. A woman she had never had a hope of being friends with. She could just imagine how Ashlee would be seething at her return. To everyone it would look like Darcey was trying to get Scott back.

Well, aren't you?

She suspected a great many women regretted their divorce, no matter how long the marriage was. As she drifted aimlessly around her bedroom in her blue negligee and robe, her eyes fell on the small pile of presents she had bought on a shopping spree for the family. She had included one for Clarry, who she knew would never leave the MacArthur family's service. She had intended to hide them away in the pile Sophie and Samantha had already placed around the tree. Why not now, when no one was about? The family had retired hours ago. It seemed the right time to head downstairs. She placed the four beautifully wrapped presents back in the carry bag, taking hold of the plaited string handle. She needed to do this in private.

When she reached the bottom of the staircase, she found the silvery moon making glorious rectangles of light through the tall windows. All that light made it easy for her to make her way to the tree with its sparkling ornaments and jewelled glints. She had just placed the carry bag gently on the floor—there were bottles of beautiful expensive French perfume inside—when she heard a sound, soft, unidentifiable, maybe a faint scrape. She looked around. She saw nothing. Nothing was moving in the dimness beyond.

Maybe it was Santa arriving early?

The fanciful thought eased her slight panic. There was no one here to hurt her. Swiftly she brushed back her long fall of hair, allowing it to tumble over her shoulders. In her working life she always pulled her hair back. It made her feel more professional, more in charge. She couldn't help knowing people found her beautiful as her mother had been beautiful, but she concentrated on being the ultimate working woman.

She took a few more steps towards the tree when a powerful arm suddenly came out of nowhere. It snaked around her waist, nearly lifting her off her feet. She kicked and struggled when she already knew who it was. Frozen stiff in a snowdrift, she would still be able to recognise his touch.

"That's enough now," he whispered, his sensuous mouth pressed against her ear.

"You frightened me!" All the nerves of her body were jumping at once. Her heart palpitated, a fevered by-product.

"Darcey darling, I wouldn't hurt you for all the world."
He sounded amused.

"Are you going to let me go?"

The pity of it all is that he did.

"As long as you promise you won't scream for help," he
said, breathing in the subtle fragrance of her. Not some
created perfume, but *her*. He had never forgotten. Darcey
exerted a gravitational pull like the moon with the tides, he
thought, entrapped yet again.

"What use would a scream be?" she asked. "I only
wanted to put a few presents under the tree."

"It couldn't wait until morning?" he queried with heavy
sarcasm.

"I couldn't sleep. Besides, I didn't want to draw attention to myself."

"That's a joke, right? Darcey, you were *born* to draw
attention to yourself."

She might as well have been naked, so acutely did she
feel his touch on the flesh of her body. "Hardly my doing.
Are you going to let me go?"

He laughed quietly. "If you know anything at all, you
know I love holding you. But don't worry. That's the extent
of it. A man can become starved for the feel of a woman
in his arms."

Tremors were passing through her limbs. Tremors he
had to be aware of since he was holding her so tightly. "As
if you couldn't find such intimacy tomorrow. You could
have your pick of any number of women."

"Maybe," he agreed. "What is the difference between
women? Beautiful women a man can admire or women
that can fill a man with a pain-filled desperate longing?
I've been shocked to find I don't hanker for any woman
at all."

"I'm glad!" She couldn't help her little outburst. She couldn't bear any other woman to take her place.

"You would be," he said, caustically. "As I recall, you wanted me damned."

She leaned her upper body forward over his locked arms, to ease the pressure on her heart. "I didn't. How can you say that?"

"You *said* it," he replied with a voice full of sharp accusation.

"I didn't *mean* to say it. I was half out of my mind."

"Indeed you were," he said, handing down his harsh judgement.

"You'll have to find the right woman sooner or later," she said, bringing herself upright again. "You need an heir. You need a woman for that."

"That much is very clear, Darcey darling, only a lot seems to have gone wrong for me. *Your* fault, of course. I'm not really sure why you came downstairs at this time of night? You must remember I do a lot of prowling about."

Her voice sounded unconvincing, even to her own ears. "I promise you, Scott, I never thought for a moment I would meet up with you."

"I think you did. Somewhere some part of you did." Very slowly his hands moved up from her waist to her breasts. She was utterly ensnared. "I think I deserve a little something from you, Darcey."

She let him do it. Caress her, her breath coming shorter and shorter. The roughened tips of his long, elegant fingers teased her sensitive nipples, calling up wave after wave of sensation that rolled in like surf. Deliriously erotic.

He laughed softly, turning her in his arms. "I can almost forget what it was like without you," he muttered. "It's perfectly possible to want a woman one no longer loves."

She knew there was truth in what he said. "So the plan is to punish me?"

"You *used* me, Darcey." He looked down on her lovely face, her skin spangled by multicoloured lights. "I thought you were the last person on earth to betray me."

"It was the last thing I wanted," she protested in a soft, heartbroken voice.

"Yet you allowed all the accusations and lies to get a stranglehold on you."

It was something she could never deny.

"What is it you want of me, Scott?"

"I don't know yet." His hands came up to cup her face. She was as beautiful as any woman had ever been or would ever be to him. He lowered his head, pulling her to him with a frustrated oath.

She swayed violently at the first touch of his mouth on hers while he moved into kissing her as passionately as any woman could hope and pray for.

Over and over. Just like before, when they had belonged together.

Her whole body was in a state of surrender, reacting to the barely containable excitement. She remembered all the times she had climaxed with a high-pitched sound he had always muffled gently with kisses. The high keening had been her signal she needed no more to achieve ecstasy. She had already reached the stars.

The delirium abruptly stopped.

It was Scott who appeared desperate to break free; Scott who wanted to break the spell.

"God, what's the matter with me?" he asked of no one. Roughly he put her from him but continued to hold her by her slender arms. "A few kisses, a few caresses, do they actually mean anything to you, Darcey, beyond a moment's release?"

She was shaking like a leaf, unable to speak.

"You're a witch," he pronounced. "Witches can bring everything to life again."

Out of nowhere a sense of righteousness came over her. "I've suffered too, Scott. Look gently on me. I'm not a witch or a bad woman. I'm just . . . *me*."

"You are indeed," he agreed, staring down into her delicate finely wrought face. "Now," his tone sharpened, "time for bed, wouldn't you say?"

She was shocked. "I want nothing transient, Scott. I need your respect."

"I mean bed *alone*," he reproved her coolly, allowing that to sink in. "Come along, Darcey darling. I don't think you could make it up the staircase on your own."

"I'm going to try." She tightened her robe that had long since swung apart.

"Remember when I used to carry you up the stairs?" he asked. "Your head resting on my shoulder. It was pretty well madness."

"Isn't that one of the conditions of being passionately in love?"

"You have the gall to remind me?" he asked angrily.

Suddenly she was seized by a fierce exhilaration. She took flight, only he went after her, as she hoped he would, catching her up into his arms in unforgettable fashion, making for the grand staircase.

When they reached the gallery he caught his breath. It wasn't from exertion, she knew. It was one of those moments in life when things were set to explode. It was all or nothing for Scott. In anyone else it would have been a sigh of regret. Not Scott. He lowered her to the floor, putting a gap between them. "Fools rush in and so on and so forth," he declaimed in a maddeningly theatrical voice. "Goodnight, Darcey. I'm sorry I can't tuck you into bed, but sleep well."

They were staring at each other like duellists. Certainly not the loving man and wife they had once been.

"Goodnight, Scott." She found she was able to match his tone.

One did what one had to do, she reasoned. Not what one wanted to do.

Chapter Four

Scott in his everyday working gear—open necked shirt, jeans, and high boots—was striding briskly towards the front door as Darcey came down the staircase. She had risen early. She needed a head start. There were a few things that remained to be done that morning.

Scott turned as if he recognized her very footsteps. "Darcey!" he exclaimed, laying a mocking hand to his heart.

"*Bonjour* to you too."

"Couldn't sleep?"

"Lots to do."

"Ah yes! No one better than you at pulling everything together."

"Part of my training," she said, lamenting what once had been and would never be again.

"Sophie always did give you a free hand." He touched a finger to his temple as if to remind himself of something. "Since I'm first on the scene I'll tell you. You'll be presenting the Melville Cup to the captain of the winning team this afternoon."

She couldn't conceal her agitation. "You can't be serious?"

"Guess what? I am. No one but you has ever accused me of not being serious."

"But I don't understand. Surely Sophie or Sam?"

"No need to fuss. They know all about it. They even approve. It's to reassure people, Darcey. Don't you see that? It's to help make the day a success. No hard feelings and all that. We've turned our backs on the past—"

"This is ridiculous and you know it," she cut him off sharply. "We'll convince no one."

"No way you can get out of it. It's all arranged. But lighten up. It could very well be Duncan."

"Far more likely it will be *you*," she retorted. "I'm not at all comfortable with this, Scott."

"Come along now," he urged. "You'll be fine. You know the protocol. It's not as if you haven't done it before."

All of a sudden she was furious. She flew at him, astounding him by hitting him on the chest. "That's it!" she cried. "I won't have you using that quiet, patient tone like I'm some dimwit."

He caught her hands, circling her narrow wrists. "For God's sake, Darcey, what on earth are you talking about?" He appeared genuinely puzzled.

"That was the way you spoke to me, remember? As if I were a dimwit," she accused him. Her beautiful eyes flashed lightning. Her colour was up.

"What the hell!" He drew in his breath, aware of the electric buzz that surged and sparked between them. He wanted to pick her up. Carry her away where no one could get to them. Make passionate love to her until she gave herself willingly up to him as she had always done.

"Poor little Darcey!" she self-mocked. "Poor girl, missing her mother. Never grew up. Not a woman at all. Not much more than a none-too-bright schoolgirl."

"That wouldn't sit well with your IQ, would it?" he countered, continuing to hold her hands.

"Don't try humouring me, Scott. That's over!" she cried explosively, seeing how easy it was for him to subdue her. "You have no idea what you were like. Master of your universe. I wasn't your bloody subject. I was your *wife*. I was afraid of you."

Shocked, he went pale beneath his dark tan. "You're talking absolute rubbish."

"Men! I hate you." Darcey was locked into her violent jumble of emotions. "I hate your height and your strength. Your physical superiority."

It was far beyond what he ever expected. "Darcey, I would die before I ever laid a finger on you."

"I know that!" She momentarily closed her eyes so she could get a grip on herself. "It was my mind. *My mind!* Do you understand? Why did you have to get so angry with me? Why did you have to talk down to me?"

Scott's disbelief was visible in his brilliant blue eyes. His emotions were coalescing into anger and shock. "Darcey, you were accusing me of betraying you with your stupid, bloody, treacherous friend. Did you really expect me to sit still and take it?"

"Yes!" she replied, knowing how unreasonable that sounded. "Everything we both said was just *wrong*. We were so upset. The distance between us I found unbearable."

"You created it," he pointed out bluntly. "How could you possibly believe my supposed infidelity was *true?* Yet you did. You showed you had no respect for me, your husband. I wasn't the only one to raise my voice, you might remember. I distinctly recall your shouting the place down. Like now. You weren't the downtrodden little wife you're trying to make out you were. You gave as good as you got."

"Ah, the benefit of hindsight!" she said sadly. "Conclusions based on the facts. Okay, I was my own worst enemy," she admitted, the air sucked out of her. "I thought you should have been there for me no matter what. You felt the same. I'm sorry, Scott. There, does that please you? I apologize for my shamefully immature behaviour. I broke your heart? You broke mine. A lot of people have to live with broken hearts."

"Only we didn't have to, did we?" he flashed back. "That's the thing, Darcey. I didn't break your heart. You did that all by yourself with the help of your aunt. A woman as dangerous as a taipan. You chose her word over mine. I think I had every right to be appalled."

Her heart was beating so hard she thought it might fly like a bird out of her ribcage.

"I said I'm sorry," she breathed. "I just felt like a misfit."

"Misfit, when we all loved you?" he challenged hotly, unable to believe what he was hearing. "Memory is a very faulty revival system, Darcey. You've embroidered what you remembered. The things you actually heard and the things you chose to re-hear in your own mind. Becky— whatever her name was—was and probably still is an out-and-out liar. Where the hell did she get to anyway?"

"God knows!" Darcey said, feeling utterly exposed. "It couldn't have been easy to trick Aunt Rachael."

"Aunt Rachael!" There was a world of hostility in Scott's tone. "The sooner you free yourself of that woman, the better. She is *not* what you think she is. She's a woman who would have no trouble disseminating false information if it suited her purpose. You think she loved you? You think she loved your mother? You'd better think again."

"You honestly think she would destroy my life? You think she wanted to hurt me?" She couldn't accept it.

"Too bloody right!" Scott answered, forcefully. "She never wanted us to get married in the first place. Don't you remember? She couldn't wait to break us up. And you *let her*!"

* * *

Sophie, looking over the gallery, was astounded to see her son and Darcey facing each other, locked into some furious confrontation. Scott was holding on to Darcey's hands as though preventing her from lashing out at him. Gentle Darcey?

"Children, children, is anything wrong?" she called, feeling a sudden moment of panic. She was the one who had brought Darcey here. She was the one who had done everything in her power to engineer a reconciliation.

Immediately, they both looked up at her. Both wore strained expressions. "Darcey is a bit put out we've asked her to present the cup," Scott said by way of explanation.

It didn't stack up. Talk was one thing. Body language was another. Watch and one would learn the truth Sophie had found. "But surely, Darcey, it's an honour, dear." Sophie began to move down the stairs.

"Better for you, Sophie. Or Sam. Not me," said Darcey, her eyes stinging with tears.

Whatever they were fighting about, Sophie saw her son continued to keep a supporting arm around Darcey's waist. Darcey for her part appeared to be leaning into him. It had the quality of an embrace to Sophie, a recognised expert at reading body language. "I would take it as a personal favour if you would do it for me, dearest Darcey," she said, her panic ebbing away like the tide.

Darcey bowed her gleaming head in acceptance. Sophie made her feel welcome and wanted. Made her feel like she still belonged. "Then of course I will, Sophie."

"Hey presto, that's settled!" Scott announced with great irony, dropping his arm. He turned on his heel, making for the double front doors with the beautiful stained glass fan-light above. Beyond him the playing fountain shimmered like a mirage except for the presence of two gorgeously coloured little lorikeets flying to and fro in the cooling spray, dousing their iridescent feathers. The extreme Outback light was a key factor in perceiving shapes and objects, even colours.

The game of polo had originated in ancient Persia in the sixth century BC. In the modern polo playing world, a professional match lasted around two hours. Today's match was set for an hour, scheduled for three o'clock, when the heat would have started to die down. Traditionally it was played on grass on a field four times the size of a football field. Today's teams consisted of four riders each, with two mounts for chukka changeovers. The term "pony" had always been used, but the horses were full-sized, super-fit thoroughbreds with great speed and manoeuvrability.

Planet Downs polo field was a good ten-minute walk from the main compound, surrounded for shade with a great diversity of mature eucalyptus and a few introduced exotics that had managed to thrive in the Outback heat. Darcey knew it had been quite a feat keeping the playing field in good condition. The station, like the entire Outback Australia, relied heavily on the bore water from the Great Artesian Basin, the largest artesian basin in the world. It covered an area of some 1.7 million square kilometres, the only truly reliable source of water in the arid and semi-arid regions of four states, Queensland, New South Wales, South Australia, and the Northern Territory. The Melville Cup had been named after a much-loved cousin of the MacArthur family and a great horseman who had died in France only days before the end of World War One. Some six thousand Australian war horses had been sent to the front. Only one had returned home, and only then because that strong, brave horse, a "Waler" born and bred in New South Wales had belonged to an Australian general. Australians regarded horses as "mates." Horses had been the only form of transport in colonial times. Horses in the lonely and remote Outback were often man's only companion.

Darcey had been taught to ride from an early age. Her skill and her love of horses had been an invaluable asset when she had come as a bride to Planet Downs.

As she was to present the prize, she paid close attention to her appearance. She knew all eyes would be on her. Especially those of close friends and fellow conspirators, Ashlee and Julie.

In the end she settled on a white silk top, sleeveless and oval necked, and a pink loose-legged divided skirt, falling from the tightly shirred waistband to the ankle. The skirt wafted around her long legs, creating a delicious breeze much like an Arab's long tunic. Silver bracelets on her arm. Silver earrings. Silver wedge-heeled sandals on her feet. She had intended to tie her long hair back, but Sam had talked her into wearing it loose.

"What's the point of having that glorious mane if you keep tying it back?"

So Darcey parted her hair to one side, allowing her abundant mane to fall around her face, over her shoulders, and down her back.

"Perfect!" Sophie said, casting a last-minute approving eye over Sam and Darcey. "My two beautiful girls!"

Both "girls" took a bow. The news of Darcey's beauty had spread over great distances when she and Scott had become engaged. In her own way Darcey was a MacArthur legend, Sophie thought. Sam too had taken extra trouble with her outfit, a sleeveless printed top with a royal blue divided skirt echoing the dominant colour in her camisole top. The blue went wonderfully well with her hair. The two young women snatched up their wide-brimmed straw hats, ribbon trimmed, to provocatively shade their faces. An exciting day lay ahead. Hopefully accident free.

* * *

The polo grounds were in full colour. A brilliant blue sky, rust-red earth, bleached-out grass now coaxed into a wonderful green. A happy babble of voices and laughter. Flags and bunting fluttered in the breeze. The men stood around together, rehashing their own feats in the saddle; the women sat talking, laughing, looking as glamorous as they possibly could. This was a stand-out social occasion. All knew they were on show. Some were looking for husbands. This was a good place to do it. Furthermore, a few had suitors in today's match.

If the women looked their best, it was the players who were the true peacocks. The day belonged to them. To all their female fans, they looked outrageously sexy in their polo gear. All wore the traditional white cotton-denim tight jeans. Duncan's team wore red polo shirts; Scott's a light blue embroidered with black. Given the feet and lower legs were the most vulnerable areas under attack, players wore the best boots they could afford. Helmets too were extremely important. Hence, Polo Gear Extreme. No one had to be told this was a dangerous game.

Two very attractive young women, blond, blue eyed, friends from childhood, physically enough alike to be sisters, sat amid the groups of spectators, a striped, navy-fringed umbrella over their heads, sipping slowly at frosty drinks. The match was due to start in under thirty minutes, at which time they would have to leave the shelter of their umbrella.

"Will you look at that?" one of them burst out. Julie Sanderson. "How's that for disloyalty!" she exclaimed as if she had all but given up. "Didn't take Sam long to extend a welcoming arm to the traitor."

Ashlee sat bolt upright. "Where, where?" she asked, looking frantically to her left.

"Right, lovie," Julie told her, shading her eyes with her hand. "They're darn nearly hand in hand. Is it some kind of welcome back?"

"How could it be?" Ashlee felt such rage she thought she was going to be sick. "That bitch repudiated him. Scott is not a man to tolerate that. He divorced her. His mother is at the centre of this comeback. Sophie always did dote on her impeccably bred daughter-in-law. Damn. Damn. Damn," she muttered, her eyes now fixed on Darcey and Samantha strolling along most companionably. She felt shocked. Devastated. Outraged beyond belief. Both young women were smiling as though they didn't have a care in the world.

"She wants him back," Julie muttered, thinking the ex-wife was back in. She was just so damned beautiful! Worse, sexy as all hell in her supremely ladylike way. "Is it possible Sophie is working to get them together again? Don't forget Sophie is a powerful force in the family. She has tremendous clout packed away in that tiny frame."

"Too darn right she has!" Ashlee let loose her poisonous feelings. "What's so remarkable about bloody Darcey, anyway? She's skinny. No bust to speak of. The softly spoken buttoned-up lady. No personality."

Skinny? More like a nymph. No personality? Really! But Julie saw no point in upsetting her friend further. "She must be clever, though. An award-winning architect, I've been told, just like her dad. He's got scads of money. She really doesn't have to work at all. Like *you*."

Ashlee was too worked up to respond to Julie's little jibe. "I hate her," she muttered, clearly telling the truth. "If breaking Scott and me up weren't enough, she's back for another go."

Julie placed a soothing hand on her friend's arm. There was pity in her voice. "Give it up, Ash. You never had a real chance with Scott, even before Darcey arrived. A few dates in the old days. A couple of recent times. Gatherings. He never did get around to courting you. You're friends!"

"We're much more than friends," Ashlee retorted, with a kind of irrational certainty. "I love Scott. She'll only trample on him again. I have to stop it."

Julie gave her friend a level stare. "Take my advice. Love Cy Bishop instead," she advised. "You're well suited and Cy won't wait forever. I'm tempted to have a go myself."

Ashlee wasn't listening. Ashlee never listened. Her feelings for Scott MacArthur were too strong and they went back a long way. What she had to do now was devise some sort of scheme. Some sort of trap? Scott had been through the trauma of divorce. He wouldn't want to do it again. He hadn't found anyone to replace his traitorous wife. She and her mother had long since agreed all she had to do was wait it out.

If Ashlee had one great gift, it was patience.

It was Samantha who realized it was Julie Sanderson in a very stylish dress that must have rolled off the same designer line as Ashlee's who was standing up waving at them and making a great show of it.

"Oh dear, can't we just wave back and move on?" Darcey was loathe to have her pleasure in the day dimmed.

Samantha took Darcey's arm, assuming a Chinese accent. "You know what Confucius say: Keep thy enemy in plain sight."

Darcey laughed. "Sam, Confucius didn't say that. Could have been St. Paul. He was always banging on about enemies."

"Okay, try this one on. Keep your friends close and your enemies closer. Will that do?"

"*Enemies*, plural," Darcey amended. "We both have them. They're sitting over there."

"Exactly." Samantha was very disappointed in Julie and

her deliberate lies about Linc. "Some people believe all's fair in love and war. It's a psychological thing."

"Maybe it works," said Darcey.

"We'll exchange a few pleasantries and then move on," Samantha promised.

They were greeted with bright smiles albeit through clenched teeth. Ashlee's cheeks were a hectic pink, betraying the heat of her feelings. Julie was more friendly. She didn't want to fall out with Samantha MacArthur. She looked around for more deck chairs as if Darcey and Samantha would be pleased to join them.

"That's okay, Jules," Samantha said, holding up a hand. "Darcey has a couple of things to attend to. She's presenting the Cup, as you know."

"How very un-us-ual!" There was something disparaging in Ashlee's comment. "We all thought you or your mother would have that honour, Samantha."

"Who's *we*?" Samantha, the redhead, asked in a voice that bordered on snappy.

"Darcey's being here has caught us by surprise. That's all." Ashlee blinked. She had never liked Scott's quick-tempered sister. She had even worried about red hair when she and Scott had children.

"A nice surprise, I hope?" Darcey glanced from one young woman to the other. Neither of them were her friends. Or ever likely to be.

"A little jaunt Outback?" Ashlee tried a tight smile. "Then back to the city grind?" She was desperate to hear that was the plan.

"Darcey is her own boss," Samantha cut in. "We're hoping she'll stay on for a month or two."

"How nice!" Julie managed to answer for herself and

her lifelong friend. Both would need time to understand the ramifications.

But Ashlee understood all too well. With a superhuman effort, she kept her inner rage off her face. Some part of her knew her behaviour wasn't *normal*, but loving Scott Mac-Arthur was like some fundamental force in her life. How to make him love her had been circling her mind since forever. Well, around thirteen when she ran into puberty and started to let out loud squeaks of delight whenever they met up. It was a schoolgirl crush she had never got over. And nothing much she could do about it, especially when she had received unstinting encouragement from her mother, who was an all-knowing woman, like her. So she had become locked in the jaws of obsession. What of it? Only a fool said love like hers wasn't obsessive. Love wasn't a comfortable emotion. It gripped you by the throat. She was convinced it was she who had to find a way to get rid of the ex-wife. Her mother's advice?

"Mean business this time!"

Perhaps the timing was right after all? Darcey had found out about Scott and her two-timing friend. Why not Darcey's finding out about her and Scott? Her best chance, indeed her only chance, would be after the ball tonight. No use praying for a miracle. Miracles, along with the numbers of saints, had suffered a great decline down the years. Indeed, Ashlee had come to believe miracles were a lost cause. She had to help herself.

Obsessively making plans, Ashlee lost track of time for the entire afternoon, which was a pity because it turned out to be a thrilling match; fast and furious even in the intense heat.

The two captains were unquestionably the best players. Both carried the number *1* on their backs. Player number one was the front attacking player. Linc, known for his speed and quick thinking, was Scott's number two, playing

defence against his opposite number player and helping his
captain when needed. The traditional eight chukkas lasted
exactly seven minutes with a break to change ponies.
Scott's number three, a bit of a hothead, earned his team a
foul for using his mallet too forcefully, in the side umpire's
judgement. That earned him a few terse words from his
captain. The team couldn't afford a foul. The teams were
too closely matched.

It was in the final chukka that Duncan was nearly un-
seated as he tried to prevent Scott, who was brilliantly controlling the ball, shooting home the winning goal. It was just
the sort of thrilling cliffhanger finish the crowd wanted. The
grounds exploded. The resounding cheers took ages to wind
down. Now it was time for the winning captain to receive
the Melville Cup, awarded to Planet Downs for yet another
year.

Darcey was acutely aware all eyes were on her. She
wasn't simply on her mettle, she was on a high. She stepped
right up to Scott, her smile lighting her face to radiance.
Scott stood, dark auburn head down bent, regarding her
with sparkling, albeit mocking eyes.

"The great thing about you, Darcey, is—"

He got no further. Her whole body stirred under his blue
glance. Making a garland of her slender arms, Darcey
threw them around his neck, locking her tapering fingers.
Next she stood on tiptoe to bring her up to his height.

"Almost there," Scott softly taunted, his voice pitched
low so as not to be overheard.

"Congratulations, Scott," Darcey said in a clear, happy
voice. "Congratulations to your cup-winning team. It was
a great game."

"Time for a kiss, wouldn't you say?" he murmured beneath his breath, clearly egging her on.

"Which is as far as you'll get," she sweetly returned, her
smile never faltering. She kissed him on one tanned cheek,

then the other, her body reacting to the polished warmth of his skin and the stunning male attraction that bloomed out of him. She didn't stop there. This was a little game. She awarded him three kisses in all, to delighted if somewhat mystified applause. Everyone remembered the divorce and the horrendous fallout. The MacArthurs were such proud people. And rightly so. They had earned their place. Two years had gone by. Were Scot and his beautiful ex-wife on the verge of making up?

All kinds of currents began to run through the crowd. Anyone who took the time to shoot a quick glance at Ashlee Warrender looked away quickly. Reconciliation between Scott and his ex-wife appeared catastrophic for Ashlee. Everyone knew Ashlee was and always had been a bit on the crazy side about Scott MacArthur. To be fair, she wasn't the only one.

In response, further fuelling the flames, Scott bent to kiss Darcey's cheek before slipping an arm around her waist. They looked the *perfect* couple. Just like the old days.

Cameras clicked. Gossip *flew.* It scattered around the compound like trained pigeons on a mission. Human beings loved gossip. There was no telling what might happen at the ball. Some went so far as to predict an announcement. After all, the ex-wife had never been replaced, for all the raised hopes. Whether the ex stayed or went, Scott MacArthur needed a wife. As master of historic Planet Downs, he needed heirs. Scott was as much aware of that as anyone. Empires were lost without heirs.

Chapter Five

Isolated from the big cities, from ordinary everyday life, the Outback went to town with their celebrations. The Mac-Arthur annual polo match followed up by the annual ball was a huge event on the Outback calendar.

The MacArthur mansion was alight, as fantastic a sight as one would ever see in a desert landscape. The extensive home grounds were so bright it wasn't all that far off daylight. The immense vault of the sky was crowded with stars in all their unearthly brilliance; the Milky Way they had grown up with. Their own Southern Cross glittered above them as it did on the great monoliths of desert sand dunes that rose out of the surrounding endless plains bristling with spinifex. Van Gogh, who passionately loved stars, couldn't have wished for a more glorious, a more paintable, sky. The aboriginal people who had settled the remote continent some sixty thousand years before worshipped the stars as the homes of their ancestors. Darcey often had conversations with her mother, up there in the glorious stars.

Inside the Great Hall lovely perfumes softly mingled. Young women who spent their days in shorts and cotton tops, their hair scraped back into ponytails, now looked

like goddesses in their beautiful ball gowns that created
dramatic plays of colour and style. Most gowns were strapless, bare shoulders a must. All gowns were long in a variety of luxurious fabrics, silk, satin, taffeta, chiffon over
petticoats. Most had indulged their love of *real* ball gowns
with billowing skirts that showed off taut tiny waists from
their preparatory workouts. The best six-piece band, who
loved travelling to exotic locations where everything was
laid on, had been re-hired. The entire Outback found dancing a delight. Indeed, the musicianship of the band was
making the general enthusiasm take flight.

   Some idiot as about as exciting as a tree stump vacated
Ashlee's side. She doubted he would be stupid enough to
ask her for another dance. Her heart had picked up some
maddening rhythm she prayed would pass.
   On the bright side, she knew she looked wonderful. So
many people had told her, had complimented her on her
gown, which had cost so much even her mother had gone
into shock. She had waved admirers away with a smile.
Julie too was looking very nice, not as good as her, of
course, but pretty nevertheless. She and Julie had a very
special friendship.
   So far, the anticipated belle of the ball hadn't arrived.
Ashlee felt her cheeks grow hot as the many comments she
had overheard flashed into her mind. Too bad most of the
comments were wrong. She had to be seen by Scott's ex-
wife as seducing him in some way. Better the other way
around, of course. She was actually holding out hope for
some show of lust on Scott's part. Alcohol was flowing
freely. The drinking would go on for hours. Surely no
virile man could ignore her? Especially if he couldn't see
her coming.

Thirty minutes passed and still no sign of the ex-wife. Could she have been taken ill?

No such luck.

As if she were waiting for precisely the right moment, Darcey entered the Great Hall.

"Shouldn't there be a fanfare or something?" someone hissed into Ashlee's ear. It was Julie, who had flown to her side.

It was a question Ashlee didn't think required an answer. The ex-wife moved among them smiling like royalty. Even Scott, who had been so betrayed, had been drawn to her side.

"Not a one of us can compete," Julie moaned. "What a fabulous ball gown! I'd like to tear it off her back. And the *colour*! I've always loved purple, but it makes me look washed out."

"Oh, do shut up." Ashlee didn't bite back her anger. "This is the bloody Outback, not New York. Can't you see she's *overdone* it? No wonder she's late. It must have taken ages to attach those cabbage roses, peonies, whatever to her hair. An alternative to no jewellery?"

"Actually, I think the roses look great! Especially against her elegant hairdo. She doesn't need any jewellery." Julie was plainly in awe of Darcey's appearance. "She *is* wearing diamond earrings, don't you see?"

"She had to hand over everything Scott had given her," Ashlee pointed out as though that had great meaning.

"According to Sam, she handed everything over *without* being asked," returned Julie. "Including *that* engagement ring. The MacArthurs aren't ordinary people, are they? They're so *rich*! Dad says Scott is a brilliant businessman. He's *hugely* increased the family's fortunes. Which is great in itself, but you know what the Bible says."

"What?" Ashlee asked explosively, her emotions in full flow.

"It is easier for a camel to pass through the eye of a needle than for a rich man to enter the Kingdom of Heaven."

"Sometimes, Julie, you don't seem normal to me." Ashlee gave her friend a look of cold, hard appraisal.

"Ditto. A curious one is this Darcey," Julie remarked, undaunted.

"We don't need her around." Ashlee felt just about ready to choke her friend. The days, the weeks, the years she had spent planning the best way to land Scott MacArthur could not go to waste. Willpower alone wouldn't work. He had escaped her once. Twice was one time too many. This time it was nothing less than war.

Ex-wife or not, everyone seemed glad to see Darcey. If Scott's impulse had been to claim the first dance, Linc got in first. After that, she had a long series of eager partners full of extravagant compliments, which Darcey accepted with a grain of salt. The Great Hall was air conditioned, but the desert sands cooled down dramatically at night, so the temperature was just right.

At one point Darcey looked over at Samantha folded in Linc's arms. Sam's radiant head was thrown back. She was laughing, a bright clear bell of amusement. It had to be plain to all Sam and Linc were very interested in each other. Darcey had to wonder whether Linc's father would drop his harsh stance and one day recognize his fine son. Any father would be lucky to have such a son. She was also aware something had been nagging at her all day. She couldn't put her finger on it, yet it was like a persistent whisper in her ear. There was something she had omitted to do. Something she had to do.

* * *

The magnificent buffet offered astonishingly good food. All manner of seafood—lobsters, prawns, scallops, oysters in their beds of crushed ice. There were succulent hams, turkey, chicken, and crisp delicious salads to freshen the palate. Champagne continued to flow. Some couples had moved outside, to take a stroll beneath a billion stars. A star wasn't simply born on its own. A star was born together with tens of thousands of siblings.

The band took the opportunity to segue into the great love themes, the ones that had stood the test of time. Couples began to move around the dance floor dreamily now, with arms wrapped around each other. Darcey felt she needed a moment's pause, shaking her head at an approaching admirer, only to see across the hall her most persistent partner heading towards her.

"May I?"

Thank God!

Darcey turned into Scott's arms. A singing started up in her blood. She felt totally reborn. "I didn't think you were ever going to get around to asking me," she confessed.

"Maybe I've been too dazzled," he said, holding her body close to him. "Now I can see why you needed a whole suitcase for the skirt of your gown," he said, with a twist of humour. "The top would fit into your wallet. You look very beautiful, Darcey." His eyes were moving over the heart-shaped bodice of her gown, lingering on the creamy upper curves of her breasts, the mauve shadowed V that dipped between them. His eyes had never been far from her all evening. He had in fact studied her endlessly in her ravishing gown, from the top of her raven head to her silver evening shoes. Darcey. *His* Darcey. He was tired of watching her dancing with other men, friends of his or not. "One sight of you is never enough," he said, staring down at her.

She had to wait a moment before she could speak. There was an answering melancholy in her smile. "I remember the first time you said that to me."

"It was the first time I met you. I fell in love on the spot."

"You *knew* me." The wonder of it took her straight back in time.

"I thought I did. I allowed you to escape me. I won't do it again."

"How?" She stared up into his bluer than blue eyes. "Lock me up?"

"I expect I won't have to," he said, with his mocking white smile. "You elected to make this journey, Darcey."

She moaned softly. "I've missed you all so much." She felt she didn't have to explain further. Her body had to be doing the talking for her. Her body always had had a singular way of letting him know how much she wanted him. Nothing had changed. Nothing had altered.

"You missed *me*," he corrected her. "Can't you say it? You can't deceive me anyway. I've been inside your body, Darcey. I've tasted your skin all over. I can taste it now. Neither of us can erase our memories. I didn't fail you. You were my wife."

She tried to keep the emotional tears at bay, but a single teardrop rolled slowly down her cheek. "I failed *you*," she said. "I was caught in a nightmare just like I said. I adored you too, Scott. Everyone knew it."

"Hush!" He gathered her closer, protectively into his arms, shielding her from the sight of the other dancers. "Darcey, don't cry. I just might lose it entirely."

"Sorry."

"We're going in circles again," he muttered against the flawless skin of her cheek. "It can't happen. I want you. You know that."

"You want me. You have me," she said. She lifted her dark head, three beautiful full-blown roses, richly purple, tucked behind her left ear. It was a colour that accentuated the flawless white of her skin. She stared intently into the eyes of the man she loved—would always love. "Didn't I give myself to you, body and soul, long ago?"

It was well after two before the band put their instruments down and everyone, including them, made their way to their appointed sleeping quarters if only for a few hours. Breakfast would be served from eight o'clock onwards. Lots of piping-hot black coffee to kick start the day. The MacArthurs had delivered yet again. The ball, like the afternoon's polo match, was voted a resounding success.

Darcey moved on winged feet, altering a few things in her room. It had been decided Scott would come to her. She was as much in urgent need of him as he was of her. She took her mother's diamond pendant earrings off, then popped them back in her handbag, zipping the smallest inner pocket. They would be safe there. It was then she decided to remove the half dozen cards inside. She really should have opened them up before this. The handwriting on the top one looked familiar. Not a good hand. A bit of a scrawl. London postmark.

"Aaah!" Recognition hit hard.

She put the other cards down on the dressing table, debating whether to open Rebecca's letter.

Read it. Rebecca has a secret.

Only she didn't want to read it. She wasn't afraid of what Becky had to say. She knew now Becky had lied. She just didn't want to be sullied by any more lies. Not now. Not tonight. The letter could well contain a plea for another handout. Becky probably would never get herself together.

Read it.

So prompted, but with grim resignation, Darcey shook
out the single closely written page. Becky had always been
on the mercenary side, but strangely enough she had liked
her. She had been kind to Becky, perhaps more than she
should have.

Dear Darcey . . . .

There was no "dear" about it. Odd how even the coldest
letters began with "Dear Someone or Other." What she had
in her hand was a document that testified to Becky's guilt.
And that of one other. Co-conspirators who were ready to
hurt her badly. If possible, destroy her marriage.

At long last Rebecca had released the heartbreaking
truth.

She had to show the letter to Scott. She had to beg his
forgiveness all over again. She had questions that demanded
answers. She vowed she would get them.

She's a sociopath.

Her inner voice delivered its judgement. The aunt she
had shown such respect, the aunt she had believed unquestionably loved her, was in fact a traitor. A far bigger traitor
than Becky, her pawn. Becky had suffered a long travail as
a consequence of her actions and her desperate need to be
more financially secure. But Becky had arrived at the point
when she desperately wanted to confess. She had visited
her parish priest. He had told her to clear her conscience,
and to gain forgiveness she had to let the truth be known.

Darcey moved swiftly down the long gallery to the right
wing where Scott had his rooms: bedroom, study, sitting
room. Her eyes were glistening with unshed tears but she
would not permit herself to cry, even given the gravity of
her aunt's crime. When and why had her aunt hatched such
a cruel plot? Had she so deeply resented her turning to
Scott? Was it all some bizarre form of jealousy? Or had her
aunt a forbidding darkness in her soul? Her aunt had lost
the one man she had loved. Why shouldn't his daughter

suffer the same fate? That had to be the motive—to separate her from Scott.

Well, Aunt Rachael had succeeded for far too long.

She tapped on the heavy mahogany door, before pushing it open. This had been their bedroom. Their sanctuary. Their love nest.

Only Scott wasn't alone.

Ashlee was there too. She was standing directly in front of him, her blue eyes glowing, her skin turned alabaster white. The strapless bodice of her gown had slipped so low it was barely covering her breasts. She seemed equally triumphant and equally unnerved.

A woman in the grip of a grand passion. Darcey drew her conclusions on the spot. "Hello there, Ashlee," she said with as much composure as if they had just met up in the gallery. "I want to speak to Scott, so could you please leave? Pull up your top while you're at it. I suspect you became overexcited. Is that it? Time for a change in your frame of mind. Scott doesn't love you, Ashlee. He never did."

Ashlee looked back at Darcey with loathing. She offered a disbelieving laugh. This wasn't what she wanted. She had expected Darcey to cry out, seared to the soul, hopefully creating a great scene. Scott, for his part, wasn't moving. He didn't speak either. He just stood there like an observer, with his dazzling white dress shirt hanging open, showing his strongly muscled tanned chest.

"Why don't *you* go away," Ashlee cried, trying to conceal her amazement at Darcey's calm demeanour. "You know all about Scott and me."

"I know about *you*, Ashlee," Darcey countered gently. "And I pity you. No doubt you thought you could carry off a seduction scene. It was a pathetic attempt. You've lived so long with your hopes you've wasted years of your life. I know it must be extremely painful loving someone who doesn't love you, but tonight is nothing more than a crude attempt to make trouble. Please go. This will never be spoken of. You have my word."

"And mine." Scott moved at last. He went to the door, holding it wide open. "Put it all behind you, Ashlee," he said, crisply. "Tell your mother to do the same. Now go. I did regard you as a friend. Now you're nothing to me."

Nothing! Nothing! Nothing!

Ashlee fled along the silent gallery, the word pealing deafeningly in her ears.

Clear-headed, Darcey put Becky's written confession into Scott's hands. Neither mentioned Ashlee, as though she had never been there.

Scott muttered aloud even as he read it, the expression on his handsome face grim.

Finally he raised his head, a hard sparkle in his eyes. "My God, I wasn't mistaken in claiming your aunt had a hand in breaking us up."

"What was her motive, for God's sake?"

"You already know, Darcey. She wanted you to suffer. It wasn't about me. It could have been any man. It was *you* she wanted to punish. She's a very strange woman."

"Strange indeed. Two different women," Darcey mused. "One did love me. The other saw me as my mother. We know now Aunt Rachael was in love with my father. Perhaps the only love of her life. My mother unwittingly took him from her. It was love at first sight. My father wasn't aware of the depth of Aunt Rachael's feelings. She's a woman whose feelings would go deep. When she looked at me, she couldn't help seeing my mother. She was witness to my happiness. She knew how much I loved you. It all got too much for her."

"So she hit on the brilliant idea of breaking us up," Scott said, deeply contemptuous. "She paid poor unprincipled Becky to lie. She wouldn't have had much difficulty. A hundred thousand dollars would have seemed like a great deal of money to Becky."

"It *is* a great deal of money, Scott, especially to someone who doesn't have any."

"So instead of being one of the have-nots, Becky would join the haves. The idea would have been irresistible. All she had to do was leave the country. Head for her relatives in Ireland. She's given no return address?"

"No. The envelope was stamped London."

"I can have her tracked," Scott said.

"I'm inclined to let her go. It's Aunt Rachael who's in the firing line. But I'm guilty too. I believed her. It would never have occurred to me in a million years she could sink so low."

"I don't want to talk about her," Scott said crisply.

"What *do* you want to talk about?"

"You and me. I love you, Darcey. I've never stopped loving you even when I came close to hating you."

"I was lost, Scott," she said quietly. "Now I'm found."

"Thank God it has happened."

"God *and* Sophie working as a team. Would you mind helping me out of this elaborate gown?"

There could have been no more compelling task. "It's gorgeous! Almost a pity I have to take it off. I'll lock the door first in case Ashlee comes back."

"Poor Ashlee!"

"I can't find an excuse for her." Scott went to the door, turning the lock. "So we stay here?" He turned back with the question. She stood in front of the Regency mahogany dressing table he had bought her with its giltwood over-mantel mirror. Even at the worst of times, he had never thought to shift it out of the bedroom. Her image was reflected in the mirror, so he had two of her. She looked so impossibly beautiful he had to stand still, watching her removing the big violet roses that clung to her head. Once undone, her hair, black and glossy, tumbled down her back.

"Why not?" she answered over her shoulder. "This is our marriage bed, after all."

As if he needed a reminder. He went to her. Swung her around to face him. "Stay with me, Darcey," he said, his breath rasping in his throat. "Never leave me again."

She put a hand to his cheek. "Never!"

"Love me?"

"Let me show you."

"First we'll have to get you out of this dress."

Now his strong elegant hand worked the long zip of her gown. It fell away from her upper body, exposing her delicate white breasts. He held her while she stepped out of the billowing skirt.

"There's only one thing more beautiful than you in that dress."

"Oh?" She had to breathe out, the rising excitement was so fierce. There was nothing but the thought of having him inside her. Swiftly he arranged her ball gown over a high-backed armchair. The rich material glowed.

"That's you naked," Scott said.

He pulled her to him. He kissed her mouth, her throat, her eyes. The kisses continued moving down over her body. Her little moans were the trigger. He lifted her high in his arms, laid her on the huge four-poster bed. The rich brocade bedspread was still in place.

Darcey, wearing only her lacy briefs, rolled over. "We'd better take the quilt off."

He shot her a smile. "No problem."

The bed linen beneath had been freshly laundered and pressed. It smelled just as it used to of the native boronia.

The sheets were sinfully smooth. She ran her hands over them.

"Is this one of the wonders of Christmas, Scott?" she asked, her heart in her eyes.

"It is to me." He lifted the last scrap of lace off her. "How different this Christmas will be! Perfect, to my mind." His eyes burned over her like blue flame. "I have you back in my life. Back in our bed."

"Where I belong." She reached out her arms to him.

Immediately he began to strip off his clothes. His body in the golden glow from the bedside lamps was as strong and beautiful as any man's could be.

On their bed his arms encircled her. He held her tight. She could feel his powerful arousal pressing against her mons. Scott had always positioned his tall body to fit hers in the places where it was most needed. She arched her back. Slid her long slender legs out, a tingling running like electric currents down to her toes. She wanted him so much it hurt. But not yet. Even as her nails were scoring the sheets.

Her pink nipples were like berries to his tongue. All the yearnings inside him needed to be assuaged. Nothing compared to the exhilaration of being with his wife. His Darcey.

Their tongues entwined, he abruptly broke off, kissing her to shake his head. "God, Darcey, do we need protection?" In the heat of the moment, the thought hadn't entered his fevered brain.

Darcey reached up to trace the line of his finely cut lips. She was ready now for that first thrust. She was ready to be filled with his seed. "It's about time we had our first child," she said.

Epilogue

Two weeks later

As soon as Darcey was settled in their Brisbane apartment, she rang her aunt.

"So you're back from that godforsaken place," Rachael gritted. "I can't for the life of me think why you went. That Sophie, I expect. I knew she wouldn't give up."

"Shall we say one o'clock?" Darcey broke in.

"Well, sorry, one o'clock doesn't suit."

Darcey ignored the standoffishness. She was being punished. That was clearly Rachael's intention. "I'd come to the gallery, only I need to speak to you privately."

"About what?" Rachael showed her impatience.

"Just family matters."

There was a moment's silence. "Are your father and that woman back in town?"

"No. They're still in London. I nearly dropped the phone when they told me their wonderful news. Anne is pregnant."

"NO!"

Even down the line Darcey caught the blast. "Great news, I thought," she continued. "She and Dad are thrilled. Anne was once told she could never conceive a child because of some abnormality, so another Christmas miracle." She didn't add she was hoping for one of her own.

"She's too old," Rachael said with a hiss of scorn.

"Forty-five. Anne is quite a bit younger than Dad."

A loud sniff. "I doubt this child will come to term."

"Her obstetrician has assured Anne it will."

"And what about you?" Rachael demanded to know. "What about your inheritance? You'll only get half of what we expected if this baby does actually get born."

"That's more than enough for me, Aunt. So are you coming or not?" She wasn't sure her aunt would. Maybe she shouldn't have told her about the pregnancy, but she couldn't resist it.

"Make it three o'clock. I'll only stay for coffee."

"I'm at the MacArthur apartment."

Darcey heard the gasp. "What is all this?"

"I have permission to use it," Darcey said, as though it were in no way out of the ordinary.

"Good God!" Rachael couldn't hide her disgust.

"You sound upset."

"Disappointed, Darcey. I thought you'd cut ties with the MacArthurs forever."

"Don't worry," Darcey replied. "The MacArthurs won't hurt me. See you at three." She hung up before her aunt had the chance to deliver another damning word.

Rachael's face went white as she read Becky's letter. When she finished, she curled her fingers into claws, bunching the cheap sheet of paper into a ball. Her dark eyes blazed at her niece. "You got me here to read that piece of garbage? How could you?"

"Because it's true, though no confession will make

up for the loss of two years of my married life. Becky's conscience got the better of her. You, of course, have none. Why did you do it?"

"You can't mean this!" Rachael barked a laugh.

"I certainly do. You're lucky Scott didn't come with me, but he had meetings he couldn't get out of."

"So he's still in the picture?" Rachael's brows rose superciliously.

"He was never really out of it. I know you want to ignore me, but you can't. I have a right to hear why you deliberately set about destroying my marriage. I trusted you. You banked on that. Please try to find the decency to tell me why you did it. Do you hate me?"

Rachael didn't meet her niece's eyes. "It wasn't about you," she said, sounding almost genuine. "Not strictly. It was about me and my sister. You don't know the half of it. How she stole your father out from under my nose. She knew how much I loved him. The only man I've ever been remotely attracted to."

"So revenge was at the heart of it? You were avenging yourself on my mother through me?"

"That just about answers it," Rachael admitted as though to a minor offence. "I went a little crazy when the two of them got married. Ysobel was callous enough to ask me to be chief bridesmaid. I was good looking enough then. Of course I had to refuse her. I didn't attend the wedding at all. I claimed illness, and it was true. I *was* ill. Dangerously ill. Imagine how I felt raising you, made in Ysobel's image."

"You didn't exactly raise me, Aunt Rachael. My mother and father did that. Do you realize you're unbalanced?"

"Don't be ridiculous." Rachael flushed.

"I can't think of anyone who wouldn't agree if they heard what you did, paying a third party to do your dirty work."

Rachael bent to snatch up the balled letter.

"That's okay. I've got copies."

Rachael straightened, trying to regain her composure. "You'll do no good opening your mouth about this." The angry flush had faded to ashen.

"I just need you to admit what you did. It was criminal."

"God knows it was easy enough. You thought I was special. As for that grasping little slut, I'll go after her. She stole my money."

"Don't go any further with that," Darcey warned. "Rebecca has paid for her part in the whole sordid affair. Hound Rebecca and I'll come after *you*."

"You wouldn't do it," Rachael said, contemptuous of Darcey's resolve.

"Try me. It wouldn't be just me. Scott and I are remarrying."

A sick sweat broke out on Rachael's pale forehead. "No, you're lying."

"You wish." Slowly Darcey removed a white gold ring from her right hand to push it over the knuckle of her fourth finger, left hand. She turned the ring to expose a magnificent diamond-encrusted engagement ring, the central diamond some four flawless D color carats, flanked by diamonds of just under one carat each.

Ferocity slipped from Rachael's dark eyes to be replaced by shock. "You're playing with fire when you play with him," she cried. "Women won't stop chasing him."

"No question about it. Only Scott loves *me*. I notice you haven't mentioned how many admirers chased me? None of them mattered. There has only been Scott. We're so, so happy to be back together again."

Rachael's breath came in a laboured groan. "I'm not a monster, Darcey, really I'm not. Your mother was responsible for my suffering."

"Sure it wasn't you who knocked her off her bike?"

"I probably would have had I been out that day."

Darcey instantly rose to her feet. "Best you leave now. Your reactions prove you *are* a monster."

"And you're a fool," Rachael countered. "Don't ever think of running to me again."

Darcey walked her aunt to the door. "On the contrary, I never want to see you again. I'm not going to threaten you with disclosure. This remains in the family. But I will never permit you to go after Rebecca."

"She's too worthless for me to bother."

"Good. That Dad was ever in love with you is an image constructed by your imagination. To this day, he doesn't know how you felt. My mother didn't know either. I'm certain of that. You've always hidden your feelings rather too well. Obsession is a terrible state of mind. I've seen it in action. Unlike you, I don't believe in revenge. I leave that to God. Not all my good memories of you have gone," she added quietly. Even with full knowledge of her aunt's betrayal and her hatred of her own sister, Darcey still felt pity. "Goodbye, Aunt. I wish you well. I am so happy with my life now I can say it and mean it."

There was no response whatever from the frozen-faced Rachael. No attempt at an apology. Rachael made a grab for the doorknob and then let herself out, giving the door a hard solid bang behind her.

Darcey found herself laughing. Well, that was over! It hadn't been as bad as she had expected. Perhaps that was because she had so much happiness and peace within her. Her aunt was sick in her mind. With the proper help she could save her soul. She had told Rachael that Scott couldn't be there because he had meetings. Quite true. She didn't tell her the meetings weren't at Planet Downs but with the state premier and two of her ministers in town. Scott would be home around five o'clock. They were going out to dinner. She had already made the booking.

Their festive season, the best ever, was far from over! The new year had commenced. Darcey hoped with all her heart, but at that point couldn't possibly know, that the year ahead would herald in the birth of their son, the excitedly awaited, adored by all, MacArthur heir.

Don't miss the next exciting book in
Lindsay McKenna's series,

Wind River Valley.

It is time for Noah's romance in

WRANGLER'S CHALLENGE,

coming in November 2017.
Turn the page for a sneak peek!

The door opened and closed. Shay lifted her head. "Oh! That must be Noah!" and she straightened, looking toward the kitchen entrance. "He's home early. Wait 'til you meet him! You'll love him!"

Dair barely had time to choke down the roll and turn her head before the wrangler entered. He was in his sheepskin coat, taking off his tan Stetson, when she gasped. It was Noah Mabry! Oh, my God! All she could do was stare at him as he jerked to a halt, his gaze fixing on her.

For a moment, there was crackling silence in the kitchen.

"Dair?" he asked, disbelief in his voice. "Is that you?"

Shay frowned and halted by Noah. "Do you two know each other?"

Gulping, Dair whispered, "I didn't know you were here . . ."

Noah smiled a little, his hat dangling between his fingers. "Yeah, we do know each other, Shay. Met nine months earlier at the Danbury Farm in Maryland." He shook his head, giving Dair a questioning look. "You're here for the assistant horse trainer job?"

Her throat closed with terror. "Yes."

"Noah, come over here," Shay invited. "You're just in time. Go get rid of your coat and hat out in the mudroom. I saved two cinnamon rolls for you. Would you like some coffee, too?"

He managed a shy nod. "Yes, please, Shay." And then he looked at Dair. "I'll be right back. Don't go anywhere . . ."

Dair didn't know whether to be happy or sad about seeing Noah again. Why didn't she put it together? He'd said he trained horses when they'd met in Danbury. But that burning, slow, hot kiss he'd shared with her, melting her into his arms, made her face burn with a blush. And he hadn't forgotten it either, if she was any judge of the look gleaming in his light gray eyes. Did he seem regretful that she was here? Dair wasn't sure of anything at the moment, feeling like an IED had just exploded next to her.

"I didn't know you two knew each other," Shay said, bringing the plate of cinnamon rolls to the table, setting it near where she sat.

"Well," Dair managed in a strangled voice, "I lost track of him. I didn't know he worked here, Shay. When you used his first name, I wondered, but you know—Noah is not an uncommon man's name." She saw understanding in Shay's eyes as she sat down.

"I think it's a great sign!" she said, excited. "And you met at Danbury Farm. Noah is good friends with Henry Danbury."

"Yes, I saw them together in the training arena at that farm." Dair saw the amazement in Shay's eyes, a dreamy look. She wasn't sure what that meant. Nerves skittered through her and she was suddenly afraid she'd not get the job. She wasn't sure how Noah felt toward her, either. She'd not had the guts to email him after meeting him at Danbury. *Oh, God.*

* * *

Noah took his time wrestling out of the thick sheepskin coat. He'd already hung his Stetson on a nearby peg. Of all people he never expected to ever meet again it was Dair Wilson. Stunned by the turn of events, he ran his fingers through his hair, taking a deep breath, centering himself. He hadn't missed the surprise in Dair's beautiful golden-cinnamon colored eyes. She looked like a deer paralyzed by a set of car headlights. And he'd kissed her in the tack room. Long, slow, deep and forever . . .

Just thinking about that life-altering kiss he'd shared with her, anchored him to where he stood. His heart was flip-flopping in his chest, humiliation and feeling badly that he'd never emailed her, gripped him. He'd wanted to comfort her, but she was in rehab with a partial loss of a leg to an IED. And now, she was here. Asking for a job. How the hell had that happened?

Rubbing his brow, Noah knew he had to go face her. And Shay seemed giddy about having Dair apply for the job. Never mind that Garret had stopped him the minute he'd parked his truck and got out. He'd grabbed him by the shoulder and said, "Hire her. She's the right person to help you." And then, he'd walked away without any other explanation. What the hell!

What was worse? Noah couldn't justify the sudden sexual urge running through him. That was embarrassing. Dair was a beautiful woman. There wasn't anything to dislike about her; otherwise, he'd never have kissed her. Because he'd wanted more, much more from her.

But it had come at the wrong damn moment in his life. He had no job, he was aimless and what could he offer her? *Nothing.* Besides, he knew she had at least another six months in rehab, stuck at Bethesda Medical Center. He was a tumbleweed, unsure where he would go next, looking for a job.

Hell, he was in a fix and he didn't know what to do.

Turning, Noah strode toward the kitchen. Entering, he saw Shay gesture for him to come over to the table. And he saw the stark uncertainty in Dair's darkening, worried looking eyes.

Sitting down, he thanked Shay for the coffee she'd put in front of him. He figured he'd better start eating the rolls or she'd start poking at him and asking him why he wasn't hungry. Noah didn't want to go there with her.

"How did you two meet?" Shay demanded, all ears.

Noah cut her an uncomfortable glance and forced himself to eat. "I was at Danbury to ask Henry for a job. He didn't have one and he didn't know of any other breeding farms in the region that were hiring, either." He moved his gaze to Dair. "And the reason I didn't contact you by email after we met was because I had no job, no apartment, no nothing. I needed to get one, so I headed west after meeting you."

"That's all right, Noah, I understand," Dair said.

"It wasn't like we had much time to talk," he apologized to her. No, they had been so damned drawn to one another, social conversation evaporated into that hot, melting kiss they'd shared.

She shrugged. "Life happens. I'm in your boots now. I need a job since the medical center cut me loose."

Noah was careful not to bring up her amputated leg. He didn't want to embarrass Dair in front of Shay. He knew that Shay and everyone realized she was probably an amputee, already. It wasn't table talk and he had no wish to make Dair feel any more uncomfortable than she looked right now. "I do need an assistant," he added quickly. "Since Shay and Reese had the arena raising, I've been overwhelmed."

"Shay said you were the manager of the arena, plus schooling horses," she ventured.

"Right." He smiled a little over at Shay, finishing off the first roll and wiping his fingers on the paper napkin. "We have snow here eight months out of every year and Wind

River Valley has a lot of quarter horse people who show their animals around the nation. They need somewhere that's enclosed to continue to train their horses throughout the winter months. Our newly built arena has been a godsend to them and a financial windfall for the Bar C."

Shay glowed. "But the people coming are here because of you, Noah. You've made a name for yourself since you've started working here."

Lifting a shoulder, Noah said, "In part, Shay. But the rest was your brilliant idea to build an arena in the first place." He glanced over at Dair, wanting her to feel a part of the conversation. "Shay is always looking for ways to make money for the Bar C because her father lost all the summer grass leases five years ago. Now, this place is getting re-built, literally, from the ground up. Me and the rest of the wranglers do fence mending every week. We try to do it every day, if our schedule allows." He thumbed toward a side window in the kitchen. "But when you have five feet of snow out there, it's impossible to do any fence mending."

Dair nodded. "That's true. So with the arena built you can train horses all year round?"

"Yes," and he took the second roll in his large hands, opening it up. "The problem is me. We've got a state-of-the-art facility for boarding, riding and training, but too few personnel to run it. I'm looking for an assistant who does a lot of the training while I manage the place, giving riding lessons and ensure the boarded horses get cleaned, fed and watered daily."

"How many horses are boarded?"

"Twenty-five," Noah said.

"And by the time he's done watering, feeding and clean-ing their stalls, most of the day is gone." Shay gave him a worried look. "Actually, you could use two more hands plus a horse trainer."

"I can clean stalls," Dair said quickly.

"Well, what I'd like to do," Noah said between bites of the tasty roll and sips of coffee, "is take you out to the arena and give you a sense of it all. And if you're up to it, I have a nice, well-mannered horse I'm training for a ten-year-old little girl that I'd like to see you work with for a bit. I need to get an idea of how you are around a horse. That's not something that you can put on your resume."

Dair knew Noah had refused to hire two earlier applicants for the position. "Sure, not a problem. I've brought my tool box, my gloves and working gear. It's in the truck."

"Great," he murmured, licking the last of the frosting off his fingers. He looked over at Shay. "I'll drive her down to the arena and we'll finish the interview there."

"That's fine. But you need to know that everyone wants to hire her, Noah."

He managed to give her a sour look. "I'm listening, Shay."

"Good," she said, standing and patting his broad shoulder. "It's gonna take a few hours, maybe until four p.m."

"That's fine," Shay said.

Noah was concerned about Dair's performance. He remembered nine months earlier she had been unsteady walking on uneven ground. Yet, when he studied her beneath his lashes, Dair looked confident. Maybe it was her high cheekbones, her burnished skin, those incredibly beautiful eyes that he could lose himself in. At the same time, he cautioned himself. Their kiss had meant something to him. He wasn't sure what it had meant to her. It had been a damned long time that he'd kissed a woman and her lips were like a soft welcome against his mouth as he tasted her fully.

He nodded to Dair and stood up. Trying not to stare at her as she rose, he wanted to assess her balance. Knowing she was nervous, he understood better than most. "This should be a piece of cake for you," he said, wanting to tamp down the sudden tension he saw in her body as she stood and squared her shoulders. Dair relaxed a bit, and that was good. He'd been around all ten of those military vets for a day and a half at Danbury Farm. And it struck him as never before how lucky he was to have his arms and legs.

Leading the way down the hall to the mudroom, he saw her old Army jacket and picked it up, handing it to her.

"Thanks," she murmured.

"It's warming up out there," he said. "But it's about fifty-five out in the arena, a good temperature."

She shrugged on her coat and buttoned it, pulling the red knit muffler around her shoulders and neck. "How many people are down there riding right now?"

If Noah didn't know she was an amputee, he'd never have guessed it. Dair wore Levi's and thick, rugged looking sneakers. She walked with balance and with ease. "Probably five or six." He looked at his watch. "It's getting close to lunch time, so most of them will be gone soon. We'll probably have the arena for an hour or so to ourselves." There was relief in her eyes. No one knew better than he that when some horses got around one another, territoriality ruled. Especially with stallions.

Opening the front door for her, he said, "Let's get your tack gear. We'll take it down to the arena in my truck."

"Okay," she said.

There were steps to go down and Noah watched her from behind. She had a fine butt, of that there was no question. He watched her reach for the rail with her gloved hand, probably to balance herself. Otherwise, he'd never have suspected she didn't have two good legs. At the bottom, he gestured to his truck that was parked next to hers. "Why don't you climb in? Your gear on the seat of your truck?"

"Yes, in a cardboard box. Nothing fancy," and she managed a half smile.

Noah opened up the door on his black Toyota truck. He started to cup her elbow, to help her climb in.

"No . . . I can do this by myself," she said.

Stepping back, he gave her room. Noah remembered their conversation when they were together. Dair had been working to appear not to be an amputee. That had been her goal. She didn't accept help or handouts as he'd found out at Danbury. She hauled herself up and although a bit awkward, she climbed into the truck just fine. He knew she had powerful upper body strength in order to compensate for that leg that wouldn't always act like a real one would. He closed the door for her.

Walking over to her parked red Dodge Ram truck, he opened up the passenger side door and pulled out the box that contained her gear. He set it in the back of his pickup and climbed in. The sky was getting less gray with more blue spots opening up the lowered cloud ceiling. The wind was brisk, off and on. But it smelled clean. Shutting the door, he started the engine, turning to her.

"What time did you get here?"

"0900," she said, falling into familiar military time.

He grinned. "Well, it's 1030 now. Let me get you to work with Thunder, a nice five-year-old gray mixed breed mare. They want her trained for their ten-year-old daughter, who's horse crazy."

"What's the girl's name?"

Noah backed out and then turned down the muddy driveway, heading down a narrow graveled road between the wrangler housing area and a group of pipe corrals. "Lori. She's a cute little red headed kid with huge freckles across her cheeks and nose. Her parents bought the mare and she named her Thunder."

"Oh? Is that because she is?"

Noah tried to quell his sensitivity toward Dair. He wondered if she even remembered their kiss. She was a damn fine looking woman any man would be proud to have on his arm. He tucked that all away. "No. Lori loves storms. The mare is sweet, quiet, and she listens well. I don't think you'll have any problems with her."

"Where are you at within her training schedule?"

"I'm longeing her daily, using voice commands right now at the walk, trot and canter. This is where I start the basic foundation work."

"It's a solid plan," Dair agreed.

"Here's the arena," he said, gesturing with his gloved hand in that direction.

"It's huge."

"Only one in Wind River Valley. Shay struck it rich on this idea. It's bringing us in badly needed money for the ranch as a whole. It's going to allow her to probably hire two more wranglers before late spring. And we desperately need them."

He pulled into the asphalt parking lot next to the huge Quonset-hut looking building made out of aluminum and glass. The green tin roof was shaped to make the arena look like a loaf of French bread that had risen. The curved roof forced the heavy snow to automatically slide off it so the structure remained sound and sturdy.

"Okay, here we are." He pointed to a red door on the side. "That's our office. We'll go in there first." And then he hesitated, realizing he'd used the word 'our.' It was probably just the team spirit that the Bar C wranglers had with one another, as well as with Shay and Reese. But maybe it wasn't. Maybe, Noah thought as he climbed out and pulled her cardboard box of gear into his arms, he'd already made up his mind to hire Dair even though he'd not seen her work with a horse. That flummoxed him because he was conservative and careful about people being around a horse he was training. Not all horse people knew everything they needed to know about a horse, how to ride it, how to care for it or train it. He needed to see that Dair was at that pinnacle where she had enough experience. Walking around the truck, he opened the door for her, noticing she had a bit of a slip on the icy area. But anyone would, not just her.

In the next hour he would know whether he was going to hire Dair or not. And as much as he personally liked Dair, he wouldn't put his horses at risk with anyone who didn't know their horses a hundred percent. He hated having to be the teacher rating the student, but that is what this was all about. And judging from Dair's unreadable expression, she knew it too.

How badly Noah wanted her to pass in flying colors.

If you enjoyed

HER OUTBACK HUSBAND

by
Margaret Way,

be sure to watch for

THE ROAD HOME.

Coming to you in November 2017.
Turn the page for a sneak peek!

"Some place, bro!" the cabbie hooted, torn between envy and entrenched resentment of the Super Rich. "It's a bloody disgrace, all them lights." He spoke like a man committed to having the issue addressed a.s.a.p. "Looks like the Q.M.2 at sea, don't it?"

Bruno had to agree. The Lubrinski mansion was *ablaze*. Even he, close friend of the Lubrinskis, had to drop his eyes. He reached in his wallet, took out a couple of crisp fifty-dollar bills. "Keep the change." He put the notes into the man's outstretched hand. "You wouldn't expect them to hold a big charity bash in the dark now, would you?"

"That's what it is then?" The cabbie acknowledged the size of the tip by landing a friendly punch on Bruno's shoulder. "Thank you kindly for that, bro!"

"That's what it is most of the time," Bruno said, stepping out of the cab without further damage to his person. "These people are among the biggest philanthropists in the country."

"Yeah?" The driver wasn't about to let it rest. "All to do with their tax, I reckon. Okay, bro, enjoy yourself now. Me, I have to get back to the grind."

"Take care, bro!" He stood for a moment in the golden

gleam of the street lights, watching the cab driver perform a perfect U turn, and then scoot off with a friendly wave. The guy was right. The house did look like a liner at sea.

He was late. Couldn't be helped. He'd got caught up with an old University friend he'd made a bundle for, allowing his friend to pay off his mortgage. There was satisfaction in that. He liked helping people. Just like his dad. As he made his way up the broad flight of stone steps he could see guests milling around the huge brilliantly lit entrance hall. They formed a living, moving kaleidoscope of multicoloured gowns, emerald, scarlet, amethyst, silver and gold, set off to perfection against the sea of black dinner suits. It all looked sensational. People had been known to fight for Marta Lubrinski's invitations. Often it came down to hissy fits.

Beautiful music was issuing from the living room, soaring above the hubbub of voices and laughter. It conveyed a broad spectrum of human emotions, joy, love, sorrow, hope. He hadn't started out life as a classical music lover though he'd been fed a lot of Italian opera in the womb, Puccini, Verdi.

He loved jazz. He had a big collection of the world's greatest jazz musicians. It was Marta, his self-appointed honorary aunt, who had taken charge of his classical music education, starting with A for Albeniz, the great Spanish virtuoso pianist and composer. He was still working his way through the B's. Bach. Beethoven. Brahms. Marta had unloaded one hundred CD's on him, exhorting him "Play them, darlink. Listen, Listen. Give your soul wings!"

Tonight was one of Marta's famous "dos" with wonderful music and equally wonderful food and wine. It was taken for granted he would attend, especially as he had been, and still was to a certain extent, her husband, Ivor's protégé. Ivor Lubrinski had started his new life in

Australia, as a seventeen-year-old Lithuanian emigrant with ten pounds in his pocket, an unshakeable belief in his destiny and an incredibly astute business brain. Ivor was also notoriously society shy. He rarely attended his wife's grand soirees. It was Marta who had control of that side of things, as brilliant in her fashion as Ivor was in his.

Bruno was devoted to them both. Their philanthropy was legendary when he happened to know Ivor was as careful with a dollar as his own Scottish-born dad had been. Neither man ever forgot their roots. Hungarian Marta had to a mind-blowing extent. Marta had the craving for luxury lodged in her very being.

As he stepped into the Rococo-on-steroids entrance hall with its glittering travertine floor, his eyes gravitated automatically to the magnificent Bohemian chandelier at its centre. The hundreds and hundreds of crystals bounced light off every surface. If it ever fell it would surely kill anyone directly beneath it and injure those in the vicinity. It had been his suggestion to place a large library table beneath it to bear the brunt in such an eventuality. Marta had come up with an extraordinary ebonized and parcel gilt centre table with really weird claws for feet.

The table now held a great pyramid of flowers. It must have been arranged *in situ*. No one could have walked with it. He guessed it was the masses of Asian lilies, pink and white, showing off their beautiful dusky pink faces that gave off the heady perfume that tickled his nose.

Eventually he was able to move through the throng into the voluminous living room as big as a football field. A series of open arched and shuttered French doors gave onto a brilliantly lit pool side terrace. It too was paved in travertine and beyond that a magnificent panoramic view of Sydney Harbour, the most beautiful harbour in the world and he had seen them all in his travels.

Along his way he received choruses of hellos; claps on the shoulder, air kisses from the women, some grasping his hand with faintly glazed eyes. He had to know he was one of the most eligible bachelors around. It wasn't a good position to be in. In fact, he hated it. Being a bachelor didn't trouble him at all. He had turned thirty, was coming at thirty one. Being vigorously pursued by young women and determined cougars did his head in. He was in no hurry to get married. He hadn't met the woman of his dreams. In truth he was beginning to wonder if he ever would. He *did* have dreams, but they were locked away somewhere inaccessible even to him. It was too damned hard for him to forget the disastrous breakup of his parents' marriage and the way his staggeringly beautiful Italian mother had taken off and left him and his dad, an incredibly nice guy, to fend for themselves.

He well remembered the waves of grief that had come crashing down on them. They had adored her. Even now he couldn't think about his mother without feeling a deep, angry hurt. Those early years had been bad, missing his mother. It wasn't until he turned twelve that he had really toughened up.

He'd got the hang of cleaning the house, shopping and preparing meals for him and his dad. His mother had been a wonderful cook. He had watched her often enough, so he soon became a dab hand with pasta, al dente of course, matching the right pasta to the right sauce. It'd got to the point when one evening after a great dinner of spicy calamari followed by *Linguini Al Frutti di Mare* his dad sat him down asking very seriously. "Do you want to become a chef, son? You know whatever you want to do I'll back you."

A chef! A great job certainly if one had a mind to it, but he was on course to secure a place at University. He wanted to finish with a double degree, Master of Laws and Bachelor

of Commerce. He could do it in five years, working part
time. He was smart. What a good laugh they'd had when
he'd explained his ambition. His culinary skills had been
inherited from his mother; Italian blood and the love of
good food. That was it! Another area where he had shone,
was organizing the household accounts. He saw they were
paid on time. He even found better alternatives. He managed the budget far better than his dad. He had made his
mark at school, both in the classroom and on the playing
field. His father had told everyone who would listen he was
meant for big things. Nothing had mattered more than his
dad be proud of him. They were survivors. Mates.

Taller than most, his eyes ranged easily over the heads
of the usual crowd, the movers and shakers, the society
crowd, the hob-nobbers and the fringe dwellers. He recognised the piece the quartet Marta had hired were playing.
Borodin. The Polovtsian Dances. The reason he knew was
the Polovtsian Dances had opened the Winter Games in
Sochi. He, Ivor and a couple of Ivor's cronies had been
witness to the dazzling opening ceremony when a beautiful Russian girl had flow across a winter dreamscape to
that music. He recalled how the works of Russia's greatest
classical composers had filled the stadium, rousing every
heart, including his, with a highly emotional Ivor in
unashamed floods of tears. The same beautiful Russian
music was now being generated in the Lubrinski living
room. The musicians were very good as was expected.

The work came to an end. The applause began. He
moved further into the monumental room that certainly had
the wow factor if you didn't shy away from opulence.
Sumptuous silk-taffeta gold curtains with tasselled tie-
backs swept the floor, a pair of antique Italian chandeliers
hung from the elaborately plastered ceiling, a huge portrait of a striking looking woman stood on a gilded easel.

Marta allowed people to think it was a portrait of her great
grandmother. Of course it wasn't.

Loads of Louis XVI furnishings were mixed in with the
plush modern stuff. Not Louis-style, the real McCoy. Marta
had a gimlet eye for such things. It made a praiseworthy
balance, since Marta was as devoted to her charities as they
were rightly devoted to her.

He was getting his first clear view of the musicians of
the group, first and second violins, viola and cello. He started
to lift his hands to join in the wave of applause, only they
fell back to his side as shock took over. He couldn't believe
his eyes. He probably would have given vent to a gasp only
his breath was lodged in his throat.

The focus of his attention was the cello player, a young
woman in her early twenties. He knew the group from other
occasions. An attractive, plump young woman showing a
lot of bosom played viola. The second violin was a tall,
earnest young gent with a mop of unruly black curls, a pronounced Adam's apple and black rimmed glasses to lend a
bit of gravitas.

The cellist was new. A replacement for the evening. She
could even be a graduate from the Con. She was that young.
In a huge room, surrounded by many attractive even beautiful women, she stood out as a single red rose would be a
standout in a bouquet of carnations. He had no interest in
other members of the quartet. His sole focus was the girl.
He was staring, when staring wasn't his style. Not that he
was the only male caught out looking his fill. He didn't
think he had seen anyone as sexy as this beautiful girl with
a gleaming cello propped between her long slender legs.
The length from the knees was tantalizingly on view as
the sheer top layer of her long black skirt fell away. Not
that she gave off any overtly sexy aura. She looked chaste.
Absolutely. Ultra-refined, very romantic. The princess in a
fairy tale. A magical creature.

Curling masses of titian hair flowed away from her face, and over her shoulders. Her porcelain skin, face, throat, décolletage were shown to priceless advantage against the black lace of the sleeveless V necked bodice. She would be above average height when she stood up, and willow slim. She had light eyes. At this distance he didn't know if they were blue or green. He was prepared to bet they were green if only because he had seen a blown-up photograph of a large bravura portrait of this girl's double. People did have doubles in life, he reminded himself, only he had the certainty this girl had Hartmann blood.

A Hartmann, for God's sake!

He was so certain, his nerve endings were doing a slow *burn.*

A seminal moment in your life, McKendrick.

Through his late father, Ross McKendrick, a private investigator and a former ex-chief of detectives, he had developed a fascination with the so called "cold cases'; the mysterious disappearances of certain individuals, male and female, that were never solved. The old Hartmann case was one his dad had laboured over to the point of obsession. It was as much a mystery today as it had been twenty years earlier.

Not anymore.

Tonight had opened up a powerful new lead. The young woman he had under close observation *had* to have Hartmann blood in her. That was his gut feeling and he trusted his gut feelings.

At one time of his life, after the untimely death of his father in a hit-and-run accident—the culprit never found—he wanted to crack the case if only to finish the job for his father and give closure to the Hartmann family. Other ambitions had got in the way. He now ran his own wealth management company, The Fortuna Group. His company was getting bigger by the day. He was very good at whatever he did. Consequently he was doing extremely well. An increasing number of other people were doing well because of him. To be a success had always been expected of him. No way was he going to let his dad down. He honoured his memory.

It's her.

She who had been lost is found.